Linda

SHOWCASE

Special Books by Special Writers

YOU AGAIN

by Peggy Nicholson

Dear Reader,

Some books happen where ideas intersect.

For instance, in my single years I had one dating rule: Never date a man who doesn't like cats. (I sought a strong but sensitive male, subtle, with a great sense of humor, who'd appreciate an independent, adventurous woman. Such a paragon was bound to adore cats, I reasoned.)

Wrong. Instead I met a man who thinks all cats are...brats. Selfish, slinky, arrogant critters. He explained this politely and at great length to Yaffa, resident computer-cord chewer in these parts, though in the end it didn't do him much good. (If you want to learn how to seduce—inch by inch, month by month—watch a cat. A paw oh-so-casually rested on a thigh, then withdrawn, a silken flick of the tail.)

While I was observing unwilling man/relentless cat, I was playing with the idea of myths: how to relate them to the present? A myth that spoke to me was that of the animal wife, the selkie. A man weds a beautiful, mystical stranger. She's woman, and maybe, late at night when the moon is full or the tide runs high, she's...other than woman. Will love bridge their differences? Or will her otherness tear them apart?

Finally, I've always wanted to be the fly on the wall, the unseen observer. How would it be to watch the man you love when he thinks he's alone: to hear him speak from his heart when he thinks there's no one to listen but a worthless cat?

Myth, man versus cat, the fly on the wall—I started writing. Hope you enjoy.

Peggy Nicholson

Peggy Nicholson
YOU AGAIN

Harlequin Books

TORONTO • NEW YORK • LONDON
AMSTERDAM • PARIS • SYDNEY • HAMBURG
STOCKHOLM • ATHENS • TOKYO • MILAN
MADRID • WARSAW • BUDAPEST • AUCKLAND

To R. duPrey
and with special thanks to Chris Canham,
who said,
"What if you made the shrink a she?"

ISBN 0-373-70698-7

YOU AGAIN

Copyright © 1996 by Peggy Nicholson.

This edition published by arrangement with Harlequin Books S.A.

® and ™ are trademarks of the publisher. Trademarks indicated with
® are registered in the United States Patent and Trademark Office, the
Canadian Trade Marks Office and in other countries.

Printed in U.S.A.

If called by a panther, don't anther.
—Ogden Nash

"Well, that ol' black cat followed us all the way across Texas. Each night, after we'd made camp, there he'd be. He'd come stalkin' up to the fire with those big shinin' green eyes of his, and he'd say, 'I'm hungry, too! Fix me some bacon, tooooo!'"

—from a bedtime story told
by my grandmother,
Lula Grimes

CHAPTER ONE

WHEN SHE WAS A CHILD, Jessica Myles's worst nightmare—or rather, one of her nightmares—had involved an elevator. Being trapped in one. Having to spend hours and hours trying to converse with total strangers while they waited for rescue.

The image returned to her with wincing vividness as the elevator doors rolled open, and five men regarded her with interest. Jessica didn't rock back on her heels, but for an instant she pictured herself turning. Striding across the hotel corridor to the elevator set in the opposite wall. Riding up to the rooftop health club in blessed isolation and silence.

The man nearest the front grinned as he put out an arm to hold the doors open. "Thank you," Jessica said, unsmiling, and stepped aboard. *Shows how little imagination I had as a kid,* she told herself, as the doors closed and the car lifted skyward. *I could've imagined myself trapped in an elevator—with five doctors.*

For though, with typical male arrogance, not one of them was wearing his convention name tag, each of her fellow passengers might as well have been dressed in a white lab coat, with a stethoscope dangling from his neck. They had that faint but unmistakable aura of self-congratulation and assurance, that *I've made it, but what about you?* air that marked the typical physician—at least the male of the species.

The man across from Jessica bent to study the name tag pinned to her suit lapel. His eyes lingered at breast level a moment too long, then lifted to her face. "Rhode Island General, huh? Do you know Bob Daley?"

A surgeon, Jessica recalled. She'd heard him paged over the hospital PA system, but in the month since she'd been admitted to practice at RI Gen she'd yet to fit a face to the name. "I'm afraid not."

"Slice and Dice Daley, they used to call him," the man continued to the group at large. "Bob could whomp out an appendix faster than you could cross yourself and say Hail Mary. I remember the time we admitted this kid, he presented like an absolute textbook case of..."

Tuning him out, Jessica suppressed a sigh and glanced up at the numbers above the door. Some forty floors to go. With any luck, the pool would be empty. She'd chosen the breakfast hour on purpose, hoping that most convention attendees would be below in the banquet hall, sucking down a last cup of coffee before the first seminar of the day.

"That was some party last night, huh?" said the doctor on Jessica's right, leaning close to her ear. "The one in the Merck Labs suite? I saw you there, didn't I? On the far side of that vat of beluga?"

"No, I didn't make that one." Nor any other of the private or promotional parties given last night, though she'd been invited to half a dozen. Jessica had bolted the hotel, desperate for fresh air, natural light and any sound at all but medical babble. She'd ridden the Staten Island ferry back and forth till the sun went down in the smoldering sky over New Jersey, and Manhattan turned into the jeweled city of Oz. Later she'd nibbled on a spinach salad in some nondescript midtown restaurant while she read a *New England Journal of Medicine*. She touched her briefcase now, thought of pulling one out to bury her nose in, then reluctantly dismissed the impulse. Only twenty floors to go.

"You wouldn't have the time, would you?" the man on her right persisted.

"I would," Jessica said, and was tempted to leave it at that. She had no doubt that if he lifted his own wrist, a gold Rolex would gleam from beneath his cuff. Her father had awarded her hers, along with six lab coats with "Dr. Jessica Myles" embroidered above the left breast pocket, on the day she received her M.D. She consulted her watch gravely. "It's seven-forty-four."

"Not seven-forty-five?" There was a smile in his voice.

"Not for another twenty seconds."

The car's floor pressed up against the soles of her feet, then the doors slid back. Jessica seized the moment and moved away from her inquisitor, making room for the two men who stepped aboard. " ... tempted to cut out of here after the ten-thirty seminar," one of them was saying, "since Jorgenson's wimped out on us. The only thing deadlier than the guest speaker at the closing banquet is a last-minute replacement."

"Maybe not this time," said his companion. "I hear they've come up with a powerhouse pinch hitter." He leaned close to his friend and whispered, while everyone else averted his eyes and strained his ears.

Jessica frowned. Had she caught the magical phrase "Nobel prize," or had she only imagined it? Imagined or real, the phrase brought a face with it. With a ruthless efficiency born of years of practice, she slam-dunked that laughing image into the back closet of her mind. Slammed the door shut on it. *No.* Not here. Not now. *Not ever.*

The first doctor let out a low whistle. "No kidding? How'd they corner *him?*"

Some other him, of course. Who'd won the Nobel in medicine last year? Or was due to win it this?

"He's an old buddy of Vincent's, the conference chair. I hear he was passing through town on his way out to some do in San Francisco, and they yanked him off a jet."

"Guess I'll stick around. He puts on quite a show, they say."

The car stopped again, and three doctors exited. The rest of them stepped off at the concierge level. Jessica breathed a silent thanks and moved to the front of the car. With any luck she'd have the pool to herself.

But as she neared the end of the corridor that led to the health club, a man pushed out through the steamy glass doors. Toby Morrison—hair still wet from his swim, a towel draped around his neck.

Toby had been a Fellow at Boston Charity, the year she'd been a wild-eyed, frantic intern. Funny that she hadn't thought of him twice in the past five years, and now they'd be speaking for the second time in less than a month. Though this encounter hardly rated as coincidence. This conference was the biggest event of the year for internists and general practitioners, and she and Toby both had their professional training to upgrade.

"More gorgeous than ever," Toby pronounced her with a grin, holding her hand longer than was strictly necessary.

"We all look better without the bags under our eyes." A hundred hours a week on call was typical for the first three years of clinical training. Jessica could still fall asleep in ten seconds flat. They'd had to snatch every wink of blessed unconsciousness, learn to sleep on their feet like horses in harness. She remembered falling asleep once, her forehead pillowed against an old man's chest, while she was checking his heartbeat. Remembered another intern who'd fallen facedown in his plate of mashed potatoes and gravy at the free late-night meal the hospital cafeteria provided for house staff.

"About that phone call last month..." Toby reminded her, as she'd feared he would.

She shouldn't have called him. Wasn't sure yet why she'd called him, why she hadn't simply minded her own business. "Oh, that..." She shrugged, making light of it now. "About Grenada?"

Toby was one of those few-and-far-between American doctors who'd attended med school offshore, then had managed to gain accreditation in the U.S. system. In his case he'd attended St. George's University, on the island of Grenada. He'd graduated there the year of the revolution, which had ended with Reagan's sending in the U.S. troops.

Late nights on the ward, when admissions were slow, Toby had had some fine tales to tell of street fighting and burning buildings, of students sharing a bottle of cane rum in the bunkered basement of their dorm while American shells whistled overhead, of working long, bloody hours in a bare-bones island clinic under fire and threat of being taken hostage. If even half his tales were true, he'd seen more excitement in that one week than the rest of the house staff had seen in the whole of their short, privileged lifetimes. They'd all been green as their operating scrubs with envy listening to him, though one second-year resident privately swore that Toby had actually skipped the revolution altogether and had spent that week golfing on Barbados.

"Anne Talbot," Toby prodded. "Why'd you want to know about her?"

Two weeks ago Jessica had called Toby in Baltimore, after tracking him down through the friend of a friend. Though she'd tried to disguise it, she'd had a purpose beyond the what've-you-been-up-to-the-last-five-years chatter. She'd casually asked if he'd known a Raye Talbot on Grenada—an American med student graduating from the school and the revolution the same year he had. A student who'd gone on, like Toby, to pass the brutal Foreign Medical Grad exam, winning the coveted right to take her clinical residency in the U.S., in psychiatry.

Jessica had made that call in the hope of gaining some insight into what kind of person Raye had been in her student years on Grenada. Because Jessica was still trying to comprehend just who or what the woman was *now*. Any clue Toby might give her to the puzzle that was Dr. Raye Talbot—consulting psychiatrist to the patients and staff of RI General, would-be friend to Jessica, charmer, raconteur and attempted cat killer—any clue at all would be more than welcome.

But Toby hadn't provided another piece to Jessica's puzzle—he'd swept the whole jumbled pattern right off the table. Because Toby hadn't known a Raye Talbot at med school—he'd known *Anne* Talbot. "Yeah, Anne—a mousy little lab rat," he'd recalled when she asked. "From some place way down South—accent thicker than kudzu."

That hadn't sounded like the Talbot Jessica knew at all.

"I just assumed you'd known my Dr. Talbot and would love to hear where she ended up, but apparently I got my facts muddled," Jessica said now. It was best to drop the matter, leave Toby out of this.

"Maybe your Talbot went to some other offshore school. Guatemala? Or Guadalajara? Sounds a lot like Grenada, after a drink or two."

"It does." But Raye had said Grenada, after four drinks. Still, Jessica shouldn't have drawn Toby into this. All the same, she couldn't resist adding, "You said your Talbot was a blonde? But are you sure she was a natural blonde?" Raye's hair was black and shiny as a crow's wing, her eyes so dark there was almost no line between iris and pupil.

"Dead sure." Toby's grin was too smug by half.

Poor little lab rat. Jessica remembered why she'd never liked Toby very much.

"But to heck with ancient history," Toby was saying. "Have supper with me tonight? And maybe a show? Last night to take a bite of the Big Apple." *And of each other,* his eyes suggested.

Jessica smiled gently. "Thanks, Toby. But I'm afraid I have somebody waiting for me back in Providence, and I promised I'd be home before dark." Cattoo was waiting. No doubt she'd finished her three-day supply of dry food by now and had started in on the spider plants.

"*So*—" if he was disappointed, it didn't show "—the Ice Maiden took someone at last? Good for you. Well . . ." He shifted his weight, signaling an end to the encounter.

"Ice Maiden?"

"What we called you back on the wards. You didn't know? We had a pool going—who'd get you by the end of the year. Nobody ever collected, so we used it to buy you that monster bouquet, remember?"

Face scarlet, she remembered the armful of white roses. "And I was touched. You *creeps!*"

"Temper, temper." He patted her shoulder and drifted on down the hall. "It was meant as homage," he called back, walking sideways. "To something rare and wonderful—the last virgin at Bos Char." He blew her a kiss. "Be well, Jessica."

Virgin—huh! Jessica glared after him. By the time she and Toby met at Boston Charity, she'd been a divorcée for four years.

She turned and pushed through the doors, her eyes fixed on something far beyond the misted glass. *Ice Maiden.* Still, repugnant as it was, she had to admit Toby and his sex-fiend pals had gotten that much right, anyway.

Because Dr. Jessica Myles had stuck her heart in the deep freeze the year she'd turned twenty-one.

BUT THE PAST WAS OVER... done with... gone. She swam thirty laps stroking those words out through turquoise water, leaving them frothing, then sinking in her wake... Swam another twenty laps willing her mind to believe those words—gone was gone, gone, *totally and forever gone...* Swam another ten laps wiping the very words from her mind, seeking first blankness, then serenity in the sterile water sliding past her skin... Swam a final ten laps wondering if she could swim just ten more...nine more...eight more laps without drowning.

When she emerged from the pool at last she was shaking with cold and fatigue, but the fit was past. She felt clean and hollow as a shell washed up a beach. *Cold.* Shuddering, Jessica glanced at the door to the sauna room beyond the deep end of the pool. But when she'd tried the sauna yesterday, its steam-making device hadn't worked well. The little redwood room had hardly warmed up at all. A long hot shower, then...

Half an hour later, dressed again, with hair blown to smooth and shining perfection, makeup subtly applied, briefcase swinging briskly and only minutes left before the first seminar of the day, Jessica hurried back to the pool. She'd left a medical journal lying by a chaise longue before she dived in. Her eyes swept the room—no one here at all—then fixed on her magazine, halfway down the length of the pool. Heels tapping, she picked her way between puddles, leaned to collect it and—

"Damn!"

With that yell echoing off the tiled walls, Jessica spun—
to see the sauna door crash open. Her heels snagged on
something. She stumbled, the backs of her knees bumping
the chaise longue—and sat down hard. A steam-wreathed,
near-naked shape erupted into view.

"Yoww!" Waving something shiny over his head, the
man took two running strides poolward, then launched
himself into the air. *"Son of a—"* The curse ended under
water. Bubbles rose.

Openmouthed, Jessica sat, pool water raining down
upon her head and shoulders.

Clouds of steam rolled forth from the sauna.

Diminishing echoes . . . pool water lapping out from that
perfect cannonball . . . the gentle hiss of steam . . . Her apparition writhed deep underwater, flesh-colored but for a
scrap of red she hoped to God was a bathing suit.

The lunatic was drowning. She was a doctor, and she
ought to save him. Jessica pushed back a strand of damp
hair and looked around. Wasn't there *any*one else to—

"Damn!" A dark head broke surface. He sucked in a
lungful of air, then rolled under like a dolphin.

Jess stared as a pair of very large bare feet pointed, then
arrowed gracefully back toward the bottom.

She stood. So he wasn't drowning. He was—whatever he
was doing, she didn't want to know. Was too enraged to
trust herself to ask politely. She'd have to change clothes
now, skip that first seminar.

As she turned toward the exit, she heard him break surface again.

"Hey, you! Miss! Ms.?"

Jessica Myles stopped. Closed her eyes. Opened them
far, far too wide, then shook her head slowly. No. *Oh, no.*
It was just because she'd been thinking about him all
morning.

"Ma'am? Would you happen to have a dime?" asked the
voice, a shade deeper than whiskey tenor, still with its hint
of Texas drawl, still with that undertone of laughter.

Jessica closed her eyes again. Usually he carried a Swiss
army knife, but when he didn't have that—

"I'll give it back, Scout's honor, I just need it for a—"

"Screwdriver." They spoke the word as one.

She nodded, eyes closed, resigned. Reaching blindly for the clasp of her briefcase, she groped inside. It had to happen someday, somewhere, somehow. But could she live through it without crying?

"Jess?"

She'd always seen his voice as a color—sunlight through honey, Southern Comfort by firelight. She found a coin, looked at it, then turned. "How about a quarter, Sam?"

He breaststroked toward her, his eyes locked on her face, something silver and metallic held aloft in one hand. "You've . . . cut your hair."

He'd always liked her hair. He'd gathered fistfuls of it sometimes when they made love, his hands gently, fiercely possessive. She'd cut it the day after she left him.

"Would a quarter do?" she repeated patiently. He'd never stuck to one topic for long. He was as right-brained and scattershot as she was linear and left.

"Nope." He dragged a muscular forearm across his face, wiping dark hair from black brows. "Too wide for the slot." He deposited the piece of metal at her feet, like some treasure he'd brought back from the depths just for her.

She flipped the quarter over his head, watched it sink. Steam hung in swaths from the ceiling, a cloud pressing down on them, pressing down on her heart. "You burned your fingers."

He stopped swishing his hand through the water. "Didn't think it'd come apart at that joint. Was trying to free the valve just above."

Sam Kirby had never met the gadget he didn't think he could improve. When he didn't lose the parts or wander off to his next project, leaving a pile of metallic rubble in his wake, he was generally right.

That trait had been endearing for the first six months, a source of irritation, then despair for the last six, when her life was already crumbling into chaos. She hadn't needed Sam's help creating more. Jessica remembered coming home exhausted to find their cuckoo clock, a wedding gift from Sam's lab mates, reduced to its cogs and springs. She'd followed the trail of components from the living-room coffee table to the kitchen counter. The cuckoo itself had been left inexplicably in the fridge, nesting in a bowl of salad he'd forgotten to cover. She remembered sitting huddled at the table, clutching the bird to her breast, sobbing her heart out, till Sam returned with the takeout Chinese he'd dashed out to buy. He'd dumped his bags in the sink and carried her off to bed.

Later she hadn't been able to tell him why she'd cried.

She slammed the door on that memory. "I suppose you're the substitute speaker for the banquet?" Sam's Nobel last year had been awarded in molecular biology, not medicine, but his field of pure research was impinging more and more on the practices of her world. Gene therapy was no longer science fiction, but the coming reality. Thanks in no small part to the man at her feet.

"'Fraid so. Doug Vincent shanghaied me on my way back from Holland. We were supposed to meet at the airport, suck down a few brews, before I made my connection to San Fran. I'm presenting a paper out there..."

He gave her a lopsided smile. "Vin had to bribe me to pry me off that plane. Claimed the best *pad thai* in the world can be had right here in the city, and he'd prove it if I'd please, please entertain his quacks for him." Dark eyes— gift of his Italian mother—caressed her face as if he was memorizing it, feature by feature. "Waste of breath and good money," he added absently. "All Vinnie had to do was tell me you'd be here and—"

"What's *pad thai?*" she cut in. Dear God, how was she going to end this? Get away?

"Lord, Jess, where've you been living—in a medicine cabinet? Thai noodles—with peanuts, shrimp, all kinds of good stuff. First time I tried it I swore off *mu shi* pancakes and General Tzo's forever. We'll have to—"

"No." She shook her head as she took a step backward.

"Wait." His "shucks, ma'am" manner dropped away in a word. His brows drew together. "We have to talk."

"That's what we've been doing." Like water bugs skating across the surface of a swamp. It was *just* possible if you didn't stop. "Congratulations on your Nobel, by the way." Not that his winning one had been a surprise. Everyone had been predicting it since the day he published his first paper, demanding it after his book came out.

She remembered the first time she'd heard that prediction, her happiness dropping out from under her like an elevator with a cut cable. The moment when it finally had hit her that he was brilliant—not just a whimsical, wonderful, bumbling space cadet, but a true rocket scientist—in that moment, she'd known it was over. That she'd never keep him. Though she'd tried. God knew, she'd tried.

"I meant to send you a card." Congratulations would have been the gracious gesture, the proper one. Some three centuries of WASP forebears demanded she make that gesture. She'd gone as far as buying the card, something tastefully understated, of course, an embossed scallop shell, sand on cream parchment, no preprinted message. But she hadn't been able to form her own message, let alone mail it.

"I sent *you* one—a postcard from Stockholm," he reminded her. "You got it?"

"Yes." His had been rude, funny, not tasteful at all—she'd dropped it in the trash can.

"And the birthday card I sent you last year?"

She nodded. She hadn't opened the envelope, but his handwriting—she'd known it the second she saw it. That card had wrecked her sleep for weeks. "Look..." She took a deep breath. It would only hurt more if she waited. *Get it over with.* "Look, I'm going to be late for the first seminar. I've got to go."

"Stay, Jess."

Did he choose those words on purpose? It was all he'd said that first night, when she'd meant to duck out his apartment door after her chemistry lesson. "Stay, Jess," he'd whispered, kissing her eyelids, the tips of her ears, the angle of her jaw. "*Stay...*" When he'd found the corner where her neck met her shoulder, she'd whimpered and dropped her books. He'd laughed then deep in his throat, knowing he'd won, and at last kissed her on the mouth, and she'd been lost. Had never regained herself, not in eight years of trying. *Damn him*.

"Stay..."

Damn you! "I can't." She backed up another step, but couldn't tear her gaze free from his, couldn't turn away until she did.

"*Talk* to me, dammit!" His voice was no longer honey smooth.

"Look..." She retreated another step, shaking her head. "It's over, Sam. Let it go." *You're such a moron, thinking we can talk it out, patch it up, end up as friends.* Not in this lifetime. *You never knew me at all, if you don't know that.*

"Jess—"

"Look—" *It's dead.* "Let's not talk it to death."

"Talk it to—*huh!* You wouldn't say a *word*. Not... one...damned...*word!* Wouldn't return my phone calls. Sent back all my letters. Cut and ran every time I hit town. Only word I ever got from you was my quickie divorce papers. Talk it to death—God give me *strength!*"

"There was nothing to say." And in her family, even when there was, you didn't say it. Silence and dignified withdrawal, that was the way you handled anger and pain.

"Nothing to—God, Jess, how about why? You could have started with that."

"You know why." Her throat ached with the words.

He shook his head, slinging drops of bright water.

"You *do.*" How could he not admit it? She'd never seen him as a coward, even when she'd hated him. She couldn't bear to see him so now. "You know."

"Okay. He wiped a hand upward to catch a drip, left his hair standing in spikes. "Okay...so maybe I do. I'm not a total idiot. Still, Jess, you owed me the *words*. You still owe me. Are you going to stand there and say them at last, or turn tail and run like a rabbit again?"

"A rab—!" If she'd had something besides her brief-case to throw at him, she'd have thrown it. It had taken every last ounce of her courage and dignity to break away

from him, and he'd seen her as a *rabbit?* Hands clenched,
she stalked toward him, stood over him, her blood thumping in her ears. *"All right then.* If it'll make you feel better
to hear it, Sam Kirby, then I'll say it, and-I-hope-you're-
satisfied!"

He cocked his square chin, with its cartoon-hero cleft, up
at her. "So lay it on me, baby. I'm all ears."

"I left you…" Her voice broke and she gritted her teeth.
She *would* say it if he insisted on hearing it. She wasn't the
wretched, heartbroken child she'd been eight years ago. She
was a doctor, her own woman, nobody's baby. *Nobody's
fool.* "I left because you cheated on me." Her eyes filled
instantly with tears, and she spun away. She wouldn't cry,
she would *not!*

"I *what?*" she heard him say as she started toward the
door.

So she'd cry, but she'd be damned if she'd let Sam watch
her—or worse, try to comfort her. "You heard me!"

As she reached the exit, she heard the splashing sound of
a large wet body lunging from the pool. "I what? What are
you—Jess, come *back* here!"

"You go to hell!" She shoved through the doors, hiked
up her skirt and ran like a rabbit.

CHAPTER TWO

EIGHT YEARS APART, ten minutes reunited, and they were doing it already, Jessica fleeing in frozen silence, Sam pursuing at the top of his lungs. "Dammit, Jess, come back here!"

She couldn't think—had never been able to think—when he yelled. It didn't matter that he'd never once laid a hand on her but with tenderness. Didn't matter that he came from a family where his mother broke plates and swore in Italian when mad, his father roared and stomped, and all their arguments ended behind a closed bedroom door with peals of laughter.

In Jessica's family emotions were controlled, or hidden away until they could be. Anything else was unthinkable. Jessica banged through the glass doors and out of the health club.

An approaching woman stopped short and lifted her gym bag to fend her off. "Sorry!" Jessica gasped, dodging around her. Sixty feet down this corridor, turn the corner, then another sixty feet to the elevators, she calculated as she ran. She'd never make it.

Behind her the doors slammed back. "Jess! *Oof!*"

The woman squawked.

Jessica stole a glance behind. Skidding down the hall, Sam waltzed his partner around and around in a desperate effort to stay upright. Wrapped in the arms of a virtually naked and dripping stranger, the woman let forth with another shriek while she thumped him with her bag.

That wouldn't hold him for long. Jess wrenched open a door marked Fire Exit and flung herself into a dimly lit stairwell. Only fifty floors to the lobby! Heels clattering on iron steps, one hand riding the cold steel of the banister, she plunged down the stairs. *Get away, hide, sort it out later!* Her heels rattled across a landing, clattered down the next flight of stairs.

Above her the door crashed open. "Dammit, Jess, you'll break your fool neck!" The sound of a heavy body taking one flight in three bounds. "*Listen* to me!"

"Just leave me alone, Kirby!" Briefcase flailing, panting for breath, she wheeled around a landing and rattled down into darkness. He would catch her. Images of laughing games in the night, mock pursuit, hide-and-seek through their darkened apartment, her delighted shrieks when he pounced from the shadows. Being carried off to bed upside down over his shoulder, giggling and kicking helplessly, his hand on her bottom. *No!*

"Jess!" He was closer.

Tears streaming, she flew down another flight, landed on her toes. She couldn't win this race. *So change the rules!* She groped for the door, found its knob, wrenched it open, stumbled into the bright light of a corridor, staggered toward a corner and around.

"Jess, dammit, which way did you—"

Ahead, an elevator, the light lit above it. Two men moved toward the opening doors, then turned to stare.

"*Wait!* Hold it for me!" she squeaked, racing at them. "Please, wait!"

The bald one shrugged and stepped on board, the other grinned as he braced his forearm to hold the doors open. Looking past her, his grin faded. "What the—?"

She didn't look back, knew who was gaining. "Please!" she panted as the man grabbed her arm and swung her inside. She fell against the control panel, punched buttons at random. "The door button! Where's the—"

"*Hold it!*" Sam's arm and leg thrust through the closing gap, followed by his head and shoulders. His teeth were bared. His wild eyes found Jessica just as she slapped a last row of buttons. "*Jess—*"

"Forget it!" yelled the man beside her. Lunging to meet her pursuer, he flattened his hands against Sam's chest—

and shoved. Sam's scowl turned to surprise as he toppled from view. "Catch the next one, buddy!" crowed Jess's defender. The doors closed. The car started down.

"What the hell was *that?*" muttered someone.

Gasping for breath, Jess turned—to find half a dozen men, doctors all, no doubt, their brows raised and eyes entranced. Scarlet-faced, she spun away and swiped at her tears. No nightmare could top *this* reality!

Beside her, the bald man had collapsed against the wall. Clutching his ribs, he seemed to be choking. No, it was laughter.

"What's so funny?" demanded the man who'd pushed Sam.

"G-good going, Ed! You just came as...as close as I bet you ever come to a Nobel prize," gurgled his friend. "That was Sam Kirby, the guest of honor, you just shoved ass-over-teakettle!"

Drop-jawed, Ed stared from the giggler to Jessica, then back again. "It was?" He swung back to Jessica. "That was Sam Kirby? The Sam Kirby who cloned the Bouncer gene? Who wrote *No Nonsense?*"

Jessica hunched her shoulders and nodded.

"Did he hurt you?" demanded her knight.

"Oh, no! No!" This was the crowning humiliation, and there was no way to explain. Jess shut her eyes and shook her head. "No, nothing like that at all. No. *Absolutely* not. Just a...disagreement."

The elevator bumped to a stop, the doors rolled open. Nobody stepped out. "She pushed every button," someone reminded the group.

Across the hall, the arrival light above the opposing elevator blinked on. Its doors rolled open—to reveal Sam, slouched against the back wall, his arms crossed, a thundercloud scowl on his face. Their eyes met and he bolted upright.

Someone leaned past her to jab frantically at the door-close button. Jessica aimed a finger at Sam, nailing him to his spot by sheer willpower. "You just stay where you are, you...you *Texan!*"

"Hate t'tell you, babe—" Sam started out his door, then stopped as her doors drew together. "That's not an insult, where I come from."

"And that's *precisely* the problem!" Jessica called through the gap.

"You tell him!" someone chuckled.

"Shuddup," another man grunted.

Jessica closed her eyes and willed herself to the ends of the earth. Not fifteen minutes in Sam's company, and he'd dragged her down to his level. She'd felt more emotions in the past quarter hour than she had in the past four years. How did he *do* it? Her control was in tatters, and with it her pride.

Her eyes snapped open as the car stopped. She heard the faint sound of six people each sucking in a breath and holding it.

The doors opened, then ... nothing. The light across the way stayed unlit. Everyone breathed out.

"He can't know which floors you pressed," a basso profundo voice noted behind her.

"Must be ahead of us now," someone else added as the doors rolled together.

Two floors down, the elevator stopped again.

As their doors glided open, across the way the doors to Sam's car were just closing. They jolted to a stop, then reversed as Sam slapped his door-open control.

Jessica mashed her door-close button.

"No, the problem is your dad—the walk-on-water, world-famous, kiss-my-sweet-fanny surgeon!" he yelled, starting out of his car, then ducking back in again when he realized he'd never catch hers.

"You leave my father out of this!"

Sam's bellow carried faintly through the intervening steel. "That's all I ever asked you to do! Leave him out of our..." His voice faded as the car dropped below floor level.

A doctor leaned in from each side to study Jessica's name tag. "Your father is Dr. Myles?" asked one after a pause. "Myles, the neurosurgeon?"

Jess shook her head wearily. "That's my brother." Winston. Who had almost eclipsed their renowned father's reputation, if that was possible, since he'd given his name to the Myles Procedure for Parkinson's disease.

"Your father's *Terence* Myles? The cardiac surgeon?" Her other inquisitor answered her grim head jerk with a drawn-out, admiring whistle. She was heir to as prestigious a medical dynasty as could be found in the country, one that stretched back three generations before her father. They'd been wizards with scalpels, every last one of them.

"So why aren't you a surgeon?" wondered Ed, the brash one.

Jessica shrugged and looked at her toes. *I wasn't good enough.* Sure, she'd had the hands, but she lacked what doctors call "aggression," that superb self-confidence that sets the surgeon apart from other doctors.

Because surgeons had no room for doubt, not with life ebbing away beneath latex-clad fingertips. No time to second-guess themselves, when time was measured in heartbeats.

Whereas Jessica had spent her whole life doubting. Her whole life second-guessing herself. All her life holding back.

All but for six precious months when she'd doubted nothing. Dared all. Thrown herself into life with a vengeance.

And look where that got me! She glanced up at the numbers above the door to find that they'd already passed her floor. Not that hiding in her room would've helped for long, with Sam on the rampage. No, she had to skip town. She carried her wallet and her keys in her briefcase, that was all she'd need. The concierge could send the rest on.

The elevator stopped. Everyone groaned. The doors opened. Across the hall, the light signaled Sam's approach, and Ed jabbed the door-close control. Before the doors met, Sam appeared, leaning out from his car. "Is *that* what happened? Your dad told you I cheated on you?"

Jessica moaned and covered her face with her hands. Was it the hot Latin blood? Or the Texan, bred to shoot from the hip? Whichever—he thought it, he said it, and damn the torpedoes. And of course, he had it all wrong. Had her father known Sam was cheating on her, he'd have never said a word. Emotional messes were to be avoided at all costs.

"He cheated on you?" demanded Ed, the thwarted Sir Galahad.

"Mind your business," warned his bald friend.

Someone stirred at Jess's back, then spoke in his basso profundo. "Look, Dr. Myles, if that's all this is, it's no big deal. All guys cheat. It doesn't mean anything."

"Speak for yourself!" snapped another man. "I don't cheat on my wife."

"How long have you been married?" retorted Basso Profundo.

"Nine months," muttered the faithful one. "But—"

A chorus of knowing laughter drowned him out.

I hate men! Jessica decided behind her hands. *Give me cats any day.*

The car stopped again. The doors opened—to a mass of flowers. The blossoms advanced on two blue-clad legs, forcing everyone toward the back.

Jessica found herself nose to stamen with a tiger lily. She refocused to find a freckled face peering at her through a cloud of baby's breath. "Are you Jessica Myles?" asked the young man holding the arrangement.

Resigned to it, Jessica nodded.

"Guy in a red bathing suit said if I saw you, I was to give you these," the kid explained. He thrust the "bouquet" at her, but she crossed her arms and shook her head.

"How the hell did he *do* that?" wondered Baldie.

"They're for a wedding party on thirty-three," the boy admitted guilelessly. "But this guy in the swimsuit promised me fifty if she dropped by and I gave them to her. Think he's good for it?"

"Oh, he's good for it," Jessica muttered.

"See, what did I tell you?" Basso Profundo rumbled at her ear. "He cares. But you can't have a marriage if you won't forgive and forget."

"That's what you'd do?" the faithful one sniped. "If your wife cheated on you—you'd forgive?"

"Ummmmmmmm..." It was a long, considering drone, like a bumblebee choosing which flower to land on. "That's not the same thing."

"Huh!" the faithful one snorted.

"No, come on, you're a scientist. You know it's true," insisted the bass. "Women are by nature monogamous. And men are instinctively—"

Jessica had had enough—too much. The car stopped, and she crashed past the flower arrangement, batting lilies out of her way.

"Hey!" Ed yelped. "You're leaving us?"

Jessica jabbed the call button on the opposite wall, then swung around to nod and wave goodbye. Sam might be as naturally and innocently polygamous as her advisers, but he was no fool. If his car was now several floors below...

"When he asks, tell him I'm heading up to my room and once I get there I'm phoning security," she called as her fellow travelers vanished.

A moment later her new car arrived, rising to collect her. With no Sam aboard. Which meant he was somewhere below, just now boarding *her* car, she'd bet the farm.

She went up to the twelfth, giving him time, then hit the button for the ground floor. He might be the rocket scientist, but this rabbit had a few slick moves of her own. By now he'd reached the lobby and was no doubt doubling back up to the convention's hospitality desk on floor three to try to bully her room number out of some clerk.

But if her calculations were logical, they'd omitted, as they so often did, the human factor.

Jessica stepped out of her elevator and into a tableau. Across the way, Sam stood in profile, one arm hugging his flower arrangement, his other hand holding Ed up on tiptoes by his tie. To one side, the delivery boy shuffled from foot to foot, wanting his fee, no doubt. Baldie and two other doctors were talking loudly and earnestly while they tried to part the opponents. Others hurried from all sides to join the fray, among them a grim-faced security guard and several joyful bellhops.

For just an instant Jessica stood frozen. He'd filled out, she could see now. Her lanky grad student had gone rock hard and muscular. Nearing forty, he was a male in his prime, with his father's magnificent build. And only the most confident of Americans—or any Italian—would have worn that sneeze of a Speedo. A gift from his mother perhaps?

"There she is!" boomed the shortest man in the circle around Sam.

Jessica stood for a split second longer, astounded—that graying shrimp with the horn rims was Basso Profundo, cheat, romantic and—she glared at him—traitor? But as Sam swung her way, she took to her heels. A taxi, if she could just catch—

"Jess! Dammit, will you just—"

"Say, why can't you leave her alone?" chimed in a voice that had to be Ed's.

Behind her she heard the sound of shattering glass— flower vase hitting the floor? Then the unmistakable *whap!* of fist meeting flesh.

Jess spun out through revolving doors and into the hotel's portico, where a cab stood, its back door open, an elderly man just taking his seat. She landed beside him, slammed and locked the door, leaned forward to the startled cabbie. "Kennedy, and step on it!"

"Yeah?" Unmoved, the cabbie looked her over. "You got a fire to put out maybe?"

Jessica fixed the man with her best intern-wilting glare. "The fire is I'm a doctor and this is a matter of life and death!"

"Long as you tip like it, honey, sure it is." Wheels squealed. As they shot out onto the street, Jessica looked back. There was no sign of Sam. She'd slipped him at last.

Beside her, her elderly companion found his voice. "Considering that this was my cab, would that matter of life and death include time for a detour by way of Grand Central?'' His eyes twinkled.

"Oh, please!'' Jessica agreed, her face warming under his worldly gaze. "By all means. My treat?''

While he leaned forward to amend the route to the airport, she sank back against the seat and closed her eyes. She'd outwitted Sam... Inhaling deeply, she willed her heart to slow its rocking-horse pace and pushed back further into the cushions. She'd beaten him...so it ought to be triumph she was feeling...or maybe rage, since she would never—*ever*—live this day down. Instead...what it felt like was...desolation.

THREE HOURS LATER she slouched back in a cab that carried her from the Providence airport north to the city.

Why did you leave me?

Because you cheated on me.

But that wasn't why—not really. Jessica sank lower, arms crossed over churning middle, eyes closed. She hadn't left Sam because he cheated on her, though that had shredded her heart....

She saw them again—eight years of trying, and she'd yet to erase the image: framed by the window to the right of the front door, the blonde stood in Jessica's living room. A dreamy smile curved her lips as she unbuttoned her blouse. Against its black velvet, her breasts glowed pearl white. The widening gap in the velvet revealed crimson lace, more skin....

Sam entered from the kitchen, a wineglass in each hand. He'd seen the blonde, stopped, then set the drinks down on a bookcase and advanced, a tiger stalking.

Outside on the front walk, Jessica had put her key ring slowly, with exquisite care, back in her pocket. Squinching her eyes, she wrapped her arms around her middle, then stood there, swaying in the midnight darkness, whispering, "No...no...no...oh, no..."

Knowing all the while it was *yes.*

She'd meant to surprise Sam, coming home a day early. But it was she who was surprised, stupid little fool, though she shouldn't have been. They had been coming to this for months—ever since she'd changed her mind and decided she'd attend med school, after all. Because that decision had marked the beginning of their end.

When she forced her eyes open, Sam held the two halves of the blonde's shirt. His face gaunt with passion, he looked down at her breasts.

The woman's arms had dropped to her sides. Her head was tipped back, her long blond hair brushing slender hips. She swayed limply in against him and—

Jessica had turned and gone. It was over.

But she hadn't left him because he'd cheated, not really. She'd left because his cheating proved what she'd fought so hard against knowing, those last bitter months of their marriage. That, happy as they'd been for a little while, Sam had never really loved her.

That he'd married her for all the wrong reasons, on a champagne-inspired lark. Just one of his whims.

No, whatever Jessica felt for him, it wasn't love Sam felt for her. Not love, but two parts lust, one part friendship, perhaps three parts pity. Sam Kirby had always had a soft spot for waifs.

And for blondes.

"The East Side, you said?" asked her cabbie, turning to look at her just as they swept into the Thurber's Avenue curve, that reverse-graded bend in the highway where half the wrecks in the state occurred.

"Yes, Prospect Street."

To their left, the medical complex loomed handily above the road—RI Hospital, cheek by jowl with RI General and the Hasbro Children's Hospital. Jessica didn't spare the buildings a glance. She wasn't expected back till tomorrow.

Ahead, Narragansett Bay narrowed to a river, which wound between the compact clump of skyscrapers that was downtown Providence. The cabbie—a native Rhode Islander by his driving—sliced across three lanes of horn-blaring traffic to take the fork of the elevated freeway that split the city.

Beyond the river, the steeples and rooftops of College Hill carved a serrated and leafy curve against the night sky. Jessica sought the shape of her town house, still more than a mile distant, clinging to the steepest shoulder of the ridge. She'd chosen it for its view of the city. *Cattoo, I'm almost home. Can you feel me coming?*

Sam might not love her, but someone did, thank God. The Ice Maiden had found someone who loved her for who and what she was at last.

While the taxi drove off, Jessica unlocked her door and entered. Stepping over the pile of letters below the mail slot, she closed the door, stood listening. *"Kiiiii?"* she called at last on a high-pitched, piping note.

A trilling sound from upstairs—eager, plaintive—hurrying closer, along with that soft, weighty sound of a cat thumping down stairs. *"Mm-mm-mm-mm-rrrr?"* Cattoo flowed into view round the landing, a black stream of continuous cat, her song of woe wavering at each step. She leapt the last four, landing on her black catcher's mitt paws with her usual clumsy grace, sat up on her haunches as Jessica leaned to lift her. "Mmmrr?"

"Caught you napping, did I?" Jessica laughed, her laugh shaky.

Nose touch—then the silky-soft head burrowing beneath her chin. Black klutzy paws spanned her neck in a desperate embrace.

"Yike, watch the claws!" She hugged the cat back. "I missed you, too, fuzzbucket."

Another nose touch, then a rubbing of cheeks and noses back and forth—*Eskimo kiss*—then Cattoo nudged beneath her chin again and started to purr. "Thought I was never coming back, huh?" Jessica headed for the kitchen. "Thought you'd have to go back to being the Cat Who Walked Alone, Cat-Who, huh?"

Cattoo lifted her head to voice her agreement, a woeful, full-throated yowl this time.

"Ahhhhh—no one *loves* me?" Jessica rubbed Cattoo's furry back, scratched her ears, stopped to flick on the kitchen light. "I'm all *alone* in the world? Ain't true, kid, but I know just how you feel."

Cattoo yowled again—there was Siamese somewhere in her ancestry for sure—then pushed off from Jessica's chest, twisting in her grasp.

"Okay, okay—I'm *sorry*—but I had to go to New York." Jessica set her down, ran a finger down her spine, straightened. "I explained all that. So how can I make it up to you?"

Wading through a river of plaintive and scolding cat, she made it to the cat feeder on the floor by the windows. "You ate it all, you little pig?" Cattoo had been a half-grown street cat when Jessica spotted her just a year ago, scrounging in a hospital Dumpster. It had taken a week to catch the scrawny, wild-eyed waif with the laughable paws, another month of cuddling and cosseting to convince her that she was safe—safe and home at last.

But there was a trauma all the loving in the world apparently couldn't erase—Cattoo was never sure there'd be a next meal when Jessica went away. In that case, by feline logic, apparently the best bet was to eat what there was *now*—be it one day's ration or three. This time, Jessica had left enough food in the demand feeder to last any other cat a week.

"No wonder you were sleeping, you piglet. You were sleeping it off! See if I ever feed you again."

Cattoo tipped back her head and emitted a hollow, lost-kitten moan.

"All right, all right, more food, but you won't eat it."

She didn't. The plate of her favorite canned tuna wasn't the point. It wouldn't cure Cattoo's fear of abandonment any more than it would have mended Jessica's aching heart. Cattoo stood by the dish, staring up accusingly, treading her weight from one ridiculous paw to the other.

"I told you, paddlefoot." Cattoo was a "double-pawed" cat, with an extra two toes on each foot, a genetic oddity. The effect was comical, that of a child in fuzzy, outsize bedroom slippers, rather than the ballerina on-point grace of the usual cat. And Jess loved her all the more for the flaw. Like her owner, Cattoo was a freak, a misfit, a klutz among swans. They belonged together, two against an unkind world.

"How about a hug, then?" She picked up the cat and wandered into the living room, one cheek nestled in fur, one hand patting the cat's back with that slow, jiggling rhythm that comes instinctively to women.

Sam, coming from his large family, had wanted babies—had blithely assumed babies followed marriage as flowers follow rain. He'd assumed she felt the same.

But there was no way Jessica could have borne a child and passed med school. No way she could have managed a family for years after that if she trained as a surgeon, as she'd assumed she would back then. And if she survived the brutal term of surgical residency and then a fellowship, well, then the first few years of establishing a private practice were even *more* exhausting, as her father had pointed out. It was no accident that most women physicians were childless, at least till their late thirties.

"Wait ten to twelve *years?*" she remembered Sam shouting in disbelief. "In twelve years, Jess, I'll be forty-one, if I'm not dead and buried or gone senile. By the time they'd be needing braces, I'd be ready for dentures!"

And after six months together with never a cross word, *she* couldn't believe he was yelling at her! Couldn't believe he was yelling at her in *public,* on a city street, since they'd been walking back from his lab hand in hand when she told him. She'd left him without a backward glance—had hopped on a passing bus. Hadn't returned home till midnight.

And their reconciliation had made the fight almost worthwhile. They'd made passionate, remorseful love till dawn and hadn't argued again—for a week.

Stop. She stood very still, eyes shut, breath uneven. *It's over, done with, gone. So just stop it.* But he'd ripped the wounds open. How long would they take to heal this time?

A soft tap on her cheek—cat's paw. Jessica opened her eyes to find Cattoo staring at her. Cattoo reached up tentatively... oh, so delicately... to touch her face again.

"You're right, I have you." Jessica bent to touch noses, paused nose to nose. Neither of them blinked. Their eyes were *precisely* the same color, not quite green, not quite topaz. But the effect was more striking contrasted with Cattoo's midnight fur.

Jessica's chin-length hair was a light honey brown. With tawny skin and bronzy eyes, the effect was... monotone. Good bones were all that saved her from total obscurity. "But I have you, if I don't have looks. Who could ask for more?"

Besides, asking had never meant getting in Jessica's world. Not the one thing she really wanted.

Stop.

"We get any exciting mail?" She moved to the heap of letters on the floor. Juggling cat from one shoulder to the other, she scooped it all up, settled them both on the couch with the mail beside them. "Hmm, Victoria's Secret, you going to order that red silk teddy you've been drooling over for three catalogs now? Ohhhh, don't think I didn't notice. I saw you'd marked the page."

Cattoo wasn't telling. Her paws were spread on Jessica's chest, the claws lightly hooked in the lapels of Jessica's suit. Limp, Cattoo gazed up at her, lids half-mast, pupils expanded to pools of darkness, purr midtempo.

Red silk teddies... He'd given her a dark green one their first Christmas together, though he'd addressed the gift-wrapped package to himself, opened it with oohs and ahhs of astonishment, then generously offered to share it with her.

Jess tossed the catalog aside, sat staring into space like her cat for a moment, then shook herself and went back to the mail. She flipped past a bill or two, then paused as she noted a return address. "Grenada."

She'd half forgotten. Last month, after she'd phoned Toby and found only more mystery, she'd written the dean of the med school in Grenada.

"Fast response." But whatever it was, she couldn't deal with it, not tonight. Intellectual puzzles were the farthest thing from her mind. Raye Talbot would have to wait.

In fact, everything could wait. Right now she needed—
A laughing image rose in her mind's eye. She shoved it back
into the farthest cupboard of her mind, slammed the door,
locked it, nailed a board across it and stood. She needed
obliteration. "Let's go to bed."

Lights off below, they padded upstairs, Cattoo half a step
in the lead, tail primly erect, ears cocked back to monitor
Jessica's progress.

"Move your fuzzy butt. Do you want to trip us both?"

Cattoo stopped midstair to consider that. Jessica made
a frantic sidestep, clutched at the banister. "Blast!" She
shook her head, laughed under her breath and went on—
almost tripped again when Cattoo shot past, ears rakishly
flattened, to skid around the bedroom door.

She was sitting demurely on the bed when Jess arrived,
with a "What took you so long?" look on her face. On the
bedside table, the answering machine blinked its tiny red
eye.

One or the other of Jessica's new partners had taken her
calls while she'd been gone, and would continue doing so
until morning. Barring a full-scale emergency, any messages from that quarter should be waiting for her at the office.

And, new as she was to the city, her social life was min-
imal, close to nonexistent. Not that it was ever—

"Mother?" she guessed, while she rewound the tape.
Jessica had told her last week she'd be out of town. But,
senior partner with one of the hottest corporate law firms
in Chicago, Eleanor Myles always had a thousand things on
her mind at any given moment. Remembering Jessica's
itinerary would hardly be top priority.

"Raye?" Jessica hoped not. The psychiatrist had suggested they go out for supper twice since that first time two
weeks ago, and Jess was running out of plausible excuses.

The tape turned, and his voice, with all its heart-tugging

memories, leapt out at her. *"Jess . . . Jess, you've got to listen to—"*

Her finger mashed down on the stop button—pressed it till her fingertip turned white. Eyes spilling tears, she shook her head. *No . . . No, Sam, no, I don't.*

CHAPTER THREE

SHE DREAMED ALL NIGHT, but could barely recall her dreams at dawn—something about falling.

Nothing unusual there. Since her fall from a tree at age eight, she'd feared heights, and it often showed in her dreams. Besides, as a therapy-minded friend had once pointed out, falls symbolize loss of control, something she dreaded.

Whatever, this time she didn't fall alone. Sam was there, or at least his voice was, wordless, warning, chasing her down into rushing darkness. Colors and images streamed past as she fell, her hair like a comet's tail rising above her.

But if her dreams were all black and rushing colors, her mood on waking was gray. She dressed in gray sweats, fed the yawning cat, then went out into a gray dawn to run her depression off. Five brisk miles through the misty, sleeping streets of the East Side and her gloom gradually withdrew, like a tide ebbing out to sea.

And like a tide, it would return. But meanwhile she had morning rounds to make at the hospital, then a full day of appointments scheduled. Work had saved her before. It would save her this time. All she had to do was give herself to its incessant demands, heart, body and soul. There'd be nothing left of her to grieve or even think about what might have been.

THERE'D BEEN TWO new admissions while she'd attended the conference, bringing her patients in hospital up to five.

"Next guy is a twenty-five-year-old white male, adult-onset diabetic, not complying with his regimen," med student Chris Carson reported as they strode along the corridor. "Came into ER last night in a coma, then admitted. He's come around nicely. His mother's still upset."

She was. "Another one!" she exclaimed when Jessica and Chris entered the room. "How many people are going to poke and prod him? And where's my son's doctor—Dr. Neuman?"

"Dr. Neuman moved to Hawaii. I'm Dr. Myles. I've been hired by his partners at Diagnostics to take over his practice."

But why did Neuman abandon the practice? Jessica wondered not for the first time. After twelve years of building it up, that wasn't something a doctor did lightly. It was too hard to pull up stakes, then try to start over from zero somewhere else. And Hawaii... That was as far from Rhode Island as a doctor could travel and still practice medicine.

"You're a doctor? A real one, not just a student like..." The woman jerked her chin at Chris, who stood at the foot of the bed.

"Yes, I'm a real doctor. A general internist like Dr. Neuman, board certified." She moved to the bed and lifted the young man's wrist. "How are you feeling this morning, Richard?"

He gave her an embarrassed grin. "I'm feeling better. Much better."

"Good." She made a notation on the chart Chris handed her, then sat down at bedside. "So let's talk about how we can keep you feeling that way." He was old enough to accept that he had a chronic disease and cope accordingly. *Or maybe he isn't,* she thought, as his mother hovered, trying to read his chart over Jessica's shoulder.

Perhaps a session with Raye's in order? Raye Talbot was the attending psychiatrist for RI Gen, after all, there to help doctors answer just such questions. Because to cure the body, sometimes you had to start with the mind. But after the Coffman case Jessica had referred to her... *Not just yet,* she decided. "So tell me about yesterday. What did you eat?"

Once she'd made her rounds, Jessica had almost an hour to spare before her first appointment. Breakfast, then, she decided, though she had no appetite. But that was another thing she'd learned during residency, when opportunities for food and sleep had been sporadic at best. How did that rule for interns go? *When you see a chair, sit on it.* When you see a bed, lie on it. And when you found a chance to eat, you ate. If you lived like a machine, then you must refuel like one, appetite or no.

In the doctors' dining room, she took her tray to a table near the windows. She sat with her back to the center table, where several residents and attending physicians were carrying on an animated debate about the latest episode of a hospital soap opera that was currently the rage.

She could have joined in. She'd be welcome at their table, and she'd seen the episode they were shredding one of the nights she'd spent hidden away in her room at the conference.

"Does anyone besides me know that you're shy?" she remembered Sam asking that first week they'd met. They'd been lying on a blanket down by the river, their shoulders touching, her organic chem book spread before them. Another kind of chemistry on their minds. "Does anyone else know you're shy, or do they all think you're snooty Ms. Perfect Princess, too busy scoring straight A's to stop and play with the po' folks?"

Stung, she'd rolled away from him and thrown an arm over her eyes. "Is that what I seem like?"

"To those who can't look past the wrappings, I imagine it is," he'd drawled, reaching for a lock of her hair. "And it's a pretty slick package. All that poise and brains, you scare people, I bet." He pulled, and she felt the tug down to her toes. They'd made love perhaps a dozen times by then, and he could melt her with just a look now that she understood what his looks promised. He tugged again and her back arched in lazy, inevitable reflex. With a rueful groan he rolled over on top of her, his weight braced on his forearms.

"Not that I'm complaining," he murmured, brushing her eyebrows with the tip of his nose. "Not since I'm in on the secret. Ms. Jessica Myles, shy...proud as the devil...and *hot.*" Laughter quivered in his voice as she arched up against him and moaned a little wordless plea. "No, babe, I'm not complaining at all."

Stop! She turned her face to the window and stared out at the garden, not taking in the view. Oh, he'd ripped open the wounds, all right. She hadn't let herself think this way in years. Not in the daytime, anyway. *Think of something else.* She picked up her coffee, drank it black and grimaced, then remembered the letter. From Grenada. She'd tucked it into her briefcase to read sometime during the day. And now was the time.

Addressed to the dean of the School of Medicine, St. George's University, Grenada, her question had been simple. Had either a Ms. Anne Talbot or a Ms. Raye Talbot attended the school roughly twelve years ago?

The dean's answer was equally simple.

Miss Anne R. Talbot of Decatur, Alabama, USA, had graduated from the School of Medicine, with honors, class of '84. If the dean could be of further assistance, she was welcome to call him. His number was—

So that's that, Jessica thought, folding the letter and tucking it back into its envelope. *You were worried about nothing.* "R" stood for Raye of course. Anne Raye Talbot, of Alabama. She frowned. But Toby's Anne R. was a blonde...

So he'd confused some other student, some poor little mousy blonde, with Anne Raye Talbot. It had been years ago, and Toby probably staggered through med school with a bottle of rum under one arm. And no doubt it was bodies Toby remembered best, not the names attached to them. *So forget it. Mind your own business.* Just because the woman made her...uneasy, that didn't mean—

Someone sat down heavily at the next table, and Jessica glanced over. Jon Cooper. The first-year resident sat staring into space, his big hands clenched around a cup of coffee.

Jessica waited. Had he truly not noticed her? Or did he want to be alone? But if so, why come and sit near her? "Jon?"

"Huh!" He jerked around. The cup of coffee tipped over. He stared at her wildly, then looked down at his mess and started to curse.

Jessica stood and handed him her napkin. "I'll get you another."

Leave him alone, or try to make him talk? she wondered, waiting in the serving line for his coffee. She didn't really know Jon that well, though he was as close to a friend as she'd made in her month at RI Gen.

When Jessica had first arrived, Jon was nearly through his six-week rotation on Med-2, the ward to which her patients were generally assigned. The night they'd sat out a death watch together, Jon had talked and she had listened. And listening, she'd found they had much in common.

Like many who entered the profession, both of them were doctors' kids. Both of them had thought they'd be surgeons—Jon still thought he might be. Both of them wondered if they should be doctors at all.

And neither of them was happy, though neither had admitted that.

It had made for a strong bond of sympathy. "There's no law that says you have to be a doctor!" Jessica had insisted. "Just because your father wants you to be..." She'd paused, shocked to hear the echo of Sam in her words. He'd said precisely this—how many times? But she hadn't listened.

As Jon couldn't listen. He'd gone too far down the road—four years of premed, four years of med school, a year of internship, now four months into his residency After all that time spent, all that tuition—all financed by his father of course—how could he walk away now?

"You just do it!" Jessica had cried. "This is the only life you've *got,* Jon. If this isn't what you want to do with it..." She'd wanted to shake him, make him *see* somehow before it truly was too late. He thought *he'd* gone too far down that road? Then where was she, five years ahead of him on the same path?

But he hadn't listened. His talk had swerved to his wife and what was happening to their marriage under the pressure of the hundred-hour work weeks. He was terrified she'd leave him.

It was no empty fear. Between them they could have named a dozen wrecked marriages. *My own*, Jessica had thought, though she and Sam hadn't even survived med school.

"Sometimes, after nights on call, I'm too tired to love her," Jon had confessed, staring down at his hands. "And she understands, but..."

But it was hard to ask one partner to forgo all his or her needs for the other year after year. The essence of love was that you were there for the other. And it wasn't simply physical exhaustion. What if you felt and felt and felt till you shut down all of your emotions in self-defense? *Sorry, dear, but I already gave at the office.*

Perhaps the wonder was that *any* of them stayed married. And looking at the older doctors, Jessica had to wonder what some of the surviving marriages were like. Look at her own father's marriage—she'd shied away from that thought.

But even if she could have—should have—taken another path and had lacked the courage to do so, still, it wasn't too late for Jon. Jessica had urged him to talk with Raye, whom she hadn't met at that point. But the consulting psychiatrist was available to house staff, as well as patients. "Just a session to help you sort out if you're doing what you really should be doing," Jessica had suggested. Might not help, but how could it hurt?

Jon had gone to see Raye the day before he'd rotated up to surgery, and Jessica hadn't seen him since. A chat with a shrink couldn't hurt him, but perhaps Jessica's pushing him into that chat had hurt their friendship.

She bought a fresh coffee for herself, as well, checked her watch, then returned to his table. "So how have you been? How's surgery?"

"Fine."

Maybe it was, but something wasn't fine. Seeing him full face for the first time, Jessica looked quickly down at her cup. Those rings under his eyes hadn't been there two weeks ago. His cheeks had hollowed. Lost a good five to ten pounds, she figured, and his *eyes*... Surgery was that bad? Or his marriage?

"We miss you on Med-2," she said lightly, and proceeded to tell him about the ninety-year-old woman who'd tired of the med students' attempts to insert an IV last week. Jessica was just reaching the point where the chief resident had entered the fray and the woman was threatening to insert the needle herself, when—

Beep, beep!

They both glanced down at their beepers. Jess looked up with relief—it wasn't hers—to catch an expression of—what?—loathing?—on Jon's face as he slapped a hand to his belt. "Mine." He stood, then gazed down at her.

Surgery was *that* bad it could make him look like this? So the talk with Raye hadn't helped. "Come see me sometime, Jon? My office is on third in the professional building, if you don't catch me on the wards."

He nodded absently, tried to smile. "Be well, Jessica." He strode out of the room, a big, good-looking, miserable young man.

"Be well, Jon," she whispered after him. He wouldn't come for that visit. Whatever was going on with him, their friendship was clearly over. She wouldn't see him again, except by accident.

That accident happened less than twenty minutes later. Jessica had stayed to finish her coffee; sometimes caffeine helped with the blues. With minutes to go before her first appointment, she took a shortcut through Med 1, on the third floor. An elevated, glass-sided walkway connected the end of that wing to the professional building across the street.

Hurrying down the deserted hall, she was approaching the intersection where the wing met the walkway in a T when, ahead of her, a door slammed open with startling violence. Its knob hit the wall, then the door rebounded. Jessica stopped short. A tall figure in white lunged into view. Without looking her way, the man—Jon Cooper— lurched off in the opposite direction. He turned right when he reached the T, a route that would take him back toward another wing of the hospital.

What in heavens? If Jessica wasn't mistaken, the door led to a supply closet.

The door moved again—someone inside the closet was pushing it open. Reacting without thought, Jessica stepped backward into one of the recessed window bays that lit the hall.

Out in the corridor, the door shut softly. Then footsteps—not stunned and lurching like Jon's, but smooth, deliberate . . . a woman's. Moving away. Jessica stood still as the *tick-tick-tick* of high heels grew fainter, then died. Whoever it was had turned the corner into the passage.

Jessica gave her a minute more, then followed, frowning. She'd have sworn, from the way he'd talked, that Jon Cooper loved his young wife. She stopped by the door he'd burst out of, hesitated, then opened it.

It was a closet all right, not even deep enough to merit a light inside. Her nostrils flared at the scent within—a hint of perfume, a whiff of something earthier— She shut the door hastily. So maybe Jon loved his wife, but that didn't stop him from loving someone else in a linen closet.

Back in New York, Basso Profundo would've argued that there was no paradox here. Men were instinctively polygamous. It had nothing to do with love.

But why follow your instincts if it made you unhappy? The way Jon had moved, like something wounded. Something trying to escape . . . Jessica turned the corner into the walkway, and stopped again.

Far down the passage, moving with the sliding grace of a tiger, a tall, slender woman strode on high heels. Raye Talbot . . .

ONCE JESSICA REACHED her office, there was no time to consider the question, or any question outside of medi-

cine. Her dance card was full with scheduled appointments, and three work-ins before noon.

Though the doctors of Diagnostics, Inc., also accepted
their own patients, the partnership specialized in referrals
from primary-care physicians. With a rheumatologist, a
cardiologist, an oncologist and Jessica—the generalist—on
staff, they consulted on the mystery cases of internal medicine, where a diagnosis had yet to be reached. But to keep
those referrals coming, you had to make your referring
physicians' worries your own. That often made for a hec-
tic schedule.

For lunch she ate yogurt at her desk, the history of her
next patient spread before her, her favorite reference book
to one side.

Her phone rang. "Call for you on line four," Caroline
Hardy, the office receptionist, said when Jessica picked up.

"Who?"

"Wouldn't say. A woman." Caroline clicked off.

Jessica punched the blinking light.

"What do I have to do to get you to come out and play?
Slash your tires?"

Raye Talbot. As with Sam, there was always a current of
amusement flowing through her voice. But with Raye
somehow the effect was dark, self-contained, not open and
sunny like Sam. It wasn't laughter, ready and waiting to be
loosed on the world, but a purr of private satisfaction.

Slashed tires—that was why Jessica had gone to supper
with Raye in the first place. It had been raining when Jess
left the office late—only to find that the back tires of her
car had been slashed.

With RJ Gen's inner-city location, vandalism was a frequent problem in the parking lots. Acres of poorly guarded
cars were a sure invitation to roaming delinquents. Jessica
had counted herself lucky that was all the damage they'd
done. And she'd been lucky Raye had happened by just
then, in that driving rain, to offer her a ride home.

Though the ride had turned into more than she'd bar-
gained for...

"Jessica?" Raye prodded, still amused. "Supper? Tonight? I want to hear *all* about your adventures in New York."

It was Raye who had adventures, not Jessica. For the life of her, Jess couldn't see why the psychiatrist would seek to befriend someone as tame as herself. That was part of her uneasiness, that and Raye's persistence. Jess had given her no encouragement—had dodged her at every turn—these past few weeks. Yet she kept on coming.

"Cat got your tongue?"

"No—oh, no. You just surprised me. I was trying to think if I had any..." She didn't want to go out to supper. For one thing, she didn't drive with people who drank, and Raye had sucked it down that last time. Afterward Jessica would have insisted on driving, but Raye owned a gleaming black Corvette with half a city block of engine under its hood, a car of unnerving power. And even if she'd dared take its wheel, Jess didn't drive a stick shift.

And calling a cab had been out of the question. The part of the city where Raye had taken her, cabs didn't venture after dark. So the drive home had been hair-raising.

"Any plans? You have a hot date tonight, Jessica?" Amusement and disbelief curled around the words.

"Well, actually, there is some work I need to catch up on, and—"

"All right. Then what about tomorrow?"

"Ahh..." She'd never been good at lying. And she needed friends. Shy as she was, she was always slow to make them in a new setting, but was this the friend she—

"Good. I'll pick you up at eight, then on to the *bon temps*. I have a new restaurant to show you— Oops, call on line one. See you tomorrow."

Jessica sat, listening to a dial tone. *Why me?* And remembering the perfume she'd smelled back in the closet...

Groping for something to talk about early on that evening they'd gone out, she'd asked Raye about her perfume, a nose-stirring blend of musk, cinnamon and something more exotic. Raye had pulled a vial from her purse. "It's called Adventuress." Uncapping the vial, she'd upended it against her fingertip. Then, abruptly, she'd reached across the table to touch the back of Jess's wrist, leaving her scented for the night. "Like it?"

"Very nice." Jess had hidden her shock behind her wrist as she sniffed. But somehow the gesture hadn't felt nice. Oh, she knew she was too touch-me-notish. Far too inhibited. Knowing Sam for almost a year, she'd learned that much of the world touched each other in spontaneity and friendship, sometimes simply to make a point. Had learned to love it, when it was Sam doing the touching.

But what was the point here? Animals marked their territory with scent, to claim it. Perhaps her revulsion was on as instinctive a level. She didn't care to be . . . annexed.

Or perhaps it was simply that she preferred florals. Her own scent was the cool, clean sweetness of freesias.

Musk . . . Then the page Jon had received down in the dining room—that must have been Raye. She'd summoned him for a quickie in a closet.

And he hadn't gone smiling—

The phone rang again. "Mrs. Dabney's ready for you in room one," said Caroline. "Mr. Mendoza just walked in, and when you have a minute . . ."

She didn't have a minute again until eight-thirty that night. She would have stayed later—there was one case in particular she needed to read up on—but there was a certain cat to consider. Jessica might have saved her from life in a Dumpster, but having done so, she was obliged to provide companionship and amusement to replace the outdoor stimulation Cattoo had lost.

They played Cat in a Box—black, starfish paws groping frantically from within the cardboard den while Jessica's fingers crept mouselike across its sides—until Cattoo purred with contentment and Jessica was holed silly. Then they holed up on the couch, Jessica reading, with Cattoo draped across her stomach.

The phone rang, upstairs and down. Both of them turned to look. "For you?" Jessica suggested. "That orange tom you've been ogling?" She'd caught Cattoo last week perched on a bedroom windowsill, crying and doing her best to butt her way through the screen, while the orange tom sauntered a good sixty feet below. The tom might be to die for, but—given the sheer drop onto rocky ground, to say nothing of the wrought-iron fence—Jessica was keeping that window shut till she found a way to reinforce the screen.

The phone stopped ringing. Upstairs her answering machine would take a message, if there was one. Jessica sighed and set Cattoo to one side. It was her night on call.

The message was a long time rewinding. The tape clicked to a stop, then started rolling. "Listen to me," Sam insisted. "We've got to—"

"No." She hit the button, sat for a second, then fell backward on the bed, rolled onto her stomach and dragged a pillow over her head. *No, we don't, Sam.* Couldn't he understand this wasn't a game for her? That she couldn't do it—couldn't be friends, couldn't stay in touch? Sure, he probably worried about her, wondered if her life was going well, but she couldn't help him.

Because she was the little Dutch boy and he was the ocean. The only way she could live, at all, with Sam Kirby in the same world was to build a dike between them—a dike high as the sky, wide as all creation.

But breach that dike with one pinhole, let even a drop of water seep through, and all would be lost. The hole would grow and grow till the dike collapsed and she was swept away.

Talking to him was the pinhole; she couldn't do it.

But this isn't much better, she thought, rubbing her face back and forth against the bedspread. *I can't spend my life with one thumb stuck in the dike. Blast him!*

A weight landed on top of the pillow. Cattoo padded across, then stepped off the other side. "Mrr?"

"Go 'way!" Jessica hugged the pillow to the back of her head. What had set him off the past year, after seven long years of silence?

The last time she'd seen Sam, before yesterday, was the time he'd talked his way past the doorman of the apart-

ment she'd rented near her med school a month after she'd
left him. He'd pretended to be a pizza deliveryman. She
could still see him standing outside her door, his hawk nose
made enormous by her fish-eye peephole, a pizza box in
one hand, a bouquet of red roses in the other, a wide, uncertain grin on his face.

Instead of flinging open the door, she'd run down the
back stairs, left town, hadn't stopped running till she'd
reached Guatemala, where she'd obtained her quickie divorce. After she'd sent him the papers, he hadn't bothered
her. Until those two cards this past year.

Soft scrabbling along the edge of the pillow—Cattoo
trying to push her nose beneath.

"*Beat* it! No, I didn't mean that." Jessica tossed the pillow aside and rolled over. Eyes closed, she reached for the
cat.

Whiskers brushing her face, so different from a man's
whiskers. Sometimes he'd scratched her raw making love in
the mornings, and she'd loved it.

God, stop it! Think of something else—anything else.
The cat squeaked a protest as she hugged her.

Raye, think of Raye, then, if that was all there was. Raye
and a young man with fear and loathing in his face... Jessica focused on the problem, replacing that laughing,
wicked grin with a boy in trouble. *Focus.* It was the one
thing she did really well. She could aim her mind like a laser, shutting out everything beyond its beam. She never
would have survived the past eight years without that gift
of concentration. Some people were brilliant—Sam, her
brother Winston, both her parents... Jessica regrettably
was not, but oh, she could concentrate. On Jon Cooper...and Raye, who was a tall, sleek brunette, not a mousy
blonde . On Jon, who'd gone to Raye on Jessica's advice
and was therefore her responsibility.. And then there was
Robert Coffman, the first hint she'd had that something
might be wrong.

"If you're a trained hypnotist," she'd asked Raye the
first time they met, out in the corridor that separated their
offices, "can you cure smokers?"

"If the motivation is strong, certainly," Raye had assured her.

And so Jessica had sent Raye Robert Coffman, who was flirting with emphysema. A head of a corporation here in the city, an educated, intelligent man with a young family and a wife who begged him to quit, Coffman was surely someone who could stop smoking with a little help. Given the right patient and the right hypnotist, hypnotherapy could work wonders.

But something had happened. Coffman had kept his appointment with Raye, then he'd canceled his follow-up with Jessica. When she'd called him to find out why, he'd laughed—not a pleasant laugh—and slammed the phone down. She hadn't been able to reach him since.

So she'd called Raye.

"Couldn't help him," Raye had explained briskly. "The first thing you do, Dr. Myles, once you've taken someone under, is to simply ask: why do you smoke?"

"And he told you?"

"Oh, *yesss*..." Again, that undercurrent of amusement. "He said he wanted to kill himself."

"He *what?*"

"Oh, it's not that uncommon, Dr. Myles. Or may I call you Jessica? I've run across it before. Some smokers smoke for pleasure, some for...darker reasons. But if that's the reason, hypnotism isn't the answer. You just say thanks very much, and you bring him back out of trance.

"Now if Coffman wanted to try long-term therapy...if he wants to get to the root of his problem..."

But Coffman wanted nothing more to do with either of them. A letter requesting the transfer of his medical records to another internist had followed a few days after that.

The incident had been troubling, but such things happened. Patients got into snits. Or sometimes the chemistry between doctor and patient simply wasn't there. But usually the break was a matter of polite disinterest—a drifting apart, not a bitter rupture.

A few days later, Raye had given her that ride home, by
way of a tiny, cockroach-ridden café in Providence's most
blighted and dangerous slum.

Sam would say— No! Concentrate...on Raye, who came
from Alabama, according to the dean of her med school.
Raye, who spoke without a trace of a Southern drawl. Jessica set the cat to one side, rolled over and reached for the
phone book.

The area code for Decatur, Alabama, was 205. And information listed only five Talbots in the city. The first two
weren't home; the third was.

"Anne R. Talbot?" the man drawled above the background babble of a TV set. "Annie's my sister. No, she
doesn't live here. Who's this?"

To explain would take half the night. "Jessica Myles. A
friend of mine knew her in med school down in Grenada.
He was just wondering if..." Jessica stared at the ceiling.
"He was wondering if she ever became a psychiatrist, the
way she was planning to?"

"Annie?" Talbot hooted. "Annie wanted to be a head-
shrinker? Now that'd be the day! No, she's an ophthal-
mologist. Practices down in New Orleans. You sure you got
the right Anne Talbot?"

"I'm beginning to wonder," Jessica admitted. "But
could you tell me one thing more?"

"Sure, if you make it fast. It's Auburne's third and ten
on their twenty-yard line."

"Oh, sorry. Is Anne's middle name Raye, by any
chance?"

Her brother snorted. "It's Roberta, after our grandmother. You've got the wrong doc, honey, and now—
Oooooo, shi—ngar! Damn! Excuse me, ma'am, but that's
the ball game. *Butterfingers!*"

With a hasty thanks, Jessica hung up. Slowly she sank
back to stare at the ceiling. Anne *Roberta* Talbot, mousy
little blond lab rat, now practicing ophthalmology in New
Orleans, could not be stretched to become tall, raven-haired
psychiatrist Raye Talbot of Providence, no matter how you
tugged at her. They were two different people.

Both had gone to St. George's in Grenada, both had graduated from there in '84, though neither the dean nor Toby remembered Raye Talbot, a woman whom no man, in his right mind, would ever forget. "Makes no sense, cat." Not a good kind of sense.

The phone rang. She should hit the mute button. Instead, her head turned slowly, her hair rasping against the bedspread till she stared at the answering machine. Her message tape rolled. Somewhere, water spurted through a pinhole, tearing chunks away... *So speak, then, damn you.*

"Jessica?" said her mother's voice, cool and hard as cultured pearls. "If you're there, will you pick up, please?"

So much for that! She wanted to laugh, needed to cry, couldn't do either. Jessica reached for the phone, then her hand fell back to the bed. The best way to hide your feelings was not to talk when you were feeling.

From half a continent away, her mother's little hiss of exasperation came clearly across the line. "Jessica, I have a message for you from Sam—Sam Kirby?"

As if there'd ever been any other Sam. Jessica shook her head, kept on shaking it. He was shameless—when he went for something, he went all out.

"It was so nice to hear from him after all these years." Her parents had loathed Sam for the first six months of her marriage, seeing him as Jessica's academic downfall. Her father had been appalled when he found that, at twenty-nine, Sam was only just completing his dissertation. Once it was published and Sam's portrait appeared on the cover of *Time,* along with a strand of DNA, they'd adored him.

For his part, Sam had remained steadfast in his distaste for her parents, though he'd always managed to be polite. Their late-coming approval hadn't changed his opinion at all.

"He said he was having trouble reaching you, and that he wanted me to give you a message." Her mother laughed uncertainly. "I believe I have it right. He said you should think about uncles and falcons, whatever that means. And his number is 415-555-6846. That's San Francisco. He's giving a paper out there at some conference. He said you could reach him any time at all tonight—he's given up sleeping." She chuckled indulgently. "I presume that's a joke. Or maybe it isn't? Einstein only slept three hours a night, they say, so—"

Jessica's finger came down on the mute button.

Uncles and falcons... "Tired? *Who's* tired?" She'd been so sure of herself those first few months with Sam. Somehow he'd made her brave. She'd sat up, turned onto her knees, slid a leg across him to kneel astride, her fingers spread on his hairy chest. "I'm going to love you, Sam *Antonio* Kirby, till you holler uncle!"

"Oh, yeah?" He'd reached for her breast.

"Yeah!" She'd caught his wrist, caught the other one, swung his arms over his head to pin them to the mattress.

Laughing, he'd let her have her wicked way. They'd ended half an hour later in a tangle of bedsheets, heads off the foot of the bed, Jess on the bottom, back arched, her breasts pressed to his damp chest, her hair sweeping the floor. Only Sam's braced arm kept them defying gravity. "Uncle?" he panted.

"Uncle," she admitted, cupping one hand to his hip. Content to be dropped on her head if it pleased him. Content...

"'Bout time you learned, babe, what they say in Texas," he drawled, nuzzling her ear, already half-asleep.

"Wha's that?" she murmured, drifting herself into darkness.

"Don't f...um, fool with a falcon, till you learn how to fly."

Startled awake, she'd laughed, and they'd slithered right off the bed. The tenant downstairs, old crabby Mr. Hadley, had started thumping his ceiling—their floor—with his broom. They'd had to press their mouths to each other's shoulders to stifle the laughter.

Goddamn you, Sam. Damn you for making me love you, when you couldn't keep loving me yourself. If I wasn't happy before you found me, at least I was... whole.

His message ... uncles and falcons ... Arrogant as ever, he was telling her he could make her cry uncle. Make her talk to him.

"Not anymore, Sam," she whispered, and wondered if he could hear her three thousand miles away. "Not this time. I'm a big girl now."

And no longer a fool. With the mark of talons still striping her heart, she'd sworn off flying. And falcons.

CHAPTER FOUR

SHE FELL AGAIN in her dreams, this time with a falcon diving beside her. Woke to the sound of purring; Cattoo liked to sleep on her pillow, nose jammed in Jessica's ear, one of their few points of disagreement. Ran five miles through the dawn-lit streets, her breath smoking—autumn was coming fast. Saw five patients for morning rounds, though Richard, the diabetic, would go home that day.

Jessica walked in the doctors' door to Diagnostics by nine. Telephone held to one ear, Caroline looked up from the appointment book and rolled her eyes. "If you're having heart palpitations, Mr. Kirby, then I really think you should see our cardiologist, Dr.— Oh? Well . . . If you're sure . . . Let me see if Dr. Myles can work you in this—"

She stopped as Jessica shook her head frantically. "Um, just a moment, Mr. Kirby, while I put you on hold." She hit a button, then cocked an eyebrow.

"*Samuel* Kirby?" Jessica demanded. It was six in the morning in California, for Pete's sake. Maybe he *had* given up sleeping.

"Yes. I guess he knows you?"

Apart from Sam's side of the equation—his family, plus a motley crew of lab mates, professors, janitors, jam-session buddies, weight-lifting pals and whoever else he'd buttonholed on the street to tell on a whim—only Jessica's parents and a few select friends from college knew she'd ever been married. The less people the better, as far as Jessica was concerned. It was nobody's business but her own.

"I've met him, but I don't want to take him on as a patient. None of us would want him. Why don't you recommend Dr. Rheinhardt?"

Caroline gave her a look, but she nodded and hit the line button. "Mr. Kirby? I don't believe we can help you here. In fact, I'm sure we can't. Could I recommend another doctor?"

Jessica moved on toward her office.

Behind her, Caroline said, "Dr. Rheinhardt's a, er, proctologist— I *beg* your pardon?" She slammed the phone down. "Well, *really!*"

Ducking into her office, Jessica closed the door, leaned against it and blew out a breath. He'd learned where she worked through the convention roster, she supposed. Or perhaps he'd wheedled it out of her mother?

Jessica had never explained why she'd left Sam—it had been too humiliating. And naturally her parents would never ask, if she didn't volunteer the information. Still, she'd always suspected they'd been disappointed by her divorce.

But then, what had she ever done but disappoint them? If she couldn't be a brilliant surgeon like her brother, Winston, the very least she could have done was to marry someone brilliant—then have the grace to stay married.

Instead, she'd left her husband just as he was making it to the big time. Her father couldn't even drop Sam's name at parties, *my son-in-law, a Nobel laureate, you know, molecular biologist* . . .

Jessica blew out another breath and crossed to her desk. Time to prep for her first patient. Work—it would save her, if anything could. *Uncle, my ass, Sam Kirby.*

She focused ferociously on medicine till noon, and when she did break concentration, it was to contemplate her other problem—Raye Talbot. After a moment's thought she picked up the phone.

"Dr. Talbot's office," answered Raye's receptionist, Tiffany, in her breathy, baby-talk voice.

In Jessica's estimation, this young woman's sole aim in life was to grow the longest fingernails known to man. It was odd that Raye wouldn't want someone with Caroline's tact and common sense to represent her interests before the public. But then, wasn't this just one more oddity among dozens? "This is Dr. Myles. May I speak to Dr. Talbot, please?"

"Oh, she's wandered off somewhere. D'you want me t'take a message?"

"No, thanks, I'll try back later." Jessica had made up her mind. There was no way she'd see Raye socially, not until she'd sorted out just who and what the psychiatrist was.

Most likely, she kept telling herself, there was some perfectly innocent explanation for the anomalies she'd uncovered. But what that explanation was, she couldn't begin to guess.

And she'd placed herself in the awkward position of knowing more than she should, yet not being able to ask for clarifications. *Raye, I've been snooping around in your past, and I have just a few questions.* Right.

It was an awkward position all around. Without asking, she might never learn the truth of the matter. Yet without knowing, she wasn't willing to further the relationship. The best course seemed to be to mind her own business, as she should have done from the start.

But meantime there was young Jon Cooper, with misery written all over his face—what about him? Jessica gritted her teeth and went back to work.

She tried once more to reach Raye, without success, then didn't try again until she found a gap in her schedule at three. Jessica dashed down to the cafeteria for a cup of soup. Returning to the professional building, she paused outside the door to Raye's office.

It would be easier to do this by phone. Raye had a certain...power, especially face-to-face. A way of sweeping you along with her plans, whatever your own desires. *But not this time*, Jessica told herself. Sam might call her a rabbit, and maybe sometimes she was, but not this time. This time she'd simply say, "No, thank you." Lifting her chin, she opened the door—to find the waiting room empty.

The glass slider that walled off the pass-through to the receptionist's office was open, but the lights were switched off in there. *They've gone home for the day?* Jessica frowned. Great, she didn't have Raye's home number and would bet it wasn't listed. Yet it wouldn't be fair to leave Raye thinking she had a companion for supper, much less make her drive by Jessica's house for a no-show.

Besides, if Raye made it as far as Jessica's doorstep, would she take no for an answer?

"Hello?" Jessica leaned over the counter. There was only one door leading from the receptionist's cubbyhole. That was to her left, opening onto an inner hallway apparently. That door was closed.

On a side table, a computer sat, with its screen-saver program turned on, the monitor glowing in the dimness. A kaleidoscopic pattern expanded, changed from blue, to lavender, to rosy pink, to blood red—collapsed. A new design formed slowly from the rubble, spinning, shapes within shapes, strange patterns teetering on the brink of consciousness and recognition.

If the computer was still switched on, then they hadn't shut down for the night. Someone had to be around. "Hello?"

Jessica pushed away from the counter to study a closed door in the waiting room—the only other door in sight. If this suite was like the Diagnostics suite across the hall, then this door led to a corridor, with exam rooms off it. Raye's office would be somewhere along the hall. Perhaps she was in, even if her secretary had stepped out?

Jessica opened the door. "Raye?" The suite was much smaller than Diagnostics'—hardly surprising, she supposed, since Raye worked without partners. The first door to the left led to a small washroom. To the right was the door to the receptionist's room. Beyond, there was one more door.

"Hello?" Jessica knocked, and when no one answered, she entered.

The office was larger than she'd expected, and empty. Empty, yet filled with the essence of its owner. Jessica stood in the doorway, sniffing musk and cinnamon, her eyes probing the shadows.

At the near end of the room, a sweep of gleaming, asymmetrical ebony formed Raye's desk. No papers, framed photos, pen stands—none of the usual office clutter or personal knickknacks marred its glossy surface, except for... Jessica's eyes stopped on the round, dark shape.

Shoes sinking into misty blue carpet, she crossed to the desk and reached for the object.

It was a stone, black, not quite a perfect egg shape, its silky smoothness conforming perfectly to the palm of the hand. *Some people stroke black cats, all warmth and softness and grateful noise,* she found herself thinking. *Some people stroke cold—* She put it down where she'd found it, within easy reach of Raye's black leather swivel chair.

I shouldn't be here. The feeling of intrusion was intense. Jessica turned to face the couch and chair at the far end of the room.

One chair. So Raye took the classical approach—patient lying on couch, analyst seated near the patient's head, just beyond his field of vision. *In control.* Many therapists had moved away from that autocratic model to a more egalitarian relationship—two cozy chairs facing each other, the occupants partners with a shared goal.

Couch, chair, walls, ceiling, the carpet, all were that same shade of misty, shifting blue. Raye had been a sailor before she entered medicine. *A boat bum,* she'd called herself with a mocking grin—the big sailing yachts, Bermuda, across to the Med, down to the Caribbean. It had been the cane rum she'd drunk with their meal at that little Jamaican dive that had set her to reminiscing.

The entire room was an ocean of color. Would you feel as if you were floating, lying there on her couch? *Or drowning?* Jessica shivered, and swung back to the desk. *Leave a note, then get out of here.*

But facing the desk, she noticed something else this time—the framed diploma on the wall beyond.

The parchment certificate was impressive, and nearly illegible—dense with medieval lettering, flamboyant signatures, ancient seals. A diploma from the School of Medicine, St. George's University.

Hands spread on the desk, Jessica leaned close to study it. The diploma had been awarded to—she squinted—

Anne? No, too long for Anne, though that capital was surely an *A*. And that letter had to be an *n*, just after. She walked around the desk to stand, her face only inches from the glass.

The diploma had been awarded to Ann—ette R. Talbot. *Annette?* Jessica put a hand to the frame and leaned even closer.

The first four letters of the name were sprawling, bold. The last three were cramped, as if the calligrapher hadn't foreseen his available space.

Darkness moved in the glass—a reflection. "Find something interesting?" Raye drawled from the doorway.

Jessica spun, her fingers jarring the diploma's frame as she let go. It swung on its suspension point, then swung back, ticking against the wall like a tapping finger. *Here, here, here...* "Oh, Raye!" She smiled, all too aware that her face was red and growing redder. "You startled me."

"So I see." Raye glided into the room, her head tipped slightly to one side. Her fine, dark eyes were wide and unblinking. She set a foam cup of coffee on her desk. "Find something interesting?"

"Not really. I was just admiring the...the calligraphy on your diploma." She'd never lied well, wasn't lying well now. Jessica swung to straighten the picture frame. "I *like* calligraphy."

"Do you?"

Now the frame was tipped too far the other way. Jessica leveled it precisely with a fingertip. "Oh, yes..."

Raye's silence beat at her like the waves that follow a stone dropped into a pool. She babbled on, willing the other woman to speak, to help her over this moment. "And I didn't know Raye was your middle name, not your first. Annette, that's quite pretty. Why don't you go by Annette?"

"Never cared for it."

The frame was level now, but Jessica didn't turn. She stood, staring at the glass. She could see the dimensions of the taller woman standing behind her, dark shape against misty blue. "I know what you mean. I hated Jessica when

I was little. But my parents always insisted on calling me that. They refused to shorten it. I got used to it finally, I suppose.''

"You let someone else name you." Raye's words were weightless, hanging between them.

"I suppose so." Jessica tried to laugh as she turned. "Most parents do name their kids."

Sometimes Raye's smile was like a shrug—a quick lift and fall of the long, red lips.

Jessica circled the desk, drifting toward the exit.

Raye didn't step back to maintain the correct social distance.

To approach her was hard. *And she knows that,* Jessica thought, suddenly angry. Everything was a game with her, a testing, the way Cattoo would prod a potential toy in hopes that it was alive. *Well, I've had enough. I want no part of this.*

Still, Raye's silence battered her. "If you don't like Annette, have you ever gone by Anne?" Perhaps here was the key to the riddle, though she was too rattled to put it together right now.

Raye had been reaching for her coffee as Jessica spoke. Her hand stopped. "Anne?" The gesture continued. She pulled the top from the cup, crossed to a trash basket, dropped the lid from eye level. Her eyes tracked its fluttering fall. "Ohhh, perhaps I've called myself Anne once or twice in my life. When I wanted to sound reliable."

She's laughing at me. That's why I don't like her—she laughs behind her eyes. Or am I imagining it all? Whichever, the way was clear now, and Jessica took it. Then paused when she reached the door. "Oh, why I was in here—"

"Yesss?" Raye smiled without smiling—something in the voice.

"I was looking for paper to write you a note. I can't make it tonight. I'm really behind, you see, after all the time I lost going to New York."

This time, Raye did smile. "I do see. Then I'll just have to catch you later, won't I?" She turned away, reached across her desk and picked up the stone.

THREE LETTERS that didn't fit the line they were written on...a woman smooth and self-contained as a stone...a young man bolting out of a closet...a rock-headed Texan who wouldn't take no for an answer.

"Mr. Kirby says his heart problems are getting worse," reported Caroline with a straight face at four o'clock. "He says if you won't treat him, he's considering a malpractice suit."

She's beginning to enjoy this, Jessica realized wrathfully. And Sam certainly was. Clearly he meant to nag her till she cried uncle and picked up the phone. "The next time he calls, tell him *I'm* considering a harassment suit!"

She turned back to the articles she'd downloaded from a medical data base. *Concentrate on my work, but how, with all this pressing in on me? Shut it out, forget it...* "The patient presented with the following symptoms...dyspnea, tachycardia—heart palpitations." Why had he said that? She'd never broken his heart. It was *he* who... *Stop it!* "...presented with the following symptoms..."

She stuck it out until eight—would have stayed longer, but there was Cattoo to consider. Perhaps she should find Cattoo a playmate, a second cat to keep her company, but Jessica balked at the notion. Right now she was first in Cattoo's heart. Nice to be first in someone's heart, even if it was only a cat. Still, she should consider it. This wasn't fair.

Cattoo agreed with that assessment. She met Jessica at the door with an accusing yowl, then darted away before Jessica could pick her up. Her lost-kitten wail echoed back from the kitchen. *I'm all alo-o-one! Nobody lo-oves me.*

"We'll play!" Jessica called, dropping her briefcase on the coffee table, then slipping out of her jacket. "Honest, fuzzbucket, we'll play all night if you want. And tomorrow's Friday. Hang on *one* more day and—"

Dong!

She spun around to face the door. Now who?

Sam! But no, it couldn't be. He'd called Caroline from San Francisco just as the switchboards shut down. Had tried to bribe her with a lifetime supply of Ghirardelli chocolates if she'd put Jessica on the line, Caroline had reported, giggling—a phenomenon that Jessica had never seen before.

Dong-donga-dong-dong. Dong! Dong!

With a hiss of exasperation, Jessica opened the door.

"Surprise!" Raye Talbot caroled, standing on the doorstep. Her eyes snapped with excitement, her teeth gleamed. Her cheeks were flushed—this was Raye at her most effervescent, the polar opposite to the still woman of this afternoon. She waved a bottle of wine before Jessica's face. Her other hand held a pizza box. "If you won't come out and party, then the party has come to *you!* Let me in, it's cold out here. *Brrrr!"*

"But—" hanging on to the edge of the door, Jessica stepped back half a pace as Raye swayed closer "—Raye, I can't—"

"Sure you can!" Raye laughed, nudging Jessica's wrist upward with her forearm. As Jessica let go the door and retreated, Raye advanced, holding out the bottle. "Take this, would you? I'm about to drop it." She shut the door, locked it, swung back again. "Oh, lovely! It's warm in here."

She swept past Jessica to set the pizza on the coffee table. Then shrugged out of her black mink jacket and tossed it on the couch.

Beneath that she wore a black turtleneck, black jeans, black boots. She shook her long, shiny hair out from her collar and gave Jessica a vivid smile. "Where's the kitchen? We really ought to warm this pizza up for a few minutes but only a few. I'm *starving!"*

Jessica didn't move. "Raye."

Carrying the box, Raye was halfway across the room already. "Through here?"

Jessica raised her voice. "Raye, I'm sorry. But I meant it this afternoon. I'm busy tonight. I'm sorry..." she repeated as the psychiatrist turned, her delighted child's smile starting to fade.

"No. Oh, no, *I'm* sorry." Raye shrugged. "It was just that..." Again she shrugged. "Forget it. I'm being pushy, aren't I? I do that sometimes."

"No! It was a charming idea. It's just that..." *I don't like being invaded. I don't like someone who blows hot one minute, cold the next.*

"Today's my birthday," Raye said, looking down at the pizza box. "I didn't like to say, but I sort of... felt like celebrating. With somebody." She looked up with a rueful smile. "Silly me."

"No. Oh, *no,* not silly at all!" Jessica had been there, how many times before? Marking a birthday with a deluxe pizza for one, a split of champagne, a rented video. Lying to her parents when they called to wish her a happy, claiming she'd be going out come the weekend with friends to celebrate. "You should have said so, Raye!"

So this was what underlay Raye's polished armor, a loneliness as deep and wide as Jessica's own. A pride that wouldn't let you cry uncle no matter how you might long to do so.

She took the box from Raye's unresisting hands and started for the kitchen. "Which birthday, or dare I ask?"

"The big four-oh, shit!" Raye admitted, following at her heels. "But really, Jessica, if you don't have time..."

"For birthdays, I make time." Jessica twirled the oven knob, slipped the pizza box inside, straightened to look at her guest.

Raye stood frozen, staring past her.

Expecting a rat, a cobra, perhaps an ax murderer, Jessica spun to see. Cattoo crouched on a counter, her tail the size of a bottle brush, eyes like green saucers. Fixed on the psychiatrist.

"I didn't know you had a..." Raye's breathless voice trailed away...

. . . As Cattoo's rose into audibility, just the thread of a moan, weaving a hypnotic little song of menace and fear. *Keep back, keep away from me! I have claws. I have teeth.*

Raye backed right out of the kitchen.

"Raye!" Jessica hurried after her. "She's *very* friendly. You just surprised her."

"Yeah, that makes two of us!" Raye stood behind the couch, her teeth clenched, eyes riveted on the kitchen door.

She should have thought—had been so focused on Raye's invasion, then the reason for it, that she'd forgotten the incident that had made her call Toby in the first place.

Raye had let her off in front of her town house that night, returning from the Jamaican café. Jessica had bounded from the car, grateful to be alive, made it to her door, then hesitated. She should make Raye sleep on the couch, shouldn't let her drive farther, drunk as she was.

Too late, she'd turned to the sound of screeching tires. The black Corvette leapt from stillness to speed in one heartbeat, went roaring off into the night. *"Raye!"* She'd run out into the street to stare after.

Eyes blazing green in the oncoming lights, a cat crouched in the road.

"No!" she'd cried, and run, as if she could somehow stop what was coming.

The cat came to its senses—dived for a car parked alongside the curb.

And the black car swerved to follow.

Jessica's cry had merged with the *crack!* of metal and the roar of the engine. Taillights zoomed into the distance, two red eyes receding, winking at the corner, rushing off into the dark.

Panting, she'd knelt by the parked car to peer under. "Kitty? *Kiiii?"*

No cat. And no cat smeared in the roadway.

No cat thrown into the bushes, though she'd searched the block foot by foot. He'd made it, she concluded thankfully at last. He'd dived under the car, then kept on running, as any sensible cat would. The only damage done was to the parked car. Its sideview mirror lay shattered thirty yards down the street. Raye had cut it that close.

Jessica had returned to her house, picked up her own cat, marched straight upstairs to call Toby...

It was only later that she'd begun to doubt what she'd seen. It had happened so fast, after all. And she'd had a drink herself. And perhaps her angle of vision had made it look worse. Or perhaps Raye had never even noticed the cat? That swerve could have been the aftermath of five rum-and-Cokes, not a hatred of fuzzies.

But now...

"I should've known you'd have a cat." Raye's jaw tightened as Cattoo edged into view. Her tail was still puffed, her head stiffly lowered, her ears folded back. As if treading on hot coals, she took three tentative steps along the wall in the direction of the staircase, then froze, eyes fixed on the intruder.

Perhaps it was the musk in Raye's perfume that offended? Musk was animal scent, after all. Or maybe Cattoo was reacting to the smell of fear itself. Whatever, Jessica knew better than to pick her friend up at the moment. "She doesn't meet many strangers."

"That figures..." Raye flicked her scowl toward Jessica, then swung her head back to follow Cattoo's progression toward safety. "Is that the only one you have?"

"*She's* the only one I live with, yes."

Cattoo had reached the bottom of the stairs. There she dithered, one paw on the first step, perhaps fearing to turn her back to escape upward.

"Go on," Jessica said softly. "It's okay. Don't be afraid—"

"Be scared witless!" Raye stamped her boot. *"BOO!"*

Inflating with a hiss like a blown airbag, Cattoo shot up the stairs and out of sight.

"Did you see that?" Raye threw back her head and laughed. "Nyah-nyah-nyah! *Scaredy*-cat!"

Jessica wished she'd never opened the door. This was going to be a very long night.

CHAPTER FIVE

"IT'S ONLY THAT I'm allergic to cats," Raye said contritely while she opened the wine.

"Really?" Setting plates on the kitchen table, Jessica didn't look her way. Raye had none of the signs, no red eyes, no sniffles. No, this was something else, a phobia or, at the very least, a deep-seated distaste.

Not that distaste was a crime. Who was she to say that Raye should like cats, just because she loved them, but still... "How 'bout a salad for contrast?" For the moment she'd rather stand at the counter chopping vegetables than sit across a table from Raye. Her doubts would show in her face. Sam had always claimed she was transparent as glass, that he could see right through her. And Raye was quite as acute.

"Super." Raye brought her a glass brimming with red wine. "Drink up."

Jessica smiled and raised it. "Happy fortieth."

"Is there such?" Ray made a comical face and drank. "Mmm, not bad." She licked her upper lip corner to corner.

It wasn't bad at all—a big Beaujolais, harsh on the tongue, mellowing as it went down. Jessica preferred something more subtle, a white, generally. She peeled three carrots, the tiny *snick* of the peeler filling the silence. Still...because you loathed cats, was that any reason to try to kill one?

You don't know that she did. Not for sure. But the way she'd looked at Cattoo...

"This reminds me of a wine we had chartering out of Antigua," Raye said, holding her glass up to the light.

"Every time we sailed down island, we'd buy it by the caseload in Martinique, imported from France. Owner of the boat thought he was *some* connoisseur." She laughed softly. "Just for the hell of it, the captain and I bought a case of rotgut red, cost a tenth of what the real stuff cost. We tried cutting the good stuff with the table wine, fifty-fifty, and he and his guests liked that just fine. Meanwhile, back in the galley, *we* liked the real stuff. So, we ask ourselves, if he can't tell the difference in the *half*-blend, will he notice..."

Jessica switched to her chef knife and chopped hard, drowning the story out. This was what disturbed her about Raye, had disturbed her from the start—listening to the stories. They all had an edge, a cynicism that would have bothered her coming from anybody. But coming from a shrink, a person trained to heal wounded spirits?

"Hey, don't you like it?" Raye appeared at her shoulder holding the bottle.

"Sure I do." Jessica lifted her glass, took a sip to prove it, set it aside.

Raye refilled the glass and moved to the oven. "I'll turn this baby down. Two hundred?"

"Fine." *Baby*... or babe—he'd called her either and both. *Stop.* Her thoughts ricocheted, to a sea story Raye had told over a last rum-and-Coke at the café...

"Was that boat owner, the wine lover, the same one you lost overboard during the hurricane?" Raye had painted that tale with nostalgic gusto, limning every color and texture of the storm. Jessica could see in her mind's eye the owner, standing forward, swaying with one elbow hooked around a shroud, silhouetted against elephant-gray seas while he relieved himself over the side of the boat.

"Had to go forward," Raye had explained, grinning, "since we were running downwind. One second there he is, giving me a show of his family jewels. Since I'm the one steering, I can't help but look, and he knows it.

"The next second I...lose it, can't—*quite*—keep the stern square to the wave that's roaring up our ass. Whoops! Over we go, green water to the midline, and when I get us under control again . . .'' Raye had kissed her fingers, then waggled them goodbye.

"You didn't go back for him?" Jessica had whispered, horrified.

"Kiddo, we had fifty knots plus on the *tail!* Nobody else was on deck. By the time we could have horsed in the main and turned back . . .'' Raye had shrugged. "And going up-wind against those seas, the boat'd never have punched through them.''

"What about the Coast Guard?''

Raye had laughed outright. "This is offshore, Jessica, another world. The rules don't apply. No cops on the corners—nobody out there to pick up the pieces, not within a thousand miles. It's every man for himself.''

Or every woman.

Raye frowned now, repeating, "The same one we lost overboard? Oh—*him.* No. This was another guy, just as big a loser.''

Jessica didn't dare glance at the clock above Raye's head, but she could feel the second hand jerking slowly round its dial. *Move faster,* she petitioned it silently, and picked up her glass to help move it along.

The evening did move, with that disconnected, running-through-water quality of a fever dream. They ate the pizza, drank the wine, while Raye spun her outrageous, laughing stories, bright and cruel-edged as shards of broken mirror. Jessica retreated behind a polite smile and let her talk. Soon, very soon, she'd find a kindly way to bring this to a close.

The kitchen phone rang and Jessica swung to look. Her eyes nailed it, then lost it again, as it reeled farther around the room.

"Oh, *don't* answer that!''

"No fear. It'll only be—'' Jessica pressed her fingers to her lips. She didn't want to talk about Sam, not with

"Be who?''

"Be-who, be-who,'' Jessica murmured, savoring the sound of that on her tongue. "It *behooves* me to let the . . . *answering* machine find out . . . who." She got it out triumphantly, then made a face up at the ceiling.

Upstairs, the machine must have switched on. The phone went silent.

"Nut!" Laughing, Raye emptied the bottle into her glass.

"No." Jessica shook her head solemnly, and again the room followed the motion. "*I* don't need that."

"Who's talking about need? I needed to turn forty? Like a hole in the head!" Raye lifted her glass. "Forty."

Jessica raised her own glass obediently. "Forty."

Raye drank deeply. Jessica sat, staring at her uplifted glass. She *hated* heavy drinking—despised the loss of control that went with it. She'd been confining herself to sips the whole night long. Yet she was feeling as if—

"Jessica." Raye's voice was a laughing purr. "That was a toast."

"Oh." Jessica took a tiny sip, then set the glass at arm's length.

"You know—" Raye lounged back in her chair, hands clasped behind her head "—I'd like to hypnotize you sometime."

Jessica smiled, shut her eyes, shook her head. "Now why . . . would I let you do that?" Perhaps that was the secret to dealing with Raye. You had to remember one tiny word. No. *No, you can't come in my house. No, stay out of my head.*

"Ohhh, for the fun of it? And it's great for tension. You're always strung tight as a guitar string, girl."

Jessica sat, listening to one pure, vibrating note—as if someone's finger plucked a taut, protesting nerve.

"Why don't we try it tonight? " Raye's voice was feather soft, inviting.

I may be drunk, but I'm not crazy. Smiling, eyes closed, Jessica shook her head. "How did you learn hypnotism?" she asked, to change the subject.

"Would you believe I was a nightclub hypnotist once 'pon a time? You get some stuffy geek up from the audience, you know, to do a striptease, tell his wife who he *really* loves, bark like a dog..."

Jessica's eyes snapped open. "You're not...*serious!*"

Raye's eyes were black, no line between iris and pupil. "Sure, I'm serious. And you'd believe anything I tell you...*won't* you?"

It was a dare—*jump, jump, why don't you jump?* She'd jumped at eight on a dare, broken her arm. Jumped at twenty into Sam's arms, broken her heart...

"*Won't* you?" Raye repeated, looming ever so slowly closer.

Jessica closed her eyes. "I won't." She held her breath and waited, praying for the phone to ring, for Cattoo to come thumping downstairs. Anything to break this moment of awful, spinning stillness. "I *won't!*" she repeated, her voice high as a child's. And found she'd broken the moment herself. She opened her eyes.

Raye's chair creaked as she sat back. "So you won't," she agreed, her words without inflection. She gave Jessica her shrug-for-a-smile. "And no, Jessica, I was never really a stage hypnotist. Just kidding."

I don't believe you. Jessica stood—too abruptly. This time the room spun from north to south. *Much* worse. "Okay." She flattened her hands on the table to stop its moving. "You know...I don't...feel very well." What was wrong with honesty, after all? *Nothing,* she decided, and clung tight to that notion.

"You don't look so well," Raye agreed. "Time to call it a night. Let's get you up to bed."

Raye in her house was bad enough. Raye upstairs was...unthinkable. "I can manage." Jessica drifted toward the living room, leaving the shrink to follow.

"I'm not so sure." Raye's laughing voice came close to her ear. "You really packed it away tonight, kiddo."

"I didn't. Had *exactly* one glass." She was sure of that. Surely?

Raye chuckled. "If you say so. All the same, I'm helping you upstairs. You're not so steady on your pegs."

It was true, Jessica realized on a wave of shame. She'd never felt this way before. *Hated* it. Hated Raye for seeing her brought to this. To be out of control, that was the cardinal sin in her family.

One step behind, Raye splayed a friendly hand between her shoulder blades and steadied her up the stairs. Shrinking from the woman's touch, Jessica focused on staying upright, moving deliberately. Then as they neared the landing, she remembered. "Cattoo's upstairs."

Raye stopped. "Your cat . . ."

"I can make it from here. Really. I'm all right."

"Well . . ." Raye's hand eased, then dropped away. "If you're sure . . ."

"Very sure." Jessica just wanted her gone. She ought to offer her the couch, since Raye had drunk most of the bottle, but she wasn't going to do that. She wanted her gone.

"Okay." Raye withdrew a step, turned to look back. "How do I lock your door?"

"Turn the button in the handle," Jessica said gratefully. She'd forgotten that. "Slam it hard, then check to see if it's caught."

"Will do." Raye stood looking over her shoulder at Jessica a moment, then she started down. "Thanks for the birthday party!"

"You're welcome," Jessica said entirely without irony. Wading through shadows like water, she made the top of the stairs, then paused in the hallway, swaying.

Below, the lights went out. Then came hard, booted heels, crossing the floor, then the sound of the front door opening. A cool draft riffled up the stairwell. "Night!" Raye whispered from below.

Jessica made no answer.

The door shut solidly.

Thank God. Jessica wobbled into her room and fell across the bed. Whiskers brushed her cheek. Touch of a cool, questing nose. She flung out an arm, hugged squeaking softness, and slept.

SOMEWHERE, SOMEONE was running a table saw. And doing it poorly. The blade whined, a rising, falling song of protest as the wood was forced in crosswise.

Sunlight glowed redly beyond her closed lids. What idiot would run a saw at dawn? Jessica opened her eyes to see, and saw candles. On her bureau across the room, their flickering flames doubled in the mirror.

Inch by inch, she turned her aching head. More candles burned on the bedside table, their flames glimmering off silver—the candelabra that had been a graduation present from her mother.

The whining song still rose and fell. Who'd run a table saw in her bedroom?

Beyond the table, something moved in the shadows. Raye Talbot sat in Jessica's bentwood rocker, rocking gently. Their eyes met, and Raye's smile slowly widened.

Raye...But this wasn't the zestful raconteur of Jessica's kitchen. This was the Raye who stood in an ocean-blue office. The woman of stony stillness and smiling lies.

Candles...but not the little kind. She ought to blow them all out, anyway. Get her wish this time. Wish Raye out of her bedroom. Wish Sam back in her bed. "It's not...not your birthday." Her head hurt when she spoke.

"Got it in one, kiddo." Raye rocked, at ease, smiling her smile that was not a smile.

"And you...did it on purpose." It felt so good to speak truth at last.

"Drugged you? Right again."

Jessica shook her head, stopped when it hurt. "You drowned that man. Made him fall overboard."

Raye's teeth gleamed in silent laughter. "D'you think? I've never been sure about that one myself." Gently she rocked. "Either way, the prick deserved what he got. And believe me, it was worth it—that look on his face when he went over the side."

"And you slashed my tires that time."

"You wouldn't come out for a drink. What's a girl to do?"

Still the table saw whined. No. That sound was...
"Cattoo!" Jessica tried to sit up—made it halfway, her elbows braced against the mattress. "Where is she?"

"In your closet. Fuzzy bitch didn't like my candles."

Neither did Jessica. "What are you doing here?"

"Waiting for you to pass out again so I can light your bed."

She should be terrified. Wasn't. Valium, maybe—one of the tranquilizers, anyway. A shrink could prescribe drugs. Raye would've had her choice. "Why...would you do that?"

"Don't really know." Her teeth gleamed again. "Professional courtesy?"

"No, why would you...kill me?" It was so easy to be detached. A stupid, stupid woman lay on the bed, lit by flickering candles. While Jessica Myles cowered in the closet with her moaning cat. *I'm not here. This isn't happening. Not to me.*

"You broke my one rule, Jessica—never let anyone get in your way." Raye's hand moved to her hip. "After you asked me about Anne this afternoon, I thought I'd better check." She drew something from her pocket—a folded envelope. "Too bad you got nosy."

The letter from the dean in Grenada. Raye would've found it in her briefcase. "You...never went to med school."

"Nor college. Didn't even finish high school. Think of it, Jessica. I lived nine years out in the wide, wide world, while you slaved over your books. Grubbed for your A's like a good girl. Who's the stupid one?"

Me, me. Oh, it was me. All those years when I could have been with Sam. "But how did you—"

"Manage it? It was easy. Most things are. It's not having the nerve that stops people." Raye got to her feet, pocketed the letter, then laced her fingers and stretched luxuriously, arms overhead. "I was in Grenada, staying on a boat in the harbor when the marines landed. We'd been there almost a month—engine trouble. I'd been hanging around with the U.S. med students, boffing two or three of them, bored to tears with all their bragging about the money they'd rake in once they became doctors.'' She circled the rocking chair, stood behind it, rocked it restlessly. "When our boys landed and the bullets started flying, everyone stampeding for the hills... It's times like that, with a world cracking open, you can do whatever you please.

"I paid a kid to find the registrar's office at the university. To bring me back all the transcripts on two or three med students, women. And to burn a bunch of the registrar's files, so they wouldn't notice later that papers were missing.''

"And so you... became Anne Talbot.''

"She was the nerd with the best grades of the three. And I became Annette, with a little diddling. Because once Anne got her papers dup'ed, and presuming she passed her Foreign Grad exams, she'd be practicing in the U.S. of A. Sooner or later we'd show up on the same computer list. This way, Annette R. comes right after Anne R., on the list, and nobody thinks twice—except you. What made you start wondering, I wonder?''

Whatever she did, she mustn't betray Toby. *Change the subject.* "But...but you still had to pass the Foreign Grad Exam.''

Raye shook her head. "*Somebody,* with her hair rinsed black, had to pass my Grad exam. With all the debt-ridden interns back in the States, that wasn't a problem.''

"And your residency.''

Raye shrugged. "Hey, I'm a quick study. And you know yourself, clinical training's a hands-on apprenticeship. The senior residents and nurses back you up every step of the way. The eight years of book learning before it, I don't know why more people don't just skip that.''

At the first ring of the phone, Raye slid around the chair. As it rang again, her hand came down on the receiver—just as Jessica started to reach. "Don't even *think* about it.'' She caught the heavy candelabra, raised it with her other hand, held it poised.

The answering machine clicked, and the message tape rolled.

This wasn't happening. *Couldn't* be happening. She should do something, but first she'd have to rise from the bed. And if she could manage that, Raye still outweighed her by thirty pounds.

The machine clicked, then Sam spoke. "No more fun and games, Jess, and don't you *dare* touch that dial! We're talking, if I have to chase you to the ends of the earth."

"Masterful!" Raye murmured on a breath of laughter. "Who's this?"

"Come midnight, I'm catching the red-eye to New York. I'll be on your doorstep by nine. Be there, or beware—I'll track you down at the hospital, have conniptions in your waiting room, howl under your window, whatever it takes. We're having it out. You owe me, babe. Catch ya tomorrow."

"My kind of caveman!" Raye chuckled as he hung up. "Who was that?"

Jessica simply looked at her. *I wouldn't tell you about Sam, with my dying—* Her thoughts shot away. *Sam, oh God, Sam...*

"Whoever, he'll be a day late and a dollar short. Think he'll need comforting when he finds you committed suicide?"

Jessica shook her head violently. "I *never*—"

"Sure you did." Raye set the candelabra down. One flame blew out with the movement. "Promising young doctor succumbs to stress from overwork? Everyone at RI Gen knows you work yourself to the bone." Raye pulled a candle free, relighted its fellow. "Or maybe she killed herself out of depression? It's clear to anyone who looks that you're dying of loneliness, Jessica. That you won't let yourself accept the attentions the men would gladly give you."

Raye pressed the first candle back into its socket, then looked up with a musing smile. "Or *maybe* ... this fellow set you off? Who is he, an old flame? Ex-fiancé? Who-

ever, he's plainly been pestering you, trying to force an un-
welcome reunion on you and maybe you just…snapped?"

Oh, God. "Sam would *never* believe…" Would he? And
if he did, would believing kill the laughter in his voice?
Jessica struggled to sit, but this time her arms wouldn't
obey. Cattoo moaned from the closet.

Raye shrugged. "Hey, I'm easy. So maybe it wasn't suicide. Maybe you just goofed? Took too much Valium.
Everyone knows doctors are prone to drug addiction. That
they prescribe for themselves. So you took too much Valium, lit some pretty candles on a whim, lay down. Then,
when Sam phoned, you half woke up, reached for the
phone and—*uh*-oh!—you knocked the candelabra over
beside the bed."

It was believable. So elegantly simple that anyone could
believe it. Just Jessica screwing up one last time. Her parents would buy it, even if Sam didn't.

Because Sam was the only one who'd ever believed in
her, even if that was only for a little while. She supposed
that was more than some people got in a lifetime. *But it's
not enough. I wanted more. I wanted tomorrow, with Sam
at my door.*

"Play it any way you like, kiddo." Raye knelt beside the
bed. "The mattress caught fire, and you and your bitch cat
burned to death." She reached behind the bedside table,
then sat up, the phone cord dangling from her fingers.
"Oops, what d'you *know?* Here's the first thing that
burned." Stretching the wire between her hands, she held
it over a flame.

The stench of burning plastic turned Jessica's stomach.
"You're crazy!"

Absorbed in her task, Raye laughed under her breath.
"Careful with your terms, kid. You're talking to a shrink.
The correct word is sociopath."

The cord parted. She blew on the melted ends, then,
cocking her chin toward the ceiling, recited, "The diag-
nostic criteria for antisocial personality disorder are as follows: patient shows a history as a child of, one, truancy;

two, lying; three, running away from home.'' She smiled at
something only she could see. "Four, forcing someone into
sexual activity with him or her. What else? Oh, stealing—
with or without confrontation with the victim. And—*most*
common—setting deliberate fires.''

"You're nuts, Raye.''

"Not at all. That's just what society would have us believe. And, let's see ... The adult patient shows, one, fail-
ure to respect the social norms of lawful behavior; two,
impulsive behavior; three, recklessness regarding her own
or others' safety. There's several more, can't remember 'em
all, but I s'pose the last one sums it all up.''

She leaned in to the wall. There was a tiny *click* as the
stub of the phone cord was pushed back into its jack. Then
she straightened with a smile. "The patient shows...*no
remorse.*''

"You are crazy.''

"No, kiddo, sociopaths aren't crazy. We have our place
in the world, whether society wants to admit it or not. *We're
the wolves.* Put here to trim the flock, to pull down the
fools and the cripples. Witness you.'' She arranged the
other end of the phone cord beside the bed.

"I'm not—''

"Sure you are. Rich kid with brains, beauty, doting parents, every advantage, every reason in the world to be
happy, and you couldn't even manage that. You had your
chance and you blew it, kid. So just—'' the venom died
abruptly from her voice "—just go to sleep, Jessica.''

Tears welled. Raye was right, she *had* blown it. Thrown
happiness away with both hands. "I won't.''

"You will,'' Raye murmured tenderly. "Let's count some
sheep. I see *one* sheep, heading for sleep—''

"I won't!'' Cattoo moaned hoarsely from the closet.

"Sure, you will. You *want* to sleep. It'll be so much *easier*... *Twooo* sheep, sleeping so deep...''

She could see them—couldn't help but see them—sheep
white as smoke, their fleece soft as smoke...Sam was there,
too, herding them all to safety, and Cattoo...

"*Threee* sheep, longing to sleep."

No, oh, no ... The sheep were leaving, white smoke streaming over the crest of a green hill ...

"*Foour* sheep ..." Dying to ...

CHAPTER SIX

SHE WAS FALLING...through clouds, Cattoo cradled in her arms. And falling, Jessica knew the secret at last. There was nothing to fear, the clouds were lovely and soft. And somewhere far, far below the clouds, Sam waited with open arms to catch them.

But Cattoo hated falling. She clung to Jessica's neck and screamed her fear. *"Rrrrrrowwwwrrrr! Yuh-rrrrr-owwwwrrrr!"*

"'S'all *right,* you silly ca—" Her words ended in a cough. Rolling over, Jessica pushed up on her forearms and fought for breath. *It's all—*

"Rrrrrrowwwwrrrr!" The yowl jumped half an octave to a full-throated feline scream. *"RRRRRRRROWWRR!"*

Something wasn't all right. Jessica opened her stinging eyes. Saw flames and billowing smoke.

"Meeeerrrrr-rrrrrrrow!"

"Cattoo!" In the closet. Jessica rolled off the bed, started crawling. Raye. Raye had shut the cat in the closet. Or had she dreamed that?

Her eyes watered and burned. She closed them, found the wall with a sweep of her hands. Oh, God, it was hot! She crawled to the right, found the closet door. Cattoo screamed.

Coughing, Jessica hung on the doorknob for a moment. *If I can't catch her...* Let Cattoo slip past her and she'd be lost in the smoke. And would die. *We'll both die.*

And Sam comes in the morning. Or was that part of the dream?

"Meeeerrr-roowwwrrrr!"

Jessica cracked the closet door. A soft, frantic shape butted at her fingers. She slid her hand through the gap, caught Cattoo by the scruff. "It's all—" Her words turned to coughing.

She hugged the flailing cat to her chest—cried out as claws bit into her shoulders. Frantic furry paws clinging to her neck. Pain like a head-clearing shock—galvanizing her. Cattoo mustn't die for her stupidity. On knees and one hand, she hitched toward the door. The flames and smoke came from one side—from her burning bed and the wall behind it. There was still time, if they could breathe for just a minute more.

The door was locked.

But that couldn't be true. She turned the knob back and forth, back and forth, ten times, twenty, refusing to believe.

"*Merrr-rrrowwwrrrr!*" Cattoo yelled at her ear. *Believe it!*

She had rented this house because the old-fashioned hardware had charmed her so. The brass dolphin knocker on the front door. The antique brass door locks with their old-fashioned keys. The key should be right here in its lock where it always stayed.

But it wasn't.

"*Rrrrrrowwwwrrrrr!*" Cattoo's voice was failing. She coughed, her ribs heaving against Jessica's supporting forearm.

Air. They had to have air. There was nothing left but the windows.

When she opened her eyes, the room had grown lighter, brighter—white cloud cover of smoke, undershot by lurid flames. *Sundown.*

The windows were somewhere above those clouds...and she was growing dizzy. So tired...

"*Yowrrrh!*" It was more croak than yowl.

Hang on, baby. Jessica shook her head to clear it, closed her eyes and started crawling. The window beside the bed wasn't possible. The other one, then, the one nearest the tree.

Her head bumped the wall—a small pain compared to the claws digging at her shoulders, the smoke clawing at eyes and lungs. She groped up the oven-hot wall with one hand. *If I can't find it—*

Her fingers touched a hard ledge—the windowsill. *And if I can't stand...*

But if she couldn't, Cattoo would die, and that wasn't fair. Cattoo had known not to trust Raye from the start. Fingers clutching the sill, she dragged herself up into the smoke.

She would fall to the floor any second—couldn't breathe. Couldn't open the window one-handed. *Trust me.* She let go the cat, pressed frantically upward with both hands against the sash.

A draft of cool air hit her face. Sobbing, Jessica threw the window all the way up and caught the cat with both hands. She leaned out into the blessed night. *Air!*

Cattoo found her breath, found that they leaned over a sixty-foot drop in the same instant. Keening her terror, she clung like a burr.

"It's all right!" Jessica tried to tell her, but her voice was gone. Far down the hill, a mile or more away, she could see whirling red lights. Hear the sirens. The firetrucks were coming.

They would come too late. A wave of rolling white belched out the window, wiping out the world. The fire needed oxygen as much as Jessica and Cattoo did. It dragged air from their lungs, offered them smoke to breathe instead.

Cattoo moaning in her ear, Jessica peered down through watering eyes. Sixty feet below those clouds lay a stony slope, and the spiked, wrought-iron fence that closed off her property. She'd always feared falling. Somehow she'd always known. *There's no way down.*

And no time left. Her back, the backs of her legs, were burning hot. Her lungs burned. Cattoo wriggled desperately.

Smoke billowed, then parted, as a breath of wind stirred. Gulping at the life-giving coolness, Jessica saw the tree— the big elm whose highest limbs always blocked her view to the south. Ten feet from the window, one branch beckoned like a friendly arm. *Jump. Jump to me and live.*

It was a jump no human could make.

She should try to straddle the window, pray the firemen found her there. But she had only one effort left, and still the branch beckoned. *Jump. Jump to me.*

Sam laughing at her, his arms spread wide. He'd taken her on a rock climb, she couldn't think when or where. *C'mon, chicken! Jump, I'll catch you.*

She'd been too afraid to jump. He'd had to peel her off her rock, lift her down to safety.

Cattoo could be safe. Didn't deserve to die. Downhill the sirens wailed, *too late, too late!*

Jessica peeled the crying cat from her shoulder. Held her struggling over the chasm, then cupped her ribs with one hand, her rear with the other.

One effort left, one breath left, only one chance. The branch beckoned, faded before her tearing eyes, came clear again as the smoke lifted and the air swirled in. Jessica drew the cat in against her face. *Softest fur.* She pressed her lips to the nape of the cat's neck.

Then, sighting between those flattened ears, sucking in her last breath, she heaved the cat with all her might. *Cattoo, go live for both of us!*

Black cat, flying out into the night. Then falling.

Falling...

Falling through the cool dark, through twigs and rushing leaves. Claws snatching. Stars and city lights wheeling as she fell.

Go live for both of us.

SHIVERING, HER BODY flattened to a branch, Jessica watched the trucks arrive, two on the street at the front of the house, a truck and ladder on the road below the ridge.

Shouts and booted men in black raincoats rushing around. Ruby, whirling lights. Sounds of smashing wood from the front, a ladder elongating till it reached the rear bedroom window, where a column of smoke gushed out past a motionless, sagging form.

Two men stormed up the ladder. The awkward bundle was dragged across the windowsill and draped over a broad shoulder. Jessica watched them carry her down, lay her on a litter...

She narrowed her stinging eyes. *Lay who?*

They lifted the litter into the back of an ambulance. Doors slammed. The vehicle raced away, its departing siren so loud it was a physical pain.

That was me, they took away.

But if that was me, then who...am I?

More men rushed up the ladder. A hose pumped shafts of looping, silvery water. Flames broke through the walls, then the roof. The men yelled and retreated.

There could be only one answer. That was her body they'd taken away. While Jessica's abandoned soul clung, shivering, to the branch of a tree.

With not a clue what to do next. Or where to go.

It was an enormity beyond comprehension. Beyond sorrow. Looking up, she could see the shape of every leaf and twig against the dome of the night sky. A bat flitted overhead squeaking like a lost soul. Jessica shuddered. Maybe if she waited, something...some*one*...would come along, tell her what happened next?

Meanwhile, she might be a soul, but she was an aching and exhausted one. Were the dead allowed to sleep? And if she *could* sleep, should she? Or might she miss something vital?

Didn't matter... Sleep—or maybe *this* was the final obliteration—reared over her in a curling black wave. *If somebody comes, will you please, please wake me?* she petitioned, and let the darkness take her.

So it wasn't till dawn that she noticed the paws.

SOMEWHERE, SOMEONE was frying bacon. Off toward the bay, a sea gull cried, its voice echoing over the rooftops. Blocks away, a bus labored uphill from downtown—Jessica wrinkled her nose at the diesel fumes. The wind caressed the right side of her face, then eddied, bringing with it the stench of smoldering wood. And remembrance. The fire...

And I'm dead. She smiled—it felt odd when she did so—and lifted her head. Death wasn't possible in the same world with bacon and sea gulls. It had all been a dream...a nightmare of astounding vividness.

She opened her eyes to see two long, slim, black forearms stretched out along a branch. Pale claws curved into brown bark. Oops! Jessica closed her eyes. *Still dreaming.*

The wind swirled, returning to the south. She smelled the bacon again, and with it— *You're burning your toast,* she warned the breakfast maker, wherever he was. *Chook!* Her ears swiveled as the toaster ejected the— Her ears... swiveled?

Jessica opened her eyes. Slim, black-furred forearms, sexy as those of a woman in elbow-length gloves, stretched before her face. Their grace ended at the wrists—in two black, fuzzy catcher's mitts, tipped with razor sharp nails. Cattoo's double paws.

Nooooo...couldn't be... She closed her eyes... *Outrageous* dream. Maybe Raye had given her a hallucino— *Raye!*

Jessica opened her eyes. Turned her head. Saw the burned-out roof of her house and let out a...*yowl.* She tried to clap a hand to her mouth to quell the appalling sound, but something wrenched at her fingernails. Her hand—paw— *Hand* was hooked to the branch.

Dreaming! She tried to say it aloud. "Merrowrr!" Drug-induced, without a doubt. Closing her eyes, she propped her chin on her forearms. *Wait it out.* Sleep long enough, and somebody would give her back her own body.

Except that there was no way to go back to sleep, with her thoughts darting like panicked squirrels. At the image, her stomach rumbled, then turned. *Oh, no!* No way.

That brought another issue to mind. *If I were a cat but of course I'm not—but if I were, then where would... Cattoo be?*

The sound of purring gradually filled her mind—that idling, sotto voce purr Cattoo used when she was nearly asleep, utterly at peace. As if Cattoo lay on the pillow beside her, nose pressed to Jessica's ear, Cattoo was...*here*. With her. Happy, as always, just to be near.

What a dream!

In the dream last night, she'd told Cattoo to go live for both— *No.* Jessica tried to shake her head—it was an awkward, unnatural motion. Her whiskers brushed her arm, sending an electric thrill to her cheek, and the nerve endings beneath the fur on her arm.

For a dream, it had its own kind of loopy logic. She'd taken Cattoo in, from a fearful, scrounging life. Now Cattoo had returned the favor—had taken her in when she'd had no place to go but a burning building.

Jessica dropped her chin back on her paws. *Wait. This'll pass.* The best way to deal with unreality was to refuse to deal with it.

A car drove along the upper street, the hum of its engine punctuated by the soft thumps coming from lawns and sidewalks. Jessica didn't bother to open her eyes. *The morning paper.*

Soft *whoosh* of a well-insulated door opening, then a few hesitant steps. A man's grunt—he must be stooping? Then the sound of a rubber band being rolled off a folded newspaper. Rustle of pages as he opened it.

Tap, tap, tap came the heels of a woman down the sidewalk. They slowed, then stopped. *"God!"* she said fervently. "Was anybody hurt?"

"The woman who rented the place," said the man. "They took her off in an ambulance. Don't know if she lived or not. Guess the *Journal* had already gone to press. There's nothing here." He rustled his paper.

Jessica opened her eyes and stared straight ahead. A gorgeous mosaic against the blue sky beyond, the leaves turning from green to gold. As she watched, one leaf let go its twig and spiraled down. She didn't track its fall. *So maybe I am dead, after all? But I didn't become a soul, exactly. I moved in with a cat.*

Nooooo. Not possible. *Wait till you wake up.* Her stomach rumbled. *Shut up!* she told it fiercely, and tried not to think about bacon. Or squirrels.

The branch lifted in the rising wind, then dipped lazily, and her stomach swooped with it. Her claws—fingernails—whatever, flexed and bit deeper into the bark. How far to the ground?

No distance at all. I'm still in my bed. All the same, she wasn't about to look down.

Perhaps she'd have stayed there forever, locked in a state of fierce and categorical denial. But sometime later, her ears swiveled to the sound of a car idling down the street. It stopped before her house.

Jessica refused to look. She'd had quite enough of this dream, thank you.

The door of the car opened. A light scuffing sound as a pair of shoes found the ground. The car door didn't close again. Slow steps crossed first sidewalk, then lawn.

Jessica opened her eyes.

Sam drifted across the grass, eyes fixed on what was left of her house. His face was the stunned face of a sleepwalker.

Sam, oh God, am I glad to see you! Dream or no, there was no one she'd rather see.

Sam's eyes rose to take in the burned-out roof. They moved to the tree, skimmed over her branch, then returned to the front of her house. His hands clenched suddenly as his chin jerked up a notch.

"Sam!" Jessica called, and didn't give a damn that it came out a feline yell. *"Sam!"*

He shook his head, but not at her. He was simply denying

Across the street, a door opened, then closed, and a gray haired man started down the walk to his car. When he saw Sam, his steps slowed. But something about Sam's stillness drew him on. He crossed the road, then stopped beside him.

"When did this happen?" Sam murmured without turning to see whom he addressed.

"Last night. Around midnight." Jessica's neighbor shifted from one foot to the other. "Did you know—"

"Is she all right?"

"*Yes*, I'm all right," Jessica yelled. "I'm right here!"

Neither of the men looked her way. "She...wasn't burned."

Something in his voice jerked Sam around. He reached for the older man's shirt, but his hand stopped midair. His fingers clenched, flexed wide, his arm dropped. "Then what...*was* she? What's the matter?"

"Smoke inhalation. I asked a fireman last night, then we heard the rest on the news this morning. She was a pretty little thing. Always smiled at us when we passed on the—"

"*Was?* My God, are you telling me—" Sam grabbed him by the shoulder.

"She's in critical condition," the man blurted. He reached up awkwardly to pat Sam's hand. "In a coma, they say."

"*Coma...*"

A coma, Oh, God... Except that she wasn't. She was right here, awake, in possession of all her senses...trapped in the body of a cat.

No, this had to be a dream.

But if this is a dream, then please, please let me wake up! Because dream or no, she had to get to Sam, had to wipe that look from his face. "*Sam!*" she cried, and rose to a shaky crouch.

Then looked down past her branch for the first time. Looked down some sixty feet—but it was more like looking over the rim of the Grand Canyon. A howl tore out of her throat.

"Where?" Sam demanded. "Where'd they take her?"

"Rhode Island General." The older man patted Sam's hand again, then lifted it from his shoulder. "I'm sure she'll be all right."

"You better believe she will! Can you tell me how to get there?"

"Sam, wait for me!" Jessica cried, but he and her neighbor were already headed for Sam's car. "*Sam!*" She had to get to him, touch him. If he'd only hug her, she'd surely wake up.

Right now she couldn't even turn around. She faced outward, away from the tree trunk. To turn, she'd have to hang her head one way over this yawning chasm, while her tail— Her...? Slowly, filled with a dreadful surmise, Jessica looked over her shoulder.

Given all the rest, it should've come as no surprise. Still, that supple black...appendage, swaying behind her like a furry cobra—her eyes went round when she caught sight of it. The tip of it...*curled,* as if saluting her, then the whole thing puffed up as her shock hit home. "I *am* a cat!"

This wail was so wholehearted the neighbor stopped his directions and turned. "Looks like she's stuck up there." He nodded toward the tree.

"Stupid cat," agreed Sam, sliding into his car. "She'll figure it out." And he drove away.

AND SO SHE DID figure it out, cursing Sam Kirby's blindness every inch of the way. What she figured, after half an hour of near paralysis, was that it was best not to think about what she was doing. Like the Zen archer who shuts his eyes to find the bull's-eye, she did best when she concentrated on the goal and let Cattoo's instincts handle the enabling details.

Or to put it another way, it was best not to sit there and agonize over how to bare your claws. Or how to sheath them, once you'd nailed yourself fast to the side of a tree. Think about it, and you tended to stick.

Determinedly not thinking about it, she hugged her way painfully down the trunk. And that, of course, was only the start of her problems.

RI Gen lay a mere three miles away as the crow flew. But between Jessica and her goal stretched the Providence River, two eight-lane highways, all of downtown Providence. And countless dogs. The day that had started out a nightmare went downhill from there.

SOME EIGHT HOURS LATER, Jessica crouched beneath a seat
on the filthy floor of a city bus, watching a pair of white
tennis shoes. The shoes were laced to the feet of a nurse,
who, pray God, was headed for the medical center.

After that last incident with the Yorkshire terrier—Jessica still seethed at the memory—she'd given up trying to
walk to RI Gen. The daytime city just wasn't meant for
cats.

Not that buses had been an improvement so far. There
was no direct bus from the East Side to the hospital complex, for starters. So there wasn't one bus she had to sneak
onto, but several.

By now she'd perfected her technique of slipping aboard
by the rear door, just as the last rider got off. People might
look back in amusement, but no one was going to stop the
bus, tell the driver he now carried a nonpaying passenger.

But once she was tucked safely under a seat, she faced
another problem. She couldn't see where they were going.
Had no way to know which stop was her stop.

And even if she figured that out, what was she supposed
to do—jump up and yank the cord? Not that she couldn't
have done so, but she'd always been a private person. People staring, that had never bothered Sam, but as for her,
that was something she avoided like the plague.

Well, that shyness had cost her today. So far the bus had
zoomed twice past the med center, once going, once returning, without stopping. She'd ridden to the end of the
line, had her tail stepped on twice on the return trip. This
time, if she was wrong about the nurse's destination, Jessica was going to pull that cord and let them all stare. She
had to get to Sam.

Her stomach turned at the thought of not reaching him,
then turned again from hunger. *Sam, if anybody can help
me, it's you.* He was the smartest person she knew, after all.
She'd hated that about him once—the last thing she'd
wanted in a husband was another superachiever to measure herself against and be found wanting, but now... *Sam,
you've got to be there. Wait for me.* Because if she couldn't

find him at the hospital, how would she find him at all? And if she couldn't find him—

The nurse's shoes shifted. She stood, then reached for the cord.

When the bus pulled over, Jessica shot between the woman's legs and out the back door. She hit the ground running, her ears swiveling back to note the screech of surprise. Silly woman. *It's not as if I were a rat, you know.* Her ears switched forward. *Where am I?* Her pace quickened as she recognized the buildings in the distance. Just a hundred yards more.

She'd figured out her strategy while riding to hell and gone. Sam would exit through the lobby of the hospital, as all visitors did. That was the only way she'd find him, since he could've parked in any one of several parking lots. *But what if he's left already?* It was nearly dark.

That didn't bear thinking about, and not just because she needed him to help her snap out of this. But after all, there was no reason for Sam to hang around waiting for her to wake up. It wasn't as if they were married. Ex's weren't obliged to worry and wait.

But somehow she knew he'd be here. Somewhere. A low hedge of boxwood edged the walk that led to the main entrance of RI Gen. Jessica found a spot beneath with a clear view of the doors. She was learning that cats were safest out of sight. *Come, Sam, come to me.* The air was cold, the damp earth colder, and by nightfall— She shuddered. By nightfall she wanted her breakfast, and Sam's comforting, clearheaded logic on her side. Without him, the night would be chilling in every way.

But while she sat and worried, her front paws grew warmer. Jessica looked down to find her tail curled neatly around her toes.

CHAPTER SEVEN

NIGHT CREPT over the city. Jessica's stomach growled. Somewhere deep within, Cattoo seemed to stretch, then stir. *What are we doing here?*

Jessica fought down the feeling of restlessness. *We have to find Sam.* She glared at the hospital doors, willing him to appear. *Sam, come to me.*

Because of her fierce attention, she almost missed him. Across the street, the revolving door to the professional building spun. Jessica's ears flicked, then dismissed it. People had been coming and going there for hours.

Leather shoes on heavy feet hit the sidewalk. The door hummed and spun again, then another man, lighter on his feet, joined the first. "Thanks, Mac," drawled a familiar voice. "There is a way you could help. I want longer visiting hours—could you fix that? Or better yet, how about a cot in her room? I'd like to be there when she wakes."

Sam! Jessica bolted out from under the bush and scurried up the walk, then stopped, watching from across the street. Sam, and somehow he'd connected with Mac MacKenzie, one of her partners at Diagnostics.

"Sam—" MacKenzie jammed his hands in his pockets and rocked back on his heels "—you can't sleep there. They don't want you underfoot in the intensive-care unit, and they don't have facilities for overnight visitors. Besides—" his gaze slipped away from the younger man to fix on the sky, the sidewalk, Jessica across the street "—besides, she might not regain consciousness...right away."

Or at all. Jessica had delivered too many heartbreaking prognoses herself not to recognize the signs of Mac's discomfort, what he hated to come right out and say.

"Or she might wake any minute. They said that, too. The neurologist told me there are no signs of brain damage."

"Good, good," Mac said heartily. "That's excellent news."

But you'd know that already, Jessica realized, sinking to a crouch. The word went right round the hospital whenever a doctor was admitted. Mac or another of her partners would've gone up to her room, read her charts. Talked with the physician in charge.

"But all the same, you'll have to pace yourself," Mac continued. "You could be in for a long haul."

Sam shrugged. "Whatever. But can you see about extending the hours?"

Mac nodded. "Soon as they consider her stabilized, in a day or two, I'm sure I can arrange it."

"Thanks." The two men turned and paced down the walk toward the parking lots, their eyes on their shoes.

Across the street, Jessica prowled in parallel.

"Funny," murmured Mac. "But we never even knew she'd been married, let alone to..." His voice trailed away.

Go on, say it, Mac, Jessica thought bitterly. *To somebody like you.* It was plain for anyone to see, wasn't it, that she'd never been a proper match for Sam. There should have been a law about truth in packaging. If she'd known what he was to become, that first day when she'd hired a bone-lazy grad student to tutor her in organic chemistry, she'd have turned around and run for her life.

Sam shrugged. "She never talked much about herself."

Except to you. Jessica trod across a sheet of damp newspaper, pausing to shake a paw with each mushy step.

"Except to me," he added under his breath.

"Huh?" Mac glanced at him.

Huh? Jessica paused in the midst of a paw shake. It was almost as if Sam had heard—

"Nothing." Sam walked on, scowling. "Okay, here's something maybe you could do. I hate hotels. If I'm going to be around awhile, I'll need someplace quiet to stay where I can work when I'm not here. Know anybody who'd rent an apartment, short term? Not too far from here?"

Yes! Jessica jumped for sheer joy—batted at a moth, which was fluttering overhead. *Sam, you're really going to stay? See me through this?* If so, she had a chance. Once she'd made him see what was going on, once he'd turned his mind to the problem ...

"As a matter of fact, I might know just the place." Mac jingled his car keys in his pocket. "The doctor whose practice Jessica took over, Harry Neuman, he and his wife lived over in the Jewelry District, in a loft. It's something between funky and swank, fantastic windows, a converted mill building."

"Sounds perfect. That's for rent?"

"I'm s'posed to be selling it for him. He left town in, uh, something of a hurry. But the realtor hasn't had a nibble on the place. I think, as long as she had permission to show it if a buyer came along..."

The two men stood arranging the details. Sam would stay in a hotel overnight. Mac would bring him the keys tomorrow. Jessica waited. Mac's route would turn from here toward the doctors' parking lot. Sam would have to cross the street to reach the public lots. It would be best if he was alone when she approached him. She wasn't sure yet how she would make him see. But she would. He'd have to smuggle her into his hotel tonight, she supposed. *Room service,* she thought ecstatically, and her stomach rumbled agreement. Perhaps a steak, juicy and rare? Or maybe fish? Most definitely the coffee she'd never had this morning.

"When does her family arrive?" Mac asked, interrupting her plans.

"They're not sure yet." Sam's voice was carefully neutral. "Seems her old man has operations scheduled till Christmas the year after next. And her mom's a hotshot in corporate law. There's some deal she's cutting. General Motors and half the Third World might roll belly-up if she dropped the ball this week."

Business as usual. It was no more, really, than she would have expected. And Jessica knew it would have been far otherwise if there'd been anything useful they could do.

"Her dad phoned Fisher, Jessica's doctor—really put him through his paces, Fisher tells me. And then he had a pal of his, some rock-star neurosurgeon out in San Diego, call for a phone consultation. Then her brother called from Europe, put him through it one more time."

"Lucky Fisher," Mac said with feeling.

"Yeah, final-exam day. But apparently he passed. Jess's dad tells me he's a good man and he's doing everything anybody could..." Sam's voice went husky, and he swung away to glare at Jessica.

"Sam!" She sat bolt upright. "Yes, *look* at—"

He swung back. "Anyway, they don't think it'd be good to move her right now."

"No, that's the last thing she needs. And she'll get the best of care here, Sam, believe me. We take care of our own."

"Yeah...yeah, I'm sure you do."

The catch in Sam's voice made Mac shy like a nervous horse. "Well..." He socked Sam on the bicep, then took a step backward toward safety. "Gotta go. The wife, you—" He stopped abruptly. "Supper..." he added lamely.

"Good idea," Sam said with a parting lift of the chin. "Me, too." He turned and—

"*Don't!*" she cried as he stepped off the curb, his eyes focused on nothing. Springing into the path of the oncoming car, she crouched, teeth clenched, eyes wide, staring it down. Tires screeched. The car loomed horrifically, then lurched to a stop some ten feet from them.

"Holy..." Sam's voice trailed away. His spread hands were still raised to fend off the hood. He dropped them abruptly.

The driver leaned out his window. "Would've served you right, you moron! You wanna walk around blind, go get yourself a cane!"

Jessica dodged over to almost sit on Sam's feet as the car swerved around them and roared on by, its driver still swearing. She let out a shaky breath.

"Whew!" Mac called from the sidewalk. "Take it easy, Sam. Maybe I should give you a lift?"

"Nope. I'm fine. Catch you tomorrow." Sam turned away, looked both directions, then plunged on across the street.

Jessica caught her breath and bounded alongside. "You...*idiot!*" It wasn't the first time he'd done that. His mind was often three jumps ahead of itself, off in the clouds somewhere, leaving the rest of him to muddle on behind. It was one of the reasons you tended to underestimate him. "You want to get yourself killed? Or end up in a bed beside me? Maybe they'll give us the family suite."

"What are you meowing about?" Sam muttered, striding along. "That car would've squashed you flat, cat, if it hadn't been for me."

"*Oh*..." She stopped short with outrage, then galloped after him. "That's rich! You saved me?" She'd forgotten how long his strides were. She'd always had to step double time to keep up, when she was hu— She winced. This was no time to be yelling at him, not when she needed his help.

And they were nearing the parking lot. Sam cut down a slope, through a bed of low rhododendrons, toward the sub-street level of the lot. Scurrying in his footsteps, she caught a branch full in the face, let out a squeak of exasperation.

Sam glanced back, but kept on striding. "Weren't you headed the other way? I mean, don't let me change your plans or anything. I'm sure you've got mice to catch, people to see."

"It's you I need to see! Sam, would you just stop for a second and *look* at me?"

"Look..." He stopped and looked down at her. "I've had a rough day. I'm not in the mood for company, okay?"

"Sam, just look at me! *Hear* me."

"You hear? Go bug somebody else." He turned and walked on.

If anyone—anyone in the whole world—could see her for who she really was, it was this man. And if *he* couldn't—

"Sam!" She tore after him.

"Give me a break, cat." He fumbled a set of keys from his pocket, then stopped beside a car with rental plates.

If she could only get closer to him. Look him straight in the eye. When Cattoo needed to do that, she... Jessica threw herself at the hood of his car, quite the highest jump she'd attempted so far.

If she hadn't thought about it, the leap would have gone fine. But thinking about Cattoo's hindquarters launching them gracefully off the ground, and whether it was her front feet or her back that were supposed to land first— Jessica hit the dew-damp metal, fumbled and, claws screeching, skidded to an inglorious pileup against the windshield.

Sam blinked, then threw back his head and hooted.

She'd never liked to make a fool of herself. Without competence, you were nothing at the best of times. And right now, on this, the most humiliating day of her life... Picking herself up, she glared at him. Her tail slashed the air, once, twice. She glanced back and flattened her ears at it. *Stop that! I'll handle this myself.*

"I thought cats' one excuse for living was that they were graceful!" The laughter had returned to his voice for the first time that day. "So what happened to you? New feet?"

"I have a perfectly reasonable excuse. In fact, that's *precisely* the problem. If you'd just let me explain—"

He turned the key in the car-door's lock. "Okay, enough of the fun and games, cat. Beat it." He opened the door.

"Sam!" She let out a wail of pure desperation.

One foot inside the car, he paused, then sighed. "What is it, cat? You subscribe to that Chinese theory—once you save somebody's bacon, you're stuck with the bozo for the rest of your life?"

"Yes—I mean, *no*. . .but that'll do for now!"

"Go sell it somewhere else, cat. I'm tired, I'm sad, I'm outta here." He slid into the car and slammed the door.

This could not be happening. This, *this* was the final nightmare, that Sam could look at her and not know her. "Don't go! *Please* don't go, Sam." She put her nose to the windshield, peered straight into his eyes.

She jumped as the engine started with a roar—her tail puffed up in alarm. Inside the car, Sam smiled and shook his head. The car edged out of its parking place.

Jessica hooked her claws—at least tried to hook them—to his windshield wiper. "Where you go, I go. You're my only hope." The car picked up speed, gliding between the rows of parked cars. Jessica hunkered down, hung on.

Sam rolled down his window. "Cat, I'm warning you..."

She flattened her ears, narrowed her eyes, hung on.

The car coasted to a halt. They stared at each other through the glass. Sam rammed the car's shift lever into park. He stepped out, strolled around the door to the hood, loomed overhead.

She'd forgotten how much she'd always loved his bigness. On some shamelessly unliberated, purely instinctive level, it had always thrilled her how much taller and wider and stronger he was than she.

It wasn't a thrill tonight. He looked enormous. Dangerous. She gulped and stood her ground. "Sam, I...need you." *There*. She'd never been able to say that before. Saying it now was...a relief. *I need you!* The magic password that must surely open his heart.

"I don't need this, cat. Not tonight."

For a moment she felt only the pain, worse than any blow. Then hearing the words, she stared up at him. "You *do* hear me, don't you? At least a little bit?"

"So hear me and hear me good." He bent till their eyes were on a level. "I...don't...like...*cats.*"

If he'd said he approved of cannibalism, she couldn't have been more astounded—then dismayed. She'd never known that! But then, why would she? In their first six months together, they'd been engrossed in each other. The issue of pets had simply never come up. Nor had it in their last six, with her commuting a hundred miles a day to med school, and Sam settling into his new research lab—when he wasn't jetting around the country giving papers—while their life as a couple stretched and stretched till it shredded.

"Nothin' personal," Sam continued, his drawl soft and deadly earnest. "But I'm a dog man. I want a hood ornament, I'll put a hound up there—got it?"

You don't like cats? With all the things she'd called him in her mind, all the reasons she'd made up for hating him, she'd never once dreamed he was tasteless enough not to like cats. Why, anyone with *half* an ounce of poetry or sensitivity in his veins liked cats!

"So now that we've got that straight—unless you want me to set a new record in the cat-toss—WILL YOU GET OFF MY DAMNED CAR?"

She'd never been able to take it when he roared. She couldn't take it now. She was literally blown off the hood—landed in a hissing, puffed-up stance some twenty feet away.

His door slammed, the car raced off toward the exit.

"Sam..." She couldn't believe it. *"Sam! If you won't help me..."*

The car squealed to a halt. He leaned to the passenger side and opened the door.

"Oh, *thank* you! Thank *God!*" She scurried after him, trilling Cattoo's little hum of hope and joy.

Sam tossed something to the ground. "No hard feelings, cat. Maybe this'll help?"

She stopped beside the object, bewildered. The car rolled away.

Jessica stood, blinking down at a half-eaten doughnut. But the tears wouldn't come, no matter how they fell inside.

IN THE END, crouching under a bush, she ate his horrid doughnut. Her teeth weren't made for it and her pride revolted, but her stomach was more practical. This would have to do until morning, unless she wanted to check out the Dumpster behind the hospital cafeteria, *Which I most emphatically do not!* she told Cattoo when that thought roused a quickening interest.

Cattoo seemed to be rousing in general as the darkness closed in. While Jessica was growing numb with despair.

What would happen to her if she couldn't make Sam see who she was? What could he do, even if she *did* make him see? More to the point, what would she do tonight, with the temperature falling toward the forties and no place to sleep?

We need a warm, safe spot. Jessica couldn't have said whose thought that was, and the memories that followed were melded. Cattoo lay curled in a warm, soft lap, purring and safe. Jessica lay wrapped in Sam's arms, her cheek pressed to his beating heart. Oh, they knew what safe was, even if they couldn't find it.

It's out there somewhere. This was a conviction more than a worded thought. Cattoo stood. Rocking forward on her forepaws, she extended first one back leg, then the other, in a sensuous stretch. That done, she padded off into the night. Too tired to argue or advise, Jessica rode within, dimly aware of taut muscles sliding rhythmically beneath silken fur. Of the brush of wind, then leaves, across her whiskers . . . a feeling of guarded hope, unblinking watchfulness, then . . . darkness.

JESSICA AWOKE shivering, one paw cupped round her nose to slow loss of body heat, her back pressed to a brick wall. *Dreaming,* she told herself without much hope, and looked around. An expanse of tar and gravel stretched to the dawn-pink horizon. She lay on a roof, which topped some sort of extension from the taller building at her back.

A warm draft ruffled her fur. She lay curled directly below a heating vent, somewhere at the back of RI Gen. The smells exhausted from within were a nose-wrinkling blend of bleach and disinfectant, bodies washed and unwashed, an onslaught of detergent and floor wax and cooking food. The cafeteria roof, she realized. *How did I get up here?*

No answer.

And Cattoo was no help in finding the way down, either. Jessica had to pick her own path from ledge to wall to a loading dock, and thence to the ground.

What time do visiting hours start in the intensive-care unit? she wondered, skirting the building at a hurried trot. *Have I missed Sam?*

Because, in spite of his response last night, Sam was still her only hope. Though his love for her had been nothing but one of his passing whims, she'd never once doubted his friendship, even when she'd have sooner died than accept it. But this was no time for pride now.

But how do I make him see?

By the time visitors began to hurry up the front walk and into the hospital lobby, their faces bright with hope or tight with worry, Jessica had figured the way. She'd spent the time since dawn scouring the well-raked lawns at the front of RI Gen.

Cattoo had roused enough to decide she was nuts—you couldn't eat sticks, after all, and this business was too methodical for play. Then she had figuratively rolled over and gone back to sleep, paws in the air, leaving Jessica to grip each twig she found carefully between her teeth and carry it to her staging site some twenty feet to the side of the walkway.

There she nudged and dragged her branches into a rough arrangement, which, if you looked carefully and ignored the digressions made by twigs shooting off in the wrong directions, spelled HEL. Having run out of branches just as she got to the P, Jessica had roamed to the far side of the lawn when she heard a familiar step striding uphill from the parking lot.

"Sam!" Grabbing the twig she'd just discovered, she scampered back toward her message. *Sam Kirby!* she called, beaming the thought at her moving target. *Come to me. I know you hear me, if you'd only believe your ears. Come.*

But Sam wasn't even focused on the doors he approached. He was somewhere far away, decoding a sequence of DNA perhaps, or no, something much less pleasant, judging from the look on his face. *Sam!* Jessica dropped the branch beside her crude SOS just as his steps faltered. He stopped, glancing around with the puzzled look of a dreamer awakened in strange surroundings.

Yes! Yes, I knew you could hear me! In her joy, Jessica tucked her chin, dropped her shoulder and rolled a clumsy forward somersault—one of Cattoo's tricks when she wanted attention. She landed sprawled in the midst of her own message. *"Come!"* she called again.

Sam laughed and shook his head. "You've got a serious problem, cat."

"Oh, if only you knew!" *Come. Sam, come to me.*

"Come here, then," he invited, snapping his fingers as if she were a dog.

Blast—they were so close, and yet so far. "No. You come to me. You've got to come *here.*"

"Come here, puss."

"You come to *me.*" Jessica's tail lashed its frustration. *Come!*

"Just like a cat." Sam glanced toward the doors, then back. "Won't even come when it's called. And you wonder why I prefer dogs?"

"What else would I expect from a deaf and dumb Texan?" she exploded. "Talk about not coming when you're called!"

He shrugged. "Okay, be that way. Don't come. Who wants to talk to a cat, anyway?"

"Please come here." She put her heart and soul into that meow.

He scowled. "Is something the matter with you?"

"You could say that." And the surest way to Sam's heart—no one should know better than she—was to appeal to his protective instincts. Already lying down, she allowed her head to droop pathetically to the ground. She closed her eyes. *Come. Listen to me. I need your help.*

"Dammit," Sam muttered under his breath. He took one tentative step in her direction.

Yes! She kept her eyes closed, her breathing shallow, her thoughts focused. *Come. Help me?*

Another hesitant step, then another. At last he gave in and strode toward her, his steps heavy with self-disgust. "Cat?"

Of course, she was lying in the midst of her own message. She waited till he was only feet away, then rolled carefully to her stomach. *Don't move a branch,* she warned her tail.

Sam stopped. "What is this? You're playing possum?"

Look at the ground, Sam. Jessica stood, retreated carefully, treading between the branches. She looked back anxiously. Even upside down, the word was still legible. HEL. *Read it,* she implored. "Please read it."

"Cat?" Sam took three steps forward. "What do you want?" He took another step—which was precisely one too many.

"No!" she yelled, darting at him as she realized what he was doing. Twigs crunched as he stopped—directly in the middle of her message.

"No!" She spun around and stalked away, ears flattened, tail slashing. If she'd had hands, she would have torn her hair. "You . . . you . . ."

"Make up your tiny mind, cat. Do you want attention, or don't you?"

"Never mind. Forget it." She threw herself down on the grass. "You blew it, Kirby. Smashed a morning's work to useless bits."

He stared at her, then brushed a hand up through his dark hair. Shook his head.

"You look terrible," she added ungraciously, really seeing him for the first time. Her tail thumped the ground. How had he put it that time early on, after a sleepless night of loving? *You look rode hard and put up wet.* That was it, drawled with a touch of male smugness. Not that Sam didn't manage to look good, even exhausted. He had one of those angular faces that age and wear would only render more interesting, darn him.

"Looks like *you* slept rough," Sam said, looking down at her. "What are you doing here, anyway? Got a friend in there?" He jerked his chin toward the hospital. "Is that it? It's hell, isn't it?"

Is it for you, Sam? Somehow, in spite of her frustration, she felt her spirits rise a fraction. Just to know he cared . . .

He glanced at his watch. "Blast, cat, look at the time! I wanted to catch her doctor before he disappears. Good mousing." He turned on his heel and left.

What am I going to do? Jessica flopped back to stare at a forest of grass blades, which fused in the distance to a wall of frost-burned green. How to get through to him? Even with someone as mentally flexible as Sam, there reared between them a nigh unbreachable wall of preconceptions. A cat was a cat, a dumb animal, unable to communicate on anything but the most primitive level. *Feed me. Pet me. Play with me.*

That was all she'd ever assumed Cattoo was saying. It was presumptous—downright insulting—now that she thought of it. *For all I know, maybe you wanted to discuss the latest theories on quantum mechanics?*

Cattoo wasn't saying. Jessica caught her feeling of tolerant, sleepy amusement, then the cat drifted away again.

She needed time with Sam, time when she had his undivided attention. If only he'd give her that, she would get through to him, she was sure she could. Because they were attuned. Still. As they'd been from the first time they'd met. Not that they'd spoken the same language, even back then . . .

"LET ME get this straight. You want to take organic chemistry over again?" He hadn't taken his boots down from the desk where they were propped. His chair was tipped back so far on its hind legs he might've had some private arrangement with gravity. Or maybe a death wish.

Clutching her books to her chest, Jessica nodded doubtfully. When she'd asked for a tutor, the head of the chem department had recommended Kirby, a grad student and teaching assistant, but someone who slept at his desk at ten in the morning? Where she came from, energy was equated with brains. And brains were everything. To be less than brilliant was to be nothing at all.

"Yes. I'm allowed to throw out one grade per year. And since I took classes last summer, I'm ahead on my degree. So I'm going to take organic chemistry again. But I thought a few weeks of tutoring before the semester starts might—"

"Might help you improve a 3.9 average?" He rubbed a chin that could've used a shave, made a comic face, then shook his head. "Most people would give their left . . . arm for a 3.9."

She shrugged. What satisfied most people had nothing to do with her. What her parents expected of her. What she'd come to demand of herself. "I was ranked second in the class last time. I need to be first."

"You already look like a first to me."

She hadn't known how to take that, or the slow smile that followed when he saw her confusion. From the first day her mother dropped her off at an exclusive day-care school, she'd been too busy earning top grades to learn about boys. Somewhere along the line, the boys had turned to men, but she'd been even busier, with every year a harder grind than the one before.

His boots swung to the floor. "Let's go get some breakfast, and we'll talk about it."

"I had breakfast, um . . ."

"Quite a while ago? When do you eat breakfast? Seven?" Standing, he topped her by almost a foot.

"Six." After her five-mile run.

"Well, come have some lunch while I eat my breakfast, then."

"You always eat this late?"

"Only when I stay up all night." He steered her through the office door and into the lab beyond.

She shot him a wary glance. There was a note of laughter shimmering beneath his every word. Everything he said sounded like it might be a joke. "Why the overnighter?"

"Was watchin' some cells divide. Sort of lost track of the time."

Definitely a joke, she decided. Still, she followed him home. He'd had to do some fancy talking to get her through his door when she realized that was where they were headed, rather than the campus cafeteria. But once he'd coaxed her inside, he cooked her *huevos rancheros* on a solar-powered grill set up on his back deck—his electric stove being mysteriously disassembled at present.

And after that, he serenaded her with Brazilian sambas on his acoustic guitar, singing what she suspected were wicked, nonsensical suggestions in a soft pidgin mix of Italian and Portuguese, his voice a plaintive whiskey tenor.

Finally, at her insistence, he'd walked her through two hours of organic chemistry with a lucidity and playful enthusiasm that had made the lesson seem more like a romp through Disneyland than her usual teeth-gritted slog.

And someplace in that long, lovely, eye-opening day, he'd seduced her—had seduced her hours before he'd ever laid a finger on her. Oh, they'd been in tune all right, even if they'd spoken different languages, his joyful Texan to her worried WASP.

So he'll understand me now, if I can just get him alone and listening. She needed to beard him in his den, not out here in the open with people marching by, distracting him. She needed to confront him in the apartment he'd be subletting as of tonight. Harry Neuman's loft, less than a mile away, in the Jewelry District, Mac had said.

Yes! She sat up, turned to give her spine an automatic lick. That was it. She'd find a phone book, look up Neuman's old ad— She froze, eyes rounding in horror, tongue touching fur. *Oh, God, look at me, licking my—*

"*Kitteee!*" Staggering footsteps cut off the walkway and thumped closer across the grass. "Kitty-Caaa!"

Jessica whirled to see a child, perhaps two, chubby hands extended, smile ecstatic, trundling determinedly toward her. The toddler's mother looked up from the prescription she'd been consulting, then started after her offspring. "*Mia!*"

"Kitteee!"

In your dreams, kid! Bolting for cover, Jessica ran like a scalded cat.

CHAPTER EIGHT

THE NEXT TWO DAYS gave Jessica a new perspective on the phrase "run ragged."

Her search for a phone book the first day had been unsuccessful. Within a quarter-mile radius of the hospital, she couldn't find one outdoor phone booth with an unstolen book. So much for that plan.

Proceeding to plan two, she decided to try the honey hunter's approach for tracing Sam to his lair. The hunter watches the bee fly its beeline toward the hive till he loses it from view. He then walks to that point, waits till another bee wings past and tracks that bee hiveward till it disappears. Before long, he's standing beneath the bee tree almost tasting the honey.

It had always sounded easy in theory. But Sam Kirby was no one-track honeybee. Jessica waited that first evening on a slope just beyond the highway underpass, through which Sam would have to travel to reach the Jewelry District. Given the height of her spy post, she'd be able to follow his route down the seedy avenue that paralleled the bay, with any luck see where he turned off it.

But she waited till dark in vain. Either Sam had gotten lost, or he'd circled the long way around, exploring the tougher side of town, where hole-in-the-wall Southeast Asian cafés sat cheek by jowl with pawnshops and grafitti-sprayed Laundromats. He'd always had a weakness for exotic foods, and if he was eating Thai nowadays, that was where he'd find it. *Or Jamaican.* She shivered remembering Raye's sleazy café, then thrust the shrink from her mind. *Later.*

But if that was the roundabout route Sam had chosen, Jessica couldn't have followed even if she'd spotted him. He'd cover roughly six miles, circling clockwise over the freeways and back through the city to reach his destination just a mile from her vantage point.

No, she had to go the shorter way. Cats were built for sprints, not distance.

And she couldn't bear to wait until the next night, then try again. So plan three was to simply walk to the Jewelry District, then search for his parked car till she found it. How hard could that be? The district of defunct mills and costume-jewelry factories, bounded on two sides by freeways and the third by the bay, was no more than a mile square.

But neither the district, nor its approach, proved to be feline-friendly territory. What wasn't vertical brick or granite building, was horizontally paved—heavily traveled, truck-filled streets. Barren parking lots without a scrap of cover. Dark, dead-end alleyways. Chain-link fences with humorless Dobermans guarding whatever dubious business ventures lay beyond. A hard, stone-cold world, without one sanctuary tree in sight.

Even in human form, Jessica would have hesitated to walk the Jewelry District after dark, though she'd heard the area was also home to tiny jazz clubs, cutting-edge art galleries and hopeful young restaurateurs with more creativity than backing.

As a cat, it was a nightmare, without a clawhold anywhere. But she did what she had to do, scuttling from shadow to shadow, *becoming* a racing black shadow when she darted past oncoming headlights. And if doing what must be done included staying awake most of each night to hold Cattoo to her purpose, well, Jessica could do that, too. Though she felt like a slave-driving ingrate—the guest who'd come to dinner and long since overstayed her welcome.

Not that Cattoo complained. Much. But the cat was growing bone-weary with all this searching and sneaking, as weary and ragged as Jessica herself. Time spent checking every alley and street and parking lot in the district for Sam's car was time lost from sleeping and hunting, after all.

At dawn of the third day, Jessica took refuge between two trash cans at the mouth of an alley to examine her sore paws and consider. Perhaps she should have stayed at the hospital? Tackled Sam again there?

But she hadn't. *No use crying over spilt—* Her stomach turned over and lunged at the image. She put it hastily from mind.

Or perhaps Sam had changed *his* mind, left Providence entirely. She wouldn't find him here. She wouldn't find him back at RI Gen. And if he'd given up and gone home, back to the research lab he directed in North Carolina, she couldn't imagine how she would follow him there.

At the thought of all the hostile miles that might stretch between them, she tipped back her head, closed her eyes and shuddered. Cats didn't cry real tears—she'd learned that the hard way these past few days. But, oh, on the inside... *Sam. Come to me? Please?*

When he drove by a second later, headed out of the alley, he was simply an extension of her need—a starvation-inspired vision, not a frowning, flesh-and-blood man in a rental car. Jessica blinked at where the car had been only a second before. It had turned left toward RI Gen. *That was Sam.*

Cattoo didn't care. She needed sleep. She needed food. She needed a serious, whisker-to-tail grooming. She wanted her spot in one of their ground-floor windows next to a tasty spider plant. The sun always warmed that sill first thing in the morning.

We can't go back to Prospect Street, Jessica insisted. *That's not home anymore.* Home was... home was where Sam was, at least until he'd helped her out of this jam. Beyond that, she couldn't let herself think.

Cattoo was thinking of sleep. But this spot was too open to be safe.

So let's see what's down here. It was a shameless ploy, but it worked. Or perhaps Cattoo simply humored her.

Jessica shoved herself stiffly to her feet, padded on aching paws deeper into the shadowed alley.

Cold granite walls reared close on either side—six-story wings of the same mill complex. Up ahead towered a cylindrical brick smokestack with the words "Clarke Street Mill" painted on its side. Beyond the stack loomed the blind face of the factory that intersected the two wings. The alley ended below the stack in a tiny, rectangular courtyard, with two parking spaces to either side.

A sign was fastened to the wall above each empty parking space. "Miller" and "Feldman," read the signs to Jessica's left. On the right, the spots were reserved for "duPrey" and..."Neuman"!

Yes! Legs shaking, Jessica sat and heaved a sigh. This was the converted mill Mac had described. The place to which Sam must surely return.

If I could just go upstairs and wait for him...

Not a chance. The entrance to each wing was a massive, eight-foot, modernistic glass door with an impressive lock. The two polished brass buttons beside each door would be the means by which visitors gained admittance. A day before she could have managed the leap up to ring the bell with the neat Neuman placard beside it, but today? Hypothermia, she diagnosed, exacerbated by not nearly enough food. And when had they last found something to drink? She remembered and immediately tried to forget. No wonder cats needed nine lives.

Besides, what use would it be to ring the bell? she reminded herself. Sam was gone, probably till this evening.

Climb to his loft? She sat and looked up, scanning the walls overhead. Black iron fire escapes zigzagged their way down both wings. But they ended in up-folded ladders one floor above the ground. Besides, even if she could have scaled the first twenty feet of these sheer stone walls, she had no idea where Sam's loft lay.

I'll have to wait here.

That resolution brought an instant protest from within. There was no sunlight here. Not a scrap of food. Worst of all, no cover. This place was a deadly trap if a dog came along.

In the end, they compromised by hunching behind the garbage cans at the head of the alley. It wasn't much safer, but at least they had a choice of two directions to flee if danger discovered them. But it was too precarious a position to sleep. So Jessica crouched there hour after hour, eyes wide open, but glazed from exhaustion, nerves jangling, ears flinching at every passing sound.

By sundown, Cattoo was in full rebellion. They must go. Somewhere there would be mice, or something else to eat. There *must* be something, somewhere. But to find it they couldn't stay here, they must hunt.

No, safety is here, if you'll only be patient, Jessica pleaded. *Trust me.*

Still she found herself on her feet, peeking out past the cans at the barren street, every feline instinct demanding that she move or die.

A pair of headlights turned the corner in the distance, coming from the direction of RI Gen.

Oh, please. She wouldn't be able to hold Cattoo here more than a minute more. *Oh, please, let this be . . .*

The car slowed, then swung into the alley, its headlights sweeping across the cans, blinding her when she peered around them. It rumbled on down the passage toward the courtyard. As it turned into its parking space, she made out the vehicle's shape and color. This car was white and low slung. Not Sam's blocky gray sedan at all. Not deliverance.

That's it, then. This wasn't a worded thought, but nevertheless, it was a decision carved in stone. Jessica found herself padding away from the alley, her own tottering hope no match for Cattoo's determination, Cattoo's resolution growing with every foot of distance she gained between them and Jessica's obsession.

Another set of headlights turned the corner and approached. *Wait,* Jessica pleaded, stopping as the lights slapped her full in the face.

The car slowed, its driver seeing two blazing emeralds embedded in a crouching black shadow, she supposed. *Oh, please.*

The car picked up speed. Drove on by.

That was it, then. She had no right to demand that Cattoo stay and starve, no way to make her see that waiting was the wisest choice. But if they left now, something told her they'd never make it back here at all. Weakened as they were, this could well be the night they became the hunted, rather than the hunter.

Hardly slowing, the car wheeled into the alley.

Jessica turned, staring back over her shoulder. Had it been gray? *Oh, let it be gray!* "Sam!" she cried, hurrying back to the alley's mouth.

Two red taillights glowed at the end of the passage. They turned as the car parked on the right.

Sam! Because it must be he, she was sure it was. "Sam!" Trilling a cry of desperate welcome, she scurried down the alley. Her body was too weak to break out of a trot. *"Sammmmmmmerrrrrowww?"*

Up ahead, a car door slammed shut.

Sam, I'm begging you! Don't go. Wait for me!

A tall silhouette moved out into the center of the courtyard and stared back toward her hurrying shape.

"Oh, Sam!"

"You!" He stared down at her, then started and lightly slapped his temple. "No, what am I thinking? It can't be you."

"Oh, but it is! It really *is* me! I know it's crazy, I can't begin to explain, but—" She let out a little rippling cry of relief. Thank God, he could see her at last! And with Sam on her side...

He laughed to himself and shook his head. "No way could you be the same black cat that was hustling me back at the hospital, could you? That's over a mile away."

He didn't see her. Saw nothing but another cat. She let out a sound that was as close to a sob as a cat could come. "Sam, just *look* at me!"

"All cat's look alike in the dark, huh?" He took a step toward the glass door, then jabbed a finger at her when she followed. "Uh-uh. Stay away, cat. I've had 'bout all the bad luck I can handle. Last thing I need is a black cat crossing my trail."

"You haven't a *clue* what bad luck is . . . you . . . you . . ." She sank to the frigid ground. It was useless. He couldn't see past the fur. Never would. "If I'd turned into a damned poodle, would you take me in, damn you? Or is it just that you don't have a heart?"

Sam stirred uneasily, glanced back toward the door. He slapped the paper bag he held against his thigh and swore softly.

"I know you, even if you don't know me. I bet I'm the only one in the world, outside your family, who knows your middle name's Antonio. It was your mother's brother's name and your dad's idea of a joke. Your mother nearly killed him when she realized he'd let her name you for a city."

"Look—" Sam backed another step toward the door "—I really don't like cats. Can't you go put the moves on somebody else?"

"There's nobody else, Sam. There's only you." She'd always known that. Not that knowing it had done her much good. Love was a tie that must bind both. Let only one be stupid enough to feel, and it became a noose, drawn tight around the heart.

Sam sighed, then dropped to a crouch. "Ever tried General Tzo's chicken, cat?"

"That's not what I want!" she yelled, even as her mouth started to water. General Tzo's. She'd have burst into tears if she could have. That had been their special treat. They'd sampled that dish in every Chinese restaurant they'd ever tried. A white box of General Tzo's was what Sam had brought home most nights when it had been his turn to cook.

"Haven't tried it myself in about eight . . . oh, for a long time," he muttered, opening the bag. "I've probably lost

my taste for it entirely. You can't go home again no matter
how you . . ." His words trailed away.

"You missed me, too?" she asked in a tiny voice. There
was no particular reason that should make her feel good.
Of course, he would've missed her. They'd had some wonderful times together. But Sam was such an extrovert he
could've enjoyed the company of any of a hundred different women. Would've missed any one of them after the relationship ended.

He tore open the bag, spread it out on the ground,
opened the white box. Using a pair of chopsticks, he raked
out two hunks of steaming chicken, then a puddle of the
pungent sauce. "If I'd known you were dropping by, I'd
have brought you some chopsticks." He closed the box.
"Guess you'll just have to lick your fingers." He grinned
at her. "Your toes. Whatever." He rose to his feet.

Crouched, Jessica stared from the food up to his face,
then back down. "This isn't what I want, Sam. I mean,
thank you, but—"

"That's another thing I can't stand about cats," he said
without rancor. "Every one of 'em's a blasted five-star
gourmand, with his nose stuck in the air. You wouldn't
catch a dog wasting General Tzo's."

"I'll eat it," she said wearily. She stood and sniffed at the
food.

"Good." He turned and left her.

If it wasn't what she wanted, at least it was warm. Gulping it down, she did her best to block out the images that its
sweet-and-sour taste evoked. Sam leaning across their
kitchen table to feed her a tidbit from his own chopsticks.
The time the brute had smiled tenderly into her eyes—then
dropped a sticky chunk down the neck of her blouse. He'd
insisted on retrieving it himself, licking the golden sauce
from her skin, then licking all the spots that the sauce by
rights *should* have splattered, till her cries of outrage turned
to another sound entirely. It hadn't been uncommon, their
first six months together, for supper to end in the bedroom.

Stop, she warned herself. Memories like that could drive a person crazy. *And you're not even a person anymore.*

Still, the hot food heartened her, and also Cattoo. *Just take it one step at a time.* She'd found where he lived. The next step was to survive the night, which was going to be a fierce one. Their coldest yet.

It wasn't easy, but she managed the leap to the hood of Sam's car. Assuming the cat's classic loaf-of-bread position, front paws tucked under breast fur, back legs folded beneath belly, tail curled tight to one side, Jessica crouched on the hood, soaking up the last of the engine's heat. Overhead, lights had switched on in the top floor. *So that's where you are.* She tried to picture the space, but it might as well have been heaven—Sam eating General Tzo's on a warm, fluffy cloud. She shuddered, and this time the shudder didn't end—it diminished to a faint, steady trembling. She blew out a breath, and it clouded whitely round her whiskers.

We can't stay here, Cattoo seemed to say within. The night was clear, ice-bright stars winking in the patch of sky overhead. No cloud cover to hold the heat in, all of Earth's warmth leaking out into the pitiless black above. The car cooled beneath her, making tiny ticks and squeaks as its metal contracted.

And I can't leave. Jessica closed her eyes stubbornly, drew inward around her shivering center.

Perhaps they would've gone, perhaps they would've stayed till they froze to the car. Sometime later, Jessica slit her eyes to the sound of a door opening, then slamming shut.

Keys jingled, then Sam loomed over the hood. He blew out a smoky snort when he saw her. "You again! Would you gimme a break?" He unlocked his car door. "Shoo. Sssszzzt!"

Jessica stared back at him. "I'm *not* moving."

"Oh, yeah?" His hands closed around her, one cupping her breast, the other her rear. "I'm late, cat. Got to get to the airport. No time for fun and games." He dropped her gently on the ground to one side. "Now stay out from under." He slid into the car, slammed the door.

For a second she stood there, too stiff to move, still paralyzed by the feel of his hands on her body. Then it hit her. "You're catching a plane?"

The engine revved. Apparently he thought he could scare her into standing clear.

But nothing scared her, compared to his leaving. And that fear was nothing to do with the fact that they wouldn't last the night if someone didn't take them in.

Desperation gave birth to invention. Stand clear, he'd said, but what if she didn't? What if she...

The car eased backward, reversing in a curve toward the end wall. He'd have to back and turn to leave the courtyard front first. Lurching into motion, Jessica trotted close alongside his door. Unless he looked straight down through his side window, he wouldn't see her. He was probably looking over his shoulder, gauging how far he could go before he touched the wall.

Still moving backward, the car was coasting to a halt.

Now! Jessica shot under the front bumper, threw herself down on the ground barely two feet ahead of the car—as if he'd caught her with a rear wheel, then backed on over her pitiful body until she was now revealed. Closing her eyes, she clenched her teeth. *Sam, look what you've done!* He'd always had a soft spot for waifs.

She heard the transmission shift from reverse to forward. The front wheels slowly rotated as he prepared to drive ahead.

Sam? Jessica's eyes slit open a crack.

One rolling wheel, the oncoming chrome cliff of the bumper filled all her vision.

"*Rrrrow!*" She shot to one side, flattened herself to the ground, the left wheel missing her tail by half a whisker. The car passed overhead, a black shadow of death hovering, smothering, now its back wheels grinding across the pavement to crush her. She scrambled desperately aside, then rolled to her feet, spun to stare after the receding taillights. "*Damn* you. Why don't you watch where you're—"

But it wasn't his fault; she'd positioned herself too close. The hood must have blocked his view.

And she might never see him again if he was leaving to catch a plane.

Jessica raced after the car. "Sam! *Wait!*"

He didn't hear her—or didn't care if he did. The car rolled away, relentless as the slow tilt of the Earth to winter's freezing plane. She would stop him—she *would*—if it cost her her dying breath. *"Sam, don't leave me!"*

The car paused when it reached the alley mouth. He'd heard her!

No, he was simply looking both ways. Headlights flashed past out on the street. Just as she reached his car, his brake lights went off.

He'd turn left to head for the airport. Her breath sobbing in her ears, Jessica shot out into his path as the car lunged into motion.

Sam, see me. She braced herself and squinted up into the headlights, the blaze of light blinding her.

Deafening screech of tires—he'd hit the brakes.

Again she'd cut it too close. The car was on top of her— a murderous black monster with blazing eyes, a silver smile. *I should duck,* she thought with icy clarity—and something whacked the top of her head.

The night folded leisurely down around her, cold as frozen concrete, warm with the taste of blood.

"DAMN, DAMN, damn, damn—you *stupid,* furball-for-brains, good-for-nothing *cat!*" His face only inches from her own, Sam crouched on hands and knees to peer under the bumper. That is, one and a half Sams peered at her, then reached to touch her shoulder with too many fingers.

Jessica blinked. Guess that *was* sort of stupid.

"You want to check out, that's your business. But did you hear me volunteering to help?" He touched her again. "You could've jumped off a damn bridge. Or turned on the gas."

Sorry.

He growled wordlessly and withdrew. She cried out as the engine started overhead. He was just going to drive off and leave her? *"Sam!"* she cried, but it came out a breathless squeak.

The car backed up slowly. Its headlights lit the road, casting the long black lump of her shadow before her. She lay on one side, her whiskers crumpled against the pavement, too scared to move.

The car stopped. Leaving the engine idling, Sam hurried back to kneel beside her. "Are you alive, cat? Speak to me."

"Hi." It came out the most prosaic of mews.

He let out a harsh breath. "That's a start, anyway. Now what's broken?" His fingers touched her delicately, exploring her ribs, her back, each of her legs. "Damn, there's not much to you, is there? I've met potato chips with better structural engineering. Why the hell did you want to tangle with a two-ton car?"

"You were leaving me."

"At least you can talk, blast you. Okay, now what?"

"Watch out for my spine."

"Yeah . . ." He stared off into the darkness, thinking. "We'll need a board." He stood. Hurried footsteps moved away. Something squeaked, then he was back again. Clash of metal as he set a trash can lid down beside her. "Not exactly classy, but it's the best we can do." He sucked in a long breath. "I reckon this will hurt. Do me a favor and don't take a hunk out?"

I'd never . . .

This time when his fingers approached, there seemed to be ten. They slid with exquisite care under her limp body, then he lifted, doing his best to keep her level. "E-e-easy . . ." He laid her gently on the lid of the garbage can. "There." He let out a shaky breath. "Cat on a platter."

"That's what I always loved about you, Sam. Your unfailing sense of humor."

He missed the sarcasm. "Okay, cat, let's go for a ride. Which vet do you recommend?" He lifted her and headed for the car.

"No! No vet." Not yet, anyway. She could see Sam paying the bill, leaving her in the vet's care with the promise that someone would find her a good home once she was healed. While Sam flew off to wherever, his conscience clear. "No vet. I don't want one. Besides, they'll all have gone home this time of night."

"No favorite, huh? Okay, we need the yellow pages . . ." He set her on the passenger seat, shut the door. A moment later he slid in beside her and sat, drumming his fingers on the steering wheel. "Blast, blast, blast."

Believe me, you won't find a phone book at a phone booth in this part of town. If only he'd take her home . . .

"All right, I guess the closest phone is back at my place. Hang on." He reversed the car past the alley, then turned into it. He braked as they jounced over a pothole, his palm hovering above her side. "Just hang on, fur-brain. How're you doing there?"

"Somebody's playing the end of the *1812* Overture between my ears. I suppose I'm concussed." The bumper had clipped her, she imagined.

Murmuring soothing nonsense, he carried her on his improvised litter into the building, then through a small lobby. He jabbed a button and the wide doors to a freight elevator groaned open. The lift hummed up to the top floor, where Sam had to unlock another set of steel doors marked with an enormous numeral six.

The doors opened directly onto the loft. Sam slapped a light switch. With one eye, Jessica could see dark, enormous beams intersecting far overhead, vanishing backward as she was carried across the room. Track lighting. A network of pipes enameled forest green and Chinese red.

"Okay, now what?" Sam muttered. "I reckon you're in shock. Warm you up, I s'pose." He set the lid down on a low coffee table. He came back a second later, dropped down on the couch before her. A wall of rough burgundy descended, blocking Jessica's view.

It settled around her, smelling of raw wool and that in-
definable, unforgettable fragrance that was Sam. His
sweater. He tucked it carefully around her chin. And with
that gesture, something like peace enfolded her. She shut
her eyes and breathed in deeply, savoring the sensation. She
used to lie in bed beside him sometimes, late at night, long
after he'd fallen asleep, her nose pressed to his shoulder,
simply inhaling the smell of his skin. *Oh, Sam.* Warmth
seeped into her bones, crept toward her heart.

Pages flipped nearby. She opened her eyes. Scowling with
concentration, Sam thumbed through a phone directory.

"No." *I don't want a vet. Let me stay here with you.*

"Hang on, cat. We'll find somebody." He grunted.
"Where the blue blazes is Warwick? Is that close by? Or
what about Cranston? I s'pose any place in this runt of a
state is no more than a good sneeze away." He picked up
the phone book and walked out of Jessica's field of vision.
She heard him punch the numbers, then he wandered back
into view, a portable phone pressed to one ear. "Hello?"
He stopped and swung to glance at Jessica. "Yes, I'm trying to reach Dr. Casten. It's an emergency. I ran over a
cat." He scowled and paced on past the sofa.

She needed to recover—not completely, but enough to
make him think twice about racing off to the vet, Jessica
realized, as he explained the situation to the vet's answering service. But was it dangerous to move? Her tongue
flicked over her teeth and she winced. *I bit it. That's where
the blood's coming from.* That was a relief. Next she took
a cautious, limb-by-limb inventory, stretching out each leg
in turn beneath the sweater.

No pain there, and her spine must not be traumatized,
since everything seemed to work.

"How long will it take him to get back to me? I
mean, if there are internal injuries, I don't want to...
Okay okay..." Sam let out a breath between his teeth.
"Okay, my number is..." Reciting it, he wheeled away.

Jessica half sat, then braced herself that way on her lower
elbow. The room reeled, her head rang like a distant gong.
She closed her eyes. *Hang on.*

"Hang on. I think—" Sam stopped. "No...never mind, just have him call me quick as he can, will you? Thanks."

Jessica opened her eyes to find him staring at her from across the room. He removed the phone slowly from his ear. "Don't you *dare* move." He pointed a finger at her as he advanced around the sofa.

"Wouldn't dream of it." Not till the world stopped spinning, anyway.

He sank down on the couch before her. "Are you okay?"

"That's a pretty relative term for somebody who's grown a tail in the past week. Why don't you check my eyes?"

He leaned forward and tipped a finger to support her chin. "Let's see, if you've cracked your silly skull, the symptom is, the pupils go out of sync. One bigger than the other, right?"

"Right." He was talking to her without a clue he was doing so. She looked up at him, their faces not a foot apart. "It's so good to see you, Sam." *To feel you touch me.*

"What have you got to purr about?" His dark eyes moved back and forth, comparing one of her pupils to the other. "Look about the same to me—both of 'em weird, but I s'pose that's normal. You've got eyes like a goat, cat."

"Thanks." She lifted her chin from his grasp and glared past him. "Knock me silly, insult me—go right ahead if it makes you feel better." He was right. She had nothing to purr about, not while all he saw was a cat.

"Well—" Sam reached for the phone book "—if you're feeling better, then I've got another call to make." He flipped pages, frowned, then picked up the phone.

"Yes," he said after he'd punched in the numbers. "I'd like to leave a message for two passengers who should be coming in on your flight from Chicago, the one that arrives in about five minutes. Yes, that's it."

Jessica turned to stare. So he'd been meeting a plane, not leaving. And Chicago, that could only be—

"The message is for Dr. and Mrs. Myles, from Sam Kirby. Yes, that's K-i-r-b-y. Please tell them an emergency came up and I can't meet them at the airport. But if they'll catch a taxi to their hotel, I'll meet them there by—" he turned his wrist to consult his watch "—ten-thirty latest. Oh! And would you please tell them the emergency has nothing—repeat—*nothing* to do with their daughter?"

Jessica fixed him with her weird eyes. *That's what you think.*

"Thanks." Sam put the phone down. He met her gaze. "What are you staring at? And when's that damned vet gonna call?"

Forget the vet, I'm fine. "Truly." Her parents…This trip would throw their exquisitely scheduled world into a shambles. She was surprised they had…well, bothered wasn't exactly the word she meant. Still, she'd assumed they'd oversee her condition long-distance, just as they had most of her life, like caring but overworked gods.

A nasty thought hit her. Her father would've been monitoring her condition, insisting that any change in her status was reported immediately. Did this mean… "How am I doing, by the way? Why does my father want to see me?"

"Don't you ever stop talking, cat? Or does that mean you hurt? You're maybe sitting there trying to dictate your last will and testament. I want Fluffy to have my catnip mouse, and Tiger gets my—" He jumped as the phone rang, then grabbed for it. "Yep?" He stood and starting pacing. "That's right, I hit a cat… No, it's a stray—I mean, I think it is. But that's beside the point. I'll pay whatever it…" Still talking, he wandered away.

Now. She had to show him she was all right *now.* Feeling as if she were lifting a piano on her back, Jessica pushed herself shakily to her feet. The sweater slithered off her shoulders to the floor, and suddenly she was infinitely lighter—she could have laughed aloud. She stood on the table, shaky but whole. Her tail swished itself through a slow, experimental S-curve. She seemed to be fine, apart from a wicked headache. A slight concussion, if even that.

"Wait a minute," Sam spoke from across the room. "He's up."

He? Jessica turned to stare. *My God, Sam, you don't even realize I'm a she?* She sat, suddenly, ludicrously, wanting to cry. Oh, what was the use?

"Oops, he's down. Sitting. Yeah, I looked at his eyes. The pupils look just the same... What's normal for a cat? It's pretty bright in here. I'd say they're dilated 'bout halfway, at least they were a minute ago." Sam walked across and leaned down to look into her eyes. "He's still the same."

And you can kiss my sweet fanny, Jessica beamed with teeth-gritted precision. *As they say in Texas.*

Sam blinked, then spun around to look behind him. He stood frozen for a long moment, then swung slowly on around, apparently scanning the shadows as he turned. He ended back where he'd started, staring down at Jessica, his dark brows pulled together over his hawkish nose.

"Right." *That was me you heard. And this me is not a he, thank you ever so much. If anybody should know, you should.*

"*Huh?*" Sam shook his head, a sharp jerk as if he was shaking water out of his ears, then turned away. "Do I... Uh... well, do you think I should? To take X rays or whatever? No, nothing *looks* as if it's broken. I'm beginning to think my tire didn't catch him. Thumped him good with the bumper, I'd say... Hmm? Oh, maybe five miles an hour..."

"No vet." *He doesn't want to come out this time of night, and I don't want to see him.* Jessica stood resolutely, then leapt to the couch.

"Hey!" Sam protested from across the room. "He just jumped on the couch. Yeah."

At the touch of the nubby fabric beneath her pads, some reflex grabbed hold. Her claws were too long. Jessica reached for a cushion, hooked in, and— She realized what she was doing just as Sam yelled.

"*Hey!*" He lunged across the room. "None of that, cat! He's trying to claw the couch, blast him. *You*—cut that out!"

As always, thinking in midaction was disastrous. One paw snagged, its claws still extended.

"Let go." Sam tapped her offending paw with a finger. "Yeah, I'd say he's starting to look pretty spry here. Let go." He tapped her trapped paw again.

"I'm *trying,* can't you see?" Jessica yanked again—and succeeded in toppling the large cushion down upon her. "Blast! Blast and—" It was all too much. Bicycling her back paws, she kicked at it viciously. She'd have burst into tears if she could. "I hate being a cat! I hate it, I hate it, I hate—"

"Whoa!" Sam sat beside her and lifted the cushion halfway off.

He was *laughing,* damn and blast him!

"I've got to put the phone down, Doc. He's mauling the sofa. Hang on a minute."

"I *hate* this, Sam." She lay very still as he gently pried her paw free of the fabric. "It's humiliating! And I...I'm *scared.*"

His hand came down on her shoulders, pinning her to the sofa, a soothing, commanding weight. He reached for the phone with his other hand.

"Okay... Yeah, I'm starting to think so, too. Maybe give it till morning, then see how he looks? Okay... No, I don't have a cage, but... Yeah...no, I'll figure out something." Still talking, he glanced at his watch and frowned. "Fine. Now about my bill for this consultation, do you take credit cards? No, really, I'd like to do someth— Well, if you're sure..."

Jessica remained motionless, her eyes closed, while they settled the matter, then Sam made his thanks. She was exhausted. Perhaps she should simply die right now. Just finish what she'd started in the first place, drift off to wherever, with the sound of Sam's voice in her ears...

"Cat?" Sam's face was only inches from her own. He was crouching beside the couch. "Are you with me? Damn, your pupils are sure dilated now. Are you cruising into shock?"

No, I'm just beat. I'm so tired, Sam...

He stroked the top of her head with one fingertip. "Should I call the doc back? Or have you just had a tough day?"

"The toughest day of my life." Or no, the toughest had been the night, then the day after she left him. But this one rated a mean second. The only thing that made it bearable was...

His arms slid around her. Her eyes drooped shut as he lifted her, and she drifted, breathing in the scent of his skin. She could feel his heart thudding against her ribs as he carried her. *Yes, I used to love this.* Those times long after midnight when he'd come in from the bedroom to find she'd fallen asleep over her textbooks. He'd carry her off to their bed, its sheets already warm from his body...

Her eyes slit open as he leaned above a bed. His other hand reached for a blanket, dragged it down. *Yes.* She closed her eyes. *Yes, take me to bed, hold me... Maybe this is all just a dream.* Maybe all the last eight years had been nothing but a lonely dream...

They moved on...moving as one...

When she heard the click of a switch, she opened her eyes, then squinted against the harsh glare of lights bouncing off white tiles. They passed a long marble sink and Sam reached for a chrome bar. A door of frosted glass slid to one side.

"This should keep you out of mischief."

For a moment his words made no sense at all. Why was he dropping the blanket into a bathtub? Then, as he lowered her, she realized. "Oh, Sam, *no!*"

He laid her gently on the blanket at the far end from the taps. "Get a good night's sleep, and I bet you'll be fine in the morning. Ready to take on the world."

"Ready to throw back out on the street, you mean, damn you! Don't leave me in a *tub!*" But the door was already sliding shut. "*Damn* you, why won't you listen to me?"

Because she was only a cat. Her legs gave way and she sank into the soft folds of the blanket, closed her eyes in despair.

The door slid aside a few minutes later. Sam leaned down to set a bowl of water, then another of orange glop, near the taps. "'Fraid there's no cat food on the house menu tonight, and we're fresh out of truffles. Think you could make do with canned chili?"

"Cold? I'd rather starve."

"Hmm..." He studied her for a moment, then shrugged. "Maybe it'll look better by morning." He brushed the top of her head with a fingertip. "G'night, cat. Sleep tight."

And don't let the bedbugs bite. That was something his father used to say while tucking him into bed when he was a child, she remembered dully. Sam had mumbled it in sleepy tenderness to her on more than one night. "Fat chance they'll find me in here, Sam!" But he was gone, and a second later the lights went out in the bathroom—then between her ears.

CHAPTER NINE

WATER SURGED, then gurgled away down a nearby pipe, and Jessica opened her eyes—to gaze blankly at a porcelain wall. A tub...Sam...the looming monster that was his car... Bit by bit, past and present meshed, then the glass door slid to one side and Sam looked in. "How're you feeling, cat? A little run-down?"

"Funny, *funny* man." Jessica stood, then stretched, spine arched into a tight, inverted U. "*Oof*—I feel like I slept in a tub." That movement done, she straightened, then, bowing till her elbows grazed the porcelain, stretched out her front legs. She yawned enormously. "*Erk!*" She stood again and—final position—daintily pointed first one back leg, then the other. "There." She was stiff, but she would do.

"If you're quite, *quite* finished?" Sam hooked one palm under her rib cage, the other around her haunches and whisked her out of the tub. He deposited her on a black-and-white tiled floor.

Ears angled backward, tail swishing andante, she glared up at him. "And if I wasn't?" It was disconcerting to say the least to be hoisted from here to there at a giant's whim. That the hands that cupped her body with such blithe familiarity were Sam's only made it somehow worse. Irritation melded uncomfortably with arousal—skittered along her nerve endings, ruffling the fur along her spine. And realizing that she herself had treated Cattoo with the same unthinking disrespect only made her mood the blacker.

"Not a morning cat?" Sam nudged a plastic basin with his toe. "Well, maybe this'll cheer you up. I found some builder's sand in **the** **ba**sement."

"Right." Domestic facilities had been less than ideal the past few days, but if he thought she'd use a box when there was a perfectly good toilet available, he had another think coming. They contemplated each other for a moment, she with wide eyes, he with narrowed.

Sam blinked first. "Right. I'll leave you to it, then. I'm s'posed to meet Jess's folks at the hospital by nine." He turned away, then stopped and glanced into the tub. "Didn't go for the chili, huh?" He collected her bowls and left the room.

A few minutes later, Jessica stalked into the kitchen, which was next door to the bathroom on the same side of a long hall, but closer to the living room. Sam stood at the stove, whistling "The Girl from Impanema" and scrambling—she sniffed, then her stomach rumbled—*"Eggs!"*

Sam glanced aside. "Hey, tall and tan. Facilities meet with your approval?"

"They would have, if you'd left the darned seat down." Come to think of it, they'd wrangled about that in the old days, hadn't they, teasing each other at first, then griping in earnest toward the end, when their nerves were frayed to the limit. And she'd thought she had troubles back then. It had taken her four tries just now to flush the darned thing.

"You didn't finish your chili," Sam noted, nodding at the bowl of orange mush, which now rested, along with her water bowl, on a folded sheet of newspaper below a gigantic window.

"I didn't start it." Jessica sat beside the bowls. "How about some eggs, Sam? And some bacon, if you've got any."

"Too spicy for you?" He hit the bar on a toaster, and two pieces of bread sank from view. "You wimp Yankee cats. Down where I come from, any self-respecting cat would be begging for the hot sauce, to jazz it up."

"And I suppose the dogs eat jalapeños on everything. I could do without Texas this morning, thanks all the same."

Her eyes followed his movements as he opened a bag. Her ears pricked when coffee beans rattled into the cup of a grinder. "Coffee!" Fresh-brewed. "Sam, if you knew

what I'd have done for a cup of coffee these last few days."
She glided across the kitchen to stand at his feet looking up.
"Fix me a cup? Please?"

"You little beggar." Sam hit a button. The grinder
munched beans.

Jessica flattened her ears to muffle the racket. "Please,
Sam. Make me a cup, too? Is that so much to ask?" She
rubbed a shoulder against his calf, hating herself when she
realized what she was doing, but still, if it got results...

"Hey, now cut that out." Intent on pouring the grinds
into a Melitta filter, Sam sidestepped down the counter.
"None of that slinky cat stuff."

She made another pass at his leg, a full body sweep from
her cheek to her hip, then flicked him with her tail as she
walked on, looking back at him over her shoulder. "Just
one cup, the way I like it?" *And do you still remember how
I like it?*

"You wouldn't like it. Honest." He poured boiling water over the grinds, paused to stir the eggs, hit the bar on the
toaster to pop up his toast. "Shoo. Go eat your chili."

"I'd rather die." Which was absurd, she had to admit,
considering that only yesterday she'd contemplated mice
without gagging.

"Or starve to death—it's all one to me." He raked eggs
onto a plate, added the toast, placed his breakfast on the
round cherry table that was centered in front of the window. He turned and went back for his coffee.

Jessica sat, her tail slashing great sweeps across the li-
noleum. *And I thought my troubles would be over when I
got you to take me in. What a fool I was!* "Sam, would you
just stop and *listen* to me?"

Instead, he walked out of the room. She clicked her teeth
in frustration, then cocked her head. He was headed all the
way across the living room—which meant she had perhaps
a minute?

One leap took her to the seat of his chair. From there, she
hopped easily to the table. Stepping delicately past his plate,
she homed in on the mug. Face over her goal, she paused
to wrinkle her nose at the smell, so much stronger than

she'd ever noticed before. Within, Cattoo awoke in astonishment. Cattoo had always loathed the smell of coffee.

Too bad. Go back to sleep. Jessica touched her tongue to
the brew, then winced. Much too hot, but beggars, as Sam
had so tactfully put it, could not be choosers. She let out a
little moan of bliss as the first quarter teaspoon slid down
her throat, then she hunched down, lapping greedily. He
still drank *his* black and espresso strong. She'd have preferred a teaspoon of honey and a dash of cream, but even
so...*bliss*.

Slow bliss. How could cats stand it, spooning up their
drinks drop by tedious drop, while the busy world stormed
past above them? It was a whole different conception of
time and its value. Meanwhile, paper rustled on the coffee
table, then Sam's footsteps approached. *One more sip,* she
told herself. Well...perhaps one more. Then another.

Then suddenly he was there, just around the corner. Jessica spun and leapt for the floor, twisting in midair to dodge
the seat of his chair. She landed heavily, precisely as he
stepped into view.

"I heard that."

"What?" She gave him a wide-eyed look, then, not lik-
ing his scowl, turned to flick an imagined bit of dust from
her flank.

He smacked a magazine onto the table before dropping
to his heels, cowboy fashion, in front of her. "Don't give
me that butter-wouldn't-melt look. You were on the table,
weren't you?"

Okay, so I was. Then suddenly it hit her—she could nod,
couldn't she? She nodded—it felt awkward. Supple as a
cat's neck was, it wasn't normally used this way. But she
managed a stiff up-and-down bobbing, once, twice, then a
third time. *Yes. So you busted me, I admit it.* She didn't
give a fig if they could communicate. *Ask me something
else,* she begged, beaming the thought straight between his
narrowed brown eyes.

"Guess we better get one thing straight, cat, so listen up.
Cats...don't...*ever*...hop up on the table. That's spelled

never, never, not ever, or death, doom, disaster and a good skinning. Got that?''

Got it. She nodded slowly, earnestly, three times. *And I'll accept your abject apology later, once you understand whom you're addressing. But right now, see what I'm doing?* "See?"

He scowled. "What's the matter? Does your neck hurt?"

Noooo. Slowly, carefully, she shook her head three times. This gesture felt even clumsier. She'd have to look up a cat anatomy book someday when she was back to normal. They apparently weren't hinged quite the same. *Ask me another yes or—*

The phone rang in the living room.

"Don't answer that!" *Stay with me, Sam. Pay attention.* "Oh, damn!"

Still frowning, he stood and left the room.

Blast, blast, *blast,* just when she almost had him! She turned a tight circle of frustration—gave her tail a bitter look when it swung into view, then swiveled her ears as Sam picked up the phone.

"Doc!" he said in surprise. "Nice of you to call."

Her father? But Sam called her father by his given—

"Well, he seemed fine at first. Walks without limping, seems alert, meows nonstop. He's a real talker."

Oh, the vet—Casten.

"But he hasn't touched his food yet, far as I can tell."

And has no plans to, till you offer her something remotely edible. Speaking of which, Jessica jumped back on the table. His coffee was now the perfect drinking temperature. *Wonder what my proper caffeine dosage is,* she wondered, lapping frantically. Her ears pricked as Sam's steps started down the hallway. He was bringing the phone back to the kitchen.

"Only one thing bothers me. He's started moving his head funny."

Oh, thanks. When you do it, it's a nod. When I do it, it's funny. By now, her nose was down a good inch into his coffee mug. She lapped up a final mouthful, then spun and launched herself into the air just as Sam came around the corner.

"Hey! You were up there again, weren't you, you sneaky devil?"

Jessica turned back and nodded. *Yes, as a matter of fact, I was.*

"Yeah ... He's spunky enough to raid the table, Doc, that's for—" Sam stopped to watch, as Jessica completed her third nod. "There! He's doing it now—wobbling his head up and down. Looks really weird. As if he's sprained his neck."

No! It doesn't, does it? Perhaps she should have practiced first with a mirror. Jessica tried it one more time, slower, with exquisite care. *I just look weird, Sam, because you don't expect a cat to—*

"I'd say I bumped him straight on. He was looking right at me last I saw him, before the hood blocked my view." Sam listened, still frowning at her. "Yeah, I suppose that's right ... His head would've been pushed straight back on his neck. Like a whiplash, in other words?"

"No!" Jessica wailed. "Don't listen to that quack! Can't you use your eyes, Sam?" She could've shaken him. *No, this is not a whiplash!* She shook her head no. "See?" *This means no.* She did it again. *Nooo!*

"There he goes again, but this time its more side to side. Could he be dizzy? Or not seeing straight? Damn."

Double damn! Jessica stopped moving to glare at him helplessly. *Sam, you lunk-head, what am I going to do with you?*

"What do you think I should do? Bring him in?"

Oh, no, that was a terrible idea! The last thing she needed was a vet poking and prodding her. Besides, if Sam took her out of this loft, would he ever bring her back? He wasn't exactly enamored with her charms so far. "No vet. I'm fine. *Really*. See, I'll stop nodding, if it bothers you so much."

"Okay, tell you what," Sam continued. "I can't bring him in now. I have a meeting I can't miss in twenty minutes. Guess I'll give him till this afternoon, and if he's not better by then, I'll let you check him out.''

Whew! Jessica sat down and vented a sigh of relief. "I'll be better, believe me.''

Sam smacked the phone down on the counter, then sat. He shoveled eggs onto a piece of toast, clapped the second piece on top to make a sandwich, then scowled at her. "You, cat, are a royal, pluperfect pain in the ass.'' He bit off a mouthful, then chewing, continued to glare at her.

"Well, that makes two of us. I never dreamed you were so close-minded. Where's all that creativity you're famous for? If you can imagine new functions for nonsense DNA that nobody else ever conceived of, why can't you imagine something simple like a cat talking?'' Watching him eat, she felt her mouth watering. Absently she wiped the inner side of her wrist across her lips.

That gesture set off some sort of feline reflex, Cattoo noting promptly that they hadn't had a good bath in days. Jessica sighed and licked her wrist—then rubbed it over the top of her head, back to front, feeling the hairs stand up on end. She licked again, rubbed from top of head to tip of nose, licked, rubbed, lick-licked...

Sam laughed softly. "You're something else, cat.'' He lifted his mug and drank without looking, took another enormous bite.

"What's so funny?'' *Remember how you taught me to drink tequila one night?* He'd dragged her off to some smoky little bar to hear a blues guitarist who sang like a down-on-his-luck, gravel-voiced angel. He'd shown her how to lick the base of her thumb, then salt it. To hold a wedge of lime between thumb and forefinger. You licked the salt, bit the lime, took a sip of tequila, called, "Yeah!''—or at least Sam did—whenever the guitarist picked a particularly intricate riff. She remembered thinking, *My parents would be utterly horrified to see me here.* Remembered thinking, *And I've never been so happy in all my life,* just as Sam caught her wrist, lifted it to lick the salt from her skin, his eyes laughing into hers as his teeth closed on her lime. But he'd finished the ritual that time with a leisurely, toe-curling kiss, rather than a swig of tequila. The blues player had stopped midsong to call, "Yeah!" and everyone in the bar had laughed and applauded...

"*Damn*..." Sam muttered.

Jessica looked up from her licking and froze, her wrist halfway to her mouth. His eyes gleamed too bright, light from the window lending them the sheen of liquid silver. His dark lashes batted furiously, then he swiped his own wrist across his eyes. "Hell. Hell and twelve kinds of damnation. *Why* did she have to—" He slammed back his chair and stood, grabbed the plate, stalked toward the sink, stepping over Jessica as he went.

"Why did I have to what, Sam?" Or was she even the "she" he was thinking of?

He thumped the mug into the sink, held the plate wavering over it, then turned to scowl at her. "And what do you want, good-for-nothing?"

"I just wanted to know—"

He swore, one single, vicious word, then headed for her, the plate held on high. "Okay, okay, but don't think this is the thin end of the wedge, cat. We're not setting precedents here by any means. Got that? This is strictly a one-time aberration, that's all."

"What are you babbling about?" She dodged to one side as he sank to his heels, then dumped the last of his eggs on top of her chili.

"There. Chili con huevos, fur-ball. They'd pay good money for that out in L.A. in those uptown, sissy bistros. Nouvelle Hispanic Lite. All it needs is a touch of cilantro and tarragon, and you won't be eating, you'll be having a culinary experience."

"Sam, why were you—"

But he stood, dumped the plate in the sink and strode out the door.

Jessica sat, listening to the sound of running water from the bathroom, a door slamming down the hall on what must be his bedroom. Then he stormed past the kitchen, a battered leather valise slung by its strap from one shoulder, one hand jangling his keys in his jacket pocket.

Don't I get a kiss goodbye? she asked wistfully. That was something she'd missed for years. He'd had at least twelve kinds of farewells, from tango dip to eyebrow kiss, depending on his mood when he went out the door. The kisses on his return had been even better.

She heard him halt. He took two long steps backward to aim a finger at her from the hallway. "You plan to behave yourself, cat, or should I shut you in the bathroom?"

"I swear I'll behave!" *Oh, please, not the bathroom!*

"Cross your heart and hope to choke?"

"Promise!"

"I hold you to it." He vanished, and a second later she heard the lift rising. Its doors opened, then closed, then it sank again, groaning.

Jessica sighed. No kiss goodbye. Still, she glanced down at her bowl, and her spirits rose. Lukewarm eggs had never looked so good. And off Sam's plate, they tasted like heaven. The patrons of those sissy bistros in L.A. could never have dined half so well.

JESSICA SPENT THE DAY following the sun around the loft. The two ten-foot windows in the living room faced south. Seated on one of the deep, granite sills, warmed by the morning sun, she had a spectacular view of the upper bay to the southeast. Once she glanced southwest toward the elevated highway, with the top of RI Gen rearing beyond its embankment, then she was careful not to look that way again.

That way lay all her hopes, all her worries. But today was to be Cattoo's day of rest and recuperation, she'd resolved, free from all demands. Cattoo had more than earned it.

But if Cattoo deserved it, Jessica still felt vaguely guilty. Goof-off days weren't something she'd ever indulged in, saving her brief time with Sam, master of the all-day goof-off. She remembered her father coming into a room once, when she was perhaps six. She'd found some markers that Winston used to color-code his lecture notes, was creating what she thought was a marvelous drawing—a fairy-tale garden for a fairy princess, who, in her mind's eye, looked quite a lot like herself, only taller. "Haven't you better things to do with your time?" her father had teased, then had brought her a *Reader for Young Scientists* and suggested she read it to him.

Never did finish that drawing, she mused drowsily, her eyes half-closed against the sun. If it wasn't for Cattoo, she'd be finding something better to do with her time right now, maybe figuring out a way to make Sam understand her...

But not just yet. She collapsed, beaten down by the sun's butter gold rays, then rolled over to let it warm her belly. Arching her back, stretching her arms and legs out to their limit, she groaned luxuriously, then held that stretch. *So this is what it's like to be a well-fed cat. No guilt, not one care in the world.*

Except that her coat...wouldn't quite...*do.* Jessica half sat up. Propping herself on one elbow, she took a swipe at her belly fur, then stopped, staring down at her own pink tongue. *Gack, look at me! Licking fur.*

Cattoo saw nothing wrong with that—saw quite a bit wrong with *not* doing that.

It's only what any self-respecting cat would do, Jessica ruefully agreed. It seemed hardly fair to Cattoo to stop. She sighed and touched her tongue to fur. *If I'm going to be a cat for a while, I suppose I might as well be a well-groomed cat.* That was how she'd been brought up, after all, to always be the best she could be, whatever the enterprise.

Cattoo had an even better reason. *Let's do it because it feels so good.*

Which it did. The stroke of rough tongue across her pelt was almost hypnotic. Jessica found herself drifting, sinking gradually down into sun tipped, shining black fur, imagining finally that the tongue that stroked her was not her own, but Sam's, hot and warm on her body. She sighed, smiled and slept, while Cattoo groomed on.

She awoke later to find the sun had moved. Leaping down off the sill, Jessica padded down the hall to the kitchen. *No sun here.* The window on this side faced north, overlooking the alley. Still, she hopped to the table, then the sill to inspect the view.

Beyond the glass, the black iron bars of the fire escape split the opposite wing of the mill into narrow rectangles. Tucked in at the side railing, a hibachi sat on the grid-work floor of the platform, along with a couple of flowerpots, containing the remains of two frost-seared geraniums. *Nothing much here.* Jessica peered down through the escape's gridded floor. An iron ladder led to the level below. Beyond that, she saw a corner of the courtyard and shivered. *So good to be in here and not out there!*

Thoughts of the past few days sent her in search of the sun again. Jessica padded on past the bathroom, down the hall. On her left were two closed doors. Bedrooms, she supposed, each facing south toward the bay. From the placement of the second door, it must open into a large corner room. Master bedroom, she guessed. That would be Sam's room.

The corner room at the end of the hall to her right was a small bedroom. From its north window, she could look down on the mouth of the alley. Its west window caught the afternoon light and gave her a straight shot at RI Gen. She shivered again. *Are you there right now, Sam? With my parents?*

With me? She shuddered. *How am I doing?*

And where's Raye Talbot? The thought intruded in spite of her last-second attempt to shut it out. Raye would be there, at RI Gen, of course, prowling the corridors, a smiling, two-legged predator. What had she called herself? A wolf, that was it. Jessica's fur bristled along her spine, then she shook herself. Not that she cared all that much about Raye really. She supposed she should feel anger—rage, even—and perhaps she would, once she let herself think about it. Right now she felt only a wondering incredulity—that a person's life and happiness could mean so little to another... She shuddered again. *Just stay away from me, Raye, that's all I ask!*

Not that Raye could possibly see her as any kind of a threat now. A woman in a coma? *She must figure I'm as good as dead.*

Well, I'm not! Jessica turned around and jumped down from the sill. *I may be temporarily . . . displaced, but I am not out.* Not by a long shot, as Sam would say.

SHE WAS SLEEPING, curled up on Sam's sweater, which he'd left on the couch, when he returned. Her ears twitched as the elevator grumbled into life far below. When the doors slid open on the loft, she lifted her head and blinked lazily. She stretched out a forearm, flexed her toes, yawned till her jaw cracked. "Hiya, handsome."

"Don't talk to me if you value your life, cat." Sam dropped his valise on the coffee table, shrugged out of his leather jacket, then threw it as far as he could. He followed it down the room, kicked it, then swung on his heel to scowl at her. "They caught the four o'clock back to Chicago."

"So?" She was surprised they'd been able to stay that long.

"My mama would be pitching a tent in my room, if it were me up there." He raked a hand through his hair, leaving it standing in soft spikes, then shook himself like a dog stepping out of water. "*Brrr.* She had eighteen *years* of that bullshit. No wonder she . . ."

He sank down beside Jessica, his forearms dangling between his legs. He glanced at her sideways. "Bet your mama took better care of you than that, huh? Worthless as cats are, I s'pose that's one thing you can say for them. They tend to their young." He flopped backward, stretched his legs out, crossed his arms, slumped slowly down till his narrow hips were almost slipping off the cushion. "*Whoof.*"

"They love me." Jessica stood and arched her back. "Really."

"They call that love? I call that emotional neglect. Criminal, selfish, cold Yankee negligence. Love isn't a good-conduct prize you hand out for straight A's. For high performance." He shook his head. "I'd like to sue 'em!"

"For what? Neglecting me?" But they weren't. This was just their way. They must have moved heaven and earth to win one day free to visit her.

"Poor Jess," he muttered, eyes focused somewhere beyond the darkened windowpanes. "Spends all her life half killing herself trying to please a couple of pinch-faced icebergs who couldn't be pleased. Every time she jumped, they just raised the stick higher. And then when she needs *them* ..."

"It wasn't—isn't—like that! Really it isn't. Just because we weren't all over each other like your family doesn't mean..." She felt an uncertain laugh bubbling in her throat, but cats couldn't laugh. "This is how WASPs love, Sam. At arm's length. No dramatics. Stiff upper lips all the way and oh, so brave and understated." Sam's family might show love by touching and hugging, by indulging in all kinds of emotional and sentimental histrionics. But her family loved by respecting one another's privacy. By sharing thoughts, not feelings. By sharing interests and hard-won goals. "Okay, I admit it's sort of cool and cerebral, but it's love all the same."

She searched for corroborating proof, an instance of her parents' saying they loved her, but her memory drew a blank at the moment. *It's because they don't use the word much,* she realized. *They say, "I'm proud of you," when Sam's family would say, "I love you."* But it was the same thing. Really.

Of course, she had to admit they had less occasion to say, "I'm proud of you," to her than they did to Winston, since he was far and away the high achiever—family and teachers had been comparing her to Winston ever since she could remember. And she'd been coming up short ever since she could remember. But still... "They love me."

"Now she can't perform for them, so one quickie visit, check the ol' vital signs, chat with her doc, and they're out of here." Sam hissed a breath out between his teeth, a silent, savage whistle.

"Well, what do you want them to do?" Jessica jumped to the coffee table and paced slowly around its rim. "Other people need them, too—my father's patients, my mother's clients. They can't just dump everything and camp by my bed. Besides, that would be about as interesting as...as watching grass grow. A person in a coma..." She shivered, fluffing her coat out, as she realized she was talking about herself, and remembered her mother speaking...

They'd been driving somewhere—oh, to summer camp. So Jessica would have been younger than ten, because after that, she attended computer camp, summers. Her mother had been saying how relieved she was once Jessica started talking. "I was rather...bored with you before that, I have to admit," she'd confessed, glancing aside from the road with her cool, close-lipped smile. "You were so much more interesting, darling, once you started to make sense."

And now I'm not making sense again, Jessica realized with a jolt. *How can you possibly be proud of a daughter in a coma? I'm a...a nothing.* Something worse than a nothing—a costly, embarrassing nuisance.

That thought was too horrid to dwell on. It sent her rebounding fiercely in the opposite direction. "Besides, you can accuse them of being too demanding, too hard to please. But didn't I have the same problem with you?" She swung to glare at him.

"You turned into a...a damned rocket scientist on me, once you published that dissertation. How was I supposed to measure up to that? Be your equal? Make you proud of me? Why do you *think* I changed my mind and went to med school, after all—after I'd told you I wouldn't? It wasn't to please my father, believe me. I did it in the end for you, so I'd be worthy of you. So you'd keep loving me."

"Don't look at me like that, cat," Sam growled. "Makes my brains itch." He stood abruptly and headed for the kitchen.

"So scratch them, why don't you? You could ask yourself why!" Jessica jumped down and trotted after him.

In the kitchen Sam reached for the teakettle, then moved to the sink. Filling it, he glanced aside. His brows shot together when she leapt to a chair, but he made no comment. Jessica watched him for a moment. "So I went to med school," she said finally. *But I blew that, too, in the end. I couldn't be a surgeon like my father and Winston. Didn't have the...the temperament. The guts. I'd have hesitated, and when you hesitate in the OR, it's your patient who's lost, not you.* "So I'm just an internist." She would have shrugged and laughed if she could have—a laugh that was meant to be carefree, but would not have been, quite. *So maybe Dad was right not to love me as much as Winston. And you were right, Sam, to fall out of love with me. You caught on to me, fast, didn't you, once you hit the big time?*

She was sinking rapidly into self-pity, she realized, with a shudder of distaste. An unpardonable self-indulgence. Simply not done. At least not in public. Leaping down from the chair, she stalked from the room.

CHAPTER TEN

SAM FOUND HER curled up moodily on his jacket. Something about the smell was comforting, she had to admit.

Her ears swiveled backward as he moved to the table, fussed with his valise.

He returned to set something down beside her. "Brought you a present."

She glanced down at a can of cat food. Lovely Liver. "Whoop-de-do, Sam. I'm ecstatic. Overwhelmed." Sweeping her tail to one side, she rocked back on her hips and shot her right back leg skyward. She licked her inner thigh, then paused, leg raised, gazing haughtily at the opposite wall.

"Don't fall all over yourself with gratitude," he growled, retrieving his gift. "Or is it just that you don't read?"

"Actually I was planning on sending out for a pizza."

Behind her Sam headed for the kitchen. "Come on, cat. C'mere, boy."

And that's another thing! she thought. She gave herself a vicious lick, then sat up properly. "I'm not a boy, and I'm darned sure not a dog! Don't you know how to call a cat?"

"Kitty, kitty, kitty?" he tried in a ridiculous, husky falsetto.

Better, she admitted grudgingly. But nothing would have induced her to follow that scent of third rate liver to its source. "What are *you* having for dinner?"

"Have it your way," Sam drawled, coming back down the hall with a mug in one hand. He threw himself down on the couch. "Food's there when you want it."

"When hell freezes over, I'll try it. Thank you."

He kicked off his shoes, swung his legs up on the cushions.

There'd been a time when she'd have walked over, rubbed his chest. And he'd have pulled her down to half lie on top of him, their legs intertwined, her face nestled in the crook of his shoulder. "Oh, Sam, why did we have to lose it?"

She found herself leaping to the couch to stand alongside his chest, staring down at him. "Why?" It wasn't a question—she knew why—it was simply a heartfelt protest. Why did the world have to snatch away the one thing in all life you wanted?

"Don't even think about it," he warned, looking back at her. "I want to cuddle, it won't be with a cat."

"A lot you know." She sighed and sat, but one paw lifted tentatively.

"Forget it," he said, noting the movement. "Off the furniture."

"Make me." Her tail waved a slow S-curve of defiance.

When he reached for her, she flinched but held her ground. His hand slid behind her arms, his thumb and fingers spanning her rib cage. He lifted, and her front paws left the cushion. "I'm warning you, cat..."

He was too big to fight, and with his hand warm upon her, suddenly she didn't want to. Instead, she went limp, savoring the sensation of his body fitted to hers, his hardness to her softness, his strength to her boneless compliance. *Yes.* Nothing had changed.

"Studied with Ghandi, huh? The ol' passive resistance move? Blasted stubborn cat..."

Everything had changed. Black furry forearms dangled before her. At the edges of her vision, she could make out the dark, blurred sprays of her whiskers. Closing her eyes, she let out a squeak of despair. *And it wouldn't matter even if I was a woman. I must remember that. It didn't work last time. It wouldn't work this time. Nothing has changed.*

"Mew? Not *yowrr,* but mew? So now we're tryin' pitiful, huh?" Still holding her elevated, Sam rolled halfway onto his side and touched her back. "Got to hand it to you. You're a soft one, cat."

Somehow her fur amplified his touch. Tingles spread out from each point of contact, quivered deliciously down the curve of her ribs.

His finger drifted the other way, up her spine, ruffling her hair. "If I had two dozen of you, you'd make quite the fur coat."

"Thanks." Despite the insult, this was heaven.

"Maybe a pair of earmuffs?"

A soft rumbling filled her throat. Her body tightened rhythmically, nerves and muscles pulsing with the tiny, exquisite vibrato. *Yessss.* Her eyelids drooped as his hand cupped to fit her narrow back, and he palmed slowly upward. *Yessss, you can do that forever.*

"You feelin' okay?" His voice was husky, close to her ear.

About a hundred times better than okay.

"You haven't done that weird head thing once tonight."

Her purr broke in half and, slitting her eyes, she considered. *Right, I haven't.* And didn't dare to. Tomorrow she must try to find a pencil, see if somehow she could hold it in her mouth? But right now, she couldn't think, didn't want to. Her purr deepened as his hand stroked again. *Yessss.*

His fingers stroked down her side to cup her belly. Warmth exploded within her, shot out to the pads of each paw. Her toes flexed, then relaxed, flexed... "You're pretty chub for a stray."

"Am *not!*" Jessica's eyes snapped open. "I'm just right for a healthy female. Maybe even down a pound after the last few days."

"Wonder if you wandered off from somewhere?" He smoothed a finger between her ears, down her spine. "Is somebody missing you?"

"Nobody." The truth of that snagged the purr in her throat.

"Maybe we should run an ad. Lost cat?"

Suddenly she had no taste for his petting. She planted her back feet and, rearing out of his hold, turned away. She stalked down the length of the couch to stand by his feet, her tail cutting slow, angry swathes. "So go ahead if you're that keen to be rid of me. I'll go it alone." But she couldn't and she knew it.

"You know..." Sam pulled himself up on his elbows to slouch against the couch's arm. "Now that I think of it, aren't you missing something there?"

She tilted her ears back, but didn't turn. "What?"

"I mean, what I know about cat anatomy you could fit in a thimble and still have room for your finger, but shouldn't some of your essentials be showin'?"

"My—" she swung to stare at him over her shoulder "—my *essentials?* Essential to *what?* I mean, *for* what? Half the human race does very nicely without them, in case you haven't noticed!" She spun and stalked toward him, ears angled back. "If that isn't the most flagrant example of guy-think I ever heard... You win the prize, Texan!"

He sat up and reached for her. "C'mere."

"*No.* And the magic word is—" But he'd already scooped her up. The world spun wildly, then she was lying in the crook of his arm, scowling up at the cleft in his chin. "I may never forgive you for this, you know!"

He didn't. He hoisted her rear end a bit higher and had a good look. "Well, I'll be damned."

"No *doubt.*" She wriggled, but he held her easily.

"You're a girl. A lady cat." He stroked his knuckles across her belly fur, ruffling it backward. "Well, that explains a lot."

"Oh?" She fixed him with her haughtiest owl-eyed glare.

"I thought you were kind of swish for a guy, but then I decided maybe that was just the tail."

Her tail hauled back, then whacked him a good one on the arm.

"Exactly so." Laughter shimmered in his voice. He brushed his fingers through her belly fur again.

"Watch it!" She twisted in his hold. This time he took the hint and set her on her feet. She turned to take two hurried swipes at her flank. She felt half outraged, half aroused, ruffled all over. She leapt to the coffee table and turned to glare back at him.

"Mussed your hair, did I? Yep. You're a female, all right." He swung his legs to the floor, then reached for his mug. "No wonder we haven't exactly been having a meeting of minds here."

Maybe his misconception *had* been getting in the way. Settling into a crouch, Jessica gazed up at him. *Yes, I'm a female. Now take it one step further, Sam. I'm not only a female, I'm a female you know...*

Eyes locked on hers, he sipped his tea. "Are all cats this weird? Or is it just you?"

"It's me. Because you *know* me. You know me better than anybody else in the world knows me." She beamed her thoughts between his eyes, putting heart and soul into them. "You know me, Sam."

He sipped, frowned. "You know, you don't answer very well to 'Hey, you.' We might as well call you something."

"Yes, *yes,* you're getting it! You *know* my name." She stood, hopped across to the couch, landing beside his leg. "I'm Jessica—*Jess!*" She laid one paw on his thigh.

He narrowed his eyes, but didn't protest.

She placed her other paw beside the first, then stood, elbows braced, staring earnestly up into his face. "It's *me,* Sam. Jessica."

"You're a forward one, that's for sure."

"Only with you. And I'll be as forward as I have to be to get this through your stubborn skull. C'mon, Sam, you can wrap your mind around this one! I'm *Jess.*" She stepped delicately up onto his leg, took a wobbling step, another, then reached to press one paw against his chest. "*You. Jess.*" She could feel his heart beating against her pads. She flattened her other paw against his shirt, lifting her face to his.

He blinked. His eyes were golden brown, that dot of green still there on the outer edge of his left pupil. The smell of his skin deliciously the same. "I'm Jess, Sam. *Jess.*" Slowly she brought her nose to his—*nose touch.*

He laughed softly, shook his head, leaned back out of reach. "You little hussy! Get off me."

"I'm not a hussy, I'm your ex-wife. Jessica Alexandra Myles. *Jess.*"

"Jezebel," he mused. "Now there's a name for a hussy."

"No, not Jezebel. Jessica!" Her tail stuck straight up and quivered with suppressed emotion.

"Jezebel, the cat with the green eyes," he drawled dreamily. "Only other girl I knew with—" He stopped, his face going very still.

"Yes! *Yes!* The only other girl—woman—you knew with eyes like this was me! Jessica!" She strained upward on tiptoe, trying to touch noses again with him, as if her thought could be transmitted nose to nose, then straight to his brain.

His brows jerked together. "Okay, you hussy, enough already. Down, Jezebel."

"Jessica!" she yelled, hooking her claws into his chest.

"Hey!" He jumped—spilling tea all over her, himself and the couch. "Ouch, dammit, now look what you've..." He elbowed her out of his lap, then smacked the mug down on the table. "Son of a—"

"If you'd just *listen* to—"

"Down!"

She leapt instinctively over the couch's arm, then skittered around the coffee table to glare at him from beyond its refuge, her tail enormous. "Don't yell," she said finally in a tiny, aggrieved voice. "You know I hate that."

He glared, held it, then burst out laughing. "Jez my girl, you're something else." He stood, brushed his clothes off and headed for the kitchen. "Darned cat!"

JESSICA WATCHED HIM cook his supper in frustrated silence. Doubly frustrated, since the smell of the hamburger he was frying was driving her crazy.

She considered hopping up on the counter to take a closer look at the proceedings, but decided that would be pushing it tonight. Instead, she settled for one of the chairs at the table.

"No," Sam said from where he stood chopping onions at the counter.

Want to bet? She assumed the loaf-of-bread position and returned his glare.

"Don't give me that evil eye. I said no cats on the furniture, Jez'bel."

Jessica. She held her ground.

Sam chopped harder. "That's what I love about cats. They mind so well."

"I'm not a cat."

He glanced at her again, his frown more puzzled than disapproving. "You look like a broody hen sittin' there."

"I give up! You'd believe I'm a chicken, but not a woman." *What am I going to do, Sam? Be a cat for the rest of my life?* And how long would that be? Eighteen years, if she was lucky?

On the other hand, if all she got to eat for the next eighteen years was liver, eighteen years might seem like a very long time. "What are you making?"

He'd always had a flair for cooking. They'd had many a squabble over his refusal to follow a recipe. She herself followed recipes to the letter with invariably passable results. But Sam cooked by instinct, taste and wild surmise. His meals were either superb, or they qualified for national-disaster funds.

He opened an overhead cabinet to study its contents. "Gotta go shopping tomorrow. Doc Neuman didn't leave much behind." He pulled out a can of pineapple bits and a jar of black olives. "Tomorrow... they're moving Jess to a private room." He reached for a can opener. "That's one thing her ol' man did for her, anyway. And tomorrow they'll let me start visiting for more than ten minutes every hour." He sighed heavily, glanced over at her. "Why don't you stop staring and eat something?"

"Give me something edible. And if you throw that in the pot, I'm not sure that meal's going to qualify," she added when he took a can of pork and beans from the cupboard. "Don't you have any rice?"

He studied the can, shrugged, put it back—then pulled out a pack of prefolded taco shells.

"Yuck! Maybe I'm better off with Lovely Liver."

But by the time Sam had finished, a delectable fragrance of curry, cinnamon and pepper sauce filled the air. He shoveled the meat mixture into a couple of heated taco shells, then sat across from her.

Jessica sat up and rested her chin on the table. "Smells good."

"Forget it." He crunched down on a taco.

"Fine. No problem. I'll just starve." She hopped off the chair, turned her back on him and sat.

"You don't like spicy food, remember? I had to throw out your chili."

"And you can throw this out while you're at it." Jessica stalked over to her saucer of ground liver.

"Now you're wising up. Good cat."

Unacceptable, Cattoo agreed after one sniff. A statement was clearly in order here.

Jessica found herself stepping halfway over the dish. She stopped and, at Cattoo's urging, made slow, deliberate, burying motions with her right paw, raking backward, as if to scrape sand over the saucer.

"Why you little—" Sam put down his taco. "It smells that bad?"

"Worse." With the liver symbolically buried, Jessica returned to her chair. "Now how about something to eat?"

"Nope. Pets don't eat table scrap, where I come from. Makes 'em uppity."

"I'm not your pet! I'm your ex-*wife,* sitting here starving to death. Think how many meals I cooked for you."

Sam gagged, swallowed with an effort, thumped himself on the chest, then coughed again.

Jessica reared up to rest one paw on the table. "Sam, don't you dare choke! I couldn't Heimlich you to save my life!"

Grabbing his glass of water, he gulped half its contents, then smacked it down with a splash. "All right, that's enough. How'm I s'posed to eat with you sitting there, drooling all over the tablecloth?'' He rose, went to the stove, slapped half a spoonful of curry onto a plate. He thumped it down beside her other bowls. "Here. This'll ream the purr right out of your fuzzy throat, but don't take my word. See for yourself."

She would've preferred her meal served on the table, but Cattoo was teaching her patience. One battle per night was the way to win a war.

Moving over to the plate, she sniffed—then sneezed and retreated.

"Liver looking better and better?" Sam inquired sweetly.

"Ha." This time she approached cautiously, breathing through her mouth. "Are you still Mr. Heavy Hand with the peppers?"

She took a tiny bite—and her tail stood straight out, then quivered agitatedly. He was—more so than ever, or maybe it was just the feline taste buds. Eyes watering, she sneezed again.

On his way to the stove, Sam laughed. "How 'bout some more, Jez'bel?" He filled another taco shell.

"I believe this will do me." And she'd have to finish every bite, or this was the last taste of human food he'd give her. Crouching, she ate it bit by scorching bit, with frequent interludes to cool her tongue at the water bowl.

She was still working at it while Sam loaded the dishwasher. He made himself a cup of decaf coffee—she flattened her ears when he used the grinder. Then he wandered off with his mug.

Who says I have to finish this now? Jessica realized, backing away from the plate. Cattoo generally snacked by the mouthful, running in and out of the kitchen at whim.

She found Sam in the living room. His valise was open on the coffee table. Next to it he'd plugged in—

"A computer!" Jessica leapt to the table. It was one of the laptop type, the latest Mac model, probably more high-powered than all the mini-computers they used at Diagnostics combined.

"Watch it!" Sam splayed a hand protectively over the keyboard. "Keep off, cat."

"Let me see." She nosed past his fingers. "That's *it*, Sam! I can type you a message! What word-processing software do you—"

His hands hooked under her middle. Jessica found herself taking a giant frog leap backward, then she was deposited on the sofa. Sam's finger descended to touch her nose. "Now this we don't joke about." He pressed her nose—once, twice, three times for emphasis. "I love my Powerbook like my life. There's stuff inside this baby that'll make the whole human race sit up and take notice. Or they would if they had half the sense God gave a goose. And I won't have you messin' with it."

"What are you working on?" Sam's field was pure genetic research. She remembered him explaining to her once that the role he hoped to play in microbiology—the one he'd played in that first ground-breaking paper—was that of the wagon-train scout. Or better yet, the mountain man, who came even before the scout. Sam went wandering through the trackless wilderness of the tiniest bits of the human genome, tracing this river to its source, venturing down that canyon, climbing this mountain, which might or might not lead to a pass over the range.

And like the mountain man, he did it more for the reckless joy and the pure wonder of it than for any hope of gain.

It was the diligent men in the wagon trains following in Sam's footsteps who'd apply his explorations to something useful. Sam could find the field, but they'd stop and plow it. Sam would chart the river, the ones who came after would dam or divert it.

Sam would never find the cure for cancer, but he and explorers like him were the ones who would make a cure possible. That he'd taken humanity a little way down that vital path was why he'd been awarded his Nobel last year.

Sam prodded her nose again. "Do we understand each other, green eyes? Even for a cat, it's a very simple concept. You touch this computer and I'll skin you."

"But—" All she needed was some quality time with that keyboard and he'd understand everything. There was no way he'd be able to deny the evidence of her written word. "But—"

"No ifs, ands, buts or exceptions. I'll drop you out the window and see if cats bounce. Somebody told me once that they do."

Patience. She would have to practice patience. With a sigh, Jessica sat back and stared wistfully at the means of her deliverance. So close and yet so far.

Meanwhile, Cattoo pointed out, they'd just eaten. It was time for a thorough face wash and whisker combing. Jessica sighed again, absently licked her wrist, brushed it through her whiskers.

Washing, she kept one eye on Sam's computer screen. He was checking his e-mail.

No focii yet, said the first message. Pressing on regardless. Nigel.

"Good man," Sam murmured. He hit a button, erasing that message, then another to summon the next.

Sam, what about your talk at Cold Springs next week? If you're not going, Petterson needs time to arrange a replacement. George says to tell you he got the grant. Antonia and Joaquim are feuding again, this time over the centrifuge. We missed you Friday. Liza. P.S. Your mom called, and your sister Gina. Call them. P.P.S. How is she?

"Liza's your secretary? At the lab?"

Ignoring her, Sam hunched forward and started typing. Liza, give Petterson my regrets. I'm here for the duration. Hooray for George. I owe him a beer or three. Tell Antonia to cut the petty He paused and muttered, "Not if I want peace on Earth, goodwill to—" He hit the delete key and erased that line. Tell Antonia I depend on her superb tact and innate intelligence to triumph over Latin machismo without undue bloodshed. Emphasis on undue. Tell her also that no way will I take Joaquim off this project—for better or worse, he's her bouncing baby boy. I missed you guys Friday, too. Tell all I want a one-paragraph summary,

per project, Friday mornings to keep me up to date. Sam.
P.S. What does your cat eat?

"How am I?" Jessica said, moving to sit alongside his leg. "You forgot to tell her that."

P.P.S. Sam typed obediently. She's His hands froze over the keys. "Damn, damn, damn, *damn*," he swore under his breath. He glanced down and met her gaze. "And damn your owl eyes, too—stop eyeballin' me like that. Didn't your mama teach you manners?" His finger jabbed the delete button. The cursor gobbled up the letters from right to left till the last addendum was gone.

"So I'm not good?"

But Sam wasn't saying. P.P.S. he typed. I mean to catch up on my reading. You know that tallest stack of mags in my office—the technical pile left of the window? Send me the bottom three feet or so, and bill me for hazard pay. Address is as follows:

"You really mean to stay." Jessica rubbed her cheek against his thigh. "Sam, I don't know how to—"

"No mushy stuff," he growled, fending her off.

She clicked her teeth in frustration and backed away. *Okay, be a grouch.* But he was a loyal grouch, she mused, as he finished with e-mail and launched himself out on the Internet. Through half-closed eyes, she watched his flying fingers. *What are you after now, Sam?* She blinked as a familar icon appeared on the screen. He was accessing a medical data base. One she'd tapped into herself often enough.

"Aha!" he muttered, and typed in the topic to be called up. COMA—idiosyncratic.

Jessica sat up. That's what they're saying?" Idiosyncratic was med-speak for "darned if we know." A coma of no known cause. "So it's not a matter of oxygen deprivation?" Her brain hadn't shut down for lack of air? "Then...I just panicked and...jumped? That's all this is? The spirit is missing, so the body just lies there?"

A long list of articles and studies published in medical journals appeared on the screen. Sam started down the list, selecting and saving the ones that caught his interest.

"Maybe I should've stayed in my body? Waited for the firemen? But how was I to know that they'd—"

"What are you jabbering 'bout, cat?" Sam didn't take his eyes off the screen. "We havin' a major indigestion attack here?"

"You could say that."

"Told you curry wasn't for cats." He leaned to grope in his valise, then pulled out the tiniest laser printer Jessica had ever seen. "Want some baking soda?"

"No, thanks." She watched as he hooked up the printer, then inserted a stack of paper in one end. "But is this good or is this bad, Sam? If I jumped once, could I simply choose to jump again? As simple as that? It's sure worth a try, isn't it?"

With a grunt of satisfaction, Sam hit the print command. The printer hummed and commenced printing.

Jessica leapt to the back of the couch and paced restlessly along it. "So I guess the next question is, do you think there's a range limitation? I was within ten feet of Cattoo—she in midair, me at the window—last time I . . . jumped. Do I need to be that close again?"

Sam had slouched back, his arms crossed. He sat frowning, apparently mesmerized, while the printer brought forth his articles. Jessica stepped carefully past his head. "It's sure worth a try, isn't it?" She turned to stick her nose in his ear. "You have to take me to see me, Sam."

"*Yah!*" He jumped violently, then brushed her off. "Worthless, cold-nosed . . ."

Jessica teetered and fell. "Watch it!" She landed clumsily. "Oof!"

Sam peered over the back of the sofa. "Cats are supposed to bounce."

"Depends on how far they fall." Jessica stood and shook herself. "I understand they actually do better with higher falls, up to a point. If they have time to assume a position like a flying squirrel . . ." But naturally he wasn't listening. She sauntered around the end of the sofa. "You have to take me to the hospital, Sam." She leaned against his shin and walked, stropping her side along him. "Tomorrow."

He kicked at her feebly, but didn't connect.

"Tomorrow." She leapt to the table.

He'd hunched forward to read the first article out of the printer. Jessica stood on top of it and looked him in the eye. *"Listen to—"*

With a growl, he caught her behind the arms and hoisted her so that she dangled nose to nose with him. "Listen to me, pest, and listen good. We...are...not...married."

"I know that!" *Believe me, I know that.*

"We are not engaged." He set her down on the arm of the sofa, then splayed a hand on her neck to keep her there when she would've hopped down. "We're not even going steady."

"So?" She didn't like the look in his eye.

"So, for somebody who's here on sufferance, you sure are pushing it, short stuff. One-night stands better not stand on my reading. That clear?"

"Quite," she said in a tiny voice.

"And while we're at it, let me make something else abundantly clear. This is *strictly temporary,* till I'm sure you're okay. There's no place in my life for a pet. And if there was, I'd sooner have a hound dog. Or a hamster. That clear?"

"Oh, quite!" she repeated bitterly. Twisting away from his fingers, she leapt to the floor. "Clear as clear can be, Sam, but just explain one thing to me."

She stalked across the room and leapt to the windowsill, stared at his blurred reflection. "What happened to the guy who wanted at least four children? The guy who couldn't imagine waiting till his wife had finished med school to have them?" She moved to rest her nose against the cold, cold glass. "You're thirty-seven, now, Sam, and what have you got to show for it? Not even a hamster? What are you waiting for? I had an excuse. But what's yours?" She turned.

He was sitting very still, his eyes wide, unfocused, not blinking. Suddenly his mouth twisted. He snatched up the article he'd been reading, stared at it unseeing, dropped it again.

Standing, he slapped down the lid of his Powerbook. "Screw it!" he muttered. "Screw it all to kingdom come and back again." He turned and left the room.

CHAPTER ELEVEN

By THE TIME Jessica plucked up her courage to follow him, Sam had shut himself in the bathroom. She crouched in the hall, listening to the shower run.

She had only to close her eyes to see him, his chest silvered by running water, his muscles slick and hard as rocks below a waterfall. His curly chest hair straightening in the torrent, to hang in a dark, waving fringe. All of him warm, wet and vital, inviting her touch.

Every shower they'd ever taken together surged back, drowning her in a tide of memories. She could close her eyes and feel—the chilly tiles pressed against her back, the heat of his mouth on her breasts, his hands cupping her bottom... *Stop,* she warned herself. *Just stop before you break your stupid heart!*

She couldn't stop. Trapped by the memories, she crouched there till the door opened.

"Hup!" Sam stepped sideways, barely missing her. "Blasted underfoot feline." He was naked but for the towel wrapped round his waist.

"Wow." Jessica sat up to stare after him. Memory wasn't half as good as reality.

"Hussy," he growled, heading for the living room. Lights switched off there, then he stopped by the kitchen to turn those lights off, as well. Reflected from somewhere outside, the faintest moon-glow defined the hall. Returning, he shuffled his feet, his hand brushing the wall. "Where are you?"

I haven't budged. But he couldn't see her, she realized as he moved past her. Which meant ...

As he groped for his bedroom door, then opened it, she tiptoed at his heels. Too close—her nose bumped his calf when he stopped to flip on a light switch. "Hey!" He grabbed, but she slithered past.

"I just want to see, Sam." She snatched an impression of an enormous four-poster bed, a large space, the usual gigantic windows. "Very nice."

"*No* cats in the bedroom." His towel slipped. He tossed it aside and came after her. "Here, you darned cat. *Jez!*"

"Jessica." She crouched, staring up at him, eyes rounding. "Oh, my."

He laughed. "Never seen a naked man before?"

"Not in quite a while," she murmured, making up for lost time.

He scooped her up, cradled her in one arm. "Must look pretty weird from a cat's point of view. D'you think I've slipped out of my coat?"

"I think you're beautiful." *I can't believe you were once mine.* And no wonder she hadn't been able to keep him. Any woman who saw him would want to make him hers.

Her fur stuck to his damp skin. She leaned against him, eyes closed in ecstasy, senses filling with his presence, her throat with a rasping song. Her tail curled to hug his waist. He rubbed her ears as he carried her. "Let me sleep with you?" she pleaded. "I'll just lie at the foot." It was suddenly all she wanted in the world to simply lie there, hearing him breathe, watching him sleep. Happiness could be no more than that.

He dropped her out in the hall, then tugged her tail gently. "Beat it, babe." The door closed with a decided thunk.

Jessica stood, her purr winding down to nothing, her ears swiveling to catch the click of the light switch, then the creak of his mattress. *Oh, Sam, was that so much to ask? Just to sleep with you?*

Apparently it was. With a sigh, she padded off into the dark, pupils expanding, whiskers held at the ready, heart heavy, yet strangely full.

JESSICA AWOKE the next morning to sounds from the bathroom. Jumping down from the couch, she paused to stretch—rear in the air, forelegs bowing to the first ray of sunlight. Then she followed her ears.

Clad only in a pair of jeans, face lathered, Sam leaned in toward the mirror, razor in hand.

"Morning." She yawned hugely, then leapt to the long, marble sink.

"Down." Touching razor to cheek, he scowled at her, then took a judicious swipe.

She swerved toward a steaming mug, which sat near his elbow. "Coffee!"

She'd stayed awake half the night, trying to open the lid to his Powerbook. Had ended up ready to gnaw her own tail with frustration—without thumbs, it simply could not be done. After that, she'd slept, but from the way she felt this morning, Cattoo must have prowled most of the night. She was bone-tired. "Could I have just a sip of that? Please?" She sniffed the rim.

"Get out of there! And *down,* dammit." Sam glanced at his foamy hands, at her, growled, then took another swipe. "I mean it, cat."

"So do I. I *need* coffee, Sam." His eyes were fixed on his chin as he negotiated that tricky cleft. She risked a mouthful, then winced when he yelled.

"I saw that!"

"*You* try to function without coffee." She backed off as he set the razor down to rescue his mug. "Selfish pig!"

"Animal! Lord knows what I'll catch." He rubbed the rim with a fingertip, scowled at her, studied his mug as if he might see germs dancing along its rim.

"Oh, for Pete's sake! I'm as clean as you are." She'd even managed to brush her teeth after a fashion last night, since he'd left the cap off the toothpaste—some things never changed. "Go fix yourself another if you're so afraid of cat cooties."

Apparently that was more trouble than Sam could manage before breakfast. He buried his scowl in his brew, then smacked the mug down on the far side of the sink.

"Fix me my own and I'd stay out of yours," she wheedled. "Just half a cup? With cream?"

Instead, he picked up his razor. "Get down. Go 'way."

"Grouch. You used to be a morning person. Didn't you sleep well?"

No answer beyond a grunt.

She looked up at the mirror, which ended six inches above her head. Seized by an awful fascination, she sat up slowly on her haunches. "What do I look like?" She knew, of course—she looked like Cattoo. But still... Bracing one paw against the wall, she rose to her full height and stared.

Round, gold-green eyes stared back at her. Enormous pointed ears, a fine set of whiskers, a furry, horrified face. "That's *me?*" she squeaked.

"That's you, fuzz-face." Meeting her eyes in the mirror, Sam laughed. "Want to borrow my razor?"

"Oh, it's easy for you to laugh!" She rested her nose against the glass and closed her eyes. "*You* try waking up to find you've grown a tail."

Falling back to four feet, she stood very still, trying to wipe that last image from her mind. Trying to recall the face she should've seen. "I'm *Jessica.*" Dr. Jessica Myles. *Jessica with light brown hair, a nose without fur...* She turned to look up at him. "You have to take me to the hospital!"

Still grinning, Sam tipped up his chin to scrape the last of the whiskers from his neck.

"You *have* to. I want out of here! *Now.*" She jabbed her nose against his bare ribs.

"Errrk!" He jumped. "Aw...*damn!*" Blood trickled from a razor cut alongside his Adam's apple. "GET AWAY FROM ME!"

Already airborne, she shot out the door.

SHE WAS JUST FINISHING her curry when Sam joined her in the kitchen, a scrap of white tissue stuck to his neck. "Take me with you."

Ignoring her, he popped bread into the toaster, made himself a bowl of cereal, sat and ate.

"What's your hurry?"

The toast popped up. "They're moving her to a private room today," he said, rising to fetch it. "With some peace and quiet, maybe she'll start…" He shrugged and sat again, took a bite, then drumming his fingers on the tabletop, stared out the window. "I'll have to buy a tape player. Stimulation, that's the ticket—talking books, lots of music. Wonder what she listens to nowadays?"

"Classical. Jazz. The same as always." It was he who'd broadened her musical tastes. Since him, she hadn't had much time to listen.

He shook his head. "How can I not know that? She used to like classical stuff, fifties jazz."

"Yes," Jessica said softly.

He nodded to himself. "I'll go with that."

"And I always loved your Brazilian—"

"Jobim!" he exclaimed, remembering. "That'll do for starters." He rose to dump his bowl in the sink. "And I told her old man I'd check her house."

"Why?" she called, tagging his heels to the living room.

"Make sure it's weather-tight. Valuables safe," he muttered to himself, stacking the coma articles. "Wonder if there's anything she'd like from there, something that might spark her—"

"She'd like her cat!" Jessica leapt to the back of the sofa. "That's *precisely* who she'd want, Sam! You and Cattoo. Take me with you!"

But Sam had no idea she'd lived with a cat. He collected his laptop and shoved it into his valise.

"No, at least leave that here! I'm still trying to open it."

He hooked the bag's strap over one shoulder, grabbed his jacket, headed for the elevator.

"Darn it, Sam!"

As the doors rolled open, he aimed a finger at her. "Behave yourself, jabbermouth." He stepped aboard and the doors closed between them.

"Damn, damn, damn and blast!" No hospital visit, no computer, not even a kiss goodbye. She threw herself down on the couch and lay there, eyes narrowed, tail thumping.

After a while she moved to a patch of sunlight.

SAM RETURNED around two, all his fierce expectations washed out of him. "You're back early," she observed, meeting him as he stepped off the elevator.

"The private room didn't open up today, after all." He trudged past her to deposit his valise and the paper bag he carried on the coffee table. "Maybe tomorrow..." He drifted to a window, braced his arms and leaned, staring out. "No wonder she's hidin'. All those bells and beeps from the monitors ... the smells...lousy fluorescent lights...needle in her arm...nurses and doctors coming and going at all hours...people lying there, half-dead and totally miserable. I'd close my eyes and hide, too."

Jessica leapt up to the sill beside him. "She's not hiding, Sam. She's here. With you." She touched her nose to his wrist.

Moving blindly, his hand found her. He stroked her tentatively, clumsily, his fingers unaccustomed to the shape of a cat.

Under the chin, she suggested. She'd always wondered if that felt as good as it looked. She lifted her nose to accommodate him, but he simply glanced down at her, then thumped her in the ribs. "How was your day?"

"*Oof!* I'm not a dog, Sam!" Ducking under his hand, she moved to press her forehead against his stomach. "My day? Not s'good. I found out that pencils weren't engineered with cats in mind." She had a few random strokes on a piece of paper for an hour's worth of trying, but nothing Sam would recognize as even an attempt at writing. His fingers scratched the spot just forward of her tail, and she hummed with pleasure. "Why are you home so early?"

He thumped her again and turned away. "I have a treat for you."

"Something edible? You forgot to feed me this morning." Leaping to the coffee table, she stuck her face into the bag, which lay on its side. It held a small tape player, still boxed, and several cassette tapes.

Cattoo awoke and was instantly delighted. *A bag!*

Jessica could see why she liked it. She pushed farther into the crackling cave. Light shining through the paper turned everything golden, mysterious. Promising. She reached the end, then twisted back, meeting her tail coming as she was going. Settling on top of the tape box, she faced the entrance.

Cattoo purred. *There might be mice, out there!*

There weren't any a minute ago, Jessica felt bound to point out.

But there might be now! Her pupils expanded to dark, expectant pools. Her pulse quickened.

Something scuttled across the top of the bag.

Cattoo purred louder. Jessica felt herself catching the excitement. The tip of her tail flicked, back...forth...

Something scrabbled near the entrance to her lair. A flicker of motion—she shot halfway out the bag, swiping frantically, then ducked back into cover.

Sam laughed aloud. "Crazy cat!" His fingers tiptoed across the other side of the bag.

Her tail twitched faster. *Come closer, oh, mouse!* Her muscles tensed, trembled...exploded as the sound came again. She smashed the side of the bag, paper crackling as she bit at its smooth surface. Ears flattened, she popped into view, nailed him in the hand—*Gotcha!*—then retreated to her lair.

"Maniac! I almost wish..."

Slowly, furtively, she stretched till she could just see his face beyond the rim of the bag. "Wish what?"

Sam wasn't saying. Chewing on his lip, he stared into the distance.

"Don't think! Play with me."

But she'd lost him. He stood and left the room.

She stayed in her cave awhile, tail flicking, heartbeat slowing to normal. When all the imaginary mice had crept back to their imaginary holes, she followed Sam to the kitchen.

He'd opened a new can of glop for her, something vaguely reminiscent of beef. "Cow hooves and other choice cuts?'' she guessed, sniffing, then turning up her nose. ''You call this a treat?''

Busy spreading peanut butter on bread, Sam didn't answer. He stacked three slices and headed back to the living room.

''Did you go by my house?'' she called, trotting after.

No answer. He sat on the couch, ate a bite, then leaned to unbuckle his valise. ''Wasn't much to worry about. Her landlord took care of the roof—hired a contractor to close it in with plywood. Upstairs is wrecked.'' He shivered abruptly, shoulders racking, then squaring again. ''*God, Jess.*''

''You're talking to me?'' Jessica leapt to the couch, set one paw on his knee. ''You are, you know.''

He ignored her. ''Downstairs's as good as ruined. Smoke and water damage. The plants all died. She always loved plants...''

''There was nothing I cared about, beyond the plants. It was just a place to live, Sam, nothing more.'' Then she remembered. ''My *jewelry*. Oh, Sam! Did you look in the bathroom?''

But his hand had continued its forgotten motion. Reaching into his valise, he dragged out the lacquered black box in which she'd kept her jewelry since she was a little girl.

''*Yes!* You did! You're a wonder!''

''Reckon I should send this to her mom for safekeeping?'' Idly he flipped the lid, gazed inside. ''Pearls, wouldn't you know.'' He pulled forth the long strand that had been a gift on her eighteenth birthday from her mother. ''Don't remember her wearing these. From a lover, you figure? Some Yankee stiff?''

''Hardly.'' Jessica sniffed at them as they slid through his fingers. ''Mother will be glad to see those. They were her grandmother's.''

He drew forth several delicate gold chains, a piece of beach glass, a bluebird's feather, a smaller box for the pearl-and-aquamarine studs she sometimes wore in her ears. Then his fingers closed on the one thing that mattered.

"It's still there!" she gasped in relief. "I thought maybe—" Somehow it seemed that if anything had been stolen, it would have been this.

"What the . . . ?" He shook the linked, crumpled bits of gold free from her other pieces. His brows angled in puzzlement. Then he saw, and his breath left him in a rush. "She still . . ." His fingers closed around the gold as if they cradled a butterfly. "She still . . ."

"Yes." Stepping up delicately into his lap, Jessica turned, then curled herself to fit his thighs. "Oh, yes."

For the first five days after they'd met, she'd hardly left his side. They'd made love, cooked, talked themselves hoarse, laughed themselves silly, slept, only to wake and make love again. *An enchantment,* she'd kept telling herself through those dreamlike days, *magic,* all the while knowing it couldn't last—wouldn't last. That he'd awake one morning any day now and realize she was the frog, not the fairy princess.

But, oh, in the meantime it was worth it! She'd snatch and savor every incredible moment while she could.

On the sixth day her courage had failed her. By now Sam *had* to be growing tired of her—a shy, awkward, sexually inexperienced kid? Too young for him, too bookish, too prim? He *must* be growing bored. But kindhearted as Sam was, would he ever say so?

Nothing seemed more horrible to her than to intrude where she wasn't wanted. She might be woefully unsophisticated, but all the same, she had her pride. And so, when Sam decided he had to teach an organic-chem section—he'd canceled his previous two sections by phone—she'd taken it as his signal that he wanted her to go. She could take a hint.

While he taught, she'd returned to her own apartment. Had explained, when he phoned after his class, that she was tired. That she thought perhaps she'd spend the night at her own place—alone.

Over the phone he'd sounded puzzled at her insistence. But he hadn't tried to dissuade her. She remembered lying in her own bed that night, arms clasped tight around herself, tears dripping, thinking, *It's over. It was lovely while it lasted, but it's over.*

Certain of that, she'd risen at dawn, run her five miles, then proceeded numbly with her day. She returned from the library midafternoon to find Sam lounging on her doorstep, his guitar on his lap, a picnic basket set to one side. "Ever gone on a champagne picnic?" he'd asked, his voice oddly husky.

And smiling, filling her eyes with the miraculous sight of him, she'd simply shaken her head.

What he brought for food that day she could never remember. It wasn't that kind of feast. But she could remember the texture, the colors, the precise pattern of the Indian bedspread he'd brought along. They'd spread it in a meadow near a tree, waist-high grass walling their private world, blue sky their roof and only witness.

They didn't uncork the champagne till nearly sundown, and by then, they were thirsty. Neither of them were drinkers; the wine had gone straight to their heads. She remembered lying in his arms, giggling until she whimpered for mercy, and then Sam suddenly saying, "Well, what now?"

"What d'you mean, what now?" She wound a whorl of his chest hair around her finger.

"I mean, I could make mad, passionate love to you—"

"For the fifth time?" she teased.

"Eighth or eleventh by my count, but who's counting? But if I do—make love to you, I mean—the skeeter's will probably carry us off."

"They're out," she agreed, brushing one from his hair

"Where're my manners? I should be holding the bloodsuckers at bay. Sir Walter Raleigh at your service, m'lady." He suited action to words by rolling on top of her, then they giggled some more. Finally he collapsed, burying his mouth in the crook of her neck. "I s'pose we could get a pizza," he mumbled against her skin.

"Mmm...not hungry." She was half-asleep, wholly content.

"Go see a flick?"

"Could..."

His voice was elaborately casual, almost bored. "Or we could drive cross the state line, roust out a justice of the peace..."

Her fingers stopped ruffling his hair. She could feel a heartbeat, whose she couldn't tell, its steady thump staggering, then coming faster. "And after we've rousted him?"

"Well, he could do his justice-of-the-peace shtick. Marry us."

"Oh, right!" She'd broken into fresh giggles. This was what she loved most about him—his craziness, the blithe fantasies he'd spin. "And then?"

"Well, *then* we get the pizza, unless you want General Tzo's?"

And so they'd done it, on a lark, as a whim, giddy with their own ridiculous daring. Swept away on a floodtide of champagne and giggles. At least, that was the spirit in which Sam had married her.

Beneath the nonstop laughter, *she'd* been terrified. Incredulous. Guilty as a thief snatching someone else's treasure.

And she had been greedy to snatch, foolish to agree— she'd known that from the start. She was taking outrageous advantage of Sam's crazy mood, but she'd wanted him so desperately, so wholeheartedly, she'd thrown away her misgivings and done it all the same. *"Yes,"* she vowed before the justice of the peace, ignoring the upraised eyebrows of his wife, witness to their hasty ceremony. "Yes. I, Jessica Alexandra Myles, do take thee, Samuel Antonio Kirby, to be my lawful wedded husband."

Driving back home, tired, sunburned, almost feverishly joyful, they'd passed some sort of street festival. Seeing the colored lights, Sam had insisted they check it out. So they'd eaten hot dogs for their wedding supper, smooched on a Ferris wheel, then Sam had found a pushcart vendor with jewelry for sale. He'd bought them each a gold three-piece puzzle ring. She'd never treasured anything else half so much in all her life.

"She still has it. She kept it . . ."

Yes.

"I used to tease her sometimes." Sam unfolded his fist to look. "I'd slip hers off her finger, take it apart . . ."

"And I used to wonder what you really meant when you did that." *Was it just a joke, or were you telling me something? Telling me you wanted to unmarry me? Undo our marriage?* The first time he'd done that, then sat there laughing at her while she tried to put her ring back together, she'd almost cried, though she'd been careful not to let him see. Pride . . . competence . . . She'd always had too much of one, never quite enough of the other.

"Smart as she is, she never had a head for spatial relationships. She couldn't put it back together no matter how many times I showed her how." He tossed the linked gold, jingling it, then held his palm open so Jessica could sniff the rings. "Guess she pulled it apart one last time."

"The night I left you . . ." Jessica nudged the wires, remembering again the pain in her finger as she ripped it off, a pain to match the one in her heart.

"Reckon she'd mind if we put it back together?"

"You can't, Sam. I—"

"S'pose she doesn't have to know." Resting his wrists on her back, he picked through the linked rings. "I could do this blindfolded."

"Not anymore, Sam."

His fingers paused, then frowning, he lifted the wires closer to his face. "Oh . . ."

The delicate, eighteen-karat bands were almost malleable as butter. Sitting in her car that night, staring back toward the lighted window, gathering her courage to go, she'd closed her fist over the disassembled pieces and squeezed. Those bits of gold would never make a ring again, not even for Sam's clever fingers.

"I see . . ."

"It was no more than you'd done, Sam. You pulled our marriage apart, messing around with that blonde. I pulled my ring apart. So don't look like that."

He leaned forward, dropped the gold into her jewelry box, then dropped the lid. "Damn you, Jessica." He stood, tumbling her out of his lap. "I know I can't blame you, but damn you all the same."

A buzzer blared, making them both jump.

"What's that?" Jessica looked from Sam's startled face to her own tail—three times its usual size—then back to Sam.

He was checking his watch. "She's early."

"Who?" Jessica asked as he picked her up.

"It's show time, cat. Put a smile on your furry puss, okay?"

"What are you talking about?" He was carrying her toward the elevator. She jerked as the buzzer rasped again. "Sam?"

He toggled an intercom switch beside the door. "Mary? Come on in and wait for us. We're coming right down." He pushed a button to open the lobby door.

"Sam, who's Mary?" she demanded as he summoned the elevator. "Where are we going?"

"It's your treat, Jez-babe." The doors rolled open, and Sam stepped aboard. "I found somebody who wants a cat." He hit the down button and the elevator dropped, but no faster than her heart.

CHAPTER TWELVE

"YOU'VE GOT TO BE KIDDING!" She squirmed, but he spread his other hand on her back, holding her pinned between his ribs and forearm. *"Sam!"*

"Hey, settle down." He rumpled her fur, then flattened his hand again when she struggled. "What's the matter? Are your ears popping?"

"Sam, you idiot, you can't give me away, I'm your wife! I mean your ex-wife, but all the same... Don't *do* this to me!"

The doors opened to reveal a pretty blond woman dressed in nurse's white. "Ohhh!" she crooned, coming to meet them. "Why, she's a *beauty*, Sam!" Her eyes flicked up to his face and held there. Her smile was too intimate, too pouty.

"Oh, *that's* how it is, is it?" An odd, weaving little moan sounded in Jessica's ears—it issued from her own throat. "The only pet she wants is *you*, Sam, can't you see that? I bet she hates cats!"

"I guess the elevator scared her," Sam apologized, rubbing Jessica's back. "Usually she's pretty chummy, for a cat. I can't keep her off me."

"I'm sure we'll get along *just* fine. Pussycats love me." Mary held out her hand. "Puss-puss-puss?"

Ears folded flat to her skull, Jessica made a sound like a lisping cobra. *"Back* off!"

The nurse paused midgesture, her smile wavering. "Ohhh-uh...*my!*"

Sam shook Jessica twice, briskly, then rubbed her back too hard. "She didn't mean that."

"Want to bet?" Jessica squirmed, trying to free her front paws, but Sam's arm tightened across her chest. "Let me go, Sam!"

"Oh, look, she's a double-pawed cat!" Mary cried. "Isn't she *cute?*"

"Double-pawed?" Sam caught one of Jessica's wrists and lifted it. "Looks like one paw to me."

The nurse giggled. "You *don't* know much about cats, do you?"

"And plan to keep it that way."

"She has too many toes, Sam. Normal cats have four toes and a dew claw on their front feet, and four toes on back. She has—let me see—six toes, front and back. Isn't she *adorable?* And, *my,* pussykins, what a great, big, puffy *tail* you have!" She held out her hand again.

Reaching under Sam's arm, Jessica managed an awkward slash. It missed, but her intention was clear. "Keep your hands to yourself, thank you ever so much!" She craned her neck to look up at Sam. "What *is* it with you— you and blondes? This is why you've been spending so much time at the hospital, isn't it? It's nothing to do with me— *Mrrrow!*" she exclaimed, as Sam hoisted her suddenly by her scruff. *"Don't!"*

"Don't..." he growled, dangling her at eye level. "Jez'bel? *Behave!"*

"Don't tell *me* what to do!" She took a swing at him, but missed his nose by inches. "Lemme go!" She would've burst into tears if she could've. *"Sam!"*

He brought her back to his chest and clamped an arm around her, half squeezing the breath from her lungs. "Maybe this wasn't such a good idea."

"Oh, I'm *sure* she'll calm down." Mary patted Sam's forearm, then rested her hand there reassuringly.

"Sure I will, once you get out of here—and not a minute before. Take your hand *off* him! Or do you like that, Sam? Don't let *me* stop you if this is what your taste has sunk to these days—it's hardly my business. But leave me out of it!"

"You're right, she is a gabby little thing. Maybe if we went upstairs and started all over again?" Mary suggested. "Had a cup of tea and let her sniff me in familiar surroundings?"

"Are you going to fall for that, Sam? Next she'll be offering to cook you supper while she makes up to me."

Mary glanced at her watch. "Or... I'm getting hungry. We could run out for a pizza. Give her time to calm down, then try again?"

"What did I tell you?" Jessica growled, turning to glare up at him.

Sam scowled back, then shook his head. "I'm afraid I have to get back to the hospital, Mary. I've missed half the visiting periods today. And I'm starting to think this just isn't going to work. With dogs I know you get one once in a while that's a one-man dog. Is it like that with cats?"

Mary squinched her nose charmingly. "I suppose it *could* be..."

"And then some cats just can't take hypocritical blondes!" Jessica's snarl ended in a bagpipe squeak as his arm tightened.

"That's it," he said decisively. "I can't give you a cat that might hurt you, Mary. But thanks for coming by..."

The encounter limped to its close, Mary intimating that any approach by Sam—anytime, with cat or without— would be *most* welcome, each of her progressively broader hints apparently sailing right over his head.

"See you tomorrow at the ICU," he drawled finally, walking her to the door.

They watched in silence until she'd reached her car, given them a cheery, finger-twiddling wave, then driven off, her mouth crumpling into a thoughtful pout. Jessica heaved a slow sigh of relief. "Good riddance!" Then, "*Yowch!*" as Sam gave her tail a not-friendly tug.

"Damned cat! What the hell got into you?"

"Loan me your computer and I'll tell you—chapter and verse."

They rode up to the sixth floor in glowering silence. Once in the loft, Sam marched across the living room and dumped her on the sofa. "I think it's time we had a little talk, cat."

"Fine by me." Jessica shook herself, then turned to lick her shoulder. Her tail was still outraged. She jumped to the sofa's backrest and stalked its length.

"I'm not keeping you, fur-ball."

"What's so new about that? You didn't keep me last time, either. And if you'll recall, *I* left *you.*" She sat at the far end of the backrest and gazed off into space, ears tipped backward, tail lashing. "If I was human, do you think I'd be sitting here? *Ha!*"

"Are you listening to me?" He followed and circled around till their eyes met. "You just blew a perfectly good opportunity."

"To live with a gooey-voiced, dough-faced blonde? Maybe that does something for you, Sam, but believe me, I'd rather live in a Dumpster." She spun away, stalked to the other end of the couch and sat.

"Cats, cats, cats, *cats* ..." Sam muttered, turning the word to an X-rated invective. "I should've left you in the road where I found you."

"Maybe you should've."

"Dammit, Jez'bel, do you want me to take you to the pound? You'd like that!" Looming over her, he prodded her in the ribs. "*Look* at me when I talk to you."

With insolent deliberation she tipped her head backward till their eyes met. "So talk. Tell me about the blonde—not that one, but the one I saw in our living room half-naked. I've been wondering for eight years—who was she, Sam?"

Their gazes locked and held while her tail switched once...twice...a third time. Something flickered in Sam's eyes, then he blinked. "Cats—cats with too many friggin' toes!" Spinning on his heel, he stormed from the room.

"Oh, right," she yelled after him. "Turn tail and run when the going gets rough!"

His footsteps stalked to the end of the hall, paused, then stamped back again. Ignoring her, he snatched up his valise and the bag with the tape player. "I'm outta here."

"Then leave me your Powerbook?" she said in a tiny voice. "Please? I know this seems weird, but just give me a chance and I can explain everything."

"Too late for apologies, fur-ball. And don't wait up for me." The doors rolled open. He stepped aboard, swung back to face her, started to add something—then he was gone.

He would take her to the pound, she could see it coming. Not because he hated cats, but because she threatened his notion of reality at the deepest level. He'd grow uneasier and uneasier the harder she pushed, and eventually she'd be a goner. *Or maybe, subconsciously, he knows I'm Jessica, and he's just rejecting me all over again. If he didn't want me enough to be faithful when I was human, why would he want me all covered with fur? With a tail?*

Her tail wafted into view at that precise moment and she gave it a vicious look. *Beat it.*

It flicked its tip contemptuously, and suddenly she'd had enough. "It's *your* fault!" She leaned to snap at it—and it swerved just beyond reach, then paused to beckon tauntingly.

"I mean it!" She leaned and snapped—her teeth clicking on air, then spun to follow its fluttering retreat. "Damn!" She slapped, missed, pinned it with a paw, fell over, bit at it again, and this time she caught it. *"Ow!"*

Great idea, Jessica. Slowly, panting, she sat up.

Her tail quivered with suppressed outrage.

"Truce?" she tried grudgingly.

Her tail settled warily, jumpily, at her feet.

Just do me a favor. She gave it a rueful look, then a remorseful swipe of her tongue. *Stay out of my sight, would you?*

The tail whisked from view and she sighed. The pound...Sam...blondes... *Maybe you should've left me in the road, Sam.* It might've been kinder in the end.

As always, Cattoo seemed to sense her sadness, if not the reasons for it. Jessica could feel her nudging somewhere deep within—velvet nose, anxious eyes. *Thanks, sweet. Sorry about that tail.*

How about a nap? came the suggestion. In Cattoo's world, there wasn't much a catnap couldn't cure.

Jessica sighed. *Maybe you're right.* But first she found Sam's sweater tossed on a windowsill. Dragging it by its sleeve to the floor, she curled herself into a small ball of misery, buried her nose in its folds, and slept.

AND DREAMED OF FALLING—falling forever.

Above her, Sam leaned over the edge of the world and waved. It was he who had dropped her.

Below her, rushing relentlessly closer, was the pound, a pen of dogs waiting, their slavering grins upturned. And Raye Talbot crouched in their midst—*smiling.*

"Yowww!" Jessica awoke with claws bared, fur standing on end. Panting, she lay very still but for her galloping heart and her trembling whiskers. Dream, dream—only a dream. Horrid dream. "What time is it?"

Cattoo had no idea, but she was growing restless. Time to rise and prowl.

"Sam's not back yet."

Don't wait up, he'd said. Out with that insipid blonde? Or some other woman. Rhode Island held roughly half a million. A man like Sam would have his choice.

She shivered, and shivering, the image of the pound returned. Barking dogs. Chain-link fences. Cold, damp concrete. Inedible food. A concentration camp for cats, with death the likeliest deliverance. *God, he wouldn't, would he?*

He might.

There had to be a way to make him see. There *had* to be. And suddenly she had it—not the whole solution, but perhaps the solution to this particular problem. She stood, stretched her ritual stretch and looked around. *Where's that phone?*

While nudging it onto its back, she knocked it off the coffee table. After that, it was easy to flip it over, but not so easy to punch out the numbers she wanted. Her paw was precisely three toes too wide for the buttons. She misdialed and reached some man with a Western twang and a bad case of adenoids.

"Darn." Pressing the disconnect, she tried using her nose the second time, but as she neared each key, her eyes lost their focus. This time, the woman who picked up the phone seemed to be speaking Japanese. "Sorry!" Jessica said, speaking into the mouthpiece.

Her *meow* elicited a questioning, incomprehensible word, repeated several times in ascending volume.

"Maybe Korean," she decided, disconnecting.

The third time she tried her paw again and got lucky. At least, she thought she'd dialed correctly. She hovered over the mouthpiece while a phone rang somewhere. "*Answer,* Mother. I know you're there." It could be no later than eight-thirty here, which made it seven-thirty in Chicago. Almost surely her mother would still be at her desk—which didn't mean she'd deign to pick up the phone. And her secretary, who would have, must have staggered home hours ago.

"Hello?" The cool, crisp voice, impatient at being disturbed, sounded from the earpiece.

"Mother!" Of course, the word came out "Meow."

There was a pause, then, with an edge of suspicion, "Hello? Who's this, please?"

"Your daughter! Jessica!" *Mother, Sam can understand me, almost. But what about you?* The odds were much longer here, and not just because this was long distance. There was plenty of caring, but had there ever been comprehension? Real connection? "Mother?"

"Is this a joke?"

"I wish it were! Mother, you're the only one who might remember I lived with a cat. Didn't you even think about Cattoo, wonder what happened to her, when you were here yester—"

Click

"Rats!" Luckily the phone had a redial button. She stepped on it.

The phone picked up on the first ring. "Hel*lo!*"

"Mother, think. This isn't a crank call. *Think.* Why would a cat call you? You, of all people. What could it mean? Don't you remember Catt—"

Click!

Jessica winced, then let out a yowl of frustration. She stalked around the phone three times, tail whipping, teeth gnashing. Then she paused, as she heard the elevator's groan.

"Sam?" Jessica hooked a paw under the phone, started to turn it facedown. The last thing she needed was to aggravate Sam. But on the other hand... She dropped it, button side up, then punched the redial. "Come *on*, Mother. Answer me."

Brrrinnnng.

No answer. The phone rang for a second time as the doors to the elevator rolled open and Sam stepped out.

Crouching by the phone, teeth clenched, Jessica didn't move. *Come on, Mother. Answer it! Be there for me for once in my life.* The ring of her distant phone skirled in the darkness.

And Sam's head swung to track the tiny sound. "What's that?" He flipped a wall switch. The track lights washed the room, one spot singling out Jessica, frozen to her tail tip, huddled beside the phone.

Brrrinnnng.

"What the..." Sam crossed the room in five long strides.

"Just let it ring, Sam! She'll pick up any second. I know she—"

"Blasted cat! How the devil did you—"

"*Wait!*" But his hand closed over the phone.

"Hel*lo!*" her mother barked—just as Sam punched the disconnect.

"Huh?" he said belatedly. "Who the heck was—" He shook his head and, staring at the phone, sank onto the edge of the coffee table. His gaze jerked to Jessica. "Did you... nah."

"Are you doing this on purpose? Driving me crazy? I had her! I actually *had* her and then you...you..." Fighting back a distinct urge to bury her teeth in his shin, Jessica turned in a circle of frustration, then flopped on her side.

"Maybe I'm going crazy? The strain..."

"*You're* going crazy. Try being a cat!" Her tail thumped the floor, whack...whack... "I *had* her, Sam." She leapt up and reared to nudge the phone in his hand. "Just let me hit the redial, and—"

He held it up out of reach. "Oh, no. You want to call your furry friends for a meow-along, you do it on your nickel. Better yet, act like a normal cat and go sing on the fire escape. Maybe I'll get lucky and you'll fall off." He headed for the kitchen, taking the phone with him.

Filling the teakettle, he glanced toward her bowls. "Didn't touch it, huh? Let's see, you don't eat chili, you sneer at liver, you scorn beef. Just where were you eating before you and I met up? The Dumpster behind a French restaurant?"

"I went in the front door, thanks." Jessica jumped up on a chair and hung her head over its edge. "Sam, I give up. Maybe I *should* jump off the fire escape."

Waiting for the kettle to boil, he wandered around the kitchen, opening drawers and cabinets, scowling, then closing them again. "What are you cooking for dinner?" she asked finally.

He shut another cabinet. "If you're thinking I'll cook for you, think again. I ate out. Somebody told me about this neat little Jamaican café."

"*Who?*"

"Don't yell at me. You've got food. Melt-in-your-mouth moo."

"*Who told you about that café?*" The hair shivered along her spine. RI Gen was a large hospital. There was no reason he'd cross tracks with Raye Talbot, no reason but the worst kind of luck. *I've been having any other kind lately?* "How'd you find the Jamaican place?" Anyone could have pointed him there. Sam tended to nose that sort of thing out—where to find the funkiest music, the best down-home cooking...

And he was too absorbed to receive her questions at the moment. Dropping to his heels, he opened the dishwasher, looked inside, ran the shelves out and cocked his head to look under them. "Nope." He stood, picked up the toaster, peered into it, scowled.

"What are you doing, then, if you're not cooking?"

No answer. He stopped to make himself a mug of herbal tea, then wandered over to the table and again dropped to his heels. "What *are* you doing?" She leaned to touch her nose to his cheek.

Sam jumped, grunted, brushed her aside. "Yeah," he muttered to himself. He touched the back of his chair. "That *might*—" He flipped it upside down, then propped it on the floor. "Yep." His hand groped in his pocket, came out with the Swiss army knife he always carried.

"Oh, no." But he was already flipping out the box wrench tool. "Sam, you can't take it apart! It's not yours. And it's not broken."

Pointedly ignoring her, he adjusted the wrench mouth to fit the bolts that held the oak-and-iron chair together.

They both jumped when, over on the counter, the phone rang. "Now who the..." Sam rose lazily.

"If it's your little blond friend, tell her I'm still not interested," she growled as he raised the phone to his ear.

"I'm hangin' in there, Eleanor," he responded after a moment. "How 'bout you?"

Jessica bolted upright. *"Mother?"*

He sighed, then wandered back to the table and hitched a hip onto its edge. "No change since I called you at noon. They didn't move her today. Tomorrow, they're sayin' now. Once they do that, and let me start visiting for more than ten minutes on the blasted hour, then we'll see some progress." He paused. "Umm—no, Fisher didn't say *that,* not exactly. They don't say much if they can avoid it, do they? But I'm counting on it. You can count on it. She's down, but she's not out. Not by a long shot."

Jessica leapt to the tabletop. "I have to talk to her."

Without looking, he shoved her off again. "Yeah, well, it's what anyone would..." His voice trailed off in embarrassment, then he brightened. "Yes, I did, and brought back her jewelry case. Want me to send that to you?'' He listened, one leg swinging gently.

"Isn't she saying anything about cats? Weird phone calls?'' Jessica reared up on his leg and patted his knee. "Sam, let me talk to her. *Please.*"

He cupped his hand over the mouthpiece and hissed, "You want to hush, or should I stick you in the dishwasher?'' He went back to listening, his foot swinging. Abruptly his brows flew together, his foot froze. "She had a...cat?'' He looked down at Jessica blankly.

"Yes!" Jessica slapped his knee. *Mother got it. Oh, she got it!*

"No, I don't know what happened to— Nobody's said a word, but then...'' He bent down to stare into Jessica's eyes, his own wide with shock. "Yeah,'' he murmured absently, still bent double, "the bedroom was pretty bad. Unless somebody actually went looking for a— Or maybe she was outside when it started? All the firetrucks and commotion spooked her, so she split?'' He straightened, his eyes still locked on Jessica's. "Just...what did this...cat...look like?'' He nodded, kept on nodding, face stunned. "Black, female... Anything else?''

Jessica caught the negative tone of the response.

Sam snared her extended paw. "What about toes? How many did she have?'' His thumb rubbed gently across Jessica's digits. "I hear they're s'posed to have four?''

Her mother's laughing question carried clearly.

Sam laughed, too, but he was forcing it. "Oh, no. No reason, I was just...wondering if you might've...noticed. Who's got time to go round counting cat toes?'' He let Jessica go. "Did this cat have a name?'' He frowned. "Sure...oh, sure. But if you think of it...''

"She doesn't even remember?'' Her mother had met Cattoo only once, on a flying trip through town, but still...

"Well, if it comes to you, I'd like to know. Maybe I'll hunt around her house a bit. Or run an ad in the paper— Lost cat, answers to name of Fleabaggums, that sort of thing..." He rubbed a hand up through his hair, leaving it standing in rumpled spikes.

They talked a few minutes more, Sam promising to continue his daily calls to report Jessica's condition. At last he pressed the disconnect. Eyes fixed on Jessica, he set the phone aside. *"Can't be..."*

"Believe it."

Hooking his thumbs under her armpits and lifting, he stared at her, their faces on a level, noses nearly touching. "There's not a snowball's chance in hell you could be the same..." He set her down on the table beside him. "There must be forty thousand black cats in this city alone. Every third cat you see's a black cat."

"I'm Jessica's cat," she insisted, resting a paw on his thigh. "Plus Jessica. Please believe it. *Please!*"

He shook his head. "That would be too weird for words." Abruptly he stroked a hand down her spine, then snatched his hand back as if she were red-hot. "Too weird entirely. What are the rational, mathematical chances that you and I—"

"Rational-smashional—*every*thing needs scientific proof? Can't you just take my word?"

Sam shook his head.

"Then I give up, I give up, I give *up!* Open that window for me and I *will* jump."

He cocked his head, listening to her tirade. "If you were Jess's cat—I don't believe for a minute you are—but if you were, what would she be feeding you?"

"Champagne, scrambled eggs and caviar," she growled spitefully.

He rubbed his chin. "You finished my eggs yesterday, didn't you?"

He was seriously asking? *"Yes!"* she agreed, putting heart and soul into that meow.

"Hmm..." He wandered over to the fridge, leaned in, pulled out a carton of eggs.

"Oh, *yes!*" She leapt down from the table to strop his

shins. Even if this was all the good that came out of her phone call, a square meal was not to be sniffed at.

"Little cheddar, maybe a touch of tarragon, some thyme?" he suggested, improvising as usual.

"Sounds fabulous!"

"Does sound sort of good, doesn't it?" He added several more eggs to the three he'd set on the counter.

In the end, they ate together, Sam with his plate on the floor beside him while he attacked the chair, Jessica crouched nearby wolfing hers down. "Bliss!" she stopped to exclaim at one point.

"Not half-bad," Sam agreed around a forkful. He set his plate aside and picked up the wrench.

"But why are you picking on that chair, Sam?"

He wasn't telling. Halfway through his disassembly, he stopped to rake the last of his eggs onto her plate, then went back to work. They finished at roughly the same time. "That might be the best meal I ever ate," she decided, sitting to comb her whiskers. "*Thank* you."

"Ze chef is so glad you like eet, *peti' chat*. Shall we repair to ze living rrrhhhum?" He picked up the iron weldment that had been the back of his chair and ambled off. Jessica finished her whiskers, jumped over the pile of wood and metal that remained and padded behind, tail on high.

Sam sat on the couch with his shoe in his lap, examining the sole. "Clumsy, but might do," he told her when she leapt to the table. Reaching past her to open the lacquer box, he pulled out her ruined ring.

"Sam?" In the midst of licking her wrist, Jessica froze. "What—"

"Can't make it any worse, can I?" He studied the jumbled wires, then gently pried one of the crushed rings apart. He slipped the misshapen circlet onto the end of one of the gracefully tapered iron rods that had made up the chair's backrest. "Here goes nothin'." Using the heel of his shoe, he tapped the wire, then turned, tapped and turned, delicately, deftly, gradually reshaping the softer gold against the iron.

"Oh, Sam!"

Eyes narrowed, lips pursed to a whistle, he hammered. As the ring bent back toward its original shape, it slipped farther down the rod. Whistling a halting bossa nova, he tapped, turned the wire, tapped. After a while he stopped, switched his attention to the second ring of the puzzle, started again.

"Sam, I love you." It didn't matter that he couldn't hear her, though for a second there, his eyes far away, he stopped and smiled to himself. It didn't matter that he didn't quite love her back, never had, never would. Just that this man was in the world. You didn't need to own a perfect sunrise to love it, after all. *I love you.*

At long last, all three parts of her puzzle ring curved round and smooth. He held the linked chain up for her to admire. "Now comes the hard part." Grasping the links with the fingers of both hands, he closed his eyes. "Haven't done this in eight years, y'know. Think I've still got what it takes?"

"I know you have."

His fingers moved slowly, tentatively. The frown on his face deepened gradually to a look almost of pain.

She leaned closer till her whiskers brushed the backs of his hands. That expression on his face—where had she seen it before? Oh, yes, how could she ever forget? It was the look he wore when he was holding himself back, waiting for her to come, and then—

His eyes opened as he laughed aloud. "Yep." He held out his hand with a flourish. "Voilà."

"You did it!" she cried, staring at her ring made whole. "Oh, Sam, oh, Sam, oh, Sam Antonio *mio* . . . you did it! Thank you!"

"There's jus' one problem," he drawled, his words no louder than a whisper. "I had to force the fit a touch, there at the end. I don't know if it'll ever come apart again."

Purring, she rubbed her cheek against his hand. "I can live with that."

He balanced it on top her head, a golden crown, and admired the effect. "Goes nice with all that fur."

Nicer than you may ever know.

CHAPTER THIRTEEN

FLOATING ONE FATHOM above oblivion, she wasn't aware of his touch at first. Warmth kindled in her belly, then burned outward from there, turning nerves to molten copper. A song of pleasure started softly, then grew till her body shuddered with its rhythm. "Mmmmm..." She rolled over onto her side and arched her back. "Don't stop."

Sam chuckled. Knuckles touched her taut belly and stroked upward, ruffling fur. "Lazy cat. You plannin' to sleep your life away?"

Cat? Jessica opened one eye, then closed it. "Please tell me I'm dreaming." Leaning above her, Sam was disguised as a giant. And she wore a cat costume, authentic right down to the toenails.

"I'm gone," he said, instead, giving her stomach a smack. "I left you some ham in the kitchen, sleepyhead."

"Wait! Don't go," she protested as he walked away. "Take me with you!" But she couldn't follow him without stretching—every instinct demanded that. By the time she'd pointed her back toes, he was stepping into the elevator. "Sam!"

"See ya, slugabed." The doors closed behind him.

"Rats." Suddenly too heavy for her own legs, she sat. Looked around, blinking at half speed. "How late did I stay up last night?"

She remembered nothing after she'd tried to follow Sam into his bedroom and had been politely, but firmly, shoved back out the door. "How late did *you* stay up last night?"

Cattoo wasn't saying. She was so deeply asleep not even a psychic whisker twitched.

"Talk about burning the candle at both ends..." Jessica shambled toward the kitchen. "Cup of coffee, that's what we need."

There was none to be had, not even the dregs from Sam's mug, which apparently had been loaded into the dishwasher. She studied the coffee grinder, then gave it up. "Not in this lifetime, without thumbs."

She shuffled off to the bathroom. "Could we be coming down with the flu?"

No comment from Cattoo.

"Distemper? No, your shots are all up to date." Simple sleep deprivation, she concluded, while she stepped on the uncapped toothpaste tube, then bit off a mint-flavored mouthful. There was no doubt she was usurping most of Cattoo's normal daylight hours. So Cattoo was perhaps switching all her conscious hours to the night?

And when do we sleep, in that case? Or do we?

And if we don't? Any doctor could give you that prognosis—*bad news*. No organism could function without sufficient sleep. Not for long.

"I'll worry about this later." She yawned till her jaw cracked. Right now a nap seemed in order. Trudging out of the bathroom, she looked right and realized that Sam had left his bedroom door ajar. "Aha!"

She dreamed of falling and awoke with a yell—to find the bed rebounding violently. Sam had thrown himself facedown onto the mattress beside her. "Stupid cat." He caught her and dragged her across the bedspread. "Lousy, worthless animal, how'd you get in here?" He buried his face in her fur.

"What's the *matter*, Sam?" He wasn't crying, but tears trembled in his voice in place of the usual laughter. "Sam?"

"She won't wake up," he muttered, rubbing his nose against her. "I've been talking and talking and talking to her. She's in her own room now, so we finally have some privacy, but it didn't do any good. I washed her face, rubbed her hands till I was afraid I'd hurt them, whispered in her ear, sang to her, told stupid jokes... She heard *nothing*, Jez. There wasn't a blip on her monitor. *Bloody hell."* He hugged her till she squeaked. "What do I do if..." He rolled onto his back, taking her with him. "What are we going to do?"

"We won't give up, that's what we'll do." She touched her nose to his cheek, inhaled his scent and shuddered with joy. "We'll figure it out, Sam." Somehow. "But first, would you just hug me like that one more time?"

He cradled her on top of his chest. Eyes closed, face clenched, he stroked her—ruffling her fur backward, then smoothing it down, a backward ruffle, then smooth—till she sang for joy and his face gradually relaxed. Every breath he took lifted her in a slow-motion ride of dazzled bliss. *I remember this, yesss.* Peace. Joy. Belonging. At last, heart speaking softly to heart, they slept.

Jessica awoke when he scratched her ears. "What d'you think you're doin' up here?" he grumbled. "Hussy. You better not have fleas."

She yawned deliciously. "Speak for yourself, Texan. Is *your* flea collar up-to-date?"

Rolling over, he dumped her on the mattress. Limp with contentment, eyelids half-mast, she lay there watching him. *Maybe I should just stay a cat?* It would almost be worth it, to be with him like this.

Right, she reminded herself, *and the first time he brings a girlfriend home? How happy would I be as his pet then? I'd scratch her eyes out, then go for his throat.*

"I've been thinkin', soft thang," he drawled, stroking. "How do you figure Jess felt about her cat?"

"There was only one person in the world she loved more."

"I have to connect with her somehow. Call her back from wherever she's wandered off to." His hand grew heavier, squeezing half the breath from her body, as his face grew bleak. "But maybe...maybe I'm not the guy to do it? When all is said and done, I'm the guy she nearly broke her neck runnin' from last week, down in New York."

"Oh, Sam, don't blame yourself for that!"

"And I'm the guy she walked out on, all those years ago. The guy whose postcards she'd never answer, whose phone calls she'd never take."

"Sam, I'm sorry." She'd been so busy hurting, so busy guarding her own precious dignity each time she'd shut him out, she'd never once stopped to think he might be hurting, too.

"So why should she take my call this time?" He stared past her, breath hissing between his teeth. "On the other hand, if not me, then who else is there to try?" His unthinking caress flattened her to the mattress, a full body massage. "Her idiot parents have already given up on her. They think there's nothing there to talk to. That she's gone away for good.

"So the last thing Jess needs is *them* hanging around, convincing her they're right. She's been a good girl all her life—too good—buying whatever load of crap they were selling, no questions asked. I can't have her doing that this time." His hand ruffled, then smoothed, ruffled, smoothed. A nerve ticked at the corner of his eye. "Guess it's damn lucky they *aren't* sticking around. I might kill that cocksure, son-of-a-bitch doctor-daddy of hers if I thought he was giving her the wrong notion. Probably should have, anyway, years ago."

"Oh, Sam, my maniac knight. Crazy Texan." She crept closer beneath his hand, till their noses nearly touched.

"But if I'm not the guy for the job, then maybe you're the girl?"

"How do you mean?"

"Maybe you really are her no-name cat, strolled in by some miracle. Or maybe you're just Ms. Any-Ol'-Black-Cat, USA. But does that matter? You know what they say 'bout all cats lookin' the same in the dark?"

"Sexist pig." She nuzzled him. "We have political reeducation camps for specimens like you. Ought to just put you up against the wall, but it's such a shame to waste prime beefcake."

He narrowed his eyes at her. "Sometimes . . . you make my brains buzz. Maybe I'm allergic to cats? Technically allergic, I mean."

"Or maybe you need to wash out your ears, then listen. But what were you starting to say? I'm the girl for what job?"

"Anyway, how'd you like to come have a chat with my— With Jess?"

"How'd I—" She shot to her feet. "How'd I like to own the stars, the moon, half-a-dozen Van Goghs and my own body? Oh, Sam, do you mean it?"

"Hey, hey, settle down! If you're going to run around yelling, we'll just forget all about it."

"Oh, I'll be good!" She sat, curled her tail tightly around her toes and stared at him, shivering with excitement. "I'll be so good, so discreet, so tactful, so . . . so grateful, Sam, if you'll only take me to me. Please?"

He laughed. "Much better. But can you act like that for more than two minutes?"

"Try me! Oh, try me right now!"

He glanced at his watch. "Too late to try it tonight. But first thing tomorrow? Whoa!" He laughed as she ducked under his arm and kissed him.

"I AM GETTING SEASICK," Jessica announced after the only other passenger stepped off the hospital elevator. "You've got to stop swinging this thing when you walk." The thing was a bowling-ball bag that Sam had discovered in a closet of the loft. He'd cut a few discreet holes in it for ventilation, though they served just as well for observation. He'd tucked her inside, then zipped the carrier shut.

"Shuddup," Sam muttered just as the doors rolled open for the next floor. Two nurses stepped aboard. "Howdy," he added too heartily.

"Howdy yourself, stranger," the prettier one returned, after eyeing him up and down. "Looks like you took a wrong turn on the way to the bowling alley."

Oh, very funny! Her tail lashed out, whacking the inner wall of her carrier, thump . . . thump.

Sam gave the bag a jerk. "Reckon I did," he drawled, laying on the corn-pone accent—Hicksville by way of Harvard. The flirtation continued for two floors, Sam tapping his foot to cover the muffled *thumps* coming from the bag, the nurses giggling too hard to notice. "You're going to get us thrown out of here," he muttered once the women had departed.

"It's you who's attracting attention, not me."

"Stop growling," he growled as the doors opened and a man on crutches gimped aboard.

He was right, of course, but as tightly strung as she was, she found it easier to focus on Sam's deficiencies than on the coming encounter. *Why did I have to fall for a man who loves women? Why did you have to marry me if you had no more fidelity than the average tomcat?* Painful as these questions were, at least she'd faced them for eight years. They were the devils she knew.

The devil she didn't know was looming ever closer. It was only two floors away now. Then one floor. *What do I do if this doesn't work? Oh, God, what do I do then?*

The elevator stopped and Sam stepped out. Striding down the corridor, he broke into a brazen whistle of "The Girl from Impanema." The bag swayed sickeningly to the bossa nova, and Jessica gritted her teeth. *He's as nervous as I am,* she realized as he stopped at the nurses' station to chat up the staff, then ask how she'd passed the night.

"No change, Mr. Kirby," the head nurse said in a tone Jessica recognized all too well. Chirpy briskness hiding compassion. The woman indicated one of several monitors mounted on the inner wall of the station, where a green line pulsed steadily. "She never misses a beat."

Not necessarily something to brag about. The essence of being alive was change, fluctuation—rises and falls of consciousness, tidal sweeps of hormones. Passion and stubborn will. Unquenchable longings, irresistible impulses. Change, not the endless humming of a machine, a green line pulsing steadily into a future of unspeakable sameness. *Oh, God, what if this doesn't work? Oh, God,*

Sam, I'm afraid. The bag swayed horribly, and she clenched her teeth, holding her heaving stomach at bay.

The swaying stopped. She heard him suck in a deep breath, then a doorknob clicked and turned. "Jess? It's me, Sam, your friendly neighborhood pest. Just when you thought it was safe to come out and play, the Texans have landed." He shut the door behind them. Moving around the bed, he set the bag on a wide windowsill. "How're you feeling, babe?"

He moved between Jessica and the bed, blocking her view. Pressed to a breathing hole, she could see the foot of the bed and the long slope of a pair of legs covered by a sheet. Sam sat on the edge of the mattress and leaned across it to brace one arm on the far side.

"I brought you a visitor. Nobody I'd care to meet in a dark alley, but you always had kinky tastes. And she tells me she's an old pal of—" His patter broke off as the door opened and a nurse breezed in.

"Why, hello, Mr. Kirby! How's our girl doing today?"

"*Dr. Myles* is doin' just fine," he said, a flicker of irritation underlying his response. "Shall I move?"

"No, no, you stay put. I just need to change this bag here..." She suited action to words, switching an empty bag hanging from an IV rack for a full one. "Then we'll stick this little gizmo in her ear to check her temp... *That's* good, perfectly normal, and *then* ..." She completed her inventory of the vital signs, noting them on a chart. "There, that's it for now. Let's see, she's had her sponge bath...she won't be taking lunch, of course, at least not on a tray..."

"So you won't need to disturb us for a while?" Sam suggested, though it wasn't a suggestion. "And if you don't mind, Dr. Myles would prefer you always knock before entering. Here—here's that sign I made up yesterday to remind folks." Ushering the nurse out of the room, he leaned out to hang the sign on the doorknob, then shut the door with a thump. "Whew!"

Returning, he stood looking down at her motionless form. "They're a pushy lot, even the best of 'em, aren't they? Used to bossing everybody around, I s'pose. All for their own good, but still... Brrrr..."

Transfixed at her peephole, Jessica stared. "That's me?" It was the same face she'd seen in the mirror for twenty-eight years, and yet it was not. Utterly immobile, not much darker than the pillow on which it lay, her face in profile reminded Jessica of the bronze knight she'd seen atop a sarcophagus in an English cathedral years ago—something that might lie there for a thousand years. For all eternity. The marker where once a soul had lived. *Oh, God, that's me?*

"So...'bout your visitor...".

As Sam moved toward her carrier, the old admonition popped into her head, its tone sniggering, slyly ironic: *Be careful what you wish for.* Since the fire, she'd wished for nothing but to be reunited with herself—but now that the moment was finally here?

The zipper snicked overhead, letting in daylight from the window at her back. Sam's hands slid into the bag, smoothing around her sides.

Now that the moment was here, who was to say that a reunion would play out in the happy terms she'd envisioned—one kiss from a cat, and Jessica Myles awakens like Sleeping Beauty?

"Sam, wait a minute, I want to think about this!" she cried as he lifted her out. "What if this doesn't work—I mean, doesn't work the way I'm hoping? What if I do make the jump, but then I don't wake up?" *Be careful what you wish for...* What could be more horribly ironic than to be reunited with herself—in a living death?

"Hey, take it easy." He tried to cradle her against his forearm, but she twisted to hook her claws into his shirt. "*Ouch*, dammit!"

Clinging desperately, she tried to chin herself up, bring her face to his level. "I mean there's no guarantee, is there, that I'll snap out of this coma? And if I don't, there's no guarantee that I can jump *back* to Cattoo." Compared with that flesh-and-blood grave marker, life trapped in a cat suddenly didn't seem half so bad. "At least right now I can move and think and feel!"

"*Ouch!* Have you gone crazy?" He caught her by her nape and tried to peel her off his chest.

She flexed her toes and clung tighter, pulling his shirt out in two fistfuls. "Sam, I'm terrified! Don't make me. *Please!*"

"Hey, what is it, babe?" He brought her in against his chest, winced, but held her, one hand stroking her heaving ribs. "What's the matter, Jezbel? Fuzzwuzzy? Sillycat?" He sank down on the windowsill, rubbing her shoulders. "It's just Jess, Jez—just my baby. She won't hurt you."

"Oh, God, Sam, I hope you're right." Panting, she clung to him, her heart racing against his slower, heavier beat. She burrowed under his chin.

"S'okay, babe. Honest."

Eyes closed, shivering, she breathed in his scent. "Oh, Sam, I'm so scared. I don't want to die, not like that!"

"Okay... okay, settle down, Jez-babe." He sighed, his cheek pressed to her head, fingers soothing. "Maybe this wasn't such a good idea, after all," he said at last. "I don't know what's spooked you, but we can't have you scratching Jess, can we?" He sighed again. "Guess it proves one thing, anyway. You aren't her cat, whoever you are."

"Just let me *think* a minute," she begged, shivering, her face buried against his throat. No guarantees. All her life she'd played by her parents' rules—work hard and then harder still, be a lady, pay your taxes—and reasonable success would be guaranteed, if not unreasonable joy. But here there were no guarantees, only terror and the arms around her. *I'm hyperventilating,* she realized, noting the symptoms.

He shifted, leaned to reach for something. "Okay. Bad idea. Don't reckon it would've worked, anyhow. Who'd want to talk to a bug-eyed, spooky cat?" Stroking her, he lifted her out from his chest.

She looked down to find herself dangling over the carrier. "Wha—"

"Let's go back in your cave, then, babe. You'll feel safer in there."

"No!" She'd come this far, she was going to turn tail now? Miss the one chance she had? Writhing in his hands, she twisted her feet away from the gaping maw of the bag. "No, I didn't say I *wouldn't* try. It's just—"

"Hey, now." He grabbed for a better hold, but she slid between his fingers like a furry eel. "Jez-dammit, come back."

She slithered down his leg, hit the floor, shot under the bed.

"Blasted animal!" Swearing, he dropped to his hands and knees.

No time to think, no time to cross her fingers or pray. Mad as he was now, he'd give her no second chance. It was now or never. As Sam dived under one side of the bed and grabbed for her, she scuttled out the other, gathered herself, then leapt.

She landed teetering on the mattress, staring wildly down at her own body. *And now what?* "Well...here I am." Her voice squeaked with terror. She stepped closer, fur standing on end, tail puffed enormous, eyes saucer-wide and whiskers quivering. "Take me back? Please?" She stretched to touch noses with her . . . self just as Sam sat up on the far side of the bed.

"Son of a blue-nosed, double-jointed, monkey-faced..." he swore in a reverent whisper. "Crazy, perverse, son of a *cat!*" He reached for her.

"Take me back?" she begged, closing her eyes, aiming her spirit like a hurled shaft. "I want to come *home*. Wake up . . ."

"Oh, God," Sam gasped. "Jess!" On his knees, he leaned over the bed. "You blinked, babe! *Yes!* Come on, you can do it! Blink again."

Jessica opened her eyes, but Sam wasn't looking at her. His forehead was pressed to the temple of the motionless, dreamless face on the pillow. His hand cupped her forehead, smoothing endless, feather-light caresses up into her hair. "Come on, baby, wake up now. Talk to us. We're here. We love you. Come back to us." His eyes opened, gleaming diamond-bright. "Come *on*, darlin', come *back*."

Stretching across her own body, Jessica touched her nose to his cheek. "Sam..."

"She blinked," he swore fiercely, his whisper ragged and aching. "I *swear* she blinked."

"I didn't see it." She drew her nose across his cheek to the corner of his eye, caught a tear on the tip of her tongue. "I'm sorry, Sam. I tried."

"Yeah," he said dully, his eyes fixed on her human face. "You tried. I thought for a minute there..." He heaved a sigh and continued smoothing his palm up her forehead. "Jess, Jess, Jess-babe...enough of this foolishness. It's time to wake up."

But she didn't.

After what seemed like hours, with a groan like an old man's, Sam pushed himself off the floor. He settled heavily onto the mattress. "Well..." He rumpled one hand up through his hair, then mustered a self-mocking ghost of a grin.

"What now?" Following Cattoo's instincts, she had settled at last in the crook made between her body's right arm and side. That arm was extended and fastened to a board to stabilize the IV, which entered at the wrist. Her position felt both right and utterly bizzarre. *I'm curled up with myself. Almost home, but not quite.* "Oh, Sam, what do we do now?"

"Beats me," he muttered. Gently he lifted her other arm. Spreading her limp fingers against his chest, he sat there stroking them, his face carved in stone. "So much for that theory."

And so much for hers. Proximity wasn't enough. Here she sat, her spirit not twelve inches out of place, yet it wouldn't make the leap—whatever the outcome of that leap might be. "I suppose you need some sort of stress? Last time, I was in danger of dying. Maybe it takes that kind of event, to make a...a soul disregard reality and...hop? But this time, my spirit's perfectly comfy where it is—under Cattoo's skin—so there it sits, blast it." Inertia was a force to be reckoned with in every field of science, so why not in the matter of souls?

Sam sat up straighter. "But that's my whole life in a nutshell, isn't it? Chasing theories down dead-end canyons. Not one in twenty pans out. Not one in a hundred. That doesn't mean you quit. You just go on to the next..."

"Or maybe the phenomenon has something to do with *inviting* me aboard? Cattoo knew I needed help, so she took me in? And now, since I'm...*here,* in a cat, there's nobody *there,* in my body, to invite me back home? And I can't jump without an invitation?" She sighed. Normally she'd research a problem like this, ransack the med literature till she understood every nuance of the problem. But in this case...she'd never heard of a case like this.

Because nobody ever made it back home to write about it? She shivered at the thought. Still, that made sense. Fat chance the *New England Journal of Medicine* would accept a paper from her once the editors learned she was a cat.

"So for now, I guess we just keep on keeping on, huh, babe? I'll keep babbling till I bore you to tears. You want me out of here, you'll have to wake up and throw me out."

Speaking of writing... She sat up. "Sam, you have to let me use your laptop. If I could just *explain* the problem to you, you'd help me figure out a way back home—I know you would." She winced, imagining Sam, apprised of the problem, testing out her stress theory. He knew how she hated heights. He'd probably hang her out the window by her tail—till she was terrorized back into her own skin.

Still... She looked longingly across the room to where his valise sat by the bowling-ball bag. He'd brought his computer as usual, but it might as well be on the moon. If she strolled over there and tried to open his Powerbook, he'd hang her out the window—and drop her.

"You know, I feel sort of awkward 'bout this, my touching you," Sam confessed, stroking her body's fingers. "Just because you once gave me the right doesn't mean I have any right to touch you now, I know that, babe.

And I know if you were feeling better, you'd probably slap me silly for...intruding on you, like this."

"I guess, yes, once upon a time I would have," Jessica admitted, staring up into his face. *Once upon a time, I thought pride was worth something. That pride was the last thing, the one thing, you held on to, when your world fell apart. Now I'm not so sure. Sam—I'm not sure of much, anymore.* This last week had blown all her beliefs to cat kibble.

He lowered her arm to his lap, smoothed his fingers up her forearm, then down. "But even so, Jess, everything I've read about your...condition seems to say that touch may be the best way to get through to you.

"I know you're thinking and feeling in there, even if you don't feel like answering right now. But I need to keep reminding you there's a world waiting out here. That you have a body, and it's a sweet place to come back to." Supporting her elbow on the palm of his left hand, he bent her arm slowly. Next he extended her arm, kissing her fingertips as they neared his face. His mouth twisted and his eyes closed for a second, then he repeated the exercise. "So, meantime, if I take a few liberties, will you forgive me? Or if you won't, will you please, please wake up and tell me so? You tell me to take a hike and I'll go, babe."

I wish I could tell you that I've changed my mind, she thought, staring up at him. *That I'm not so sure, anymore, that pride is the last thing you should hold on to. Now, I think maybe friendship is all that matters, when everything else in the world is stripped away. And Sam, nobody has been a better friend to me than you. There isn't a word big enough, bright enough, to tell you what that means to me.* "Thank you" *doesn't begin to touch it.*

She lay, staring up at him, the tip of her tail beating slow time to her thoughts. *I still wish I could've had your love, Sam. Once upon a time, I thought I might die without it. But in the end, it looks like I got what I needed, even if I didn't get what I want. Your friendship is the most precious thing I own—all I own. It's my fortune and my treasure.*

Sam propped her elbow in his lap again, her fingers splayed against his heart. Leaning, he rested his other hand on Jessica's furry flank. They sat like that for a long time, wordless, both drawing strength from the touch of a friend.

CHAPTER FOURTEEN

"WHEW," SAM MUTTERED, a long time later. "Gettin'
stiff." He arranged her arm carefully alongside her body,
then stood to stretch. "Don't know how you stand it, lying
there, Ms. Slugabed. Me, I'd be bored silly by now."

Jessica stood and arched into an inverted U. "Ha! That's
not how I remember it. Weekends, I had to pry you out of
bed with a crowbar." Not that he hadn't been a morning
person. He just knew what he liked to do with his mornings.

She gave a startled squeak as he scooped her up and
draped her around the back of his neck. "Cheaper than
mink," he declared, strolling over to the mirror to admire
the effect.

"And much more elegant," she agreed, drooping her
chin on his shoulder to play her part as mink stole. "Green
eyes, instead of those nasty, little, beady-brown glass eyes."

Not blinking, they studied each other in the glass. "You
know...it's the weirdest thing, but somehow this fuzz-farm
reminds me of you, Jess." Sam aimed that statement toward the bed.

"And so I ought!" Jessica murmured wickedly in his ear.

"She has your great green eyes, Mama—must be yours."
He tugged her tail absentmindedly. "Only thing is—you
probably never noticed this, moms always being the last to
know—but she's a spoiled-rotten brat. Could've used a
tougher hand in the discipline department—eat your liver,
feet off the furniture and all that. Or maybe that's where
the dad is s'posed to come in, to make the rug rats toe the
line?" He sighed, then strolled back to stand at the foot of
the bed. He stood there, frowning, rocking gently on his

heels. "You know, babe, you haven't asked me the most important question of all—why I happen to be here."

You know, I did forget that, what with the fire, then waking up in a fur coat. I guess I just assumed you came because I needed you. Which didn't make sense—he'd have had to have a crystal ball to know she needed him before the fire.

On the other hand, her view of the universe as an orderly, rational, scientifically predictable sequence of events had taken a rude hit this past week. Was precognition any weirder than the rest of this mess? "Okay, I'll bite. Why'd you come?"

"It was what you said down in New York, 'bout my cheating on you. What I was trying to ask you then, what I came to Providence to ask, was where the blue blazes did you get that crazy notion?" He laughed unhappily and swiped a hand up through his hair. "I was going to ask you that, if I had to chase you off the edge of the earth to ask it.

"But instead of running, you pull this—burn your house down, then fall into a coma. You're sure tryin' my patience, woman." He sat at the foot of the bed, took hold of one of her feet through the sheet and caressed it absently. "I wish you'd tried 'no comment' before you tried this."

"Sam..." Jessica braced her forepaws on the slope of his chest, so she could peer down and around into his face. "What the blue blazes are *you* talking about? That blonde in our living room? Unbuttoning her blouse? You're going to tell me you were moonlighting doing chest exams, while I commuted to med school?" She laughed bitterly, then leapt down onto the bed. "Don't lie to me. I'd take almost any truth from you, but please, please, *please* don't lie."

"Here I've always figured I knew why you left me—I didn't like it, but 'least I thought I'd figured it out—then you lay that one on me down in New York. I felt like you dropped King Kong on my head, complete with Empire State Building. I've been rackin' my brains all week, trying to figure out where the hell that could've come from..."

"Sam, the blonde?" She paced to the pillow, stared down at her own empty face, then swung around to stalk back. "You're going to tell me I was dreaming? Or that you have a twin brother I never met, who dropped by our house that night to seduce a blonde in the living room while you were off innocently tending your petri dishes?"

"Do you remember how we were having all those fights 'bout having kids, back about the time you left?"

"Of course I do. So what? You're telling me you meant to adopt her?" She stood on his leg and glared up at him.

"And do you remember that kid, Timmy Rafferty, who used to hang around my lab after school? His mom was Fullerton's lab assistant?"

Jessica closed her eyes, trying to remember. "Things were so crazy back then." She might have handled the three-hour daily commute to med school, or school itself. The two together, especially with her futile attempts to make the top grade in every course she took, had nearly overwhelmed her. And with Sam and her fighting about everything from the meaning of life to housecleaning on top of that, the whole period was a blur of misery, cumulating in that one searing, indelible memory of the blonde. "Timmy...you bought him a Frisbee for his birthday? Every time I'd drop by the lab, he'd be there doing his homework in your office. Yes, I remember him. So?"

"He was a latchkey kid. His dad had flown the coop years ago. His mom was scrambling to make ends meet, working all day, going to school nights to get her degree. Kid was bright as a whip, a real sweetheart, but any fool could see he was headed for trouble—twelve, mad with the world, startin' to run with the tough guys at school.

"And there I am, wishing we could start a family, wondering what it would be like to have kids, wondering if they were really as important as I felt in my bones they were, or if you were right and they were something we could postpone—maybe put aside altogether."

"I never said that, Sam! I never *thought* that! I just wanted—"

He pushed her off his knee. "Shut your mouth, cat, I'm talkin' to your mom. Anyway, Jess, there I was at loose ends, what with you dropping in and out of our marriage, sleeping half the week up at med school, straggling home when you could spare me a minute. There he was, needing a dad, so I guess I sort of fell into that role. Played Frisbee with him. Taught him how to toss a football. He asked me to take him to a father/son deal at his youth club, so of course I went..."

"Sam, what did his mother look like?" She could see Timmy, now that she thought about it, but his mother had always been a figure of hearsay, off in some other part of the lab, working for somebody else. "Was she blond? You started playing daddy and next thing you knew you were playing husband—is that how it happened?"

"Anyway, somehow his mom got the wrong idea. Katy was a pretty little thing, surely deserved some guy's attention, but somehow she got to thinking I was courting her by fathering her son. And I didn't have a clue what was goin' through her head. You know me, sometimes I'm a little out of it, focusing on tree DNA through a microscope while the forest closes in around me..."

"Sam..." *I'm not sure I can stand to hear this.* But there was no way out of the room, and she couldn't have taken it even if there was.

"Anyway—I can't put my finger on what night it was, but somewhere toward the end of you and me—Katy asks if she can come talk to me about a problem she's having with Timmy. And I say sure, figuring she'll ask me to give him the old birds-and-bees song and dance, or the Dutch-uncle routine—no big deal either way, I can handle it..."

"Sam, *tell* me, dammit!"

"So she drops in pretty late, after her night class..." He sighed, swiped a hand through his hair again, turning himself to a perplexed Mohawk. "Women..."

"Sure, you're going to blame it all on her? She seduced you, huh? Dragged a hundred and eighty pounds of whimpering, protesting male off to bed? I'm sorry, Sam, but I'm not buying."

"But Katy won't get to the point, say what she came for. So I go out to the kitchen, pour us some wine to loosen her up. I was tired, wanted to get this over, go to bed..."

And while Sam had been out in the kitchen, Jessica had entered the picture. She could almost see her younger self—as if she looked out through the window of her own living room to see an exhausted, bedraggled med student trudging home one night early, her arms full of books, her life as she knew it only seconds from its end... Pausing on the sidewalk when she sees movement beyond the glass...

"I come back with the wine, and there she stands, naked to the navel." He laughed and shook his head. "She's decided I want her, but I'm too shy to ask. That I've been taking the slow, roundabout route to her through Timmy. So here she is, unbuttoning her blouse, ready to help me over my imagined hurdle..."

"And so you...?" Jessica prompted. Her heart was pounding in her ears. She felt sick to her stomach.

"So I tell her she's beautiful—which she is—and that the men of the world are all fools not to notice that, and that Mr. Right must surely be waiting around the next corner. But there's nothing here tonight but an ol' married man.

"I remember I lied and claimed you were due home any minute—yeah, that's right. You were supposed to come home the next night, but you never came. That next night was the beginning of our end."

"No, Sam, our end was *that* night, *that* minute..."

"So I button her up. Give her a glass of wine. We're both embarrassed enough to die. She's about to cry, and I'm terrified she's going to. So I start talking as fast and hard as I can about Timmy and my latest experiment and whether the Red Sox are going to pull it off this season, and so on and so forth. Pretty soon after that, she gathers her wits together and roars on out of there—leaves rubber on the road, believe me."

And by then I had already driven off—was on my way, by then, back to med school, since there was no place else in my life to go. Nothing else to do... She would have thrown up if there'd been anything in her stomach to heave.

Wave after wave of sickness washed through her. *I walked out on my marriage for this?* One picture was supposedly worth a thousand words, but when you got the picture wrong?

"Anyway—" Sam shrugged "—it was just one of those wish-you-could-die-then-sink-through-the-floor kind of comedies. I put it behind me and never thought twice about it again—till this last week. But now I'm wondering...could somebody at the lab somehow have gotten the wrong idea—about Katy and me? Maybe Katy told somebody she was dropping by my house, and he or she jumped to the wrong conclusion? And somehow the rumor was passed on to you, though you hardly knew any of the people I worked with ... But if you really think I cheated on you, if that's not just something you said to put me off, was it something to do with Timmy and his mom? Because there was never anything else, I swear, babe."

"Oh, Sam..." If cats could cry, she would have cried him a river. She dropped off the bed, landed clumsily, then leapt to the windowsill.

"Hey." Sam turned to look after her. "Where are you off to?"

"I want my cave." Crying was another thing that wasn't done in public, not in her family. If she could only weep in her mind, still, she needed to hide. She needed to think—or perhaps never think again for the rest of her life, however long that might be. Sitting up on her haunches, she nudged her face between the two halves of the zipper, then jumped down into darkness.

Sam snorted. "Okay, snooty cat, be that way."

That's what I'm afraid of. That I'll be this way—forever. I'm sorry, Sam, so sorry, for not trusting you. But the only apology you may ever hear is meow. Curling herself into the tightest ball she could make, shutting out Sam's soft bedside drawl, Jessica cupped her eyes with a paw and dived downward into her self. Cattoo half awoke, purred drowsy welcome. Shutting out all but that rasping lullaby, Jessica surrendered to a troubled and restless sleep.

Sometime later she was dimly aware of being carried—the sickening swing of the bag as Sam walked, the acrid fumes of car exhaust and the rumble of engines in traffic, the garbage smell of the alley behind their mill, the dizzy swing of the bag again, then the rising drone of the elevator.

Sam unzipped the carrier in the loft. "You all right in there? You're being awfully quiet for a cat."

"Just leave me alone, Sam."

Instead, his hands smoothed around her and lifted. She struggled, but he flipped her gently, so that she lay, paws-up, cradled along his forearm like a baby. "What's the matter, babe? Are you carsick?"

"Heartsick." *I walked out on you when I could've stayed.* Oh, she knew it would've ended sooner or later, much as it had. She'd been no match for him from the start, and sooner or later he would've realized that.

But her damnable pride had cut them short. When every moment with him had been precious, her own stupid pride had cheated her of months, maybe years, of his company. At the first sign of rejection, she'd turned and walked, rather than stayed to demand an explanation.

It was funny—bitterly funny—how what was your strength became, in the end, your downfall. Pride had been her only defense in a family where pride wasn't half enough. But with Sam...

She spent her evening curled in a ball on the couch. Sam tried to tempt her with a bowl of corned-beef hash, but her stomach revolted at the first sniff. He cooked his own meal, worked on his laptop computer for a while, then wandered off to bed.

SHE STOOD at the edge of a cliff, wind whipping her hair. Tearing at the ring on her finger, she wrenched it free—it broke into three links as it left her paw. She hurled it from her, gold dropping into blackness—and her heart fell with it. That ring was all she'd ever wanted. All she'd ever need in life. She leaned, snatched after it—and fell. *"Yeeeeeeow!"*

Heart hammering, throat aching, she jolted awake, her scream still echoing in her ears. Had she screamed aloud or only dreamed it?

And if a cat screams in the night and nobody hears, was there ever really a noise at all?

Her tail flicked skittishly into view—puffed gigantic.

Well, you heard it, didn't you? She half fell off the couch and shuffled off to the bathroom.

Jessica had just flushed the toilet and jumped down from its seat when she heard a shambling step out in the hallway. *Oops.* She shot past Sam's legs while he groped for the light switch, then swung back to watch from the door.

Light flooded the room—her pupils contracted to slits. The last of the water swirled down the drain.

"What the..." Sam approached the fixture as if a snake might rear from its depths any moment. "How..." He leaned against the wall and stared, fascinated. "Did that thing flush itself, or am I still dreamin'?"

"You were dreaming, too?" Jessica joined him, pressing her shoulder to his bare shin.

"Wha—!" He jumped, bounced off the wall, then swung to glare. "You pussyfootin' sneak!"

"What were *you* dreaming about?" She licked his calf, savoring the taste of salt—and a deeper, muskier flavor that was all his own. He tasted . . . right.

"Weirdest dream. Jess and me, think we were parachuting. At night. She was fallin', I was tryin' to catch her before she hit the ground. She screamed—" he shuddered "—like a cat..." He hooked a bare foot under her stomach and half lifted her off the tiles. "Did you yell, furball?"

"I did, but there's no way you could've heard me, all the way down the hall with your door closed." They were in tune, speaking the same language in dreams, her cat to his sleepy Texan.

He nudged her with his foot. "Go on, get out of here. Give a man some privacy."

She sauntered off, tail disdainful, but couldn't resist stopping to look over her shoulder. Her whiskers lifted, then quivered. "And you think cats are funny, big guy!"

"Hussy, quit peekin'." He flushed, watched intently, shook his head. "Guess I better check this thing out in the morning."

"Oh, no, Sam, don't you dare!" She followed him to the sink and stood on his feet. "We're already out a chair. You tear the toilet apart and we'll both end up using the cat box. I mean that!"

"Meow-meow, meeyaw-*mew,* nag-nag," he mimicked, missing every nuance and change of tone, though he got the drift. He hit the light switch, and shuffled back down the hall. "Catch ya in the morning, cat."

But she'd already squeezed through the widening gap in his door ahead of him. Crouched under his four-poster, she waited while the mattress creaked, then rebounded above her, waited till his breathing slowed and deepened. Then, with all the grace and weight of a shadow, she leapt onto his bed.

Somewhere beyond the hulking shoulders of RI Gen, the moon was shining. Its reflected glow lent enough light for cat eyes to see.

Sam lay on his back, one arm thrown over head. As always, sleep softened his angles, gentled the force of his quirky character. He looked not a year older than the last time she'd lain awake watching him sleep. *Oh, Sam . . .*

She crept closer on cat feet. *Sam, I know sometimes you hear me best when you aren't listening, so hear me now . . . I'm sorry, so sorry, I didn't trust you, love.* Her mouth hovered a hairbreadth from his skin. If she kissed him, he'd wake and surely throw her out. Instead, she breathed out a kiss . . . breathed in, tasting his skin. *Oh, yes, I remember this, kissing you awake when I couldn't sleep.*

He smiled, stretched luxuriously, growled a wordless, sleeping welcome.

WAS IT THE PAST she was seeing, the future, or only a wistful dream, and did it even matter?

Her leg slid across his body, so that she knelt astride, no more weight than a shadow. *Oh, love...*

Her fingers spread, spanned his rib cage, rode warm velvet skin, crisp curling hair, the hard swell of his chest, till they cupped the width of his shoulders. Her lips sought the pulse at his throat and moved, one kiss per beat...kiss, pulse, kiss, pulse...her kisses quickening as his blood surged.

Her hands slid slowly outward along his arms, molding themselves to curve of muscle, angle of bone, corded sinew, till they found his waiting fingers.

Fingers twined, held. Her breasts flattened to his. Mouths fused in liquid, groaning wonder.

Silken slide of skin across sheet, hair across cheek. His lips at her breast, her cry that sounded like pain and was not.

Heart calling to heart, *Come closer.*

Wet silk sliding. Softness mating to hardness, aching emptiness to shaped desire—fusion. And then...*fire.*

Heart pressed to heart. Incredulous, breathless laughter. *Oh, yes, I remember...*

Then sleep...sleep...rocking horse hearts rocking off to sleep. Moon walking her way across the sky...

And no thoughts for the dawn.

SHE AWOKE TO THE SCENT of his skin, the safe cave of his arms, the slow distant throb of his heart. Awoke, smiling. Jessica opened her eyes to the tan, bristly curve of his throat, arching like a roof overhead. She lay on her back, cuddled tight in his arms. *Love.* She licked him—and froze. Her tongue was too pink, too long, too exquisitely curled. Not her own. *Not human.* "Noooooo!"

"Uh!" Sam bolted upright, his breath stuttering, his eyes staring wildly around the room, then down to her. "Aaagh! How did you— Where did she—" His eyes swept the room and returned, widening in horror. "Omigod."

"I was a woman last night," she wailed. "I *was.* Don't look at me like that!"

"I didn't— You didn't—" He swiped a hand up through his hair, shook his head as if he could shake the thought out. "Brrrrrrrr!"

"Oh, stop it, that was *me,* last night." Or was it a dream?

"*What* a dream." Sam shuddered. Then he scooped a hand under her stomach and dumped her off the bed. "How the hell did you get in here?"

"Ouch!" From heaven to the cold, cold floor in less than a minute. Tears gathered, found no outlet. Mortification slid rapidly downhill toward icy rage—her tail was there already, slashing the air behind her.

"It *was* a dream, wasn't it?" Sam swung his legs off the bed and sat, shaking his head. "Cats. I don't even *like* cats."

"*Oooooh!*" Spinning around, she nailed his shin with a right, then a left, not caring at all if her claws were sheathed or not.

"Hey!" He swung his legs up out of reach. "What's with you, devil cat?"

"Your morning-after manners are...are *despicable,* she hissed, backing away from him. "If that's being human, I'd as soon stay a cat!" Tail in high dudgeon, chin haughty, she walked from the room.

She cut him dead for the next hour, turning her back on all overtures, until he entered the living room, ready to leave for the hospital. He walked straight to the carrier, opened it, then turning, whistled and patted the side of the bag. "Come on, Jez, let's go. Come on, girl."

Eyes narrowed, she glanced over her shoulder. "I beg your pardon?" She looked the other way. "Is there a *dog* in the room, or just an ignorant Texan?"

"Move it. She blinked for you yesterday. From now on, you're part of the wake-up team."

"And if I don't care to go?" Though of course, she wanted to.

Sam scooped her up and, ignoring her snarls, stuffed her into the bag.

THEIR VISIT STARTED precisely as it had the day before. N
change in the patient overnight. No change in the attitud
of the nurses, who still treated her body like an oversiz
porcelain doll, inanimate, unfeeling, rather expensive. N
change in her own spirit's stubborn immobility. She sat b
her motionless body and even licked her pale face, but he
body never blinked. Perhaps Sam had imagined that.

All that had changed was their hopes. Each of them wa
noticeably bluer today, though Sam continued his non
stop, lighthearted babble. But now it held the faintest edg
of desperation. *You can't keep this up,* Jessica though
watching him from where she lay curled in the cozy angl
between her own arm and side. *You'll run out of patienc
and ideas and even time.* He was director of one of the mos
famous research labs in the country. Such an institutio
couldn't run itself for long. And then what, oh God, the
what?

No one here to fight for her, or to care. And she an
Cattoo, what would be their fate? Fobbed off on som
nurse? Or dropped at the pound on his way out of town?

"You're looking pretty glum, fur-ball." Sam slid a han
under her and hauled her into his lap. "I guess cats do hav
their uses," he admitted, directing his words over her hea
while he rubbed her back. "Furry water bottles on co
nights. Sounding boards, when you're working out a lir
of thought. Good place to stow your leftovers..." Liftir
her, he turned her and held her against his chest with or
arm while he stroked her with the other. He stared dow
into her eyes. "Something warm to hang on to, when you'
lonesome or scared half to death..." His arm tightened.

Oh, Sam. Her claws hooked delicately into his shir
*Don't leave me. Don't ever leave me again. I'll be there f
you if you'll be there for me.*

His eyes widened. His heart lurched, then gather
speed. *You hear me,* she realized. *You know this is m
don't you? Don't you?*

"Jess!" he cried hoarsely, and shook his head. "Som
times I think I'm goin' crazy."

You're not! You're just seeing me, that's all. That's everything!

They both jumped at the knock on their door. Jessica squeaked as Sam plucked her off his shirt, whipped across the room and practically slam-dunked her into her carrier. The zipper snicked overhead. "Come in," he called as he turned.

"Good *morning*, Sam," purred a gay, familiar voice.

Jessica jammed her eye to an air hole. *That voice.* It couldn't be.

But it was. Raye Talbot leaned back against the door, closing it with a slow back thrust of her hip. "Sorry I couldn't stop by yesterday." Her smile was intimate, brilliant. "But I thought about you." Her sparkling, black-eyed gaze stayed fixed on Sam even as she asked, "How's our patient doing today? Any change?"

CHAPTER FIFTEEN

"NOPE, SHE'S STILL takin' it easy," Sam drawled. "Doctor's week off." He stayed on his feet while Raye circled the bed, high heels ticking slowly.

My God, she's been here before! Jessica realized as the psychiatrist chose the chair beside the bed with no hesitation while Sam sat again on the edge of the mattress. Every hair in her pelt stood rigid as a needle piercing her flesh— her goose bumps ached right down to her toenails. A growl moaned silently within. She clenched her teeth to keep it back.

"And you, Sam?" Raye asked with a sympathy ever so slightly too soft to be professional. "How are you holding up?"

"Oh, fine and dandy." Sam's brows twitched under Raye's warm, unblinking gaze, then he looked back to Jessica's body. "I've been talking her head off, but so far she's putting up with me."

"And so she should, lucky girl." Raye reached to lay a hand on Jessica's arm. "Jessica? It's Raye, kiddo. How are you doing?"

I'll tell you how I'm doing. I'm standing here in a cat coat contemplating scratching your eyes out, that's how I'm doing! Jessica drove her claws into the flooring of her barn and shivered with horror. The smell of cinnamon and musk was so strong she could almost gag on it. *What do you want, Raye? Haven't you taken enough from me?*

But that was an easy question to answer. Raye was still following her one rule in life—*Never let anyone get in your way.* Having failed to kill Jessica outright, the shrink wanted to make certain a comatose Jessica was no threat to her interests—and would stay that way.

Jessica glanced overhead. The zipper on the carrier was an old one, softened with wear and age. She might be able to hook a claw in it, yank it open. Raye hated and feared cats, after all. If Jessica leapt out and flew at her, she could drive her right out of this room.

Shuddering, she closed her eyes. *And then, Jessica?* Raye was nobody's wuss. Raye was an attending doctor of RI Gen. Once she'd recovered from her fright, she'd gently— oh, with the greatest empathy—insist Sam leave his cat at home. This was a hospital, after all, requiring the most sterile environment. *Go for her, and you'll be bounced out of here so fast it'll make your whiskers frizzle. And you'll never come back again.*

No, she couldn't risk ejection, then exile. Not when she was the only one who knew to keep an eye on Raye. *Keep a lid on it, Jess. Oh, keep a lid on it.* Her body was humming with its unvoiced growl—it was Cattoo adding her voice to her own, Jessica realized, shivering with redoubled loathing. *Down, girl. We can't afford to. Not now. Not yet.*

"You know that dress I tried on—the other night when we went shopping at Emerald Mall?" Raye squeezed Jessica's arm. "The red silk one, cut down to here? Well, I decided you were right, that it was a dress in a lifetime. I took out a second mortgage, then went back and bought it. I'll sneak it in and model it for you tomorrow."

As if I would've been caught dead shopping with you! Or something as unsubtle as a red silk, cut to the equator? Jessica's tail lashed the inside of the bag. But there was no way for Sam to know, was there, that they hadn't been the best of friends? It would seem plausible, two women doctors in a world mainly male, their offices located right across the hall from each other. There'd be no apparent reason for the psychiatrist to lie about the relationship.

Still touching Jessica, Raye switched her attention to Sam. "Did you find that little café I recommended? The Jamaican?"

He nodded. "You were right. It was the real thing. Blowtorch jerk chicken, cane rum, authentic cockroaches skittering across the floor. The aroma of authentic Jamaican postprandial cigars driftin' out from the back room."

Raye laughed deep in her throat and nodded, eyes shining. "Well, if you liked that place, I'd feel safe recommending this little Thai place I know. It's only for the stout of heart and the cast-iron stomach, but—"

Sam laughed. "Say no more, sounds like my kind of place. You like Thai, too, huh?"

Oh, God. Jessica had thought her heart was beating at its maximum load, but now it shifted into overdrive. *Oh God—she's coming on to him like a Mack truck!* And with her damnable, unerring instinct for people's weaknesses, Raye had already found a point of connection.

"The problem is," Raye was saying, "I've only been there once or twice. It's in a part of town where a woman only goes with a...man." She looked down, as if suddenly embarrassed, then looked up with her ironic, self-mocking smile. "So I don't remember the street names well enough to draw you a map. I'd just have to show you some night..."

"Sure, we'll do that." Sam glanced down at Jessica, then took her limp hand. "I was telling you the other day, Jess, down in New York, 'bout *pad thai*, remember? I'll bring some back for you. Hospital chow isn't fit for cats." His eyes flicked to the carrier and he reddened.

Thanks ever so much, Sam. His drawl was growing more noticeable, a sign that he enjoyed Raye's attention, in spite of the fact that he was still focused on Jessica's body. But then, why should he not? Raye might not be a blonde, and she wasn't quite beautiful, but whatever she had, it was that quality that made happily married men falter, then turn to glance over their shoulders when they passed it on the street. Raye looked dangerous, and available, if only you were man enough—like a parked Ferrari, with its door ajar and its key in the ignition. *Take me if you dare.*

And Sam wasn't even a married man. *Oh, God, haven't you taken enough from me already?*

But Raye wouldn't see it that way. To a sociopath, people's transcripts, their fortunes, their loves, their very lives, were there for the taking. Jessica closed her eyes. *Stop.* She breathed deeply—once, twice, a shivering third time. *Don't panic. Use your brains, Jessica, that's what they're there for. First, what does she want? My life?*

She put her eye to the breathing hole and peered out. Raye still sat, red-nailed fingertips curled round Jessica's arm—sorrowful best friend. Swallowing her revulsion, Jessica thought. *Raye came up here the first time, because she was afraid I might recover, then talk.*

But once she'd seen me, if she'd thought I was a danger, I'd be dead by now. Because Raye could move around the hospital day or night with no one lifting an eyebrow. A back stairwell gave the staff access to every floor. Raye could have slipped up the back stairs the first night after visiting hours with a syringe full of insulin, or a barbiturate, or—Jessica shuddered—perhaps succinylcholine, used to paralyze the skeletal muscles during surgery? A drug to make the patient stop breathing on his own. A drug that metabolized rapidly—hours later, it was undetectable in the body.

Besides, if a comatose patient stopped breathing in her sleep, no one would be thinking murder, looking for lethal drugs at her autopsy—if her parents even permitted an autopsy. And that wasn't likely. Her mother would want her presentable for the funeral.

Her breath was accelerating again. She caught it and exhaled. *Okay, okay, I get the picture. But I'm not dead yet, so Raye must've decided I wasn't any danger.* She grimaced. Only too true, so far. *So why's Raye here today— to check on me?*

Raye could do that by phone—the head nurse would be happy to report her condition. *So*—she put her eye back to the breathing hole—*she's here for Sam. Why?*

That didn't take a rocket scientist to figure out, she thought grimly, studying Sam's profile. If Raye had it for a woman, whatever "it" was, Sam had it in spades for a man. Any woman would get a case of the hot fidgets, looking at his dear, rugged face. And once he started drawling...

I can't stand it. I won't! It was one thing to think of Sam involved with some faceless woman—perhaps another scientist at his lab. Much as it pained her to imagine such a relationship, it would hold only pleasure for Sam. And pleasure was what she wished for him. To be cherished by a wise and wonderful woman was what he deserved. But if Raye somehow slithered into his life...! *And she wouldn't stop with just his body,* Jessica realized, *or even his soul.*

Sam held patents to synthesized genes, biochemical processes. His salary at the research lab probably equaled or surpassed her father's yearly earnings as a top surgeon. There'd been that book of his a couple of years back that had crossed the line between professional obscurity and lucid, even fascinating science for the layman. Sam's bank account had to be as alluring as the man himself. To a wolf like Raye Talbot, Sam must look like a six-foot sheep for the shearing. Fun in the sack, then fun in the sacking. How could she resist, and whyever would she?

Her whiskers stood straight out, feeling for danger, zapping electric shocks to her brain each time they brushed a surface. *I won't permit this. I will not. It's bad enough she wrecked my life with no more qualms than if she'd stepped on a june bug, but this—hurting Sam—this I will not permit. No way. This is war, Raye Talbot, all-out war. If it takes my last breath, I'll stop you.*

But how? For the rest of the morning, long after Raye had touched Sam's cheek, then departed in response to her pager's beep, Jessica sat there, wondering how.

The simplest way was to warn Sam. He was more than a match for Raye, if only he realized she was dangerous. *have to warn him.*

No simple task that. From her position, draped on the pillow alongside her own body's head, she glanced aside to where he now slouched in the visitor's chair. Apparently he'd forgotten they'd been poised for a breakthrough when Raye interrupted. Or he'd put the moment out of mind. Denial—simple, effective, almost impossible to crack. "You knew it was me, here in the cat, for a minute there. I swear you did."

"Puss-puss?" Sam reached absently to scratch her ears, but his eyes stayed fixed on his laptop screen. "We'll take a coffee break in two shakes, Jez. Just let me finish my e-mail." Frowning, he reread a message, then fired off a key-rattling response. "It's like herding cats, Jess," he growled. "You turn your back for two minutes, and they're wandering off every which way, or having spats, or getting into the catnip. And the better they are, I swear the worse they are. Heinemann here's about to blow the doors off Tanaka's theory on the nef gene's function. What does he do last night? Gets himself arrested for riding his mountain bike through a hotel lobby full of Daughters of the American Revolution buck naked—him, I mean, excepting his helmet. Nigel says they'd have never caught him, except he tried to do a turn around the fountain, no hands, and some ol' blue hair nailed him with her purse."

"They're like your family, aren't they?" she asked softly, but his grin had faded. She leaned past his elbow to read his next message.

You haven't forgotten that you testify before the Senate week of the 8th? his secretary Liza had written. Re continued funding for the Genome Project. Don't even think about wriggling out of that one, Slick—too many people are counting on that ol' Texas charm.

"That ol' Texas charm is wearin' pretty ragged," Sam growled. He typed, "Nope," signed it and signed off, then slapped the lid down on his Powerbook.

The latch's tiny, emphatic snick might as well have been the door of a safe clanging shut. She had no way to open it.

Sam stood, drew the tape player from his valise, and punched a button. Jobim's heart-tugging, liquid guitar purled out into the room. Sam set the player on the pillow. "We'll be back in twenty minutes or so, Jess. Can I get you something? Ice-cream soda? Harley-Davidson Softtail? The Taj Mahal?'' Kissing his fingertip, he touched it to her mouth, butterfly-brushed the rise and fall of her upper lip from corner to corner, then watched intently.

There was not a tremble of eyelid, nor quiver of lip in response. He sighed. ''Back in a flash, babe. If you wake up, wait for me, hear?''

Out on the lawn, not far from the spot where she'd tried to construct her ''help'' message days before, Sam unzipped her carrier. ''I take it you know on which side your bread's buttered?'' he drawled as she hopped from the bag. ''No running off, okay?''

''Wouldn't think of it. Not while you can't be let loose without a keeper—I can't *believe* you let Raye touch you like that back there. If you knew what she'd done...'' She wandered between some nearby bushes and Sam's legs, thinking as she walked. ''But how could you, if I don't tell you? Sticks didn't get the message across. Pencil's useless. ESP gets me nowhere, you rock-headed Texan. No, I've got to get into your laptop, but how?''

Sam pulled the lid off the foam cup of coffee he'd purchased on their way out, took a swallow and grimaced. ''Lord, I hate hospitals, and everything about 'em! How can they cure people if they can't even make coffee?'' He set the container down in the grass.

''It's drinkable, if you think of it as caffeine, not coffee.'' Jess wandered back and stropped herself against his shins, still thinking. *If I had a chisel, I could open that latch.* Of course, if she could use a chisel, she could simply open the blasted laptop. If she could use a chisel, she wouldn't need Sam's computer to type him a message.

Sam turned to follow the course of a motorcycle rippling up the hill past the hospital. Jessica circled his legs and found herself face-to-face with his coffee cup. *Ah.* She took a sniff, grimaced—it smelled much worse than usual.

Still, she could use a jolt. She tucked in and sucked down, lapping greedily. *This is awful!* Cattoo awoke and agreed wholeheartedly. Jessica lapped faster. She'd hardly slept last night at all—or if that had all been a dream, then her subconscious hadn't slept. Either way, she walked the ragged edge of exhaustion today—too unnerved by Raye's appearance to collapse, so tired that everything had the hard-edged brightness of a fever dream. But every doctor learns the cure for that condition his first night on call— coffee, if you could call this that.

"Hey, you little beggar!" Sam nudged her with his foot. "Out of there. That can't be good for you."

"I could say the same about Raye Talbot, but do you listen?" She got in a few last licks.

Hoisting her out of the cup, he held her aloft, their noses almost touching. "I said *quit.*"

"Were you always this domineering? Or do you only bully cats?" She reached to touch his cheek with a velvet paw as Cattoo sometimes did with her. "Never mind, I don't care. Sam, about last night..."

He blinked, the pupils of his eyes expanding with shock. "Sam?" *You see me, Sam.*

His chin jerked in half-formed denial. "I'm going stark, ravin'—"

She let out a startled squeak as he swooped her down— then stuffed her into the bowling-ball bag. "Hey!" He yanked the zipper shut between her ears. "You're a *coward,* Sam Kirby, that's what you are! You can't face up to the evidence of your own senses! I'm Jessica, your wife—I mean your ex-whatever, and you damn well know it! Admit it and you'd save us both a truckload of heartache."

"Me*ow,*" he mimicked, carrying her across the grass. "Mew, mew, mew-Me*oww!* You plannin' to shut up, so we can go inside, or do I have to take you home?"

"No, you don't." She clenched her teeth. *I have work to do, pal.* And with a human-size dose of caffeine roaring through her veins, it was all coming crystal clear. She needed a computer to type out her warning, but who said it had to be Sam's?

Her opportunity didn't come for several hours. Jessica prowled the room, submitting to Sam's dropping her on the bed every so often—by his lights, she had a job to do, rousing her body. But she couldn't sit still. The room felt like a trap, with danger prowling ever closer—Raye Talbot, eyes agleam, teeth bared. Jessica's heart slammed out a textbook example of tachycardia, and her coat roughened along her spine. *Too much coffee, but do I care? Let me out of here.*

She was pacing the wide windowsill, staring out at their own mill building beyond the highway, tail lashing, when the knock came on the door. Sam jumped off the bed and reached for her—she leapt down to the floor.

"C'mere!" he hissed, spinning and grabbing at her tail.

She slipped through his fingers and ducked under the bed.

"Son of a blue-nosed baboon!" he whispered as a nurse pushed a cart into the room. He bent to inspect his shoelace.

"Hellooo," she caroled, "and how are we today?"

"We've been better." Sam's eyes flicked to below the bed, where Jessica stared back at him, owl-eyed. He showed his teeth, then stood.

Jessica turned the other way. Beyond the bed's sheltering darkness, the wheeled cart gleamed in the fluorescents. *Might do.* Its lower shelf was a bit lower than she'd like, but how many carts had come along today?

Sam subsided to the windowsill, where he sat, his whistle elaborately casual, the one foot Jessica could see jiggling in triple time. No doubt he expected her to saunter out from under the bed at any moment, say something inane, like "Meow," then perhaps strop the nurse's shins for good measure. The image was tempting—who would be more dismayed, Sam or the nurse? But this was the caffeine talking, making her reckless. *Nope, get to work, girl.*

When the nurse drew blood from her body's arm nearest the window, Jessica slipped under the cart. She lurked there, jittering silently while the series of samples were collected. This was the last room on the ward, the one closest to the back stairwell, she'd noted on their coffee break. In general that was bad—it would be easy for Raye to reach her body unseen. But for now this worked in her favor. She was probably the last patient the nurse needed to sample on this floor. At least she hoped to high heaven she was.

"There—that'll do for now," the woman chirped. "Sorry to bother you." She pushed the cart toward the door.

"No problem." Sam hurried to open it for her. "And thank you, ma'am."

As the cart rolled away, Jessica skulked beneath, legs bent, ears brushing the underside of the shelf. *And just where precisely is my tail?* Let the tip hang out the back, and her cover was blown. She hunched forward a few inches, to keep her nose level with the front wheels.

The cart picked up speed, the nurse's feet tramping steadily behind, and Jessica scuttled faster. This wasn't half as easy as she'd pictured!

Back in her room, Sam would've checked under the bed by now. He'd search the corners, under the sink, the chair. He'd check the tiny bathroom, since that door had been left ajar. Then he'd conclude she'd dodged past him somehow, that she must be hiding in her carrier. But once he'd searched that . . .

Just as the cart reached the nurses' station, the door to her room cracked open. Jessica didn't dare look back. He'd be peering out into the hall, swearing, still confident she hadn't gone far.

The nurse brought the cart to a halt by the elevator. She punched the button, then turned toward the desk. "Now *that's* what I call a hunk—in room 909? Eleven on a scale of ten. The husband, I mean, not the sleeper."

"Ex-husband," corrected an unseen woman. "Or so I hear. Can you believe? He's absolutely glued to her bedside. Pigs'd fly before *my* ex would—"

"Shh! Here he comes!" hissed another voice.

"Howdy, ladies," Sam said too heartily. "Beautiful day . . . still."

Jessica looked over her shoulder to see his size twelves halt a few feet away. They turned as he looked down the intersecting corridor that led to more rooms.

"Just stretching my legs," he explained, though no one had asked. He strolled across to the waiting room beyond the elevator.

It would take him perhaps a minute to check under all the couches. *Come on,* she silently urged the elevator. *Come on!*

The doors opened just as Sam returned, and Jessica choked off a groan. Within the elevator, a forest of legs rose beyond her field of vision—the car was packed. They'd have to wait for the next one.

Or maybe not. "If you'd just squeeze back there a *tiny* bit," the nurse coaxed, steely determination underlying the sweetness.

Sam's feet moved closer. "Here, ma'am, I've got the door."

As the cart was eased into their midst, the passengers' feet shuffled grudgingly backward. Skin tingling with apprehension, Jessica skulked aboard. Once the cart was wedged in place, she turned cautiously around to face the door. A few feet from her face, the nurse moved to one side of her cart and also rotated. "Thank you, Mr. Kirby."

Shut the door. Let's get out of here! Jessica glared at his feet. Give him a moment's peace to focus, and he'd pick up her thoughts, guess where she was. For better or worse, they were attuned.

The doors rolled together with all the deliberation of a glacier sliding south. Jessica watched his toes. He hadn't realized—wouldn't for a minute more. She'd done it!

The nurse shoved the cart back four inches, and suddenly Jessica found herself staring directly up into Sam's widening eyes.

His lips parted. His hand jerked up—the doors closed, and the elevator dropped.

Made it! Inching backward into darkness, Jessica let out a gasp of relief. But what now? She'd originally planned to accompany the cart down to the pathology lab in the basement. At that level, there wasn't much foot traffic. It would have been easy to reach the back stairs, climb them to the third floor; then reach her office in the professional building via the passage that connected it to the hospital.

But now, with Sam in hot pursuit? He'd ask the nurses on her ward where the cart was headed, then catch the next elevator. *Darn you, Sam. You're supposed to be helping me, not making this harder!*

Several floors down, the elevator stopped to let two pairs of tennis shoes and a pair of scuffed Top-Siders depart. From Jessica's angle, she couldn't tell which ward this was, but it was a busy one. *No go.*

The doors shut, and she danced impatiently. *C'mon, c'mon.* She could imagine Sam, floors above, also jittering as he waited for the elevator's return. Or what if he decided not to wait, decided, instead, to run down the stairs to the basement? Visitors weren't allowed to use the stairwell, but there wasn't the woman alive, from nine to ninety, whom Sam couldn't sweet-talk his way past. If he took the stairs, Jessica might dash straight into his arms. *Blast!*

But what other choice had she? The basement was a sure loser—it was the one level he'd be bound to check. The elevator stopped again. On this floor, Jessica could see three pairs of feet, all of them clustered around the nurses' station. A pair of Italian pumps stepped off the elevator to aim their toes at the desk, as well. The gap between the doors narrowed, steel plates about to clash—Jessica shot from under the cart.

Behind her she heard a squawk of surprise, cut off as the doors met. Looking neither right nor left, Jessica streaked down the hall, her ears tipped backward, tail following straight as an arrow.

But she heard no cries of surprise in her wake. *Good, good, good.* It was amazing what people missed down at floor level.

Ahead of her, a door to a room creaked as it opened. Jessica dodged under a gurney that stood along the wall and crouched there, panting, while feet clad in white tennis shoes marched past, headed back to the nurses' station. She gave them thirty seconds while she caught her breath, then she sprinted again for the door at the end of the corridor.

She reached the stairwell door with no further adventures—to find it, as always, closed. *What I'd give for a pair of hands!* Taking cover in the deep embrasure of the nearest window, she waited, ears swiveling, heart pounding, one side of her plastered to the glass. *Come on!* The house staff used the stairwell almost constantly; someone was bound to come along.

Her ears pricked as a hand turned the doorknob from the other side. She leapt down to crouch by the doorjamb, a runner bouncing on her racing chocks. The door opened six inches, then paused.

Out in the stairwell, she heard the reverberation of footsteps, then a familiar voice, garbled by echoes.

"A black cat?" asked whoever stood directly beyond the door. "Uh, no. Sorry."

The door swung open and an intern stepped forth, chuckling to himself and shaking his head. When his eyes lit on Jessica, his chuckling stopped. "Hey!"

She shot past his legs out into the stairwell, then paused, legs braced.

Floors below, she could hear Sam's footsteps pounding toward the basement. She chose the stairs leading up just as the door opened behind her. "Hey, cat, come back here! Kitty, kitty?"

Ha! She skittered across the landing above, then halted just out of sight. Far below, a good two floors down, she estimated, she could still hear Sam's footfalls. He was traveling fast.

"Hey, mister?" called the intern, leaning over the stair rail.

The sound of women's laughter floated up, drowning out his voice.

"Mister!" The young man listened a moment, then muttered under his breath, "Whatever." The door closed behind him.

Jessica let out her breath. *Good.* That was her ace in the hole. No one who worked in a hospital ever had enough time. They might be amused by Sam's plight, but they wouldn't go out of their way to help him. She turned and padded downward, noting the floor numbers painted on the wall. She was now on floor seven. Four to go.

Hours later, Jessica crouched in the third-floor corridor of the professional building. A door opened and she peered around the corner, her nose only inches off the floor. A woman exited from Jessica's own office, closed the door, then set off in the other direction, toward the walkway that passed over the street and into RI Gen. *Wait a minute,* she thought, watching the woman go. That was Mrs. Cavazos, one of her patients; she had a mysterious, recurrent case of heartburn, which wasn't reflux, wasn't an ulcer. She'd had an exam scheduled for... today, Jessica realized, and grimaced. *Time sure flies, when...* Mac or one of her other partners must have worked Mrs. Cavazos in somehow. She sighed. Truth be known, she didn't miss her practice at all, but oh, at the moment, she'd like to be a doctor—cool, collected, always knowing the answer, or at least pretending to. *Walking upright. With my own office and my own computer. And my own two hands to type with.*

She'd hoped to slip into her office, the one place she was guaranteed both a computer and the privacy to use it. Unlike Sam's folding laptop, her full-size computer's keyboard would be accessible. All she'd have to do was drag off the dustcover, push the toggle on the back of her PC, and she could start typing. She didn't even have to worry about using unfamiliar software, an issue to be considered, if she stole time on any computer but her own.

Once she'd typed out her message to Sam, she'd print it. Folding it to cat-carrying size might prove a problem, but surely not an insurmountable one.

Meanwhile, the first issue was how to reach her office. She'd made it as far as the patients' waiting room twice—on the heels of incoming patients—only to be spotted by Caroline, and firmly ejected. Luckily Caroline was too busy minding the switchboard to do more than pitch her out into the hall with a pat and an admonition to go home, silly cat.

If only Mac would come out our back door. He always seemed to hover in the doorway with half-a-dozen last-minute instructions for Caroline or the nurses. By now it was close to quitting time. He should be leaving any minute, if he hadn't ducked out already for a very cold round of golf. Let him pause in the doorway, and she'd slip past him if it killed her.

A door clicked, and she again edged her nose around the corner. This time the door to Raye Talbot's office was opening.

Yikes. The hair on her spine lifted, her tail bristled. She'd been wondering all afternoon what she'd do, faced with Raye. It was one thing to swear to bring the woman down, quite another to confront her.

Raye's bleached-blond receptionist, twenty if she was a day, teetered into view on her too-high heels—imitations of Raye's, Jessica realized. But without the psychiatrist's lethal grace, the effect was almost laughable. What was her name—oh, yeah, Tiffany—hoisted the strap of her over-stuffed purse to her shoulder and hiked determinedly toward Jessica's corner.

Jessica dropped to her belly and lay along the wall, her eyes closed to slits. The carpet was dark gray, the baseboard black. With any luck—

"Well, hi, kittycat, what are you doing up here?" Tiffany loomed above her. "Is catterkins all *right?*"

Catterkins would like very much to be left alone. Teeth gritted, Jessica submitted patiently to a pat. Ignore her and perhaps she'd go away.

"Poor pussy-wuss, is um *lost*, puss?"

Existentially, yes, physically, no. And thank you very much for your concern. Now buzz off, Tiffany.

Instead, Tiffany scooped her up and hugged her till her ribs creaked. "*Poor* puss. Why don't we go find Lost and Found, and see if some nice person is looking for you?" She turned back toward the hospital.

"*Put me down!*" Jessica hissed, glaring up into Tiffany's eyes. A throaty little moan wove out of her throat, then she hissed again. "*Right...now.*"

"Oops." Tiffany deposited her carefully on the carpet, then backed away. "Gee. Sorry about that."

Jessica shook her ruffled coat out, then glowered after Tiffany while the receptionist hesitated, then tottered off down the corridor toward the elevators. She punched the summons button and almost immediately the doors opened. Stepping aboard, Tiffany looked back, giggled, and waggled her fingers. "Bye, grouchy cat."

Jessica sniffed, then swung around as a step sounded from the cross-street walkway. A male step. Sam?

She eased her nose around the corner and blinked. Jon Cooper. An apparition from another life. She was ashamed to admit it, but the resident's existence had dropped right out of her mind this past week. Even from this distance she could see the slump of his shoulders, the raccoon rings under his eyes. *Coming to visit me in my office?* No, he'd have heard where she was, like everyone else.

The young man paused outside *Raye's* office, hand on the doorknob, and it hit Jessica like a blow to the stomach. Yes, the supply closet, Jon exploding out of it last week, then Raye sauntering out behind with a self-satisfied smirk. *Oh, God, and I'm the one who suggested he see her in the first place! That kid loved his wife, was afraid of losing her, and I sent him to Raye.* Raye, who had bragged that one of the symptoms of sociopathy was forcing others into unwanted sexual liaisons.

It's all my fault.

Jon opened the door perhaps an inch, then froze, his head drooping, his other hand flattened against the door panel as if left hand fought with right.

The absolute misery on his face was her fault, something else she'd have to rectify. Or else answer for.

The resident sighed and his left hand fell away. He opened the door wider, but still couldn't seem to find the will to pass through.

Don't do it! Jessica thought, pattering silently toward him. *Don't!* And then it hit her. Beyond that door, in the receptionist's office, was a computer. She'd seen it herself only a week ago.

The door was closing behind him, dragged by his lax hand. She skidded around its swinging edge, slipped behind his heels, then under a couch—just as the door to the inner rooms opened.

From her cover, Jessica could see a pair of slender ankles, polished black heels. A familiar voice purred, ''You took your sweet time, sweet cakes.''

Jon Cooper said nothing.

The black heels rotated in a single graceful turn, then departed in long, measured strides toward Raye's private office.

Blue you could drown in, Jessica remembered, her hair standing on end. *And a leather couch.*

Jon stood there, unmoving. Then, slowly, he let out his breath, and trudged after.

Jessica padded out from under the couch to watch him disappear down the darkened hall. *Don't go.* But if she tried to stop him, there was no retreat from this room until someone let her out the door.

Her eyes shifted to the glass panel that divided the receptionist's office from the waiting room. Tiffany hadn't closed it all the way. Between the wall and the slider there remained a gap, a passage just wide enough for a vengeful cat.

CHAPTER SIXTEEN

BUT FIRST SHE'D BETTER make sure she'd not be interrupted. Steeling herself, Jessica padded down the darkened hall. The door to Raye's office was closed. Jessica put
her nose to the gap, then winced—musk and cinnamon.
Raye's perfume—what had she called it—Adventuress?
Figures. In the original sense of that word, an adventuress
was a woman with no visible means of support, out for all
she could seize from the world.

"I'm thinking of killing myself," Jon Cooper said
abruptly beyond the door.

Raye's voice held a low amusement. "You could do
that."

"If I do that, bitch, I'll take you with me." He spoke
quickly, with an effort, as if he'd memorized the words long
ago and now could barely recall them.

"*That,* you might find a bit harder." There was a rustle
of clothing, then her voice, a laughing groan. "Speaking of
hard . . . Jon, Jon, Jon, what's not to like here? You love it
when I do this—"

His gasp was a single, extended hiss, an escape of scalding steam—perhaps scalding shame?

"And this—"

"I hate it!" His voice cracked like a boy's. "I hate *you.*
And I'm not giving you any...more...prescription blanks,
whatever you say. They're going to catch me, Raye."

Sickened, Jessica had half turned away from the door.
She swung back. *So that's it! That's what she's up to.*

"I told you, if you don't want to give me your own, steal
'em from the other doctors, a few here, a few there. They'll
never miss them."

"I won't do that. I can't!"

"Then you've got a problem, don't you, beautiful boy?"

"Don't!"

She chuckled. "Beautiful boy... Does the little wifey know how beautiful you are? Or that you're a movie star? Shall we show her our tape?"

"Do that and you're dead. I swear it!"

"Then maybe we better go on as we are? I keep your secret *saaafe,* and you bring me what I *neeed.* But right now I need ..."

Jessica scuttled back down the hall, shivering down to her toenails. *I have to tell someone about this—I have to tell Sam. He'll know what to do. How to save Jon.*

The door leading from the hall to the receptionist's cubbyhole was closed. She loped into the waiting room, then flung herself at the ledge below the glass slider. Stepped through the gap and down onto a desk. Followed the L-shaped counter around to the side where the computer sat waiting with darkened screen.

"Oh, no!" It was an IBM clone, and all her life she'd used MacIntosh computers, with their different software. *A computer is a computer,* she told herself, sniffing the back side for a toggle switch. *Punch a few buttons, and it'll all come clear.*

Brave words, soon belied. It took her five minutes by the clock on the wall to turn the malevolent thing on, another ten to get past the screen-saver pattern and into the main menu.

And it wasn't just lack of knowledge that handicapped her. Her six-toed paws spanned precisely two and a half keys of the keyboard. Even when she knew which command to type, she was quite as likely to punch three keys at once. Usually this resulted in a bemused inquiry from the computer and the condescending suggestion that she try again. Occasionally her mishits sent her off in unintended directions—opening files or menus she hadn't known existed, much less had chosen. Each of these had then to be closed before she could proceed. *All I want is the lou word-processing program!* She could have wept with frustration.

And then, suddenly, the screen blinked, came clear, and he was in. *Yes! Yes, oh, thank you, yes!*

At long last, after days of yearning to communicate, her way was clear—and she hadn't planned what to say. Where to start. She flicked her ears toward the back rooms and shivered. *How much time do I have?*

Not half enough to tell her whole story. No time at all for the social amenities, such as "Dear Sam." Quite possibly only minutes. *And then I still have to figure out how to print it.* Raising her right paw, she angled it inward so the inner toes would hit before the outer and pecked out i ' m t as—*damn*—p po—*blast!*—e d

She paused, then turned her head. Had she heard something?

But the sound didn't come again. "i'm trapped—" she read. i n sd—*what the heck, don't go back*—e. She stopped and shook out her paw; she was getting a royal cramp. "I'm trapped insde—" a... Her paw hovered over the C—and down the hall a door opened.

Transformed from sleek cat to fuzzy airbag in two seconds flat, she stared wildly at the screen. *Erase, erase, how do I— There!* She scrolled down, highlighting her message, then stomped the delete key. All that effort for nothing and still the blank screen glowed. It lit up the unlit room like a beacon, proclaiming, *She's here, she's here. An intruder's right here!* Raye would see it as soon as she stepped into the waiting room.

"My wife knows something's wrong." Jon's words carried through the door that led to the hall. "I can't go from you to her."

"Well, I should think not!" Raye laughed.

"I mean I won't, you bitch. But if she leaves me, I swear I—"

Bodies bumped up against the door, grappled, just as Jessica exited her file and returned to the main menu, with its own glowing screen. *Now shut it down, but how—*

"I love it when you get rough," Raye growled. "Makes me hot all over."

"Don't!" Someone banged up against the door as it shoved. "I mean it, Raye, you take me seriously, or we'll both end up dead. Is that what you want? I can't take any more!" His voice wavered on the raw, ragged edge of tears.

"Jon, Jon, let me show you something." Raye's voice was that of an adult, soothing a tearfully rebellious child. "Wait...wait here. I'll be right back."

Inside the cubicle, Jessica leapt to the floor to hit the surge control switch. Leaping back to the counter, she flattened her ears to lowest profile, then reared to peek over the inner ledge at her door to freedom. *Let me out of here!* Even the air in this place breathed filthy. But if Raye saw Jon to the door, then when—

"You see this stone?" Raye crooned, returning. "It's a souvenir. So's this brass key. Lovely old thing, isn't it?"

Jessica went rigid. A brass key?

"So what?" Jon muttered.

"So this stone once sat on a man's desk as a paper weight. And that man is...dead now. The woman whose bedroom key this was—" Raye laughed softly "—well, she may as well be."

Jessica's heartbeat rocked her to her toes, thud after hammering thud. *That's what you think, Raye Talbot! Oh, that's what you think...*

"My point is, you're an amateur, Jon, and I'm a professional. So don't threaten me. Or at least, you'd better smile when you do it."

She hooked her hand through his elbow and drew him toward the door, the picture of wifely affection. "You're under a lot of strain, aren't you, kiddo? Surgical rotation and all that. Could you use a little vacation?"

"Not with you," he said, head down.

She laughed indulgently. "I didn't mean that. I mean, suppose I leave you alone for a few weeks to pull yourself back together, make it up to the wifey? I have all the prescriptions I need for a while, and as far as getting my ashes hauled—" she cupped a palm to his face "—I've got oth-

fish to fry this week, lover. So...take a little break." She rose on tiptoe to kiss his cheek. "I'll call you when I want you."

Jon lunged away without a word. Switching off the last light, Raye leaned in the doorway to watch him go. The hand that was raised to her breast fondled the stone.

Jessica felt as if she were choking on her own heartbeat. *I have to get out of here. I have to go now.* The thought of being trapped in here, alone with Raye... She leapt lightly down to the floor—but not lightly enough.

"What...?" Raye spun around. Chin lowered, she scanned the shadows, foot by careful foot. She grasped the doorknob with one hand and then, quite deliberately, drew the door inward.

"No!" Jessica screamed, flying at her. *"No-rroww!"* As she shot through the closing gap, her fur slid along Raye's nylon-clad calves.

Raye shrieked—a wordless cry of fear and fury.

Halfway down the corridor, racing for the passage back to RI Gen, Jessica glanced back over her shoulder—just as Raye threw her stone.

The shape grew like an oncoming cannonball, smashed to the marble floor, then rebounded, sparks flying. Whizzing past so close it ruffled her fur, it crashed into a passage window. Glass tinkled. Skidding around the corner on two legs, Jessica shot into the back end of Med-1—

—and smack into Sam's shins. *"Ooofff!"* Shaking her head, she staggered around him and plastered herself to the backside of his legs. "God, I'm glad to see you! She's coming, Sam! She's coming."

He stooped, reached for her. She flowed into his embrace, wrapped her arms around his neck when he lifted her, burrowed her head beneath his chin and hid there, quaking. "Whew!" She would have broken into giggles, but apparently that was another thing cats were no good at—having hysterics. "Whew! Am I glad to see *you!*"

"Who threw that?" Hugging her to his chest, Sam strode down the hall to its intersection with the passage, then looked left and right.

There was no one in sight. Nothing to see but the window across the way with its spiderweb of shattered glass. And below it, lying on the marble, a smooth, black stone.

"Weird. You've been driving somebody crazy besides me, cat?"

"I was so *close,* Sam. I wrote you a letter. A little more time and I could've explained every— Oh, Sam!" She tried to squirm closer.

"Damn, you gave me a fright. If I'd lost you..." He stroked her once from head to hip, then knelt, opened the carrier he'd been dangling from one hand and tucked her inside. "Let's go home, Jez. Later, I think I'll drop you in the Providence River, but now, I've had it. Let's go home."

"Sounds good to me." *Home.* She hadn't had a home to run to for eight years.

But there was one slight delay, Jessica found, when they reached the hospital exit. Two small boys waited for them outside the doors, each clutching a black cat.

"Is this her?" they cried on seeing Sam, each raising a resigned cat for his inspection.

"Nope." Laughter shimmered behind Sam's denial. "I told you, guys. The cat I wanted got loose *inside* the hospital. Your job was to catch her if she tried to sneak out the door. Now where did you find these mangy critters? And, hey, look at that one—he's a black-and-whitie. You didn't listen to me at all!"

Negotiations followed. There was a payment for their efforts, but once two tens had changed hands, the kids were inclined to consider all cats involved to be henceforth Sam's responsibility, not theirs.

Further negotiations ensued. Finally, with Sam muttering darkly about kidnap charges and the end of his career as he knew it, they chauffeured the whining cats back to their respective points of apprehension—or as close as those points could now be determined—then the two gleefully whispering boys to their home.

"Think they really live above that video arcade?" Sam wondered after he'd handed each a second ten and waved goodbye. "And do we even care?" He thumped the side of her bag. "Free enterprise at its finest, Jez. You reckon they'll show up tomorrow with three black cats apiece?"

But curled tightly into a ball inside her carrier, plummeting downward into oblivion, Jessica was too exhausted to respond.

SHE SLEPT straight through until morning, awoke reluctantly when Sam shook her, like a drowning suicide dragged back to the surface against her will. *God, I'm tired. How could I be this tired?*

Sam deposited her in their one working chair in the kitchen while he cooked breakfast. Assuming the loaf-of-bread position, she crouched there, blinking and brooding. Raye Talbot... Jon...

The way she felt this morning, one half of her would gladly stay a cat forever, if only she'd be allowed to catnap her life away. Her other half groaned under the mounting pressure. *I've got to get back to myself, stop Raye...*

She yawned hugely and remembered. "She's blackmailing him, Sam." *Does the little wifey know you're a movie star? Shall we show her our tape?* Our tape—a tape in which both Jon and Raye played a role? She shivered, and tucked her paws further under her breast fur. Suppose Raye had some sort of hidden video camera set up, aimed at that couch in her office?

The night of the fire, Raye had claimed she'd once been a stage hypnotist, then she'd retracted the statement. What did they call that when you told the truth disguised as a joke? Joking on the level?

Wherever she learned it, she's a hypnotist. No wonder it was hard to resist her.

Supposedly a person couldn't be hypnotized against his will. But how hard would it be for a sexy female hypnotist to subtly lower the inhibitions of a male patient, who was perhaps more than willing to fantasize about a couch-top seduction? Seemingly safe in that oceanic blue room,

soothed by the confidentiality of the patient-doctor relationship, lulled into a position of trust, the average man
would think he was being given a delicious freebie—if he
stopped to think at all.

It was only later, once Raye showed him a copy of their
tape, that he'd begin to realize the cost.

And of course, Raye would have to choose married men
who valued their marriages, for the tape to be useful.
"That's what happened to Robert Coffman!" she cried,
remembering. "A patient of mine—I sent him to Raye to
be cured of smoking and suddenly he was furious with me.
She must've got him, too. God—do you think he thinks I'm
in cahoots with her?"

"Waking up, are we?" Sam raked reheated lasagna onto
two plates, set hers on the floor below the window. He
tipped her out of his chair, then sat down to his own
breakfast. "Hustle up, cat. Eat."

"Coffman had oodles of money. I guess that's what she
wanted from him. I doubt if Jon has two nickels to rub together, but she's taking his prescriptions. She must be
making them out for drugs—Demerol, Valium, controlled
substances like that—then selling them to addicts. And if
the law catches on, Raye's nose is clean. It'll be Jon who
loses his career."

Buried in one of the scientific magazines his secretary had
sent him, Sam waved a loaded fork at her. "Eat and stop
jabbering."

Jessica sniffed at her lasagna, then lifted her head and
looked around the room. "And I bet that explains this loft,
Sam! I've been wondering for months why Harold Neuman quit a perfectly good practice here and moved to Hawaii. And don't you think it's weird the way he left? He
must've just packed his clothes, grabbed his wife and
caught a plane. He left all his furniture, left the food in the
cabinets, didn't even stop to sell the place, just asked Mac
to handle it, then send the money on. He was running,
Sam—running from Raye, I'll bet you anything! And
maybe from an investigation, if Raye had written too many
prescriptions under his signature?"

And that, she realized with a gulp, just as she started to eat, *explains why Raye tried to cozy up to me!* Raye would have lost a prime source of prescriptions when Neuman left. *If she could've gained my confidence, found some sort of leverage to use on me, I'd have been her next source!*

Still reading, Sam stood, took his empty plate to the refrigerator and placed it inside. He swung back to the table, collected the half-empty quart of milk from which he'd been drinking and set it in the sink. "Let's hit the road, Jez." He stopped when she stood on his feet. "What do you want, green eyes?"

"Milk in the fridge, plate in the sink, big guy. And thank your lucky stars your head's permanently attached." When he still didn't get it, she leapt to the counter and smacked the milk carton, then sat to lick her paw and scrub her face.

"Oh." He made the trade, then turned to frown at her. "I always thought cats were one step up from guinea pigs, brainwise."

"That puts 'em two steps up from the average molecular biologist." She hopped down from the counter and trotted off to wait by her carrier.

On the way through RI Gen's lobby, Sam stopped in at the florist to buy a dozen red roses. "Should've done this days before," he muttered in the elevator. "She always loved flowers."

"I'm sorry?" said the elderly man standing across the car.

"Just talkin' to my cat."

The man mustered a wavering smile, then stepped off briskly at the next floor. They reached their own, ran the gauntlet of the nurses' station—much admiration for the roses, no change in the patient—then reached the room.

"Babe..." Sam deposited his bundles on the windowsill, then sat on the bed. "How was your night, Jess?"

No answer, not a ripple of consciousness. Her body lay like a lake beneath a windless, cloudless sky.

"I hate to leave you here alone at night. The nights are always the worst, aren't they?" He smoothed his palm over her forehead. "Jess, sweet Jess . . ."

I'm here, Sam. Jessica stood, one eye pressed to an air hole. Closing her eyes, she strained to feel the warmth of his hand on her brow. *Oh, let me be there . . . with Sam touching me. That's all I ever wanted, all I'll ever ask. Oh, please?*

No response. She stayed where she was, trapped in a bag, trapped in a cat.

"You're here, aren't you?" Sam whispered. "And you know I'm here."

No answer. At last Jessica said wearily, "Let me out, Sam." *At least I can be with you.*

Sam sighed, then straightened and squared his shoulders. "I brought your fuzzy friend again." Releasing Jessica from her carrier, he returned to the bed.

Jessica hopped up onto the mattress, then stood on his thigh. "I'm here, Sam. Right *here*. Look at me?"

Absently he scratched her shoulders, his gaze fixed on her human face. "I brought you flowers, babe, red roses. Make of that what you will. Want a sniff?" He held the blossoms to her untwitching nose, then breathed another silent sigh. "Not bad for hothouse roses, but d'you remember that old bush that grew behind our little rental house? You always thought it was something antique, remember?"

"I remember." He'd scattered the petals on her body one night. When they made love, the fragrance of the petals, crushed between them, had . . .

"Do you remember one night, we . . ."

Yes, Sam, oh, yes, I do. She reared to lean against him and kissed his cheek. *Don't cry. Please don't. I'm right here.*

He hugged her fiercely with one arm, his gaze still focused beyond her.

The door opened, and a crowd of men filed into the room.

"Hey!" Sam barked, swinging around. "You don't barge in here without knocking! Can't you read?"

Jessica's brother, Winston—or rather, Dr. Winston Myles, world-famous neurosurgeon—took half a step backward, then stiffened. "Sorry, Sam, I didn't realize that sign applied to me." In the group at his heels, Jessica recognized Fisher, her own doctor and head of Neurology, along with two other attendings, plus several residents and med students of the house staff—the usual collection of courtiers who danced attendance when a celebrity made Grand Rounds. And her brother was very much a medical rock star. Winston's eyes shifted to Jessica, hugged to Sam's chest, and his eyebrows rose. "What are you up to in here—voodoo? I thought the usual requirement was a chicken."

The doctors behind him chuckled obediently, though Fisher was not amused.

"This is Jess's pet." Sam stood and moved to the carrier. "I figured anything that might stimulate her..." He tucked Jessica into the bag, then zipped it.

"I see." Winston advanced toward the bed, and his retinue pressed closer. "Not a bad idea, Sam, but given that it's a hospital, a sterile environment..."

"Yeah, yeah, yeah." Sam lifted the carrier. "You mean to examine her?"

"Of course."

"With a cast of friggin' thousands?"

Winston smiled a smile of practiced tolerance. "That's how it's done, Sam. Would you care to stay?" He turned toward his followers and extended one arm to indicate Sam. "This, by the way, is my ex-brother-in-law, Samuel Kirby, the Nobel laureate, molecular biology. The man who cracked the code for nonsense DNA."

The rumble of approval said these men knew this already.

The tips of Sam's ears turned red. "No, thanks, I think we'll pass, but a word, Winston." Catching him above the elbow, he towed him through his admirers and out into the hall. Marching him a dozen feet from the doorway, he set

Jessica's bag at their feet. "You could've told me you were coming, Win."

"Oh?" Winston brushed off his sleeves, then shot the cuffs on his Italian suit. "Sorry, but I wasn't sure I'd be able to make it—I'm only passing through on my way back from Prague. I had back-to-back operations scheduled in Boston—special patients—yesterday and today, but this morning's subject coded last night." He shrugged. "If he'd held on one more day..." *I would have been able to save him,* was the unspoken assumption. "So my flight out of Logan isn't scheduled till this evening. And of course I wanted to see Jessica if I could find the time."

"Fine, but how many eyes does that take? You know how shy she is. She doesn't need half a dozen jerks standing around gaping, while you do your thing."

"That's the way it's done in a teaching hospital, Sam. Jessica knows that, even if you don't. And she's hardly in a position to be embarrassed. She's comatose."

"That's another thing." Sam took half a step closer. "You know as well as I do what they've learned about patients' awareness levels under anesthesia—that they hear everything that's going on in the operating room? Well, I'm working with the same premise here. While you're in there, Winston, I want you to treat her like a human being. Like your sister, not like a slab of raw meat laid out for dissection. If you have to discuss her in there, keep in mind that she's listening. I want sweetness and light, and most of all *optimism* in that room, is that understood?"

Through the breathing hole to which she was pressed, Jessica could see the muscles flutter in Winston's jaw. *Nobody has talked to him like that in years,* she suspected, not even their father. Given hands, she might have hugged herself. *Thank you, Sam.*

"You're in a position to ask that?" Winston inquired pleasantly.

"No. I'm in a position to tell you." Sam's drawl had faded to nothing. He spoke with the same clipped consonants as her brother, in the language of the academic elite, his tone so light and even it would have been a major storm warning to anyone who knew him well.

Winston was not numbered among these. "Ah." His tone condescended without conceding. *Humor the layman, then go your own way.* "If you wish."

"I wish."

Once Winston had returned to her room, Sam paced the corridor, swearing under his breath.

"You could put me down," Jessica suggested as he turned on his heel for his fourth pass. "I'm getting seasick."

"Sorry." He set her down, shortened his circuit so that he paced a dozen feet to either side of her bag. "Guess that's the end of your visits."

Yes. She'd already figured that one out. Fisher wasn't about to allow an animal near his patient. *Oh, Sam, how will I protect you from Raye after today? And how will I get back to myself? I'm going to go mad!*

They both turned when the group of physicians shuffled out of her room. Winston spoke hurriedly to Fisher, clapped him on the arm, then strode their way while the others headed for the elevator. "Sam, join Fisher and me for lunch? It's a rather good restaurant, I understand. Seafood. We'll have a drink and then we'll talk."

"Thanks, Win, but I guess I'll stay here." Sam drew a deep breath. "So tell me."

"A drink first, Sam. She won't miss you."

"No." Something vibrated deep in Sam's voice. "Now."

Winston let out an irritated breath, then turned to lean back against the wall beside him and crossed his arms. "I'm advising Father tonight that he request DNR be written on her chart."

"DNR?"

"Do not resuscitate. If she stops breathing for any reason, Sam, they won't try to bring her back. And no respirator, if it should come to that."

"Why would you recommend that?" Sam's voice grew markedly softer.

Winston sighed again. "Sam . . . we don't want to prolong this."

"Prolong—you're damn right. Let's talk about curing her!"

"Sam . . ." Winston shook his head. "She's gone, Sam. Don't think I don't care. She was my little sister, I loved her—but she's gone. What's in there . . . well, that's not Jessica. I'm sorry."

Sam was shaking his head, a nonstop, stubborn denial. "No, no, no, *no*, that's not right, that's not true! She's *there*, Win, even if she can't talk! I can feel her trying to reach me every time I walk into that room. Why, just when you barged in—"

"Sam, her brain wave—"

"Screw her brain wave, and all your other friggin' machines! I'm talking about her *heart*, her . . . her soul! She's still with us, Win. We just have to give her the chance!"

"We're *giving* her a chance—that's just what we've been doing. But the odds drop dramatically by the day, Sam. She's achieved some sort of stasis. She could lie like that for years."

"You've got to give her a chance. If it's the money, then leave it to me."

Winston snorted. "It's not the money, Sam. Don't be absurd. You think my family can't—"

"Then if it's the nuisance, the pain of facing this, having to see her like this, okay, okay, I can see that. That's okay." Sam swiped one hand up through his hair, shook his head. "In that case, just leave Jess to me. I take full responsibility. I'll move her down to North Carolina, marry her again, so all the decisions are—"

"That is *grotesque!*" Winston bounced away from the wall. "And certainly illegal—she's not competent to consent! Moreover, it's not the point."

"Who needs a point?"

"The point is that, given this condition, my sister would *want* to die. That's what her body is telling us, lying there—*I'm dead, let me die.* Jessica wouldn't want to live without a brain—that's not life!"

"Yeah, it always comes down to brains in your family, doesn't it?" Sam laughed bitterly and swung around to flatten his hands to the wall, his arms braced, head hanging. "You all lead with your heads, not your hearts. I tried to tell Jess that, but she couldn't hear..."

Winston touched his shoulder. "Doesn't it come down to family, in the end, Sam?"

Sam turned his head slowly. "Meaning?"

"Meaning, we're her family, and we know best what Jessica would want."

"You never had a clue!" Jessica cried from her carrier. It wasn't her family who had brought her rose petals by moonlight, who had showed her delight for the only six months of her life that had ever mattered. Not her family who now sat aching by her bedside.

Winston glanced at her bag, grimaced, then turned back to Sam. "Jessica wouldn't want to live like this. And I'm sorry to rub your nose in it, but really, Sam, what is this to you? You two broke up—what?—six, seven years ago. You're out of the loop now, man. This is a family affair."

His voice a raw, aching whisper, Sam thumped his own chest. "*I* am her family. Because I care about Jess the most, then *I'm* her family. Yes, we broke up, but that was her idea, not mine. I loved her with all my heart."

"Sam..." Show Winston a skullful of bloody brains and he wouldn't have blinked. Show him a naked emotion, and he quailed. He backed off a fastidious step, his face pink with embarrassment—on Sam's behalf. "Look, there's no real hurry on this. Perhaps we should discuss it later, by phone, once you've calmed—"

"And if she couldn't really love me back," Sam forged on, "that doesn't even matter in the end. I love her. I'm her family."

"Don't be absurd, man! We love her, too."

"Sure you do, but Myles love is conditional, based on performance. And now she can't perform—your perfect little doll's broken. So what good is she now to you guys?"

Winston edged back a step and glanced over his shoulder. "Sam, I've got to go. I'm meeting Fisher...lunch. You're sure you won't—"

Sam held out his hand. "Then give me your hand, Win."

Winston let out his breath, managed a smile that didn't come near his eyes and held out his hand. "Sure, Sam, no hard fee—"

Sam's fingers clamped on his wrist.

"What the..." Chin rising in alarm, Winston tried to back away but was drawn inexorably closer. His breath rushed out in a hiss, then he stopped resisting. "Sam—"

"Sam!" Jessica called from her bag. "Sam, please! Don't!"

"Nice *hand,*" Sam marveled, holding Winston's hand up to the light. "I've always wondered, did your old man choose your mom on that basis, that she'd throw brainy kids with long, clever surgeon's fingers?"

"Sam, come on." Winston tried to laugh. "Look—"

"What do you have 'em insured for?" Sam turned Winston's wrist first this way, then that, as if he admired a priceless object. "I take it you've insured them with Lloyd's? Half a million, Win?"

"A million," Winston growled. "Apiece."

With his free hand, Sam touched her brother's splayed, captive forefinger. "Two hundred thou' per finger, my, oh, *my.*" His face slowly lifted until his eyes were level with Winston's. "Your hands are your life, Win."

"Sam, look..." Winston stole a glance over his shoulder, but no help was in sight.

"You take Jessica's life...then I take yours, one two-hundred-thousand dollar digit, by one. Is that clear?" The drawl had crept back into his voice; somehow softness made it all the more deadly.

"Look, I know you're upset—"

"Who's upset, Dr. Nimble Fingers? I'm just tellin' you, if you write DNR on her chart, if you get clever and tell 'em to stop feeding her, anything tricky at all like that, I'll hunt you down and break your every damn finger. By the time

I'm done with you, they'll call you Dr. Hamburger Hands."

Winston tried to laugh, but it came out a whinny. "Get yourself under control, man! I know how you feel, but—"

"You don't have a clue how I feel, so I'm explaining, *very carefully,* and you better listen up. Now you go tell your old man that the same applies to him. I'll start with your fancy fingers, and I'll finish with his. If he takes Jess's life from her, he'll never cut out another heart. You go tell him I said so." He tossed Winston's hand aside.

Winston scuttled out of grabbing range, then halted. "I know you're upset, Sam, but th-th-this—this is unforgivable."

"Yeah." Sam swooped up Jessica's carrier.

Winston glanced toward the nurses' station, then backed away as Sam advanced. "I could call Security, have you thrown out on your ass this minute."

"I don't recommend that. I really don't." Sam paused in the door to Jessica's room.

"But I'll make allowances for your emotional state, as long as you realize—"

Sam shut the door in his face, threw the bolt, then stood there, staring at the door. *"God Almighty!"* he whispered.

CHAPTER SEVENTEEN

"SAM, LET ME OUT."

"God, what an idiot I—" He stooped, unzipped the bag and helped her scramble up into his arms. Shaking with adrenaline, his muscles pumped with it, he leaned back against the door. "I meant every word, but still..."

"Did you mean you loved me?" *That's all that matters!*

"I blew it. That wasn't the way I should have..." He hugged her fiercely, then dropped his chin on her head. "I should've had my mom call her mom, maybe that would've..." He tipped his head to rub his cheek roughly back and forth across her ears. *"Stupid!"*

"No, that wouldn't have helped. Mother always follows my father's lead, and in this, he'll take Winston's word."

"I should've handled it *some* other way, but how? When he said that, I didn't want to break his hands, I wanted to break his self-satisfied, smirking face! Lost my temper, and maybe lost Jess while I was at it," he whispered into her fur. "Talk about winning the battle and losing the war—I blew it!"

"You didn't blow it. You did your best." She lifted a paw to his cheek. "You did, Sam. Once Winston makes up his mind, you couldn't change it with a crowbar. He thinks he knows everything—so whose advice is he going to take but his own? There was nothing you could do, my crazy knight, my Texas wild man, but thank you for fighting for me. I loved it."

He sighed, and seemed comforted for a minute. Then he carried her over to the bed and knelt beside it. "Jess baby? It's me. They've gone, and it's just me. Me and my—your—our—fur-ball friend, here." He touched her body's still hand. "Could you stand me touching you, or have you had enough manhandling to last you a while?"

If it's you touching me, I could handle about a lifetime's worth. Oh, did you mean it, Sam, that you loved me?

He must have heard some part of her consent, because he sighed, then rose to climb onto the bed. He stretched out full-length alongside her body and tucked Jessica in between them. "Oh, babe..."

She twisted around to brace one paw against his chest. "You know, I always thought you married me on one of your impulses—an it-seemed-like-such-a-great-idea-at-the-time finale to a champagne picnic. And you always had a soft spot for strays, so I thought maybe that's what I was to you. Take home a shy, nerdish virgin. Show her what life and loving's all about, feed her up, teach her how to play, and if she has six happy months, then, hey, she's well ahead of most of the rest of the world, who never get loved at all. Then turn her out—now that she's tutored, she'll do just fine on her own, then it's on to the next one, a blonde this time.

"I guess that's what I thought you were doing, thinking. But was it more than that, Sam? More than kindness and friendship? Did you really love me?"

Sam tipped his head to consider her, then tickled her chin. But he was working out his own line of thought. "You know, babe, I was just talking with your brother..."

Jessica snorted. "*That* was a conversation? I suppose now I get to hear the edited version."

"He said that I was outside the loop, since we were divorced. That it was up to your family to determine your...treatment."

"As it were."

"And of course, technically, he's got me dead to rights. But what I'm wondering is—*un*technically speaking, in the court of the heart, not the law, which we all know is an ass—am I being a fatuous, sentimental, pushy fool, inflicting myself on you like this? Just because I've carried a torch for you all this time doesn't mean you remember me from Ad— Hey, stop kissing me, cat. I don't kiss anything in whiskers."

Still focused beyond her, he wiped his cheek, then sighed. "I sure wish you'd wake up and tell me a thing or two..."

"Such as?" There was nothing *she* needed to know beyond what he'd just said, if only she could believe it.

"Like I always figured I knew why we broke up—I had to work it out for myself, since you sure weren't about to tell me. But I've been wondering these last few days if I got it right, or if all this time I've been wandering off in left field?"

"What did you think went wrong?"

"Me, I figured you'd just never really loved me. I was your first man, and if *numero uno* is any kind of a semi-competent, halfway gentleman—sex itself is such a snazzy little concept—I imagine a young girl..." He paused. "And don't give me that woman's lib stuff—you were a baby, babe. Anyway, I imagine a young girl confuses all that lovely feeling with love for the first guy that helped her discover it. Am I right?"

"Maybe sometimes..." She flexed her claws against his chest, then relaxed, flexed, relaxed. "But when it's that way, wouldn't it fade once the novelty wore off? In my case, a day hasn't passed, Sam, when I didn't speak your name in my mind. I bet I've worn a groove in my brain, saying your name."

"Of course that's bound to fade, once she's learned all his tricks. Maybe she even wakes up one day and starts wondering—what it would be like with some other guy?"

"Never crossed my mind. I swear it. You don't really think—"

"And I reckon I was begging for a kick in the teeth, persuading you to marry me with a bottle of champagne. I mean, I never set out to do that, that day, or that way. I'd had in mind doing it right—full moon, roses, diamond ring—though that was a problem, since I was dead broke with tuition loans back then. You in a long dress, me in a tux on one knee, saying pretty please, violins in the background, or at least a guitar." He laughed and shook his head. "That's the way I meant to do it. Instead, I drag you off to a justice of the peace, and you don't even know what state you're in, much less what a state you were in."

"As I recall, I was in a state of terror, Sam. I was terrified you were going to sober up and realize what you were doing before you said 'I do.' But you were feeling that, too? You mean you wanted us as much as I did?"

He smoothed his palm over her body's forehead, then up through her hair. "I wanted you so much, I lost my head and grabbed, babe, just when I should have gone slow. So I guess I figured it always served me right when you woke up one day and realized you wanted out. That I was a detour, not what you'd planned to do with your life."

"Sam, I never, never, *never* wanted out. That's not why I left you. I left you because I was a prideful, silly, untrusting idiot, who couldn't believe someone as wonderful as you could love someone like me. And it only got worse once I found out that it wasn't just me—that the whole world thought you were special.

"You see, I never thought it could last, Sam. So when I saw Timmy's mother that night, I guess I'd been expecting her—or somebody like her—to come along from the very start." She pressed her nose to his chest and lay there, remembering. She'd always loved lying in bed with him, her head pillowed on his shoulder, his soft, speculative drawl rambling on for hours in the dark. "What else did you want to ask me?"

"And I wanted to ask you to forgive me, Jess, for not supporting you better, 'bout going to med school. It's just—" he sighed "—I never could believe you really wanted it yourself. I mean, I know they'd been grooming you for exactly that since the day you could walk. And Lord knows you worked like a dog to get the grades you needed. But I just didn't see you getting any *joy*, out of medicine. I thought if you lived that life, you'd be living it for your old man, not for yourself."

"And you thought right, big guy." Jessica ran a paw down the hard curve of his chest for the sheer joy of touching him.

"That's no way to live, without joy." Sam twisted around to pull a rose from the vase at her bedside, then rolled back to brush the blossom along her pale temple. "I used to notice how you'd light up, around flowers and growing things. I kept thinking you should look for something softer than medicine, something artistic, or hedonistic. That maybe you'd grow up to be a landscape designer, or a rose hybridizer, something that would let you work in the sunshine, not trapped under these damn fluorescents, and not dealing constantly with people, when you were so shy.

"I wanted you to choose your *own* direction in life, not trudge along the path your dad laid out for you. It's a setup, letting somebody else choose the game and the rules, then spending the rest of your life wondering why you don't play the game so well. Why you don't measure up to the other players."

"You wanted me to make up my own game, my own rules," she remembered softly. "I remember you yelling that at me once in the middle of one of our fights, but I was too upset to understand..."

"But I've come to realize, babe, that I made myself part of your problem, not your solution. I was just one more know-it-all man barging into your life, deciding what was best for you, then trying to use my love as the bribe to make you do it. That's not really love, or if it is, then it's a clumsy, misguided, hurtful kind of love."

He pulled the petals from the rose and strewed them softly, one by one, over her cheeks, her forehead, into her hair. Holding the last petal, he butterfly-brushed it along her lips as he whispered. "So I do beg your pardon, sweet Jessie... and I'd give anything—anything at all, babe—to have the chance to do it over again and this time do it right." A tear trickled down his nose, and he swiped it aside.

"You... love me." It was as hard to say as it was to believe—miracles didn't come easy, and maybe they shouldn't. "You really love me? Oh, Sam...Sam..." *San Antonio mio, maybe this is why I wasn't snatched directly off this earth? Maybe these are the words I was left behind in a cat to hear?* Because a universe that contained stars and roses and cats, and a love true as Sam, might well contain a god merciful enough to grant her this one last, miraculous revelation. *So if anyone's listening, then...thank you!*

Closing her eyes, she held her breath, half expecting that this was an end of some sort. That when next she opened her eyes, she'd see heavenly clouds, or see Sam, framed by a woman's eyelashes, not those of a cat.

Deep within her, something seemed to shift, to tremble, then poise itself for flight.

Sam rubbed the end of her nose. "You snoozin' off on me there? Must be nice to be a cat, nothing to worry 'bout but the next meal, where the next back rub's coming from."

Jessica flattened her ears and hissed.

"Hey, what'd I say?"

She blew out a breath, pressed a paw to his chest and closed her eyes. But she'd lost the moment, with its odd, shifting momentum—perhaps had only imagined it. *So thank-you wasn't the magic word, either, huh? And I've already tried please.* She sighed again. *Guess I'll just go back to wishing and praying.* And bargaining. *But if anyone's listening out there, I'd give anything to have a second chance. With Sam. Anything at all.* She waited, tail tip counting off the seconds...but there came no reply.

When she returned her attention to the outer world, Jessica found Sam, his lips pressed to her human temple, his breathing deep and catchy as a fevered child's, his lashes quivering to his own troubled dreams.

Who was she to stay awake when the rest of the family slept? She turned to fit spoon fashion against Sam's chest, lay, eyes half-mast, purr rising like sleepy song in her throat. *He loves me. All the time I was loving him, he was loving me.*

She stretched contentedly, and his hand slipped from her body's arm to cup her furry stomach. She kissed his wrist, then closed her eyes. *Before this, I just wanted my body back. Now, Sam, I want my life.*

SHE AWOKE SOMETIME LATER to the sound of a brisk rap on
their door. Then someone tried the doorknob. "Sam, you'd
better wake up." She sniffed his chin. He growled and
rolled over onto his stomach. "I mean it, Sam, wake up. If
they get the notion you're locking them out, maybe pulling some kind of a siege, we'll be in big trouble." Depending on whether Winston had decided to take action or
simply ignore Sam's threat, they could be in trouble already. The knock came again, louder, and with it, the
muffled sound of a woman's voice.

"Sam, *up!*" She nipped his earlobe.

"Arr!" He twisted around to clutch his ear and glare.
"Crazy, blasted animal, what was that for?"

"The door—" But the knocking had stopped. "Oh,
great, they've gone. Now you've done it."

They both sat up and stretched. "What is it?" Sam asked
around a yawn. "D'you need to go out?"

"Nothing so simple." If they left, it could well be that
neither would be permitted to return. Perhaps the same
thought had occurred to Sam. When she didn't pester him
further, he moved to the chair, opened his laptop and ac-
cessed his daily messages. Jessica leapt to his armrest.

How's it going? was the laconic query from someone
named Will.

Having a wonderful time, Sam typed back. I almost
committed murder today. Sometimes I hear voices, and—
major sign of psychosis—I'm cohabiting with a cat.
Meanwhile, Jess... His hand hovered over the keys, then
he hit the delete key and held it down until the cursor had
gobbled up every word. He typed, It's not, frowned at this
for a moment, then added, yet, but it will, Will.

"You're not going insane, Dave." Jessica reached past his
arm to tap a key. "Please, please let me use your laptop
and I'll explain everything."

"No way!" he muttered absently, reading. He elbowed
her gently off her perch, then scowled at his next message.
"No, no, no, *no,* you don't want Pilcher's medium, you
know-nothing, you've got to use—" Keys rattled, his fingers flew.

"What's wrong with this picture? You'll talk to your lab people in North Carolina, but you won't talk to me. I guess I'd have a better chance of making you listen if I was down there, with a keyboard, and you—" It hit her suddenly. "I could send you a message by e-mail!" She leapt to the windowsill, then spun around twice, chasing her tail. "I wouldn't have to worry about printing it out. All I'd need is somebody else's computer on which to—" She flopped over onto her side. "Rats. Never mind."

They both jumped as a knock came again on the door. Sam scrambled to his feet, scooped Jessica up and dropped her into her bag. "Not a peep," he warned. "We've got trouble enough as it is."

From her spy hole, Jessica watched him stride to the door, square his shoulders and open it. The tension went out of him. "Oh, it's you. Hello."

"You were expecting the SWAT team?" Raye Talbot laughed as she glided past.

"Something like that." Sam lowered his voice to a murmur and tipped his head warningly toward the bed. "I had a little set-to with my ex-brother-in-law."

"I know." Raye touched his shoulder.

Sam let out a hissing breath. "Word travels that fast 'round here?"

"Fisher called me, Sam. Your brother-in-law has informed him that you are not family and that you have no say in Jessica's treatment, and he wanted Fisher to tell you so. Also, that if you tried to interfere in any way, then Fisher was to call Security. So Fisher called me to do his dirty work. That's part of my job, you know—liaison between patients, or patients' loved ones, and the staff." She touched his arm again. "I'm sorry. I know this is hard."

"It's hell."

No, it was hell *watching* this. Jessica fought down the growl in her throat. If Raye didn't know she was here, then now was not the time to announce her presence. *What's your game, Raye?*

Sam walked to the window and stood there, staring out. He rested one hand on Jessica's carrier. "You know what

Myles wanted?" he whispered as Raye joined him. When she nodded, he sighed and curled his fingers into two of the breathing holes in the bag. "What's really hellish is, I have to ask myself if maybe he's right?"

He's not! Inside the bag, Jessica kissed his fingers, and he brushed her cheek in blind response.

Sam drew a shaking breath. "I have to ask myself if I'm being selfish wanting to keep her...keep her alive. If maybe she'd rather die, if this is the alternative." He jerked his chin toward the bed. "Lord knows, I know which I'd choose for myself. So do I have any right to ask Jess to..."

"Yes. You'll have to think." Raye's voice was a length of black velvet, dragged slowly across skin. "And there's something else you must consider."

"What?" Sam said, his tone both breathless and flat.

"Did you ever stop to think how all this started, Sam? The fire?"

Oh, you bitch! Jessica clamped her teeth to swallow a cat scream.

"They said an accident, a candelabra knocked over," Sam muttered. "That she'd apparently had a drink, maybe been clumsy. What are you—"

"It's the first thing you learn as a psychiatrist, Sam. There's no such thing as an accident. Or at least, they're much rarer than you'd think."

"You're saying *Jess*—" He cut himself off and glanced toward the bed.

Raye touched his shoulder again, then rested her hand there. "This is hard for me, too, Sam. Not as hard as it is for you, I know, but Jessica was my friend, too."

In her bag, Jessica's hair stood on end, her nails stabbed into the flooring beneath her. *You liar. You barefaced, psychopathic liar!*

"But because Jessica was my friend—your love—then it's we who must ask. What did *Jessica* want? If that's who she was setting out to do, and her attempt...miscarried then don't we owe it to her to...respect her wishes?"

He swung to catch the hand she'd laid on him. "Did she say anything, *do* anything, that would make you think

she . . ." He glanced toward the bed. "Look, we can't talk
about this in here." Plunging toward the door, he towed her
behind. Raye tripped over her high heels, laughed when his
hand effortlessly bore up her weight and hurried after. He
swung the door wide, put his fingers to the small of her
back to sweep her through, then pulled it shut behind them.

It happened so fast Jessica's first yowl of protest sounded
just as the door clicked shut. "Sam, come back here! Don't
trust her. She's a lying, murdering, two-faced—*ooh!*" She
spun around in her bag, her tail lashing, her claws slashing
at its sides. *Oh, I can't believe you'd— Just because she
looks like that, talks like…walks like…* She lifted her chin
and yowled. "Come back! Don't listen!"

But if Sam wasn't listening to someone, it was her. Five
minutes of yelling achieved her nothing but a fair case of
laryngitis. Perhaps they'd moved away from the door? She
turned her attention to the zipper and broke two claws—it
wasn't as easy as it had looked. She'd just succeeded in
shoving it an inch down its track and thrusting one paw into
the light when the door opened. *Oops.* She yanked it back
and pressed one eye to her peephole. A nurse's aide entered the room pushing a wheeled cart. She placed it to one
side of the bed, then stooped to remove a bag of IV fluid
from beneath.

Sam stalked into the room, his face grim, his hands
jammed in his pockets. He stood glowering, answering only
when spoken to, while the aide finished her chores.

Thank God! Jessica sat and rested her aching head
against the side of the bag. Raye Talbot was nowhere to be
seen. *I hope you told her to take her slimy insinuations
and— No, you're a gentleman. Oh, if I were only human,
I'd scratch her eyes out.*

The aide left, leaving the cart pushed against the wall by
the bed. Sam crossed directly to the windowsill. "The cat
wants out of her bag?"

"Does she!" She vaulted up into his arms—*nose touch.*
What did Raye tell you?

But he wasn't saying. He wasn't talking at all. Sam had
withdrawn to some hurting center, where she couldn't reach

him. He didn't even blink when she laid a paw on his cheek. He simply stood, hugging her, staring out through the glass at the tired old mills and factories beyond the elevated freeway until their windows turned bloody with the setting sun. When the freeway was a rush-hour river of lights and glinting chrome, he sighed, checked his watch, then bent to tuck Jessica into her bag.

He carried her slowly to the door, then stopped, one hand flattened on its surface. "You aren't even going to say goodbye?" she asked timidly. *God, you believe Raye, don't you? What did she tell you?*

Sam set her bag down and swung back to the bed. Sinking onto the mattress, he leaned over her body. "Jessbabe?" He slid one hand under her neck to cup the back of her head. "Babe? Somebody told me... Somebody suggested that the fire wasn't...an accident, that you *set* it, and that...that you might have done that because you were upset...depressed 'bout my coming to town, my insisting on seeing you, when you wanted nothing to do with me."

"*No,* Sam!" With a sly twist of a fact here, an ugly suggestion there, Raye had shredded the gossamer fabric of their trust. How evil could one woman be? "*No!* That's al a crock of lies!"

Sam didn't turn his head. "Babe, if that's so, I don't... don't know what to do now. Should I stay here, knowing caused this, knowing no apology I could ever make woul make this up to you? I've no right at all to be here if yo were that desperate to avoid me in the first place. I mean, knew you didn't want to see me, you made that plai enough, but I'd thought—hoped—that maybe there wa some misunderstanding, that we really had something t talk out, if I could just get you to talk with me."

He dipped his head till their foreheads touched. "God damn bull in a china shop, Jess, that's me, but this time stomping on Ming vases... If I did this to you, babe, swear I'll—"

"You didn't, Sam! Oh, Sam, would you listen?"

He shook his head, his lips caressing her eyebrows. "S I've no right to stay, but if I go, then...who fights for yo baby? Who'll be here, when..." His voice choked off on a hoarse intake of breath.

"Sam, ask me what *I* want." She beamed every ounce of her will into that demand. "*Ask* me."

"You know, it's funny," he whispered. "But sometimes I swear I can almost hear you. I know you're tryin' to reach me. So tell me now, babe, tell me what to do, what you want. Do I stay, or should I go?"

If heart and soul could be channeled to one laser beam of desire, aimed, then fired at another heart, then... Closing her eyes, Jessica gathered herself, then loosed her cry. *Stay! I love you, Sam, stay. Be here for me, as I would be for you, now and for always.*

Jessica opened her eyes as Sam let out a laughing sob that ended with his lips touching her body's lips. "You..." He kissed her mouth, her cheeks, her eyelids, her mouth. "Jess, Jess, okay, then, babe, if that's what you want, it's me and you...me and you and your crazy cat, and the devil take who stands in our way. I'm here, babe. And here I stay." He kissed her one last, lingering kiss, then straightened with a crooked smile.

In the bag, Jessica sank till her belly fur brushed the flooring, then she fell to her side. Whatever fueled the spirit, she'd spent hers and Cattoo's to the last drop, but one. *But in a good cause,* she told herself as Sam lifted the bag. *For the only cause that ever could matter.*

CHAPTER EIGHTEEN

As SAM CARRIED HER, she drifted in and out of sleep, opening her eyes once to the sickening fall of the elevator, then closing them again as they walked, somewhere still in the hospital, by the sounds and the smells. She curled a paw over her nose and drifted away. *Home, take me home.*

A door shut nearby, then a woman's voice murmured warmly in her dreams. Then Sam, saying something about changing his mind, that he was very grateful for the offer, but he'd decided he could handle his problems himself, that therapy just wasn't his—

"I'm not suggesting *therapy*, Sam," Raye Talbot protested on a note of laughter. "Think of it as a values-clarification session. Just a chat to help you sort out your options. Maybe help you reach some sort of...*acceptance.*"

Sam snorted, then turned it to a sneeze. "That's very kind of you, Raye, but on this, I reckon I'll make up my own mind. Fact is, it's made up. I've accepted that I'm goin' to the wall, if I have to. They unplug Jess over my dead body."

"If that's what you've decided, then good for you, Tex."

Right, Jessica thought groggily. *What's wrong with this picture?* She was too tired to sit up, but her tail was puffing to a furry exclamation point. *Danger, danger, don't believe a word she—*

"There's just one slight problem," Raye continued. "I didn't exactly...fib, this afternoon, but I did, umm, finesse you on one point." She chuckled ruefully. "I thought I'd get away with it since you promised you'd come and have a chat."

"I know I said that, but—"

But here it comes, Jessica thought, clutching after her scattered wits. *Here it comes.* She struggled to her feet.

"What I didn't tell you before, since it didn't seem necessary, is that Fisher and Myles were really...disturbed by your outburst this morning. Fisher's a bit of an old woman."

He's not, Jessica thought. *Anything but, from what I hear.*

"And I'm sure Myles blew the argument out of all proportion, but I guess you really rattled his cage. Anyway, they're worried about malpractice suits, possibly outright violence..." She laughed, and Sam attempted to join in, but it ended as more of an embarrassed growl.

"I know, I know, it's perfectly ludicrous," Raye agreed, giggling. "But still, the upshot is, Fisher wants me to evaluate you—assess that you're not dangerous to anyone on staff. That you'll abide by hospital rules..."

Sam snorted. "Of course I will. That doesn't mean I won't bring in a go-for-the-jugular lawyer and sue his ass from here to Hawaii if he writes DNR on her chart, but he's physically safe—till all else fails."

"I think I'll do some heavy editing before I pass *that* statement on." Her heels tapped with teasing deliberation as she moved closer. "But I'm afraid that doesn't quite solve my problem. Fisher wants you barred from his ward till I've certified you harmless. And professionally speaking, I can't pretend to have held a session with you if I haven't."

She's lying, Jessica realized. *I wonder if Fisher even called her?*

Sam blew out a breath. "And so, to satisfy Fisher, we go through the motions—is that what you want?"

"Putting it bluntly, that's exactly what I want. Come in for an hour and lie on my couch. Tell me your life story, or dirty jokes, or whatever you—"

"No!" Jessica screamed at the top of her lungs. "Stay away from her couch! Sam, listen to—"

"What the *hell* is that?" Raye's voice came from the far corner of the room. Stripped of all coquetry, it sounded almost ugly. "That's not a—"

"It's just Jess's cat, here in this bag. Fisher didn't tell you? I've been bringing her in, thought maybe she could reach Jess."

"Jessica's cat? But..." Raye laughed incredulously. "But—"

"Let's get *out* of here!" Jessica yowled. "*Now*, Sam. Please! Now!"

"Hey!" Sam dropped to his heels. "Hey, what's with you, you freaking fur-ball?" He curled a finger into a breathing hole and waggled it comfortingly. "Don't know what's gotten into her. She's been crazy off and on all day—nearly took my ear off a while back. Do cats ever get PMS?"

Jessica bit him.

"*Yowch!* Okay, okay, joke in very poor taste, you grouch. It's been a long day. Would you *hush?*"

"What color is that cat?" Raye demanded.

"She's..." Sam paused. "She's Jessica's cat."

"If you say so, but what color—" Raye stopped.

"That's right," Jessica yelled. "If you were my best friend, you'd know what color my cat was, wouldn't you?"

"I mean...I guess I'm just surprised," Raye blurted. "I thought Jessica's cat...burned. I don't know *why* I assumed..." Her laugh was shaky.

"Apparently she was outside when the fire started. Hush, now. Hush your cat mouth, babe. We're in enough trouble around here as it is." He nudged the bag with his toe. "Getting back to us, Raye, when do you want to schedule this mandatory headshrink? I know you said to stop by after hours, but it's pretty late."

"It is, but since they won't let you back on the ward till I've done my dirty work..." She laughed. "You know, that cat's *really* rattled me. I haven't liked cats since my mother locked me overnight in a closet with one."

Sam swore under his breath and took a step toward her. "Raye!" He stopped. "Oh, you're kidding...aren't you?"

"Joke," she agreed, "also in poor taste. File it under stupid shrink jokes. All the same, I've never cared for cats. They're so... so *sneaky*. What I was going to say is, she's making me so nervous, why don't we go back to my office? If we shut both doors, we won't hear her. And then there's this bottle of scotch that lives in my desk. What do you bet we can make this session just about... painless?"

"No!" Jessica wailed, but the door to the back rooms was already swinging shut behind them.

It took her three minutes and two more nails to fight her way free of the bag. Bounding to the door to the inner rooms, she hunkered down, slipped her upturned paws beneath it as she'd seen Cattoo do, flexed her claws, then pulled. *Oof!* The door creaked, but it didn't budge. The times Cattoo had managed this trick, the door had been slightly ajar. *Oof!* Another nail broke.

All right, all right, all right, stay calm.

How could she stay calm? He'd take a drink—he'd had that kind of day—and Sam had no head for drink. If Raye coaxed *two* scotches down him... Jessica shivered. *Lower his inhibitions, that's what she's up to.* And then a sympathetic chat, perhaps a spot of hypnotism if Sam proved suggestible—and he very well might, brains were no protection. And then?

She knew what then. *Oh, Sam, remember that you love me.*

But for a man, love wasn't necessarily a guard against sex with another woman. The others Raye had seduced had loved their wives, too, yet that hadn't saved them. And Sam wasn't married, after all. And neither was Jessica available. *If you touch him, I swear I'll scratch your eyes out.*

Stay calm, stay calm. Whatever was happening down in that drowning blue room she couldn't stop or change. Sam was flying solo—she flinched at the image. But in the meantime, there was the computer.

Tiffany had again left the glass slider open and the door to the inner hall closed. This time she'd forgotten to switch off the cubicle's lights. Within minutes, Jessica sat reading the main menu, her tail swishing like a metronome. *E-mail, e-mail, how do I access e-mail?* She'd never been interested enough in the so-called information highway to learn more than a few of its on-ramps and exits, all leading to medical data bases or word-processing functions she needed as a doctor. Drop her down in a different system of software entirely, and she was as good as lost, driving aimlessly along, praying the right signpost would come into view before she ran out of gas, or the Mack truck that was Raye Talbot smashed her flat.

That looks like— Nooo— Is that? Maybe? Here goes nothing! "Yesss!" she cried as a familiar command appeared on the screen. Enter your password.

Password, password, obviously it wanted the user's password. What word would Tiffany choose? Fingernail? Bubblegum? MTV? *Wait a minute.* Jessica sat back. *Why would Tiffany use e-mail? I swear she'd have trouble handling a three-button phone system. She's probably scheduling appointments, and she might be doing Raye's billing, though I'd be darned if I'd let her handle mine.*

Therefore, if anyone was using the e-mail functions on this computer, it must be Raye. So this would be Raye's secret password, chosen by same. *Pass, pass, let me pass, you wolf...* Wolf! She typed the word in—weoplf—blast these paws! She deleted and typed more slowly, clicking her teeth with frustration as she eked out each letter. wolf

Invalid password, the computer informed her with an electronic snigger.

sociopath?

Invalid.

Then try it backward—

htapoicos?

Invalid.

Not since her residency days on her rotations in surgery had she felt such pressure—the clock ticking, life dripping, her knife sliding through muscle and flesh, and all the while the need to stay calm, to think coolly and objectively, all emotions ruthlessly suppressed to the moment's need. *Not Annette, not shrink, not stone, not killer, not boat, not bitch. I haven't a clue to her real birthdate, who she is, what she is . . .*

Adventuress! She knew, even as she twisted her paw to type it out.

The screen contracted to a point of light, then expanded—and Jessica blinked at a page full of print, not a blank screen waiting to accept an e-mail message. Some other document file. A dead end on the info highway, no route from here to Sam's mailbox. She let out a squall of despair, reached to hit the quit key, saw the word bisexual, and paused.

She was looking at a paragraph that began with a man's name in bold caps—the name of no one she knew. Bisexual, Raye had noted after his name, address and phone number. Came to me, hoping to quit. Terrified his wife will find out and take the kids. Terrified his wife will contract AIDS. He's a professor, Brown Univ., salary low forties, paid twice monthly, few debts. My present take, $400 per payday. Aim higher next year if he makes tenure. Voice tape from his first session in strongbox J. (He's crying, but his voice is clear enough for his wife to recognize.)

Her fur fluffed out till her goose bumps ached. "Oh, you bitch. You greedy, horrible, hurtful *bitch!*" A blackmailing predator who might, this very moment, be sinking her teeth into Sam. Jessica let out a whimper and scrolled down.

Another name, a state politician whom even she, a newcomer to Rhode Island, could recognize. Sent to me by Larkin Raye had noted, in lieu of six payments.

"My God." One of Raye's victims had sent her another victim in place of cash. "Nothing like patient referrals to grow your practice!" The politician had a nasty cocaine habit. If that ever became public, his career was finished. Apparently, for the past two years, Raye had been helping him cut back on his usage—a good chunk of his available income now went to her, instead of his dealer. The politician's voice tape was stored in strongbox M, wherever that might be.

Jessica scrolled up and found Jon Cooper, listed logically with the C's. His videotape was located in strongbox N. (Will have to edit if I ever use it, Raye had noted. My face shows twice.)

"If she has strongboxes A through N, she's blackmailing half the state!" Jessica glanced up at the wall clock to find the minute hand had swung a quarter way round the dial since she'd last looked. *And I still haven't even found the e-mail function, much less typed Sam a—*

Wait. She didn't need to type Sam a letter! She had this, instead. Let him read a page or two of Raye's how-to-torment-and-extort list, then he'd know what Raye was. He'd be safe, if nothing else. This was the best vaccination Jessica could give him—if he hadn't been infected already.

She opened the top menu, selected the print function, hit a command key. A few feet away, the printer awoke with a whir. *Print, print, hurry and print.* Jessica high-stepped along the counter, tail flaunting itself with excitement, her exhaustion held at bay by an adrenaline tide. The printer was an older model, not likely to be fast. Lights blinked. Data should be pouring now from the computer into the printer buffer. When it had ingested enough, then— The machine purred. Jessica purred and glanced anxiously at the clock. *Come on, come on!*

Page one crept into view, then dropped into the rack below the printer, while page two inched its way into the machine. *Hurry, he's been in there almost half an—*

A door opened in the distance with a pistol crack. "...only hot, wet thing I want right now is maybe a fish sandwich," Sam drawled, his voice half an octave below normal and comically husky. "Maybe I'll send out for oyst— Nooo, cancel that. They don't have those suckers up here in Rhode Island, do they? Or *do* they?"

The second page dropped out of the printer as Jessica stomped the print cancel key. *Damn, oh, damn, I almost had her!*

"Actually, pizza's more what comes to mind," Sam continued. "A nice pizza pie. Damn. I think I better wander on out of here, Raye. My mouth's runnin' away with me and my feet better follow, 'fore they trip down my throat.''

He'd had—what?—maybe two drinks. And she had two pages, maybe enough proof if she could get them back to her bag. Sam still sounded as if he stood at the far end of the hall by Raye's office door. She might have time, if the printer would only stop *printing*. Page three of Raye's file was nosing its way into the machine, and the print menu still filled up the computer's screen. *Quit, blast you, I told you to quit!*

"Anyway, thanks for the drink and the couch time. It's been quite an eye-opener. Had no idea psychotherapy had advanced as far as it has, or in the directions it, uh...hmm.''

It was the buffer, that was her problem! The printer had gulped pages of data into its own memory bank, called a buffer, and now it intended to spit them out before it quit printing. Page three was three-quarters done. It would do her no good, but Jessica jabbed the print cancel key again, then kept on stomping. *Quit! Quit, damn you, you mindless, malicious machine! Quit!*

"Sam.'' Raye's voice held a note of laughing indulgence—*you silly boy*. "What are you afraid of?''

"Specifically? You mean what's my blackest, most subterranean angst?''

Whatever it is, don't tell her, Sam. Don't! Page three was done, and the printer was munching on page four. She couldn't wait for it. Jessica clamped her teeth on the edges of pages one through three and dragged them out of the printer's hopper and onto the counter.

"My deepest, darkest fear is that my cat's going to yell at me if I don't take her out for a walk. Critter's been cooped up in that bag for—''

"Sam.'' Raye laughed. "Sam, we're both adults, aren't we?''

Like a jujitsu master, he didn't resist, but rolled with her and kept right on rolling. "Well, actually that's a matter of intense debate amongst the cognoscenti. Some of the women I've dated will swear, and for that matter, my three sisters and my mom—and moms should know, shouldn't they?—anyway, all the above gaggle of feminine wisdom and pulchritude hold that, actually, my mental age is somewhere between fourteen years, eight months and *two* days, and fifteen years…" Word by drawling word, he was erecting a wall of inpenetrable nonsense between himself and his pursuer while he retreated along the corridor. Had Jessica's teeth not been clenched on the papers she was dragging backward across the desk, and had she not been a cat, she would've laughed aloud with delight. But to someone with no sense of humor—

"Sam, would you just…shut up? Come back here. Touch me, please. I *need* to be touched. Just touch me…here?"

Somehow Jessica made it up to the shelf below the glass slider. Her last glimpse of the printer showed her that it was working on page five. But mercifully the computer's screen had returned to the main menu. Head twisted to one side to hold the papers away from her paws, Jessica toppled off the shelf and hit the waiting-room floor.

Landing, she stepped on one page, and it tore loose from her teeth. *Rats, oh, rats, oh…* It fluttered to the foot of a chair, ended halfway beneath it. *Rats!* Get these pages into the bag, then go back for that. Then go back for the stuff in the printer, if she had any time left.

"I'd love to, Raye, but I can't. Gotta go. Prior engagements, y'know, and there's this man I gotta see 'bout a dog and— But anyway, thanks for the drink and the nap on your couch. Sorry I faded on you like that, but—"

"*Sam!*"

Rearing, Jessica tried to stuff her papers into the bag. The bag flopped over onto its side. Swearing with her mouth full, she rounded it to reach the entrance, dragged the papers inside, spun to go out again—

The door to the inner hall burst open, and Sam crossed the room in three strides, Raye hot on his heels. "What the…" he muttered, grabbing the carrier's handles and jerking it upright. "Damn cat."

Inside, Jessica fell on her back amidst her plunder. *That's done it!* But there was no going back now. She let out a squawk as he shook the bag once, apparently determining that she was indeed still in residence, then she clenched her teeth as Sam and the bag swerved wildy around.

"Damn you, Sam!" Raye's voice cracked with frustration.

"Probably. In fact, doubtless, but what can a man— Anyway, pretty lady, you be good, or if you can't, then be, er— *Yikes,* cat, exit stage left." The door slammed behind them.

"Pursued by a *bear,*" Sam added under his breath just as Jessica thought the words. Her whiskers quivered, he laughed, and they swung off down the corridor.

But, Sam, she thought after a moment, while scuffing her papers into a catnap nest. *I wouldn't call her exactly...pretty.*

"Lot a cat knows 'bout that."

WARM HANDS SMOOTHED around her and lifted her into the light. She pressed her face to his shoulder as he carried her. "I'm so tired, Sam." Could one die of exhaustion? The candle burns at both ends till the flames—cat and woman— meet in the middle? And then what? Poof—burnout? "Let's go to bed." She would show him Raye's papers in the morning.

Instead of the bedroom, they went straight to the bathroom. Sam set her on the counter, scratched her ears, then stripped off his clothes. If anything could have revived her, it was this. She fought a losing battle with her two-ton eyelids—till he stepped into the shower.

"*Yow,* that's cold!" he groaned through clenched teeth, revolving beyond the glass. "Ow-wow! Eeee!"

"Serves you right," she told him, curling into a ball. "Any man who'd fall for a line like 'Come lie on my couch' deserves to suffer." She shivered, remembering. "I wonder if Raye will spot that page in the waiting room under the chair?" That was the most damning clue she'd left, but as furious as Raye had been, she was likely to sweep past it without noticing.

"And if I'm lucky, when she turns off the light in the receptionist's office, she'll assume Tiffany left the computer on. Odds are good she won't notice those pages in the printer rack."

Come morning, perhaps Tiffany would bring them to her boss's attention. Or perhaps she'd miss their significance and blithely toss them. Either way, by morning Sam would know the score. She'd show him her evidence at breakfast. Jessica yawned and curled her tail over her nose.

She came halfway awake when Sam carried her to the kitchen. *Clean clothes,* she noted, pressing her nose to his ribs.

He set her down on his chair. "What's the matter with you, Jez-babe? Behind on your catnaps? It was a long, frazzlin' day, wasn't it? What d'you say, BLTs for supper, heavy on the bacon for you?"

"Not hungry." Curling back into a ball, she wafted away on a delicious fragrance of sizzling bacon fat and hickory smoke.

"Whew! Smoky in here. Hope you like your bacon well-done." Nearby Sam opened the lower section of the giant window that overlooked the fire escape. "Pretty warm out tonight. Indian summer. Jess used to love this season." The comforting, homey sounds of supper preparation wove into her dreams, then a distant sound intruded. A buzzer, nasty tone, nastier implications. But she was too tired to deal with it. She dived away from its significance, back into dreams. Sam's voice came from a distance. "Sam?" *Not talking to me,* she decided, and drifted off.

Then voices, coming closer. *A woman's voice.* Hard heels in the hallway. "I'm *so* embarrassed," Raye Talbot confessed as she walked into the kitchen. She was dressed all in black—black jeans, black turtleneck, high-heeled black boots, a black mink jacket thrown over all, an enormous black purse slung from one shoulder. "I am so *ashamed.* The way I behaved this afternoon was so...so unprofessional, I cannot believe that was me!'' She held a pizza box balanced on her forearms.

"It was no big deal," Sam said behind her. "Already forgotten." He held a bottle of red wine she must have handed him.

Jessica struggled to a sitting position. *This isn't real. This must be a nightmare. Tell me I'm dreaming!*

"But *forgiven* is what I'm after, Sam. I feel *such* a fool. So...this peace offering." Raye waggled the pizza box, then set it on the table. "I decided no anchovies—you don't look like an anchovy man. And a Chianti," she added, touching the bottle in his hands. "From my very own cellar."

"Nooooo!" Jessica yelled, rearing to stand, her front legs braced on the table's edge. At least she tried to yell. Her overtaxed voice came out more of an agonized squeak. Raye flinched violently at the sight of her, but held her ground.

"You didn't need to do this, Raye." Sam looked thoroughly uncomfortable. "I reckon that scotch went to both of our heads. At this point, I can't remember a thing that happened."

"You are such a sweet liar! Jessica is *so* lucky to have you."

"And Jessica plans to keep it that way! She's up to no good, Sam, coming here, can't you see that? She must have found the page I dropped." Heaving herself to the tabletop, Jessica advanced, her ears flattened, eyes flaming, a tiny, moaning song of menace weaving out of her throat. "Don't you even *think* of hurting him...not while I have claws...while I have teeth...while there's one last breath in my body..."

Sam plucked her off the table and draped her over his shoulder, pinning her there with one flattened hand. "Hush, you. Sorry, I don't know what's gotten into her. She's been kinda skitzy all day."

"I know just how she feels." Raye laughed as she retreated a step. "So have I. I wanted to explain to you...the reason I...I came on so strong today—"

"No need to explain a thing."

"The reason I came on to you like that was, well, the man I thought I was going to marry broke our engagement just last week. Jessica warned me—she thought he was a stinker, but would I listen? I was convinced he was Mr. Wonderful." She laughed painfully. "Boy, did I know from nothing!"

"This is her con, Sam!" Jessica yowled in his ear. "She's playing on your pity, just like she played on mine. There's no fiancé, wonderful or otherwi— *Oof!*" she gasped as he thumped her ribs, turning her yell to a series of bagpipe squawks. "D-d-dammit, l-l-listen to m-me!"

"So I guess today, I was just trying to wipe a bad taste from my mouth with somebody truly wonderful." Raye cut a wide detour around them to reach the hall. "But I'm sorry I came on so strong. I get pushy sometimes." Giving him her smile-for-a-shrug, she backed a step toward the living room. "Well . . . you enjoy. I'll see you tomorrow at the—"

"Wait a minute," Sam protested. "You're not going to just drop this monster pizza on me and run, are you?"

"I think I should, shouldn't I? I mean, I don't want you to think that—"

"I don't think anything of the sort. Stay and have a piece, and help me brainstorm 'bout how I'm going to handle Jess's family."

"I can't *believe* you're this stupid!" Jessica raged. "She's playing you like a hooked trout! *Listen* to me. You think her danger is that she's a sexy woman, trying to seduce you. And since you love me, you think you're perfectly safe. But *that's not where she's coming from!*"

"Well, if you're absolutely sure, then..." Raye shrugged prettily, then swung her purse off her shoulder to drop it on the counter. "All right,"

"Like, ask her what she's carrying in her purse that's so heavy!" Jessica pleaded, ears wincing at the metallic clunk. "*Please* listen to me."

"What d'you carry in there? A folding bicycle? Silverware service for six?" Sam nodded at her bag as he moved past it to the stove. He picked five pieces of blackened bacon out of a pan, set them on a plate, headed for the window.

"Oh, just a few odds and ends." Raye went straight to the drawer that held the utensils and pulled out a corkscrew. "Oh, and I bought a hammer today. Mean to hang some pictures when I get home."

"Wait!" Jessica shrieked. But Sam leaned out onto the fire escape, set the plate of bacon down near the flowerpots, then deposited her on the iron flooring before it. Below the bars of the grid, six stories of black yawning space seemed to suck at her toes. Spinning around, she lunged for the window, but he held her off and closed the sash.

His voice came faintly from beyond the glass. "Supper al fresco, fur-ball. When you're ready to be polite, you can come back inside."

Behind his turned back, holding the wine bottle, Raye gave her a long, level stare that was worse than any smirk. She dug the razor tip of the corkscrew into the cork. And twisted.

I have to stay sane, I have to stay sane. How can I save Sam if I go stark, raving bonkers? Panting, Jessica leaned her forehead against the glass and tried to think. Her mind was a reeling squirrel cage inside a tornado. *Think. Be calm and think.*

Beyond the glass, Sam left the room. Raye wrenched the cork from the bottle, dropped it aside, almost ran to a cabinet and selected two wineglasses. Groping in the pocket of her jeans, she pulled out a tiny glass vial. Head cocked toward the hallway, she dumped the vial's contents into one of the glasses.

Jessica shrieked and threw herself at the glass.

When Sam returned a moment later with a chair from the living room, Raye was topping off his wineglass. She smiled, set it before his place, poured her own.

Don't drink it! Jessica pleaded, her nose pressed to the glass, her body trembling. *Don't drink!* Focusing all heart and soul on that single command, shutting out the scents of the night breeze, the cold iron beneath her pads, the roar of blood through her veins, she closed her eyes and aimed.

Don't drink, Sam. If you love me, love your life, then don't drink.

When she opened her eyes, she seemed to see through a gathering darkness—exhaustion thick and clingy as fog. Sam lifted his glass to his lips. He frowned, hesitated, started to set it aside. "Y'know, after that scotch this afternoon, I don't think I—"

"I knew it!" Raye laughed. "You *haven't* forgiven me, have you? You're probably planning to call the hospital ethics committee first thing tomorrow—another doc puts the make on her patient."

"Don't be absurd, Raye. It's just that—"

"This is a peace pipe, Tex. A twenty-dollar-a-bottle peace pipe. And I fibbed about having it in my wine cellar. I went out and bought this especially for you. Now, are we at peace, white man?"

Not even turning his head at Jessica's screech, Sam clinked his glass with hers and nodded. "Peace, then—but only one glass worth of peace."

"I imagine that will do." Raye took a sip of her own, licked her top lip from corner to corner, then smiled. "Have some pizza?"

Forehead pressed to the glass, heart sinking, Jessica clutched at her failing wits and fading energy. *Something... must do something. Break the glass? Not possible—it was double-paned. Find a phone, call 911? Right, they'd listen to a cat. Gotta do something.* Instead, she was sucked softly, slowly, irresistibly down into echoing darkness. *Oh, Sam... Sam... Sam Antonio mio.*

CHAPTER NINETEEN

CLAWING BLINDLY UP from a pit of blackness, Jessica reached the top, then forced open her eyes. Beyond the windowpane, Sam sat motionless in his chair, his hands flattened on the table as if for balance.

Where's Raye? Hope shot up like a bottle rocket, then fizzled as Raye entered the kichen from the direction of the living room. She glided across to a cabinet, removed objects, returned to place on the table a candelabra holding four half-burned candles.

Oh, no. Jessica scrabbled at the glass. *No.*

"You know your way around," Sam said heavily while she switched off the lights.

"I've been here before, Sam. Harold Neuman was a... friend of mine." A match sparked, burst into flame in the darkness. Raye sat holding it, her black eyes reflecting the fire. "That's better, isn't it? I love candles... flames...heat...don't you?" When he nodded, she touched the match to a candlewick. Flame flickered, then danced straight and true. "So tell me, Sam...who put that cat in my office yesterday?" She blew out the match and watched him through a veil of smoke.

"Yesterday?" Sam frowned. "Yesterday...she strayed out of Jess's room. Was loose in the hospital for hours. She went to...your office?"

Raye struck a second match, held it up. "I don't believe in accidents. So *tell* me, Sam, who put her there, and why?"

This is the flip side of evil, Jessica realized, her nose pressed to the glass. Expecting evil to be done in return.

Paranoia, you wolf. Do you see enemies, wherever you look?

"If she went to your office, she must've had a reason." Sam swiped a hand up through his hair, shook his head. "Beats me. Crazy cat."

Raye grimaced and set the match to candle. Flame guttered, then rose. "So tell me, who have you met since you've come here?"

"Mac, Caroline—Jess's receptionist. Mary, Fisher, Myles. Jez, but I . . . I knew her already."

Yes, you know me, Jessica thought, shivering in the wind. *Deep down you've known me all along.*

Raye blew out the second match, gazed narrow-eyed through its rising smoke. "*Tell me,* Sam. Which one of them is helping you?"

"Mmm, Mac helped me find this apartment. Fisher's no help at all, blast him. Mary tried t'take the cat off my hands, but now I know that wouldn't have helped—I'm good as married to the critter."

A match ripped into flame. Raye leaned across the table to hold it before his eyes. "*Tell me, Sam.* Who helped you today? Who was out front nosing around my computer, while you distracted me in my office?"

"Jez messed with your computer?" Sam tipped back his head and laughed. "Damn cat! She's been after mine for days. Wonder what she—"

Raye blew out the flame, threw the match on the floor. She struck the next match under his nose. "*TELL ME.* Who's your accomplice? Not the damned cat, what *person is helping you?*"

"Jess. Jess in a fur coat." Sam pushed his glass to one side. It tipped off the table and shattered. "Oops."

"*Look* at me, Sam—at *me.* Jessica's in a coma. *Tell me who helped you.*"

Slowly he shook his head. "Jess's right here, watching you, watching me, giving me holy hell for talking with you."

Yes, yes, yes! Jessica beamed, her paws flattened to the glass. *So throw her out.*

"I give up!" Raye lit the last candle and blew out the match.

"That's good. 'Cause we're goin' to bed now. It's been one helluva day." Sam stood, opened the window.

Jessica scrambled up into his arms, wrapped her paws around his neck. "So throw her out, Sam. *Now!*"

But Raye had already gathered her purse and her jacket. "Don't bother seeing me out, Sam. I know the way."

"That's right." He swayed dizzily, and his hands tightened on Jessica. "Then we're off to bed. Blow out those candles, will you?"

"See her *out*, Sam! Make sure she goes!"

He didn't. He ambled off to the bathroom, his fingers clamping on her scruff when she tried to wriggle out of his arms to see for herself. He shut the door, then dumped her on the counter. "Whew, fur-ball, don't know what was wrong with that pizza, but I'm gonna be sick."

He was.

Good. Shivering on the counter, Jessica stared from Sam to the door and back. *Good, get it out.* Though much of whatever Raye had given him had clearly hit his bloodstream already. Still. Nerves twanging, fur standing on end, she jittered while Sam brushed his teeth, splashed water on his face, picked her up and hit the lights.

Listen to me, she pleaded. *Raye's out there, I'm sure of it. Out there with a hammer. Sam, don't—*

He opened the door—on blackness. Every light in the apartment was out. Her claws dug into his shoulders. *Don't go out there, Sam. Don't.*

"What's the matter, babe, scared of the dark? I'm with you." He shuffled along the hall, one hand hugging her, the other brushing the wall.

Even a cat can't see without *some* light, but she tried, staring back over his shoulder, her ears swiveling, straining to catch the sound of eager breathing above her own hammering heart.

They made it to the door.

No lock on it, Jessica thought as he pulled it shut behind them. *I wish we could lock it.* Maybe pile furniture up against it? No, it opened outward, and maybe Raye was here already, waiting in the room.

They made it to the bed.

Cradling her to his chest, Sam sat, then toppled slowly backward. *Don't sleep, Sam. Don't!* But he sighed contentedly, Jess rising and falling on his chest as he breathed, then his breathing deepened. Too deep, too slow—drugged.

Or poisoned? Trembling, she lay frozen, her ears flinching at every sound. *If I could get to the phone in the living room* ... She jumped violently out from under his hands, landed, hissing, as, from the hallway, she heard a soft, sliding step. *Oh, God, here she comes.*

Spinning around, she drove her claws into his shoulders. *Sam, wake up. Here she comes!*

He grunted and rolled to his side. She nailed his bicep—he yelped, jerked half-upright—pushed her off the bed.

Out in the hall, a gentle tapping sounded. Metal on wood.

What's she ...?

Again the tapping came, then again. And then suddenly, horribly, *Whock! Whock! Whock!* Steel clanging hollowly on steel—a hammer pounding a nail. Then another, and another.

Oh, god. And so now she knew. Somehow it was almost a relief. Raye wasn't coming through that doorway with hammer upraised. But then, they weren't going out. She was nailing blocks of wood to the floor along the base of the door. *Me, she locked in. But here she knew there wasn't a lock, so she came prepared.* Next would come fire.

Jessica leapt onto the mattress again. *Up, Sam! Get up!* There was always the window. Six stories high. No fire escape on this side of the building. *Up! Help me!*

The magic words with Sam. He grunted and struggled to his elbows. "Wha—? Jess-baby?"

"If you're awake, Sam," Raye called beyond the door. "Here's your last chance."

"What the hell—" Sam rolled off the bed and staggered toward her voice.

"Never *mind,* Sam! There's no way she'll let us go after this. We have to..." Jessica swatted his calves, but he was at the door, turning the knob, then shoving. It wouldn't budge.

"So you *are* awake." Raye laughed. "Listen up, beef-cake, here's your final chance."

"What are you—" Sam threw his shoulder against the door and bounced back.

"I found two pages of my special file in your cat bag, Texas. Tell me who put them there. Who's helping you? Tell me that and I'll let you out."

"Are you crazy?" Sam stopped shoving and leaned his forehead against the oak. "Nobody put anything in the cat carrier. Listen, I think there was something bad in that pizza. If you're feeling funny, then—"

"I'm feeling fine, Texas, if a bit irritated. Nobody gets in my way. I told Jessica that, and now I'm telling you. Now... if you don't want to star at your own Texas bar-becue, Tex, you better tell me—who broke into my computer? Who knows about me... besides you?"

"Open the door and let's talk 'bout this. Raye? *My God!*" he whispered.

"Have you ever seen one of these old mills burn, Sam? We lose about one a year around here. There's a hundred years of oil and grease soaked down in their beams and flooring. They burn like the wrath of God. Every fire department in the state comes out for the party, but they burn, baby. They burn till the stones melt and they see the smoke in Boston. No one will ever be sure you were even in here, you and your bitch cat. That's what you want? Now tell me."

"*God,*" he whispered. "*You hurt Jess, didn't you, you crazy bitch?*" Then, "Open the door and I'll tell you." He stumbled back to the bed to grab two pillows. Returning,

he stuffed them along the crack below the door, then
switched on the light. His head tipped back as his eyes followed the door's perimeter while his fingers traced it. The
movement made him dizzy; he clutched at the knob to stay
upright. "Be *glad* to tell you."

Hinges on the other side, Jessica noted despairingly, and
it was built solid. They'd never break it down, not in time.

"Right, sweet cakes. If that's the line you're taking, then
we've got nothing more to chat about. So I'll find out for
myself. This should smoke whoever-it-is out in the open,
don't you think?"

I've killed you, Sam. Jessica tagged his unsteady steps to
the window. *You and Cattoo. Curiosity's supposed to kill
the cat, not everyone the cat loves. Oh, Sam!*

He shoved open the lower sash of the window and leaned
out. A cold wind blowing off the bay rushed inward.
Wind...wind would fan the flames. She leapt to the sill
beside him as Sam stared left, then right, then twisted to
look overhead.

"Well, toodle-loo, gorgeous," Raye called through the
door. "I'm off to start a grease fire. Enjoy."

Jessica crowded to Sam's elbow and peered down. Her
stomach plummeted—elevator in free-fall. Below was only
the sheer drop, six stories to the pavement. The street itself
was badly lit, utterly deserted this time of night.

"Hey, look at this." Sam caught her up, cuddled her in
his arms. "Cat highway." He leaned out so she could see.
Below the granite sill, a narrow, decorative ribbon of stone
ran along the building.

The ledge was precisely two inches wide. "Oh, no,
Sam!"

"Oh, yes, you can do it. You're a cat—piece of cake.
Follow that around the building—it should reach the fire
escape. Go down, jump to the top of my car, get yourself a
life. Find some nice tomcat—"

"I don't *want* a stupid tomcat, I want you!" She was
crying, cats couldn't cry, but still the tears fell. She pressed
her face to his bicep. "*No,* Sam."

"Yes, baby. I'd come too, if I could, but ..." His hands smoothed down her body and his lips brushed her ears. "Anyway, I never liked heights."

"*You* never... You mean all those times you teased me... Damn you, Sam, you can make it!" But he swayed, then bumped heavily against the sill.

"Get going, and don't you worry about me. I won't be bored. I've got this sky hook to build, or maybe a glider. Or maybe I'll just sit here, chunk lamps and stuff at the passing cars."

"There *aren't* any cars! Sam, let me stay!" She put a paw to his cheek as he lifted her up to his face. "Sam, I love you."

"I know you do, babe." *Nose touch*—eyes holding, hearts fast. "I know you do." He juggled his hold on her, then gathered her up, one hand under her ribs, the other gripping her tail. Braced on his elbows, ignoring her cries, he leaned out over cold, yawning space to set her on the ledge. Gradually his fingers withdrew, till only his fingertips pressed her against the stone. "Now beat your cat feet on outta here. Take a right at that corner, a right at the next, and you're home free."

"*Sam—*"

"And if a cat attention span stretches more than five minutes, once you get there you might consider finding a phone, and dialin' 911. Just a thought." He smoothed his palm softly, slowly down her side. Then nudged her haunches with the backs of his fingers. "Now scoot, fuzzybabe."

He was right. If she could make the fire escape, she might find a phone. And there were other people living in this building, allies who'd object to Raye's plan, if only she could alert them. All she had to do was... She focused forward for the first time on that terrible catwalk above the abyss, lifted her face to the rising wind and wailed, "*But I can't!*"

She didn't dare turn her head to look back for Sam, and something told her he'd withdrawn. He couldn't help her now. She looked inward to the only one who could. "Cattoo? This is...your department, isn't it? Cattoo? Please?"

The candle burns from both ends till the flames meet. Deep within, Cattoo's spark glowed and ebbed. She needed sleep. *Leave me alone.*

Cattoo, please. I need you. Come?

Clawing painfully up from oblivion, Cattoo peered for one moment through her eyes. The yowl that ripped from their throat was a cry of pure feline incredulity. *"No!"* Then she was gone, crouched somewhere deep within, hiding beneath some psychic sofa, waiting out the terror as any sensible cat would. *No!*

Yes! We have to.

No answer. Catlike, she was gone.

Jessica swallowed and lifted her nose to the wind. "Fair enough, I suppose. I got you into this. So, if you won't, then..." Shuddering all over, she lifted her outer forefoot. As it swung out over the depths, the skin of her pad quivered—nerves shrinking with electric dread. Gravity ravenous and sucking. *I'm here. All your life I've been waiting.* Her claws raked out, but the enemy was empty air.

Hooking her paw delicately around the leg nearest the building, she gradually, shrinkingly, transferred her weight to it. She shuddered, then lifted her inner paw—slid it, side of leg and shoulder scraping the rough-cut stone, past the outer foot—then flattened it on the ledge. Transferred her trembling weight. *And now the back paws.* With perhaps twenty feet to go to the first corner. Then beyond that— *Don't think about it. Go.*

How much time had passed? *Don't think about it. Flow.* Whiskers sending electric shocks to her right cheek, chill wind ruffling fur on her left. Clumsy catcher's-mitt paws spread wide for balance, growing colder with each step on frigid stone. Tail outraged, incredulous, quivering as it brought up the rear. Somehow she reached the corner.

Oh, Sam, I can't. It would have been easier to be human and turn the corner standing upright, than it was to do it as a cat, where the longest part of her body—nose to tail—must be pivoted around that knife edge. *I can't do it.*

Then Sam will die. Go. Don't think, flow.

She set her outer paw on the outermost angle—her claws hooked empty air. She whimpered aloud, trusted her weight to that foot, then edged inner paw past outer, around to the side of the building she could not see. *Oh, God, who knows if the ledge is even there?*

It was.

Now her nose edged out over echoing space. She caught a glimpse of the ground—her eyes slammed shut. But she didn't need them. This was all touch, balance . . . terror. Weaseling her body around the turn, the stone edge scraping her fur in the closest of shaves, she brought her outer paw forward, and now half of her was around. Bent to a right angle, she opened her eyes—and moaned. This end of the building was longer than she'd remembered. Far longer. And the side overhanging the alley was three times as long if it was an inch. *I can't do it.*

But she couldn't stay here, halfway around, her compressed side muscles cramped and threatening to spasm. *Back legs now, but don't think, let them flow.* They flowed out, around, after, her tail whisking behind—it swung out too wide. And the wind gusted.

"Yer*rrowwww!*" Teetering on the razor's edge, clawing stone for a toehold, tail flailing, every heartbeat threatening to jolt her from her perch, she cried again, then heaved herself into balance. Mewing wordlessly, she pressed her face to the wall. *Oh God, oh Sam, oh Cattoo, I can't, I can't, I can't.*

Then Sam would die. And how much time had passed? Five minutes? A lifetime?

Some lifetimes weren't so long. *Go. Think how easy this straightaway looks compared to a corner.*

Don't think about that corner up ahead.

When she reached it, the second corner was harder. Whatever final reserves of Cattoo's strength she'd drawn on, she was now sucking bottom. Beyond her shock-dilated pupils, the night sky pulsed lighter, darker, whiter, blacker, seemingly in time with the droning gusts of the wind. Her muscles shuddered and cramped, shivered and seized. Her toes ached, then grew numb, turned to small, clumsy blocks of furry ice.

She turned the second corner by act of will alone. *Sam. If I have to walk on air, then I will.*

Rounding it, she stopped again, closed her eyes and leaned into the granite. How much time had passed?

Three lifetimes at least—Sam's, Cattoo's, hers.

How much time was left? She smelled bacon, and knew. *Bacon grease.* All Raye had needed to do was turn up the flame on Sam's skillet full of grease, crack the window to feed the fire, then walk away. Once the hall was ablaze, it wouldn't matter if Sam broke through the bedroom door. He wouldn't reach the fire escape or the elevator. The loft was a death trap.

No, not yet. Not while I live.

Now she flowed—left paw past right, scrape of shoulder, lunge of hindlegs, whiskers brushing stone, ribs heaving like bellows, eyes locked on the ever-nearer prize of the fire escape. A warm light danced on the kitchen windowpanes, turning black iron to a web of flickering gold.

So fixed was she on her goal that she nearly flowed out into empty space. Nails screeching across rock, she stopped—ten feet from her goal. "Oh, *nooooooo.*"

At some time in the past hundred years, some heartless idiot, some thoughtless monster, had cut four feet of the ledge away. Perhaps to accommodate a previous fire escape—her incredulous eyes traced rust streaks dark as blood down the granite till they vanished in a well of darkness. *No, this cannot be.*

Yet it was.

No way around that gap. And no way back. It would take her hours to back up even as far as the corner, and there was no rounding that, tail-first. If it came to that, there were more dignified ways of dying.

But if I die, Sam dies. And this I will not permit.

You've got a choice?

I have a choice. I make that choice. I would give any-thing...

But anyone? Not only herself, but—

Yes, even Cattoo, that love for this. *Cattoo, I need you. I can't do this alone.*

From deep, deep within, only the tiniest spark in answer. *Please, leave me alone... Rest...*

We can't rest here. If we stop here, we die. The building will burn. Cattoo, please...

A guttering flame at the bottom of a well. *Rest, I need—*

Cattoo, I need you. Please. I'm begging.

And she came, as in need she always had. Clawing up from the depths, she came, peered out through their eyes and wailed. *Not possible! Not even to be considered!* It wasn't the length of the leap, but the footing on this end, the landing on that. *No. Leave me alone.*

Cattoo, I need you. Please. We can do it. We must. You have to jump for both of us. For Sam.

The flames meet in the candle's middle, and the stronger flame consumes the weaker. The flames burn as one. *I would give anything.*

As for Jessica, Cattoo would give all, without hope, with all love.

Haunches sinking like a spring compressing, tail quivering, heart bolting, energy gathering, eyes narrowing as all love and will coalesce to a single spark. And the gap that must be crossed.

Tail tip shudders... then stills... Then...

Muscles *exploding* into motion—black cat rising. Flying. Limbs stretching, clumsy paws reaching...

One shoulder brushes rough-cut stone... *And the night tilts.*

Ledge rushing nearer, then there—two inches to the right, not below where it should be. Claws snatching at unforgiving stone, pupils expanding to black pools of terror, gravity ravenous and sucking... *It cannot be done.*

It must!

It must and yet—*"MERRROOOOOOOOOWR!"*

Black cat falling...

Falling through the cool dark...

Twisting...claws snatching...stars and city lights wheeling as she falls...limbs stretching as if to fly...

Pupils expanding, black as the rushing night...wide as the ending world...

CHAPTER TWENTY

HEAVEN WAS ROOFED with acoustic tiles, seven deep by... Jessica swung her head on the pillow as she counted. By ten tiles wide. The tenth tile ended above a familiar door. *The door to her private room in the hospital.*

Oh, God, could it really... *I'm not dead, I'm back?* She tried to lift an arm and could not. It was strapped to a board to stabilize her IV needle. Her other arm came up as if she dragged it through clear water. She lay smiling as she clenched and flexed her fingers before her face. Fingers! And an opposable thumb. What she wouldn't have given for—

She had. Jessica struggled to one elbow. "Cattoo?"

No answer. Not here... Not anywhere. Only darkness. *I forced Cattoo to jump, then left her to it.*

And Sam?

"*Sam!*" Jessica struggled all the way up, stopped to slide the IV needle from her arm, unstrap the board. She swung her legs off the bed, tried to stand—and failed. How long had she been in bed? A week? A cat's lifetime? Too long. Much of her muscle tone was gone.

Scrambling to the foot of the bed, she was able to look out the window. The city lights were just bright enough to let her see the mill—and the white sheet blowing like a banner from Sam's window. *Sam, you haven't quit yet!* And neither would she.

Though it seemed another lifetime, she must have fallen only minutes ago. *How long do I have left?*

No red flickered yet in the windows on this side of the mill. And if smoke rose from the alley side, she couldn't see it against the night sky. *There's time, dear God, there's still time! I need a phone—911.*

Comatose patients don't need phones, so none had been installed in the room. "Dear God . . . Sam . . ." She twisted around, shoved her legs off the other side of the bed, leaned to jab the call button, nearly fell, then caught herself by grabbing a wheeled cart, which stood against that wall. "911, Sam, oh, Sam." *But what am I waiting for?* It was after midnight. The nurses might be napping, off tending another patient, calling a doctor. "*I can't* wait." Her eyes swept the room, then swung back to the cart. *Yes!*

Minutes later, minutes that could have been a lifetime, might cost a life, Jessica wheeled herself down the hall. Flopped stomach-first over the cart, she pushed along, panting, feet slipping and sliding, like a wounded child on a makeshift scooter. *Sam, oh, Sam, would you laugh at me now! 911. Oh, hang on, Sam. I'm coming. 911!* Forty more feet to the nurses' station—where in hell were they?

A nurse stepped out of a patient's room on her right, then stopped short, eyes rounding. "Oh, my sweet heaven! What do you think you're—"

"I need a phone," Jessica panted, not stopping. "There's a fire. I have to call 911. *Help* me."

"What are you doing out of *bed?* What are you doing— Miss *Myles?* You're awake, that's wonder— But what are you—"

"A phone! Find me a phone! *Now!* It's an emergency— a fire!"

"But dear, you haven't been— How could you— First, let's get you straight back to bed," A decision reached, she hurried to the front end of the cart to stop it. Sugarcoated steel, she smiled into Jessica's face. "Then we'll call Doctor, see what he—"

"Forgive me." Jessica shoved the cart—hard.

The nurse went down with a squawk, and Jessica wheeled right into the room from which the nurse had appeared. She managed to catch the door and pull it shut behind her, swung to turn the dead bolt, turned back again. "Oh, God, let this patient have a phone!"

An elderly man sat upright in his bed, a talk show turned down low, his eyes bright with interest. "And he does." He patted the phone on the table beside him, then lifted the handset. "May I dial you a number?"

"Oh, God, *thank* you, somebody sane! Dial 911," she cried as someone rattled the doorknob and called out.

"With pleasure," was the gallant return. "I've been dying of boredom." He pecked out the numbers and handed her the phone.

As soon as the dispatcher answered, Jessica spoke slowly and clearly. "The Clarke Street Mill in the Jewelry District is burning."

"Who is this, please?"

A patient straight out of coma. Right, she wouldn't make that mistake again. "The fire is on the sixth floor, and it's a bad one. It's burning on the alley side of the building, but there's a man trapped on the bay side of the south wing. You'll see a bed sheet marking his window."

Several voices conferred in low, urgent voices beyond the door. The doorknob rattled.

"*Who* is this, please?"

"*Please* hurry. It's a mill, it'll go fast, but you still have time. *Please!* Clarke Street Mill, Jewelry District, sixth floor, white sheet."

"You'll have to tell me who's making this call, before I can—"

"I'm the man's wife!" Jessica cried, then hit the disconnect button as the door to the hall burst open. Three nurses and a very large orderly marched into the room, their faces grimly determined.

"Thank you." Jessica passed the handset back.

"Has she been bothering you, Father Houlihan?" a nurse clucked.

"Not at all. Lovely time. *Oh*, now—" he added disapprovingly as Jessica was pressed none too gently into a wheelchair. "Come back and visit me, dear, when you're, ah . . . free?"

"I will. I will, thank you!" Jessica called over her shoulder as she was whisked out the door.

The wheelchair swung left toward her room. She drew a deep breath, then spoke deliberately. "This won't be necessary—I'm signing myself out. If someone would just find me my clothes?" Surely the dispatcher would send a fire truck to check out her call—surely? But she meant to make doubly sure herself. *Sam. Oh, Sam, hang on, love.*

Someone behind her snorted. "You can't even walk, Miss Myles."

"It's *Doctor* Myles, thank you. I'll take a wheelchair to the lobby, then I can handle it from there." Somehow.

"Not until we consult the doctor, Miss, er..." The chair turned again, and she was back in her own room.

"No!"

"Now just calm down, dear."

"Wait! Please! If you'd just *listen*, let me speak with Fisher myself—"

"*Evvvvv*erything will be fine. You don't know what a lucky girl you are."

DON'T FIGHT, Jessica told herself, her teeth clenching till they ached. *Fighting will get you nowhere—got you nowhere, you chump.* Even as she thought it, she yanked her hands against the straps that held her down. *Damn!* She couldn't even sit up to see if the mill was ablaze. At least they'd had the decency to leave her legs free, so she could thrash out her frustration. Tears squeezed through her lashes, spilled down her cheeks.

Her head sank back against the pillow, and she laughed silently. *At least I can cry!* But that reminded her of Cattoo. She bit her lip. *Be patient. Fisher won't make me wait till morning, will he?*

By morning, she would be dead from not knowing Sam . . .

The door opened softly, then closed with the same stealth as Jessica opened her eyes. A dark-haired woman in a nurse's peach lab coat swung away from the door, then smiled. "Hello, Jessica." Raye Talbot glided toward the bed.

Scream! Instead, her breath came out in a series of hyperventilating gasps. Jessica tried to sit up, and the restraints yanked her back. Nightmare—the one where you can't run, can't squeak, while the monster glides closer. *"You..."*

"Me. They've had orders all along to call me immediately if you woke up. Luckily my phone rings in my office, as well as at home." She stood, looking down, her face detached, the woman of stony stillness. "I've been lobotomizing my hard drive for the last hour, thanks to you."

"To me?" Play dumb. Oh, God, where was Fisher, that grumpy nurse, anyone at all?

"That's right, you've been out of the loop, haven't you?" Raye glanced toward the door. "Wish I had time to explain, but let's just say you messed up everything, kiddo. I'd been planning an early retirement, yacht in the South Pacific, couple of nubile, tanned young crewmen for amusement. Had my sights set on three million for the cruising kitty. But the way things have been going lately, thanks to what you started, I've decided to settle for two. Just a few loose ends to tidy up, a few banks to visit in the morning, then I'm outta here."

"If they've called you and you've said you'd come, then you *can't* kill me," Jessica pointed out, trying for a tone of cool rationality and failing woefully. "There's bound to be an autopsy—one moment I'm awake, the next I'm dead?"

"Who said I picked up the phone when they called? They left the message on my answering machine. No one will ever prove I monitored. And then, of course, I came up the back stairs." With a swift yank, Raye dragged the pillow from beneath Jessica's head. "Now don't yell and make me use this. Too icky for words." She tucked it under one elbow, then drew a capped syringe from her coat pocket. "You always prided yourself on your dignity, didn't you? Stiff upper lip, WASP reserve to the end? Sooner die than whine?''

Perhaps she had, but no more. Not while there was a chance that Sam was still in the world, loving her. Jessica wriggled her feet in place as if, beneath the sheet, her ankles were also restrained. Raye's chin swerved toward the motion, and in that moment, Jessica drew her wrist inward, until its tie pulled painfully taut.

Raye turned back, gave her smile-for-a-shrug, and pulled the cap off her syringe. Pocketed that neatly.

"What's in it?"

Raye smoothed a hand up through Jessica's hair—it was almost a caress. Gathering a thick handful, she lifted it to expose nape and scalp. A needle prick there would never be noticed. "Succinycholine. Won't hurt a bit, I promise you."

"What a pal." Jessica pulled harder against her wrist strap, drew a shaking breath. *Sam, I choose you. I choose life.*

Far away, perhaps at the nurses' station, voices sounded—protesting, angry, excited.

"Uh-oh!" Raye's grip tightened cruelly. Black and serene as an oncoming shark's, her eyes widened as they neared, homing in behind the tiny, silver-bright needle.

"No!" Jessica screamed. Yanking against her restraint, she pivoted around. Her legs swung off the mattress—to slam Raye's forearm, then her ribs. "Get *away* from me!"

Staggering, Raye shrieked a wordless cry of rage. The syringe hit the wall and fell, unbroken. She dropped to her knees and scrambled after it.

Beyond the door, someone yelled. Something thumped against a wall. A woman cried out.

"Help!" Jessica squeaked, drawing in her feet and preparing to kick again.

Raye grabbed the syringe, swung around on her knees. Not bothering to rise, she hobbled across the floor, needle poised, teeth bared. "It's all *your* fault, you—"

The door slammed back, and what looked like a rugby scrum staggered into the room—Sam, face smudged black, clothes torn, with a security man hugging his waist and dragging behind, while an orderly tried to heel him by his elbow. A nurse plucked at his shirt, while another added her cries of indignation from the hall.

Raye swung around and froze.

"There. You want to tackle somebody, how about her?" Sam panted, pointing at Raye. "All I did was try to leave ER without permission."

"She was trying to kill me," Jessica added, as the guard dropped from Sam's waist to sit glowering from Sam to Raye and back again, his chest heaving. "She's also wanted for arson, blackmail and murder, and I do mean to bring charges."

"Don't be ridiculous!" Raye rose with fluid grace. Her hand fell unobtrusively to her thigh.

The nurse who had hold of Sam's shirt drew herself up to her full five foot one. "I'll give the lot of you ridiculous, behaving like this in the critical-care ward! And as I tried to explain to the gentleman, it's *after* visiting hours. So everyone out of here! *Now!*"

"Except for my husband," Jessica said, as her eyes locked fast with Sam's across the room.

BUT AFTER THAT MOMENT of suspended silence, reality surged back between them. Sam was sucked out the door on a riptide of protests, demands and explanations, none of which were deemed suitable for a recovering patient's ears. So it must have been half an hour later when a tentative tap sounded on her door. Jessica opened her eyes as the door cracked open, and Sam stuck his head through the gap. "Hi." He sounded as shy as she felt. "You still awake?"

"Looks like it." Rolling to face him, she touched the edge of her bed in mute invitation. "Everything settled?"

He seemed uncertain for a moment if he should sit, then he did so. "They'll hang on to her till we can sort it out.

The security guard started takin' it personal once she tried
to stick *him* with that syringe. He said he was going along
to the station to press charges on his *own* account. That
should hold her till morning."

Silence set in again. Too many words crowding into their
mouths at once, each begging to be the first to be spoken.
No way to know how to start, or where. Sam frowned.
"What you said about my bein' your husband . . ."

"I should have said *ex*-husband," she returned too
quickly. "Slip of the tongue." Then cursed that part of her
anatomy for a coward. Damn her pride, would she never
learn? She caught his hand as he leaned back and seemed
about to rise. "*No!* I mean—I didn't mean—" She
stopped, staring down at the glint of gold on his little finger, then gasped and pulled his hand to her lips. "I mean—
Oh, Sam, I never know what to say! I never *did*." And it
was so much easier saying it as a cat.

He laughed, a wordless, breathless, almost hurting
sound, and leaned down over her till his lips brushed her
temple. "Then try sign language," he growled. "Anything! I've been doing the talkin' all week. Now it's your
turn."

Sign language. That she could do. Tears sliding even as
she smiled, she kissed his knuckles, one by one, ending with
the little finger that wore her ring. Her tongue curling like
a cat's, she touched it daintily to the ring, then to the soft
skin between that finger and the next. Her smile widened
when he shuddered and settled closer. "So . . . if you're my
ex-husband, what are you doing wearing my ring? *My*
ring."

He swung his long legs up on the bed so that they la
face to face, his hand still pressed to her lips. "I was tryin
to figure out what to wear to a bonfire, or better yet, a
quick departure therefrom. This was the only thing I coul
think of that mattered. That I couldn't leave behind." H
reached over their clasped hands to stroke her hair. "Eigh
years, and I haven't been able to leave us behind. So I sai
to myself, self, why quit on a good thing now?"

"Don't ever quit on me, Sam. Not *ever*, not even when I—"

"I've no intention of quitting." His whisper was as husky as her own. "Not that it's exactly a voluntary process. I'd say you're stuck with me, babe, or at least my devotion. Must've been a dog in my last life, the soulful, brown-eyed, lie-at-your-feet type."

Oh, after all this, that he could still... "You don't think cats can be faithful?" For just a moment, she thought she could feel her tail lash, almost missed it.

"Those sneaky fur-balls? They're only out for what they can—" His smile ended in a gasp. "Oh, Lord, what have— Kick me for a heartless— Once they told me in the ambulance that my wife—my *wife*—had called in that alarm, I couldn't think of anything but getting to you, seein' if you really..." He frowned. "But wait a minute, how did you know your cat and I..."

She kissed his finger again, then the underside of his wrist, where she remembered the nerves lay close to the skin, smiled at his response. "If I told you, I'm not sure you'd believe."

His eyes had gone darker, his hand heavier and starting to tremble when he stroked her hair. "Right now, I reckon I'd believe anything in the world you asked me to believe," he swore in a whisper. "Well... most anything."

She brought his hand to her cheek. "Then, would you believe that I love you? That whatever I did, however things seemed, I never stopped loving you all this time—not for a day, not for an hour, not for one minute?"

He drew a shaking breath. "That's a tough one... but since it's you who's asking..."

She touched his lips, smiled when he kissed her fingers. "Believe that one thing, Sam Antonio *mio,* my knight, my lazy Texan. Believe that, and everything else is easy."

The telling would come later, after, somewhere in a bed they could call their own, her head pillowed on his shoulder, her hand stroking his chest in the sheltering, blessed darkness. But now... *oh, now...*

She framed his dear, beloved face with her palms, her thumbs—*thumbs,* by God—trembling as they traced the never-forgotten angle of cheekbone, the softness of his lashes when he shut his eyes and shivered. There was no need to draw him closer; he surged to meet her, groaning with relief. Lips met in liquid, laughing wonder. Bodies fused from mouth to thigh. Their arms wrapped and held tight as if they'd never let go. *Oh, now. Now and forever, at last, love.*

BUT IF THE REST of their life together looked easy, there was one hard thing left to do, and the sooner it was faced...

Even knowing what they went to find, they couldn't stay sad. If anything, somehow the sadness only deepened their joy. The night was all fizz and giggles, with not a champagne bottle in sight. "You're sure you're all right?" she worried as he sat down with her in his arms on the third floor landing of RI Gen's back stairs. A discreet getaway, then explain it all later, had suited them both, but still...

"Smoke inhalation isn't something to—"

He kissed her mouth shut. "I'm fine. Strong lak ze bull. The panting ain't the stairs, babe, it's the baggage. Say the word, and I'll carry you to North Carolina."

"After we see to Cattoo..." Her arms tightening around his neck, she pressed her breasts to his chest. "Yes, North Carolina sounds perfect. Let's blow this town."

For just a moment he sobered—as much as he ever did. "And your job, Jess?"

She traced the hawkish shape of his nose, the slant of his eyebrow, glorying in her fingers that could touch him. "Ohhh... I was thinking about taking a long vacation." To consider long and hard what she—she, her own sane and happy self—wanted to do with the rest of her life, now that it had been so mercifully restored to her. What else, besides loving a certain crazy Texan...

He snorted. "What d'you think you've been having a week? I'd say it's my turn to lie down on the job!"

She pulled his head to hers, to growl against his lips. 'Yes . . . fine . . . if you come lie with me.''
And his kiss was the only answer.

THEY CAUGHT a late-cruising cab down the street from the hospital. The cabbie was clearly convinced they were either drunk or insane, or embarking on an elopement, but his amusement turned to alarm when they directed him down the alley behind the mill. "Stop right here," Jessica said, "and please leave your headlights on."

"Hey, I need my fare before you—"

"We're just going over there by that wall. We'll be right back." Between them they hadn't a penny. The firemen had been in no mood to let Sam find his wallet or his keys before they hauled him to safety. After this, they would have a drive to Mac's house to borrow money, but now, that was the least of her worries.

With all their coming and going, if the firemen had trampled Cattoo's body . . . She shivered, and turned her face to Sam's neck as he lifted her from the cab.

"She made it this far?" he muttered, walking slowly, his eyes scanning the ground. "There's no chance she can't still up there, safe and sound on the ledge, givin' us a cat smirk? Only the inside of the sixth floor burned. If she kept her cool . . ."

"No. She's here." And yet not here. Jessica reached out, reached deep within, called one last time their plaintive, singing cry. *"Kiiiii?"*

No answer. Only darkness, silence, the idling mutter of the cab's engine at their backs, its lights throwing their long, knotted shadow in front—man and woman, two yearning creatures made one. Walking with one heart.

Sam stopped and his breath hissed out. "There, babe." He carried her to the front of his rental car, stood looking down into shadow. "Maybe you'd better let me . . ." He settled her on the hood of the car, then dropped to one knee.

"Is she . . . ?" Jessica couldn't see past his bent head. Didn't really need to see. Reaching out, her mind told her nothing—and therefore told all.

"Yeah . . . Oh, Jez . . ." Carefully he stood, something dark and heartbreakingly small cradled in his arms. "Little hussy, if you'd only . . ." He turned and smiled crookedly. "She's not too beat-up. Her front legs are broken. Guess she landed feet first, cats being cats, then flipped over, hit her head . . ."

"Give her to me."

"Babe, are you sure . . ."

She held out her arms. "She's mine." *She's me.*

"She was mine, too. Or maybe I was hers." But he laid Cattoo in Jessica's arms. Softest fur . . . fragile body . . . heart as big as all the night sky. She dropped her face to the warm bundle, inhaled on a shaking sob—felt the touch of a cool questing nose.

"Merrrr?" It was just the ghost of a sound at her ear, no louder than a heartfelt prayer.

"Kiiiii?" she called again, and this time heard the answer in her mind, stronger and surer. "She's—"

"Yes." His arms were already sliding around her to lift them both. "Let's go find ourselves a vet."

From deep within, the answer came once more—a painful, joyful purring. *I am here. You are here.*

"She's going to be all right, Sam! Oh, God, she's—"

"Yeah," he said, walking quickly toward the light. "Didn't I tell you, once 'pon a time, that cats are s'posed to bounce?"

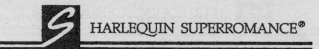

HARLEQUIN SUPERROMANCE®

Special Books by Special Writers

Under One Roof
by Shannon Waverly

The Author: Two-time RITA Award finalist and
Romantic Times Reviewer's Choice winner, she's
got fans worldwide. Shannon wanted this, her tenth
book for Harlequin, to be a very special one. *It is.*

The Characters:
Spencer Coburn. Overstressed physician, divorced father.
He's currently the sole emotional and physical support of...
Stacy Coburn, his teenage daughter—his *pregnant*
teenage daughter.
Gina Banning. Hardworking, divorced schoolteacher and
only child. She's currently the sole emotional and physical
support of...
Joe Banning, her eighty-three-year-old father—her seriously
ill father.

The Story: One of the most moving, honest and *uplifting* books
you'll ever read. And it's just plain *romantic,* too!

Watch for *Under One Roof* by Shannon Waverly
Available in August 1996, wherever
Harlequin books are sold.

HARLEQUIN SUPERROMANCE®

The book you've been waiting for
by that author you love!

A Family of His Own
by Evelyn A. Crowe

Remember Matt Bolt, the handsome ex-homicide
detective in *Fathers & Other Strangers*? Remember Matt's
dashing and delightful brother, Jason? Well, Jason's
looking for *A Family of His Own*. And while
the setting's the same—West Texas—Jason's romance
is entirely different. That's because Jason's the kind
of guy who's never met the woman he couldn't
charm.... Until now!

**Watch for *A Family of His Own*
by Evelyn A. Crowe**

Available in August 1996,
wherever Harlequin books are sold.

HARLEQUIN SUPERROMANCE®

If you've always felt there's something special about a
man raising a family on his own...
You won't want to miss Harlequin Superromance's
touching series

FAMILY MAN

He's sexy, he's single...and he's a father!
Can any woman resist?

THE TROUBLE WITH TEXANS
by Maggie Simpson

Jake Evans knows exactly what his late wife's
sister is doing in Sotol Junction, Texas. She's checking
to see what kind of father he is. Michelle Davis will no
doubt be reporting back to her mother in Boston about
how eight-year-old Brooke is being raised. And Jake
had better keep that in mind, despite the attraction
developing between him and Michelle. If she thinks for
one moment that he'd allow the Davis family to take
Brooke away from him, she'd better think again.

Available in August

Be sure to watch for upcoming FAMILY MAN titles.
Fall in love with our sexy fathers, each determined to do the
best he can for his kids.

You'll find them wherever Harlequin books are sold.

HARLEQUIN SUPERROMANCE®

RETURN TO
CALLOWAY
CORNERS

Remember the Calloway women—
Mariah, Jo, Tess and Eden?

For all the readers who loved *CALLOWAY CORNERS...*

Welcome Back!

And if you haven't been there yet or met the Calloways...

Join us!

MEET THE CALLOWAY COUSINS!

JERICHO
by Sandra Canfield
(available in August)

DANIEL
by Tracy Hughes
(available in September)

GADE
by Penny Richards
(available in October)

Look us up on-line at: http://www.romance.net   CAL1

HARLEQUIN®

Don't miss these Harlequin favorites by some of our most distinguished authors!
And now, you can receive a discount by ordering two or more titles!

HT #25663	THE LAWMAN by Vicki Lewis Thompson	$3.25 U.S. ☐/$3.75 CAN. ☐
HP #11788	THE SISTER SWAP by Susan Napier	$3.25 U.S. ☐/$3.75 CAN. ☐
HR #03293	THE MAN WHO CAME FOR CHRISTMAS by Bethany Campbell	$2.99 U.S. ☐/$3.50 CAN. ☐
HS #70667	FATHERS & OTHER STRANGERS by Evelyn Crowe	$3.75 U.S. ☐/$4.25 CAN. ☐
HI #22198	MURDER BY THE BOOK by Margaret St. George	$2.89 ☐
HAR #16520	THE ADVENTURESS by M.J. Rodgers	$3.50 U.S. ☐/$3.99 CAN. ☐
HH #28885	DESERT ROGUE by Erin Yorke	$4.50 U.S. ☐/$4.99 CAN. ☐

(limited quantities available on certain titles)

	AMOUNT	$
DEDUCT:	**10% DISCOUNT FOR 2+ BOOKS**	$
ADD:	**POSTAGE & HANDLING**	$
	($1.00 for one book, 50¢ for each additional)	
	APPLICABLE TAXES**	$_____
	TOTAL PAYABLE	$_____
	(check or money order—please do not send cash)	

To order, complete this form and send it, along with a check or money order for the total above, payable to Harlequin Books, to: **In the U.S.:** 3010 Walden Avenue, P.O. Box 9047, Buffalo, NY 14269-9047; **In Canada:** P.O. Box 613, Fort Erie, Ontario, L2A 5X3.

Name: _____

Address: _____ City: _____

State/Prov.: _____ Zip/Postal Code: _____

**New York residents remit applicable sales taxes.
Canadian residents remit applicable GST and provincial taxes.   HBACK-JS3

Look us up on-line at: http://www.romance.net

Sabrina   It Happened One Night
Working Girl   Pretty Woman
While You Were Sleeping

If you adore romantic comedies then have
we got the books for you!

Beginning in **August 1996** head to your
favorite retail outlet for
LOVE & LAUGHTER™,
a brand-new series with two books every
month capturing the lighter side of love.

You'll enjoy humorous love stories by favorite
authors and brand-new writers, including
JoAnn Ross, Lori Copeland, Jennifer Crusie,
Kasey Michaels, and many more!

As an added bonus—with the retail purchase,
of two new Love & Laughter books you can
receive a **free** copy of our fabulous
Love and Laughter collector's edition.

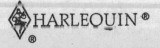

LOVE & LAUGHTER™—a natural
combination...always
romantic...always entertaining

◆ HARLEQUIN ®

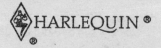

BRIDE'S BAY RESORT

UNLOCK THE DOOR TO GREAT ROMANCE AT BRIDE'S BAY RESORT

Join Harlequin's new across-the-lines series, set in an exclusive hotel on an island off the coast of South Carolina.

Seven of your favorite authors will bring you exciting stories about fascinating heroes and heroines discovering love at Bride's Bay Resort.

Look for these fabulous stories coming to a store near you beginning in January 1996.

Harlequin American Romance #613 in January
Matchmaking Baby by Cathy Gillen Thacker

Harlequin Presents #1794 in February
Indiscretions by Robyn Donald

Harlequin Intrigue #362 in March
Love and Lies by Dawn Stewardson

Harlequin Romance #3404 in April
Make Believe Engagement by Day Leclaire

Harlequin Temptation #588 in May
Stranger in the Night by Roseanne Williams

Harlequin Superromance #695 in June
Married to a Stranger by Connie Bennett

Harlequin Historicals #324 in July
Dulcie's Gift by Ruth Langan

Visit Bride's Bay Resort each month wherever Harlequin books are sold.

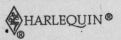

HARLEQUIN ®

BBAYG